FIX HER UP

Also by Tessa Bailey

THE ACADEMY SERIES
Disorderly Conduct
Indecent Exposure • *Disturbing His Peace*

BROKE AND BEAUTIFUL SERIES
Chase Me • *Need Me* • *Make Me*

ROMANCING THE CLARKSONS
Too Hot to Handle • *Too Wild to Tame*
Too Hard to Forget • *Too Beautiful to Break*

MADE IN JERSEY SERIES
Crashed Out • *Rough Rhythm*
Thrown Down • *Worked Up* • *Wound Tight*

CROSSING THE LINE SERIES
Risking It All • *Up in Smoke*
Boiling Point • *Raw Redemption*

LINE OF DUTY SERIES
Protecting What's His • *Protecting What's Theirs* (novella)
His Risk to Take • *Officer Off Limits*
Asking for Trouble • *Staking His Claim*

SERVE SERIES
Owned by Fate • *Exposed by Fate* • *Driven by Fate*

STANDALONE BOOKS
Unfixable • *Baiting the Maid of Honor*
Off Base • *Captivated*
Getaway Girl • *Runaway Girl*

This book is a work of fiction. References to real people, events, establishments, organizations, or locales are intended only to provide a sense of authenticity, and are used fictitiously. All other characters, and all incidents and dialogue, are drawn from the author's imagination and are not to be construed as real.

FIX HER UP. Copyright © 2019 by Tessa Bailey. Excerpt from LOVE HER OR LOSE HER © 2019 by Tessa Bailey. All rights reserved. Printed in the United States of America. No part of this book may be used or reproduced in any manner whatsoever without written permission except in the case of brief quotations embodied in critical articles and reviews. For information, address HarperCollins Publishers, 195 Broadway, New York, NY 10007.

HarperCollins books may be purchased for educational, business, or sales promotional use. For information, please email the Special Markets Department at SPsales@harpercollins.com.

FIRST EDITION

Designed by Diahann Sturge

Library of Congress Cataloging-in-Publication Data has been applied for.

ISBN 978-0-06-287283-8

22 23 LSC 22

FIX HER UP

A NOVEL

TESSA BAILEY

AVON
An Imprint of HarperCollins*Publishers*

To the youngest siblings everywhere

ACKNOWLEDGMENTS

Every year at Christmastime, Port Jefferson, Long Island, turns into a Charles Dickens village. For two days, locals dress up like chimney sweeps and carolers, greeting visitors with their cockney accents. There's apple cider, ice-skating, and old-fashioned puppet shows. Basically, it's magical. I took my family one year, and I've been charmed by the small waterside town of Port Jefferson ever since. I'm so excited to set a series in this glorious little place, and I hope I did it justice.

Thank you, as always, to my family for lifting me up when I'm down and loving me through deadline weeks. Thank you to my editor, Nicole Fischer—for helping me turn our broken-down ex–baseball phenom from swoony to OH YEAH SWOONY. Thank you to my agent, Laura Bradford, for always looking out for my best interests and helping bring this series to life. Thank you to Dansby Swanson for inspiring Travis Ford and Melissa Benoist for being my mental Georgie. As always, thank you most of all to readers who continue to invest their time in my stories—I love you all.

CHAPTER ONE

No freaking way.

Georgette Castle tucked the stolen key into her pocket, wincing at the creak as she opened the apartment door. Empty beer cans skittered along the floor the farther she pushed, the stale stench of unwashed dude reaching out and throttling her. Her older brother had tried to warn her. Had she listened? No. Did she ever listen? Also a definitive no.

This time, though, Georgie had been positive Stephen was mistaken. It didn't seem possible that the town's baseball phenomenon could fall so far so fast. Just under two years ago, she'd watched Travis Ford hit a World Series grand slam on live television, along with everyone in town, gathered beneath the new flat-screen television at Grumpy Tom's. There had never been a doubt Travis would go professional after his sterling college career at Northwestern.

No one saw the injury coming. Especially Travis.

After a year of physical therapy and being passed between teams like a hot potato, Travis had come home to Port Jefferson. Georgie could still see the heartbreak in his eyes during the sparsely attended press conference announcing his retirement at age twenty-eight. Sure, he'd been smiling. Joking about the chance to improve his golf game. But Georgie had been in love with Travis Ford since she hit puberty and knew his tells. Every expression on his face was categorized in her memory, his name scrawled on every other page in her diary, never to be discovered beneath the floorboards of her bedroom. Five decades from now, when she looked back on her youth, she would remember Travis standing at home plate on the high school baseball field, lifting his batting helmet to adjust it, allowing just a glimpse of dark auburn hair to catch the wind, before covering it back up.

Heroic, gorgeous, bursting with character, and cocky as sin. Travis Ford before.

What would the after look like?

"Hello?" Georgie called into the dark dwelling. "Anyone home?"

She kicked aside a plastic bag full of takeout containers and closed the door behind her, advancing into the apartment. Stephen had definitely been here to see his childhood friend. The untouched health shakes and UV sun lamp made that obvious. He'd at least *tried* to reach Travis. So had members of the church, old baseball coaches, and autograph seekers. Instead of being coaxed back out into the light, though, he continued to wallow.

Georgie had a better plan.

"Hey, dickhead!" Now in the living room, she stooped down and picked up a melted pint of ice cream, her lip curling in a smile. Perfect ammunition.

See, Georgie might have reached the ripe old age of twenty-three in Travis's absence, but she would always be the pesky little sister. That wasn't a label she'd given herself. But she'd heard it upward of a thousand times growing up and it refused to die. What was a girl to do besides give in and embrace it? Sympathy hadn't worked with Travis. Now she'd try her own method of breaking through to him.

A floorboard groaned beneath her foot as she stepped into the bedroom, finding Travis facedown and naked on top of the covers, that signature deep auburn hair in a wreck around his head. She almost lost her nerve then, lowering the pint of soupy vanilla ice cream to her thigh. Ridiculous that her heart should kick into a gallop and the moisture in her mouth dry right up. It was just a butt. You could go on the internet and see butts by the . . . butt load. While she was thinking about it, God bless the internet. What an invention.

Still. Throw in Travis's considerable height and naturally athletic frame, complete with ripped muscles and dark, manly hair . . . well, maybe his butt excelled over other butts. Every human in town with a preference for men concurred. Travis Ford was extraordinary.

Just not today. And not for the last month since his premature homecoming.

Georgie lifted the pint of ice cream and took a moment to contemplate the task in front of her. This wouldn't be easy. Deep down in her bones, she wanted to throw her arms around Travis and tell him everything would be all right. He might not get another chance to be a star on the baseball field, but he'd never stop being a hero. The man who left this town and achieved dreams most men let go of as children.

Unfortunately, he'd never stop being the man whose face she'd pictured while Frenching her pillow in middle school, either. As a grown woman now, she pictured him during far less innocent endeavors, which usually required a charged device and twenty minutes alone.

But she digressed.

Her infatuation with Travis was impossible to miss. Even her siblings were aware of it, but they wrote it off as their pesky little sister's silly crush. So be it. She'd be the best damn pest on this side of Long Island. An effective one, too. Hopefully.

"Hey!" Georgie reared back and threw the full container of melted dessert at Travis's naked back, watching in fascination as it spread into a Rorschach painting on his shoulders. And hair. And headboard. It was almost beautiful. "Get up!"

Travis must have gone to bed wasted, because it took a full five seconds for him to register the liquid mess seeping down his skin and onto the bedsheets. His head came up, right wrist swiping at the ice cream on his forehead. "What the fuck?"

His gruff tone made Georgie think of teeth marks and massage oil—seriously, God bless the internet—but she ignored the reaction. "I said get up. You're disgusting." She bent down and picked up a pair of stiff boxers, dangling them at the very tip of her index finger. "Only two outcomes are possible here. Your face is eaten by rats. Or this place gets condemned by the fire marshal."

"Georgie?" Facedown again, Travis turned a little to confirm her identity. There it was. An expression she'd had thrown at her since birth. The perfect combination of irritation and dismissiveness. It screamed, *Go away, you are irrelevant!* without making a sound. Georgie hated that expression but, somewhere along the line, had been given no choice but to lean into it.

If you can't beat them, join them, right?

"I'm surprised you recognized another human being through your own self-pity." Georgie sighed and sat on the edge of the bed, taking the opportunity to memorize his concrete-slab buttocks. "I saw a container of lo mein on the way in here. Figure I'll throw that next. It'll pair nicely with vanilla. Probably. I'm not a chef."

"Get out, Georgie. What the fuck? I'm not even wearing clothes."

"I've seen naked men. Tons of them." On the internet, God bless it. "You used to be a nine point five, but you're slowly bottom-ing—ha—into a seven."

"Really? Because I can feel you staring at my ass."

"Oops. I thought that was your face."

Cool. Good one. Five minutes around this man and you're ten years old again.

Travis's snort sent Georgie back out into the living room. She toed open a bag of Chinese food, confirming the lack of vermin before extricating the lo mein. One step into the room and she let it fly, noodles and rotten chicken raining down on her brother's oldest friend. "Might need a pinch of salt to bring it all together."

"I can't believe you did that," Travis roared, sitting up and throwing his legs over the side of the bed. Anger radiated from every inch of his baseball player body, veins protruding from the sides of his neck, his cut biceps. She'd never seen him with a beard before, but the uneven state of it told Georgie the facial hair was definitely the product of laziness instead of a style change. "Go!" he shouted, dropping his head into his hands. "Don't make me throw you out."

She refused to acknowledge the sharp pain in her chest. "I'm not going anywhere."

"I'll call your brother."

"Do it."

Travis surged to his feet, turning a storm of rage in her direction. The noodles in his hair would have been comical in any other instance but this one. Clearly remembering his naked status, he whipped a T-shirt off a nearby chair and held it over his lap. "What do you want?"

Now, that was a loaded question that could be answered in two parts. She wanted one person in her life to see her as more than the annoying hanger-on. As far back as she could remember, she'd always wanted it to be Travis who listened to her. Told her she was special. Right now, none of those hopes and dreams would be useful. Probably never would be. "I want you to stop being a selfish asshole. Everyone is worried about you. My brother, my parents, the local doe-eyed groupies. Spinning their wheels, trying to figure out how to cheer you up. Maybe you just enjoy being the center of attention whether it's negative or positive."

His arms shot wide, bringing the T-shirt along for the ride.

Penis.

There he sat. Long and thick and crowned like a king. They didn't call him Two Bats for nothing. Ever since he'd been snapped by the paparazzi in a compromising position with a Swedish pop princess during his rookie year, the media had been fascinated with Travis, documenting his never-ending one-night stands and notable conquests. "It Wasn't Me" by Shaggy would play over the stadium loud-speakers when he got up to bat. Women would shriek.

All while Georgie watched from a cross-legged slump in front of the television back on Long Island.

The Player's Player. The *Other* Home Run King. The Back-seat Athlete. Gorgeous even in his dishevelment, the cocky charm was nonetheless missing at this very moment.

"You think I enjoy this?"

"Yeah," she shot back. "I think you want to stay in here forever, because it means you don't have to try again." Working a loose-hipped swagger out of the room, she called back over her shoulder. "I think you're a wussy man. I think you've been sitting in here crying to your highlight reels, wondering where it all went wrong. What a sad cliché. I'm going to talk to my brother about finding a cooler friend."

"Hold the fuck on," Travis thundered, following her out of the bedroom, just your average, everyday, gorgeously pissed-off athlete who was once a contender for Rookie of the Year. "You're acting like I got laid off from just any job. I was a professional baseball player, Georgie. That was all my life was ever building to. There's nowhere to go from there but down. So here I am."

Surprise knocked her back a step. Travis Ford was insecure enough to write himself off as a failure? She'd never known him to be anything but wildly confident—to a fault even. Her hesitation had caused him to back slowly toward the bedroom, though, so she shook off her sympathy and pressed on. "Stay down, then. Become a pathetic has-been who tells the same bummer injury story every time he has more than two beers." She gestured to the apartment. "You're halfway there. Don't quit now."

"It's been a month," Travis seethed.

"A month you could have used to make a new plan, if you weren't a wussy man." She raised an eyebrow. "Like I said."

"You're a *kid*. You don't understand."

Oh, that was almost her knockout punch, those oh-so-familiar words hitting Georgie's most sensitive target. If she hadn't grown up with Travis, she might have left and gone to lick her wounds. But this man had sat across from her at the kitchen table a thousand times. Ruffled her hair, grabbed from the same bowl of popcorn during movies, and defended her from meanies. After all, Travis and Stephen could torture her, but when it came to other people doing it? Not a chance. If she hadn't spent her life in love with Travis Ford, she would consider him a brother. So she knew a strong, self-assured man was under this bearded freak's surface. And he needed someone to jab and punch until he was free.

"I just bought a house. My own house. I'm not a kid anymore, but even if I was? I'd have my shit together more than you do. And I'm a children's birthday party clown—let *that* sink in." Georgie paused for a breath. "Right now, everyone in town feels bad for you. They understand the loss." She poked him in the chest, right over his red-and-black baseball diamond tattoo. "But in six months? A year? People will shake their heads and laugh when you walk down the street. *Look at him now. He never recovered. What a waste.*"

By the time Georgie finished, his chest shuddered up and down, muscles jumping on both sides of his jaw. "Why did you come here? What do you care?"

"I don't," she lied. "I just came to see you for myself, because I couldn't believe it. The guy we all looked up to is a drunk slob. Now I know."

"Get out," Travis snarled, taking a step closer. "I'm not going to say it again."

"Fine. I probably need to schedule a tetanus shot anyway." Georgie turned on a heel and sidestepped a pizza box on her way to the door. "See you around, Travis. Probably on the last barstool in Grumpy Tom's muttering about your glory days."

"It was . . ."

His new, choppier tone stopped Georgie midstride. She looked back over her shoulder just in time to catch him swigging from a half-empty whiskey bottle.

"Going pro was my only way to be better than him, all right? I have no way to be better than him now. I'm nothing. I'm him."

"That is garbage, Travis Ford," she breathed, unable to speak above a whisper. "You did it. You achieved what you set out to do. Circumstances screw everyone once in a while—and they screwed you worst. But you're only him if you lie down and play the victim." She turned away before he could see the tears in her eyes. "You're better than this."

Georgie left Travis standing in the filth, looking like he'd been struck by lightning.

And he hadn't seen the last of her, either.

CHAPTER TWO

Travis squinted through his front windshield into the sunlight and wished it were raining. Maybe if the sun weren't beating down on him like a cheerful asshole, he could have given himself an excuse to stay inside one more day. Instead of his usual routine of waking up, ordering breakfast delivery from the diner, chasing it with a six-pack, and going back to sleep, he'd found himself pulling on clean pants and walking out into the daylight. His sudden motivation had nothing to do with Georgie's visit yesterday—nothing whatsoever. He'd simply hit his limit for staring at the same four walls and needed a change.

Was this the right change, though? A construction job?

He didn't need the money. If he wanted to spend the next decade living like an antisocial vampire who drinks Bud instead of blood, he had the funds to do it comfortably. Frankly, that sounded pretty appealing at the moment.

I think you want to stay in here forever, because it means you don't have to try again.

Travis pushed himself out of the truck with an annoyed growl. When did little Georgie Castle turn into such a ball-breaker? Last time he'd seen her she'd still been in middle school. She'd spoken only when necessary so she wouldn't have to show off her mouthful of braces. Far more preferable than the whirlwind who'd blown through his apartment yesterday, engaging in a one-way food fight. Some things about Georgie hadn't changed, like her uniform of ripped jeans and oversized sweatshirts, but she'd definitely found her voice. He wished she'd directed it elsewhere.

Travis tugged on the collar of his shirt, grimacing at the dampness. August in Port Jefferson. He'd been out of his air-conditioned truck for only five seconds and his clothes were already sticking to him. From his vantage point, he could follow the paths of residents hurrying down the gentle slope and curve of Main Street, rushing to get to their next, cooler destination. Beyond the town's main drag, water spread out wide and blue, boats lifting and dipping with the current. Banners stretched over the road, advertising church festivals and town hall budget votes. Whether he wanted to be back home or not, time and distance had given him enough objectivity to admit Port Jeff wasn't a terrible spot. It would just be hotter than the devil's ass until fall hit.

Travis came to a stop on the sidewalk, looking through the giant picture window of Brick & Morty. Through the gold lettering that hadn't changed since his youth, he could see his friend Stephen Castle on the phone, probably barking orders at some poor soul. Travis's best friend had been groomed to take over the family house-flipping business since high school and he'd fallen right into rhythm, inheriting the institution from his father, Morty. Right after Travis's ascent to the majors, his phone calls to Stephen had been the one thing keeping him grounded. When all the Rookie of the Year fanfare threatened to inflate his head, Stephen had no problem reminding Travis he was the same asshole who'd broken his arm at age nine attempting to ride a skateboard backward down the Castle driveway. Toward the end of his career, he hadn't needed Stephen to deflate his ego.

Fate had handled that nicely on its own.

Would his easy friendship with Stephen be the same now that Travis's identity had been stripped away? The death of his career seemed to cast a shadow over his every interaction now. He'd always been a baseball player. The game ran in his veins. It never failed to be the first thing people spoke to him about. How's the shoulder? *Better than ever.* How's the team looking for the upcoming season? *We're focused and ready to win games.* Hit me one out of the park. *I'll hit you two.* The few times he'd left the apartment since returning to Port Jefferson, the topic of baseball had been deftly avoided anywhere he went. If someone asked him about the weather or complimented his new non-haircut one more time, his fucking head was going to explode.

Was this his life now? Pretending as though the five years of his baseball career never happened? Some days, that's what he wanted. He wanted to numb himself to the memories of his injury and subsequent decline. Being shared around the league like a bummed cigarette. And finally the phone call from his team manager that was the equivalent of shooting a lame horse. Other days, though . . . pretending his career never happened scared the shit out of him.

What was the point of all that hard work when he'd ended up right back in Port Jefferson, hitting up his friend for a job, just like his father always predicted he would?

That was a reminder he could have done without today.

Knowing he needed a minute before having to converse with a real live human being, Travis sighed and backed away from the window, leaning up against the building's concrete wall. Maybe he should put this off until tomorrow. It wasn't a reunion, exactly, since Stephen had been at his place a week . . . or maybe two . . . ago. Hard to remember since he'd been knee-deep in a bottle of Jack at the time. Having a sober face-to-face conversation with the bluntest person he knew might not be the greatest idea in his shitty frame of mind.

"Travis Ford?"

He turned to find a pretty blonde he didn't recognize approaching him on the sidewalk. When all he could muster was a nod, she laughed.

"You don't remember me, do you?"

"Can't say that I do," he responded, without matching her smile. "Should I?"

Her composure faltered, along with her stride, but she recovered fast. "Well . . . we went to high school together. Tracy Gallagher. I sat behind you in homeroom senior year."

"Oh, right," he said tonelessly. "Sure."

Port Jefferson was a little bubble of a town. What happened out in the world only mattered insomuch as it directly affected the residents. But the familiar mixture of interest and censure on Tracy's face made one thing pretty obvious: his reputation as an unrepentant womanizer had penetrated the bubble. She stood there waiting for him to elaborate on his monosyllabic answers, maybe even make a pass at her, and she was about to be sorely disappointed.

"Um," she continued, seemingly unfazed. "You've been back in town for a month and I haven't seen you around. Were you . . ." Cheeks turning pink, she squared her shoulders. "Did you want some help reacquainting yourself with the town?"

"Why would I? Nothing here has changed." God, he was being a complete dick. As little as six months ago, they would have already been on their way back to his place. Good old Two Bats, always up for a lay. Until he wasn't worth a damn anymore. Everyone had wanted a piece of him until shit got heavy, right? After the trades started and his stock went down, his phone stopped ringing. Here was a woman showing him some interest. Hell, she seemed nice enough. Maybe her intentions were pure. But after the fleeting smoke-and-mirrors lifestyle he'd led for the last five years, he could no longer muster an ounce of excitement. None of it ever *meant* anything. "Look, I'm about to meet with a friend . . ."

"Tracy. I work at the boutique." She pointed south. "Down on the other end of Main Street. Glitter Threads."

He forced a tight smile. "If I ever need the perfect little black dress, I'll let you know."

She laughed as if he'd made the joke of the century instead of a sarcastic jackass comment. "Why wait to hang out? There's a new park down on the water, actually. If you wanted to check it out, I could pack a picnic lunch, or . . ."

His laugh was toneless. "A picnic."

Finally picking up on the fact that he wasn't interested, Tracy paused and her expression went flat. Irritated. Part of him felt bad for being impolite, but the other half? It felt good to *not* be the charming ladies' man who took nothing seriously except his batting average. "You know—"

"Hey, Travis," said a voice behind him. The sound reminded him of dripping Popsicles and skinned knees, but it had changed some. Grown huskier, lost the slight lisp. Georgie came into view, a ball cap pulled down low on her forehead, hair escaping in every direction. "Are you ready?"

He gave Stephen's little sister a bland look. "For what?"

"Uh. Your *doctor's* appointment, silly." Georgie poked him in the ribs. "Come on. We're going to be late."

Was Georgie swooping in to save him from Tracy? Yeah. It appeared she was. And he wasn't going to look a gift horse in the mouth. The idea of a picnic with anyone—especially this woman who probably expected him to dazzle her with stories about meeting celebrities—was right on par with water torture. "Right. My doctor's appointment."

Georgie sent Tracy a wince. "When I described the symptoms to his doctor, they asked me to bring in a stool sample right away. Whatever he's got, they haven't seen it since the nineties."

Jesus Christ.

Tracy raised a skeptical brow. "He looks fine."

"That's how it starts. One second you're feeling fine . . . and then . . ." Georgie made an explosion sound, clapping her hands together. "Pus everywhere. You wouldn't believe the pus. You can't get it out with regular detergent."

"You took it too far," Travis muttered to Georgie. "Way too far."

"I'm new at this," she shot back, out of the side of her mouth.

Obviously onto the impromptu ruse, Tracy jerked her purse higher on her shoulder. "I can take a hint, Travis Ford. And by the way, you're not as hot in person."

"Aw, give him a break. He's had a rough month."

That comment earned Georgie a glare. "Don't ever come into the boutique, Georgie Castle. Your legs are too short—even for the petite sizes."

Georgie's confidence dipped, but she lifted her chin to make up for it. "They don't treat me this way at Gap Kids—you could learn a thing or two from them."

Travis realized he was frowning down at Georgie. The top of her head only reached his shoulder. Small but fierce. Again, he marveled over the quiet girl who'd barely been capable of eye contact, once upon a time, becoming this scrappy defender of . . . him. Why the hell was she even bothering? Travis didn't know, but he felt compelled to return the favor in some small way. Probably because she was Stephen's little sister. "Your legs are normal-sized."

She stared up at him as if he'd given her a way better compliment. Just as quickly, though, she rolled her eyes. "Oh, shut up."

Tracy turned tail and stormed down the sidewalk. "Know what? I hope you *do* get some disease from the nineties, Travis

Ford," she called over her shoulder. "I don't know why every woman in town is determined to throw her hat into the ring. You're not even worth a midweek leg shave."

"Points for originality." Travis and Georgie watched the blonde until she was out of earshot. "Although, did I really hear her asking you out on a picnic?"

He sighed. "You did indeed."

"Would she have shown up with a Yogi Bear wicker basket? Would she have packed a giant cartoon ham hock? I'm disappointed you didn't say yes, just to satisfy my curiosity."

Travis knew he should say thank you, but he didn't want Georgie getting the impression he wanted or needed any more of her interventions. God forbid he formed an obligation to her. No one relied on Travis for anything now and he relied on exactly nobody. Commitments were temporary, and thus he didn't bother making them. When he'd landed in the pros, he'd allowed himself to trust teammates, coaches, managers, despite the lesson he'd learned at a young age. He wouldn't make that mistake a third time. The only exception to the rule was waiting for him inside the office, and even Stephen was kept at a comfortable distance.

"I'm meeting with your brother, Georgie." He turned and opened the door, air-conditioning rushing out of Brick & Morty to greet him. "Run along."

Georgie followed him inside. "What brought you out this fine summer day? It wouldn't have anything to do with me—"

"Nope."

"Are you *sure,* because . . ."

Travis turned on a heel and the brim of Georgie's hat drilled him in the chest, the impact knocking it off her head. He opened his mouth to tell her, no, nothing she'd said or done was responsible for his leaving his cave to meet with Stephen. It was pure coincidence. But the fallen hat had allowed her deep brown mass of hair to spill out everywhere. Over her shoulders, down her back, across half of her face. One of her green eyes peeked out through the wave of it all and he got distracted from his speech.

Yeah, she'd definitely . . . changed.

Georgie broke their stare, stooping down to grab the hat and yank it back down over her head, pulling her wealth of hair through the back opening. "What are you here to speak with Stephen about?"

The husky tone of her voice perturbed him even more, though he couldn't say why. "Can you go play outside while the adults talk?"

She looked bored, but Travis got the impression it was an act. "It's not my turn for the swing."

The sound of a phone hitting the cradle ricocheted through the office.

"Georgie," Stephen called behind Travis. "That's enough. We'll talk later."

"Right," she muttered, her smile tight. "I can take a hint, too."

An uncomfortable sensation moved in Travis's chest as Georgie backed toward the door. When *he'd* been patronizing to her like an asshole, it hadn't sounded as bad as when Stephen did it, right? Yeah. Probably. And so be it. Making this girl feel welcome wasn't his job, especially if her own brother didn't see a reason to do so.

"Oh!" Georgie stopped and spun, keeping one hand on the doorknob. "Stephen, I'm starting a new tradition this weekend. Saturday brunch at my place. Can you come?"

Travis turned to find his friend scribbling on a legal pad, barely giving his sister the time of day. "Sure, sure. I'll talk to Kristin."

"Great." She seemed to brace herself. "Travis, you're invited, too."

"Don't count on me."

She sent him an exaggerated wink. "It's the blue house at the end of Whittier. Big elm tree in the yard. I'll see you there."

"You won't."

"But I think I will," she said in a drawn-out whisper, edging into the sunlight.

Travis watched in exasperation as Georgie passed in front of the plateglass window, while pretending to be on a down escalator. "Is she always like this?"

"Who?"

Again, that weird roll of discomfort tried to pass through him, but he batted it away. "Your sister."

"Oh, Georgie? Pretty much." Stephen's voice came from right behind Travis, prompting him to turn and shake the other man's hand. "You still look like shit, but you've moved to a step above corpse."

"Yeah? I'll rebound." He forced a grin. "You'll look like shit forever."

Tight-lipped and grim-faced, Stephen wasn't a man given to laughing. His snort was his closest mirth indicator. With a chin jerk, he stomped back toward his desk and took a long sip of what appeared to be a fruit smoothie. "Saw you talking to a girl outside." His stare was baleful. "Did she land the coveted first date?"

Travis dropped into the chair facing Stephen's desk. "Come again?"

"Kristin tells me there's something of an informal competition brewing in Port Jeff. Now that you've finally emerged from your hovel, I'm guessing it's game on."

A vein started to pound behind Travis's eye. "Let me get this straight. There's a competition and the object is to date me?"

"About right."

"What I do is the opposite of dating. I do not date."

"I didn't either until I met Kristin." He nodded, obviously preparing to tell Travis the same story he'd related several times over the phone and would probably tell another nine hundred times throughout his life. Christ, his best friend was already such a dad. Travis couldn't even commit to a toothpaste brand. "She was on vacation in New York, visiting from Georgia. Saw her crossing an intersection in Manhattan. I pulled over, asked her to lunch, and she never went home."

"I told you before, bro. That sounds more like kidnapping."

Stephen let that go without comment. "What can I do for you, Travis? I'm guessing you didn't come here looking for a job."

There was a pinch in his chest at the prospect of signing

on for a daily grind. Forming a routine. Those things meant devoting himself. Having people count on him. Being on a team. When a man's usefulness ran out, Travis knew very well what happened, but he had no choice. Rotting away in a one-bedroom wasn't an option, no matter how much he wanted it to be. "Actually, I did. Come here to look for a job."

His oldest friend sat forward in his chair. "I know how many zeroes were attached to those contracts you signed, man. You don't need the work."

"Need? No." Georgie's voice caught him off guard for the tenth time that day. *The guy we all looked up to is a drunk slob.* "I just need something to keep me busy until I figure out my next move," he said quickly, trying to dispel the words in his head. "Wasn't so long ago I used to swing the hammer for extra cash during summer vacation. Your father taught us carpentry at the same time. Anything I forgot, I can re-learn on the fly."

"I hire serious candidates only." Stephen steepled his fingers. "Men looking to grow with the company and be in it for the long haul."

"I don't offer the long haul to anybody."

A muscle twitched in his friend's cheek as they faced off across the desk. Finally, Stephen picked up a pen and wrote something down, sliding the piece of paper across the desk toward Travis. "Here's the address of our current flip. This is where you'd be working to start."

Travis held up the note, giving it a cursory glance. And then he read it again, a pit yawning wide in his stomach. "This is across the street from . . ."

Regret darkened Stephen's eyes. "I know. It's a pretty fucked-up coincidence," he said. "That going to be a problem?"

"Nope. Ancient history." He shoved the paper into his pocket and stood. "See you there."

He knew if he turned around, Stephen's expression would call bullshit, so he kept walking, doing his best to ignore the foreboding in his gut.

CHAPTER THREE

Georgie gave her blueberry compote a final stir and stepped back from the counter, wiping sticky hands down her apron. Bacon warmed in the oven alongside Belgian waffles. She'd stayed up late whipping cream with her new hand mixer and had taken only seven finger swipes out of it since waking up this morning—but who was counting? In an exciting twist, she'd timed everything right for her first time cooking for more than one—painfully single—person.

It was her first time entertaining in her new home, period.

Georgie still couldn't believe it. She had a *house* now. Granted, the Castle family business thrived on the art of sniffing out real estate deals, so she'd bought the two-bedroom ranch for a song and it still needed *a lot* of work. But it was hers. Not bad for a birthday party clown. Speaking of which, she had a dozen phone calls to return as soon as this brunch ended. Port Jefferson had exactly one clown and she was in high demand. It was how she'd managed the down payment on the house. Unfortunately, half the calls were from new customers who wanted a cotton candy machine, pony rides, magicians, princesses.

And she'd have to turn those jobs down.

A familiar hint of panic crept into her throat. Her fledgling clown business, along with some help from her parents, had put her through college, but it no longer seemed as sustainable. She did her best to keep the act fresh and cater to new trends, but kids' birthday parties were a competitive racket. Parents wanting to outdo each other were beginning to look outside of Port Jeff for their entertainment needs. What was Georgie going to do about that? With a mortgage to pay, the future of her one-woman show had begun weighing more and more heavily on her mind.

Don't worry about it now. Not when there's compote to be consumed, parents and siblings to impress, and mimosas to drink. And Travis.

As if she could forget about Travis and his big, beautiful, brooding self.

Would he come?

No. Of course he wouldn't. He'd barely given her the time of day when she was a kid. What made her think this guy who'd been wined, dined, and invited to the White House would be interested in having brunch with a girl who'd chucked rotting food at his head? Still. It didn't hurt to imagine him waltzing through the swinging door of her kitchen with that amazing animal grace, that tongue tucked into his lower lip as if he just had to utilize it at all times. Guh.

Pressing her hand to her pounding heart, Georgie checked the clock on the oven. She would find out if he'd show soon enough. There was only ten minutes to go until everyone started to arrive.

Telling her nerves to hit the road, Georgie took the pitcher of mimosas out of the fridge, arranging it at an artistic angle on the kitchen table. She couldn't stop herself from taking her cell phone out and snapping a few pictures in portrait mode.

"Okay," she muttered under her breath. "I'm one of these smug foodie people now."

Before she could post the picture to Instagram, the phone dinged with an incoming text message. It was from her sister, Bethany.

> **B:** Can't make it. That asshole community theater director broke up with me during the appetizers last night and I self-medicated with Cuervo. Rain check next week?

Georgie slumped into a kitchen chair, her fingers poised to reply. She typed a message imploring her sister to come, then deleted it and sent a thumbs-up instead. No big deal. Stephen and Kristin were coming, weren't they? Her brother could eat enough to feed a small village—a way better brunch guest than Bethany, the perpetual dieter.

Fifteen minutes later, the pitcher of mimosas had started to sweat. A check of the waffles in the oven confirmed they were beginning to dry out. She paced the kitchen with her cell in hand for another five minutes before sending a text to Kristin.

> **G:** You guys coming to brunch?

Ten seconds later her phone dinged.

K: What brunch, sweetie?

Georgie's eyes closed slowly, the phone dropping to her side. The brunch had been so unimportant to her brother, he hadn't even remembered to tell his wife. God, now if her parents showed up, her father would shuffle the floor like a loose end. Without Stephen around for Brick & Morty shop talk, his restlessness would be obvious, even if he tried to pretend otherwise. Her mother would poke her husband and send him dagger eyes until he relaxed, but did Georgie *want* to inconvenience them?

Quickly, she fired off a text to her mother.

G: Mom, we're moving brunch to next weekend. I overslept.

She tacked on a befuddled emoji for good measure.

Her phone buzzed.

M: Are you sure, honey? We're halfway there. I can help whip something up.

Georgie hesitated.

G: I'm sure. Go split your favorite pancakes at the Waterfront, instead ;)

That was it. All that work and no one was coming.

She pressed the pads of her thumbs into her eye sockets

and sighed. She'd been holding out hope that buying the house would force everyone to recognize her as a fellow adult, but maybe such a feat was impossible this late in the game. Her parents loved her, but they'd been exhausted by the time their third child came along. Whereas her siblings were given careful attention and had their paths carved into the family business, Georgie had been left to figure shit out on her own. Since they'd always thought of her as the family clown, she'd embraced it. Whether she loved her job or not, maybe her career choice had guaranteed their seeming lack of esteem.

Her empty kitchen seemed to agree.

Not bothering to swallow the lump in her throat, Georgie moped over to the compote and prepared to knock it into the trash, cheap bowl and all. But then the doorbell rang before she could.

Who . . . ?

No. No way.

It couldn't be Travis.

Georgie's gaze darted around the kitchen looking for a place to hide. Letting in the local baseball god to witness her humiliation was *so* not an option. She paced to the kitchen window and peered through the lace curtain—

He was glowering right at her.

Right, okay. No way to avoid this. His body language could not be making it clearer that he'd prefer to be a million light-years away, so Georgie would merely send him packing, then spend the rest of the afternoon eating bacon and regretting it.

She sucked in gulping breaths all the way to the front door, fingers twisting in her apron. Oh my God. Travis Ford was standing outside her door. Five feet away. Maybe less. She should probably take a moment to savor that, since she'd been dreaming about it since puberty, but she couldn't stall any longer. With an inward groan, she opened the door and leaned a casual hip on the frame. The picture of complacency. Hopefully. "Hi. So sorry. Brunch is canceled." She jerked a thumb over her shoulder and winced. "Ye olde oven cut out on me last night. I didn't have your number or I would have texted you. I mean, I wouldn't *abuse* the privilege of having your number or something." Her laugh sounded painfully forced. "But I would have sent a courtesy text."

His eyes were hidden behind gold-rimmed sunglasses, but she could feel the assessment in them. "If the oven cut out last night, why are you wearing an apron covered in fruit and batter?"

"You can tell that from there, huh?" Playing it cool in the face of having her bluff called, she pursed her lips. No option but to dig deeper. "I haven't washed it in a while?"

"I can smell what's happening in there." He tucked a tongue into his cheek. "No one showed up, did they?"

Oh, this was not the time for that knot to expand in her throat. Not at all. But it formed with a vengeance, pushing out at all sides. Her eyes started to burn—and this was a disaster. Her siblings had flaked out, her parents had barely protested when she canceled . . . and they'd all confirmed what she'd already known. That they didn't take her seriously. She was going to cry in front of her childhood hero turned mega-crush turned object of her every sexual fantasy. Seriously, Travis was the reason she couldn't hear "Take Me Out to the Ball Game" without getting horny. Meanwhile if she cried right now, he'd probably lose his boner next time he smelled blueberries. Of course, while all these thoughts raced through her head, she said absolutely nothing, simply stared up at the former Hurricanes shortstop while her eyes ached.

"More food for me," Travis said finally, stepping over the threshold. "Move it."

"What?" She couldn't hide the wistfulness in her tone. "You're staying?"

"I've been eating takeout for a month." He turned and pointed at her, letting that sink in. "That's the only reason I'm here. We clear?"

She jogged to keep up with him. "To be fed. Yes."

"I guess it smells pretty decent, too."

"I was about to throw it all in the garbage," she breathed, wiping an eye with her sleeve.

He caught the action as they entered the kitchen and sent her a scowl. "You need a minute or something?"

"Why? Because there's no crying in . . ."

"Jesus."

"I'll help you. It's baseball." Georgie walked to the oven and took out the heaping plates of bacon and waffles. "That was called a segue. I'm being a good hostess by seamlessly bringing up topics of mutual interest. You love baseball. I love Tom Hanks. If we meet in the middle, we get *A League of Their Own*."

He slid into a chair and stretched his long legs in front of him, like a prince preparing to be entertained. "I just want to eat bacon."

Georgie heaped a plate full of waffles, whipped cream, compote, and bacon and slid it in front of Travis. "Okay, fine. We won't talk about how underrated Geena Davis is."

"Thank God." He picked up a piece of bacon, pausing with it halfway to his mouth. "Because Lori Petty was the standout."

"Don't." She shook her head slowly. "Not in my kitchen."

Travis snorted and threw the entire strip of bacon into his mouth, before picking up the fork, cutting off a giant bite of waffle, slopping it through the compote/whipped cream combination, and tucking it into his mouth. "Fuck. That's good."

Until he spoke around the giant bite of food, Georgie didn't realize she was staring at his mouth the way a charmed snake stares at a dangling pocket watch. She backed away from the table and started to cobble together her own plate, pleasure flooding her over his compliment, gruff though it was. "Thanks. Mimosa?"

He seemed to think about it. "Nah, I'm good."

"No longer looking for the answer in the bottom of a bottle?"

"See, I knew you were in there."

"What do you mean?"

The strong column of his throat worked as he swallowed a bite. "The girl who threw lo mein at my naked ass is not the same girl who answered the door."

She fell into her spot at the table, stabbing her waffle in the heart with a fork. "My brother and sister abandoned me and my parents are probably relieved I gave them an out. Excuse me for having a weak moment."

"I know a thing or two about being abandoned." As if he'd caught himself off guard by telling her something so personal, Travis rolled one of his shoulders. "You get used to it."

Georgie's heart skipped. "I don't want to. You shouldn't be used to it, either." Just like the morning she'd confronted Travis at his apartment, Georgie was struck by the possibility that he wasn't the flawless, invincible giant her younger self had perceived. He knew about being abandoned? How? He must have been referring to the professional teams who'd furiously traded him before that final cut. "The Hurricanes were idiots to trade you for Beckman. He couldn't find the ball swinging *three* bats."

His hand paused on its way to grab a napkin, but she thought she caught a spark of interest before he hid it with a shrug. "Nah, he's decent."

"Tell that to his batting average." It took her a few beats to notice Travis's amusement. "What?"

"Nothing." He rested his fork. "Not many people bring up the trades to my face."

"Oh." Heat tingled at the base of her neck. "I didn't mean to—"

"Didn't say I minded," Travis cut in smoothly. "How long have you been in this place?"

"Four months." Relieved he hadn't taken offense to her word vomit, Georgie forked a blueberry into her mouth and leaned back, casting a glance around the kitchen. "There's so much I want to do, but I haven't gotten around to it yet."

He made short work of a second piece of bacon. "You are aware your family owns a remodeling business, right?"

Remembering the text from Stephen's wife, she waved off his comment. "They're busy."

When the silence stretched, she looked up to find Travis watching her. Thoughtfully. Had he ever done that? "What would be your first project, if you could pick anything?"

"The fireplace." She laughed, a little amazed. "I didn't even know my first choice until I said it out loud. But definitely the fireplace. It's this old, faded brick—"

"Show me."

"But you're eating . . ." Every remnant of food had vanished from his plate. "Oh."

Travis pushed back from the table and, without waiting for her, left the kitchen. She found him in the living room, running a big, long-fingered hand over the old mantel of the fireplace. "You looking to do some stone work, cut it with a floating mantel?"

She couldn't hide her surprise. "That's exactly what I'm thinking," she murmured, brows drawing together. "Why are you asking? You're not going to do it for me, are you?"

"No, but I can talk to your brother about getting it on the schedule." A sardonic smile ghosted around his mouth. "I'm on the payroll. For now. And I can bitch at him without getting fired. If he does fire me, I'll tell everyone he used to get emotional over *Designing Women* reruns."

"You're working at Brick & Morty?" She breathed a laugh. "Why the sudden need to work? Is this because of me coming to your apartment and—"

"Nope. Keep dreaming."

"It is," she said, hopefully to herself. "I know it is."

"It's not."

"Agree to disagree. Do you want to see the rest of the house?"

His expression said no, but he gestured at her to lead the way. Sort of flustered and a lot prideful, Georgie took his wrist—*oh my, so thick*—and tugged him through the living room. "The backyard is through here," she said, presenting the sliding glass door and backyard beyond with a grand sweep of her arm. "I'm going to get a big, sloppy dog someday and this is where I'll throw his ball."

Was it her imagination or did that make him smile a little?

"You might want to adjust your aspirations to a medium or small dog." He swept her with a look. "A big dog would walk *you*."

"Sorry, my mind is set on Beethoven."

She waited, hoping he would remember watching that movie several times together on her parents' couch all those years ago, neighborhood kids sprawled on the floor munching popcorn. When recognition meandered through his expression, Georgie's heart kicked.

"'Any kind of weirdness and Beethoven is gone,'" he drawled, quoting the movie.

"'Weirdness? What should I watch for, hon? Wearin' my clothes around the house?'"

"Classic." He made an impatient gesture for her to keep moving, but she caught his lips twitching. "Show me the rest. I don't have all day."

"Okay." She had to force herself not to skip down the hallway, but her steps faltered the closer they came to the bedroom. Travis Ford was going to look at her bedroom. See it. Be near it. Were the fantasies she continually had about him going to be visible, like vines hanging from the ceiling? "Um. This is my room."

"Oh, uh . . ." He gave a tight nod, barely glancing through the doorway. "Great."

"Moving right along," she said too quickly, directing his attention to the tiny, closet-sized room across the hall. "This is my magic zone."

"Magic how?"

"I keep my performance equipment inside." His narrow-eyed interest tickled her pulse. "Normally I would charge for a show, but since you braved my cooking I owe you at least one magic trick."

He propped a shoulder on the hallway wall and crossed his arms. "Fire away. But be warned, I'm a skeptic."

Georgie gasped in mock surprise. "*You?* A skeptic?" Lips pursed, she opened the door slowly, slowly, as if it held the secrets to the universe. Maintaining eye contact, she slipped into the room and moved behind the door little by little until disappearing from view. "I'm building the drama," she said, ducking down to retrieve a few items. "Are you intrigued?"

"On the edge of my seat."

Georgie came back into the hallway and closed the door, holding a blue scarf in her hand. As she expected, Travis eyed the silk with suspicion. She threw it up in the air, let it flutter down, and caught it. "Just your average, ordinary, everyday scarf that I stole from my sister."

"Okay. What are you going to do with it?"

She tilted her head and frowned. "Do you hear the pitter-patter of rain? I think it's raining outside."

Even when Travis was patronizing, he was the sexiest man on the planet. She swore his eyes twinkled as those sensual lips tilted in a smirk. "I don't hear anything."

Really? Not even my heart? "Just in case, you should take an umbrella." With a twist of her wrist and a sleight of hand, a rainbow-colored umbrella bloomed beneath the scarf, sending it fluttering to the ground. Oh, he struggled not to be confused, but failed, quite possibly making her life complete. "I know what you're thinking. Will I perform at your birthday party? I usually only book children's events, but I'll make this one exception."

He shook his head, studying her for a moment. "You weren't always like this, were you?"

"Delightful?"

"Sure." He graced her with a too-brief smile, then pushed off the wall, moving in that long-legged stride back toward the living room. "We'll call it 'delightful' instead of 'weird.'"

Georgie caught up to him in front of the fireplace, just in time to watch his hand run over the brick.

"You haven't, uh, heard anything about some competition in town . . ."

"The competition to go on a date with you?"

His head fell back with a groan. "Oh God, it is real."

"And you're not *thrilled* about it?" Georgie mentally reviewed the conversations she'd heard around town all week. In the bakery, at a birthday party, simply walking down Main Street. "I mean, even if you're not thrilled, you're at least used to this kind of attention from women, right?"

A shadow passed over his face. "Yeah. Something like that."

A jealousy fountain tried to bubble up, but she stuck a rock in it. The green monster was useless where Travis Ford was concerned and always would be. Instead, she focused on what his body language was telling her. The stiffness in his shoulders, the bunched jaw. "You're *not* thrilled about it."

He stared straight ahead at the fireplace. "No."

"Why?"

It took him a moment to answer. "I guess I don't want to be a novelty anymore. A good time. Something easy, not to be taken seriously." He ran a rash hand through his dark auburn hair. "It's no one's fault but mine. I made myself the punch line of a bad dirty joke, didn't I?"

"I don't think of you that way. You could never be a joke," she whispered, taken aback. "I'm sorry if the mean things I said in your apartment made you feel this way."

"No. What you did was different. I needed that." He reached over and tweaked her nose. "There. You finally got me to admit that throwing food and calling me on my shit is why I'm back among the living."

If he hadn't just played gotcha with her nose like she was five, Georgie might have kissed him then and there out of pure joy. But he had. So she didn't. "You're welcome." She curled her fingers into the edges of her apron. "Ignoring the competition is only going to up the stakes, you know. Long Island women take betting seriously."

"Let me worry about that." As if becoming conscious of time and place, Travis cleared his throat hard and headed for the door. "I'll talk to Stephen about the fireplace, all right? Thanks for breakfast."

"Travis?"

He stopped with a hand on the knob, but only gave her a half-turn of attention.

"Thank you for staying."

The door closed in reply.

CHAPTER FOUR

"Take off your shirt!"

Ignoring the shouted suggestion, Travis clamped his teeth around the pencil in his mouth and focused on the laser leveler in his hand, eventually lowering it to make notations. The major downside to renovating a house was definitely the lack of windows—there was nothing to muffle the outdoor noise. A crowd of around a dozen women and a handful of men had gathered on the curb outside the flip, snapping pictures of Travis with their camera phones—and if the portable Dunkin' Donuts coffee dispenser was any indication, they were planning on getting comfortable. Yes, safe to say the Date Travis Ford competition was in full swing.

Out of the corner of his eye, Travis watched a petite redhead break from the pack, approaching a clipboard-holding Stephen with a casual air. "So . . . I'm thinking of doing some work in my kitchen this fall." Her smile broadened. "Do you think I could ask Travis a few questions? I'm trying to decide between vinyl and ceramic tile."

Blessedly clueless that he was being played, Stephen

slapped the clipboard against his thigh. "Look no further. I could talk flooring for *hours*."

The redhead's smile transformed into more of a baring of teeth as Stephen launched into a presentation, complete with hand gestures and his iPhone camera roll.

"Yo, Ford," one of the freelance workers said, wiping plaster onto the front of his T-shirt. "There's enough people wanting to see you naked out there, you could crowd-surf over them. I'm personally offended by your bored attitude."

"And here I thought I was being polite by not showing you up."

"*Please* show me up!" He gestured toward the growing crowd. "You are mocking a gift from the Lord God himself."

With a snort, Travis went back to making measurements. Once upon a time, he would have been front and center, absorbing the attention. *Basking* in it. As soon as he'd been let go from his final team, he'd learned pretty fucking fast that that kind of superficial admiration was cheap and fleeting. The women who'd once flocked to him had moved on to the next big thing, just like his coach, the team managers, and the fans. None of it had ever been real—and it wasn't real now.

There was one advantage to having an audience outside. He either ignored them or encouraged them—and it would be a cold day in hell before he did the latter. Pretending he didn't see the pack of admirers prevented him from looking outside. Across the street to the ramshackle old house of his youth.

Really, there was no need to look. He could picture every

square inch of the place. If he lifted his head and glanced out the window, his catcalling fans would be outlined by the drooping roof. The overgrown, sun-scorched lawn. Pretty ironic, wasn't it? At their backs stood a reminder of how the world *really* worked. In his parents' case, love had bred resentment and eventually eaten it whole. For Travis, affection had been given based on his success. Once that was gone, he'd been left alone. Again. Even his stardom hadn't changed the rules.

Hours later, Stephen had managed to disperse the crowd by lecturing them to death on insulation, allowing Travis to escape the flip without having to turn anyone down for a date. Going from a chauffeured SUV to carpooling in a minivan was a kick in the ass. Travis resisted the urge to hide his face as Stephen took a right turn, bringing them trundling straight down Main Street at happy hour. Port Jefferson natives were either picking up dinner or heading into one of the pubs for the liquid version. After spending the last few days working across the street from his childhood home, Travis wouldn't have minded a few slugs of whiskey, but he'd have them in the privacy of his own home or not at all. He might have escaped the uncomfortable public interest unscathed today, but its presence had mentally exhausted him.

"Mind telling me why you have a fucking Dodge Grand Caravan?"

Stephen adjusted the air-conditioning from high to higher. "I have a truck I use to transport building materials."

"Why aren't we in it?"

"Did you always complain this much?" Travis decided that didn't need an answer and Stephen wasn't waiting for one anyway. "I'm trying to get Kristin to give . . . strong consideration to children. I thought this might encourage her."

Travis frowned as a woman waiting to cross the street blew a kiss at him. "This conversation is above my pay grade." He could feel Stephen wanting to say more and sighed. "She's *not* considering having kids? Isn't that the first thing a married woman living on Long Island considers?"

"Kristin is complicated," he explained patiently. "She wants me to work for it."

"Jesus. She wants you to work for something that will be nothing *but* work?" Travis chuckled. "How many hoops did you jump through to get a yes to the marriage proposal?"

Stephen growled. "You don't want to know."

"You're right, I don't. I'll just be over here thanking God it's not me."

"Famous last words," Stephen murmured, nodding his head at a group of waving women on the sidewalk. "You could be looking at your future bride right now." He laughed when Travis shivered. "It'll happen. As long as it's none of the women in my life, we'll be good."

The idea of him settling down was so far-fetched, Travis didn't even bother addressing it. The mention of the women in Stephen's life did bring a certain face to mind, though. Georgie's, to be exact. Over the last couple of days, she'd popped into his consciousness at the weirdest times. Her red nose and damp eyes when she'd opened her front door. That sunny yellow apron she'd forgotten to remove the price tag from. It didn't seem right that her family hadn't shown more enthusiasm over her stupid waffles when even Travis had managed to drag his ass out of bed to be there. He'd told himself it wasn't his place to bring the oversight up to Stephen, but now it was Wednesday, and it was obvious that Georgie wasn't going to give her brother hell over it.

He thought she might be . . . too hurt. Or something equally unpleasant.

How annoying that it should bother him at all. He just wanted to put his head down, sweat through the depression he'd landed in after getting cut from the league, and move forward without looking left or right. He shouldn't be concerning himself with the hurt feelings of his friend's little sister. They were almost to his apartment. If he could just get through one more day without bringing it up, he'd eventually forget about all that food she'd probably spent hours making for no one.

"Speaking of the women in your life, you forgot Georgie's brunch on Saturday."

Christ. Had he actually said that out loud?

"What brunch?"

A little spike poked up under his skin. "I was standing right there when she invited you to it, man. We were in your office . . ."

"Right." A line formed between Stephen's brows. "And it was *last* Saturday?"

Travis snorted. "Forget it."

"Did *you* go?"

He coughed into his fist. "Yeah."

"You were alone with my little sister?"

Travis couldn't roll his eyes hard enough. "Stop clutching your pearls, Grandma. I didn't go there knowing I was going to be alone with her. I left after half an hour." He sent his friend a look. "Give me some credit. I'm not in the market for a woman at all, let alone the girl who used to spy on us through binoculars from the tree in your backyard. Your sister's blessed virtue was safe the whole time."

Stephen popped his jaw. "I trust you."

Travis let out a breath he didn't know he was holding. It was one thing to be the manwhore of the sports world and another to have his best friend distrust him because of that well-earned image. Was it too much to hope that one person found him redeemable? Once again, he couldn't seem to prevent thoughts of Georgie from popping up. *You could never be a joke.* "You can make up missing brunch to Georgie by fixing her fireplace. She wants to replace the brick."

The calculations Stephen was performing in his head were almost audible. "I want to, but we're on a tight schedule with three flips running at once. Two of my best guys won't be back until the summer is over, so we're short-staffed even though you're gracing us with your moody presence. It's going to have to wait."

Travis nodded. There. He'd fulfilled his job by asking. Done.

They pulled off Main Street, traveling down one of the side streets to a three-family house, of which Travis was renting the top floor. The elderly owners who lived on the first floor left him alone, and the middle apartment below him was empty. A far cry from the crowded luxury high-rises he'd lived in all over the map, but right now, the quiet was exactly what he wanted.

"I'll meet you at the job site tomorrow," Travis said as they pulled up along the curb. "I can't ride in this estrogen trap another day and maintain my self-respect."

Stephen shrugged. "Suit yourself. Don't be late." He rubbed his hands together. "Tomorrow is demo day."

"I won't sleep a wink," Travis droned, closing the passenger door behind him. "Thanks."

The horn tooted as Stephen drove off, making Travis shake his head. He entered on the first floor, climbing the stairs to the top and unlocking the door to his apartment. He'd only managed to shuck his work boots, strip off his dusty shirt, and crack open a beer when a knock sounded on the door. Who the hell? He'd paid the rent a couple months in advance, so it couldn't be the owners. Unless maybe there was a leak coming from his place? Travis plowed a hand through his hair, unlocked the apartment door—and found Georgie staring back at him, holding two armfuls of groceries.

A different ball cap hid her eyes this time, her standard ponytail sticking out through the back. She wore overalls with a loose T-shirt underneath. He almost closed the door in her face when he saw the script across the front. CLASS OF 2012 RULES!

This veritable girl-child was trying not to look at his bare chest and failing miserably. The combination of her high school memorabilia and the freckles scattered across her nose made him feel like a lecher for offering her the view, whether it had been intentional or not.

Fuck's sake. He didn't have time for this. Couldn't he just drink his beer in peace and forget he'd landed back in his hometown working a construction gig? Getting up in the morning and putting on work boots was enough of an effort when his heart was back in the dugout and aching to be lacing up cleats instead. At the moment, there was no energy left to give.

"Why are you here?"

"Um." She slipped past him into the apartment before he could stop her. "First of all, hi. Second, I don't know if you're aware of this, but it's very hard to cook for one person. They sell things in two portion sizes: family smorgasbord, and enough for two. So I keep ending up with leftovers." She snuck a nervous look at him over her shoulder and started to unpack the first bag, setting foil-covered plates out on the counter. "You can only eat so much Chinese takeout, right?"

Her comment brought on the memory of her chucking a carton at his head. The damn apartment wasn't in much better shape than the last time Georgie had been there. His laundry was still spilling out of the hamper in the bedroom doorway, unopened mail and glossy advertisements were scattered on every surface, sticky beverage rings, dust, clutter. It was nasty.

"Are you going to close the door, Travis?"

"No." He jerked his chin toward the hall. "Because you're not staying."

She turned and propped a hip against the counter. "Afraid I'll drop some more truth on you?"

"No."

"Because we need to talk about your rat infestation."

His neck prickled. "I don't have rats."

"Not yet." She went back to unloading food. "This close to the water, though? You'll have roommates within a week. They'll be even more annoying than me."

For some reason, Georgie calling herself annoying made him close the door.

The brim of Georgie's hat didn't quite hide her smile. "Okay, so there's meat ravioli—"

"That works," he grunted.

"Or chipotle meatloaf."

His beer paused on the way to his mouth. "What the hell is that? Never mind, I'll eat it."

"*Both* things?"

He gestured to her tiny frame with his beer bottle. "A portion size for you is not the same as a portion size for me, baby girl." The endearment rolled off his tongue like butter, and Georgie almost dropped one of the plates she was unloading. Why the hell had he called her that? Pet names weren't unusual for Travis, although he'd never called anyone by this one before. Still, Georgie wasn't one of the women who'd come and gone from his life at the speed of fastball pitches. She shouldn't even be here. And he damn sure shouldn't be calling attention to their size difference or making references to her body type. Not that he could make out a single curve with those overalls hanging loose around her, head to toe. He found *nothing* about that disappointing. "Look, thank you for stopping by with the food. But I don't think your brother would appreciate us hanging out."

Her nose wrinkled. "Why?"

Travis raked a hand down his face. "Come on. You have to know I've got something of a . . . reputation where the opposite sex is concerned." He waited until Georgie looked at him. "Let's just say it's well earned."

"Yes, Two Bats. I'm aware." She shrugged as if she hadn't just called out the size of his cock. "But it's not like *we're* going to—"

"No, definitely not."

"I mean . . ." She winked at him. "I think I'm safe."

"You are one thousand percent safe."

"Okay, you don't have to be quite so adamant. I do have a thimbleful of vanity and I'd like to keep it."

Travis laughed. An actual laugh that reached his stomach. How long had it been since that happened? Months. Usually he found nothing funny about someone invading his personal space, but having Georgie in his apartment was . . . surprisingly easy. He didn't even have to be nice to her and she just stuck around anyway. If he'd been required to entertain or charm someone, they would have been sorely disappointed, but she didn't seem to expect that. Maybe he'd let her stay for a few more minutes.

Ten tops.

"Okay, don't get weird, but I found this DVD . . ." As if she were unveiling the new iPhone, she pulled out a copy of *A League of Their Own* with a flourish. "We can put it on in the background while we clean this rat hole."

Travis plunked his empty beer bottle down on the counter. "You're insane if you think I'm cleaning tonight. I just spent eight hours framing a two-story addition . . ." He backed away. "Don't look at me like that, Georgie. My ass is tired."

"There's no crying in construction."

"That's not funny."

"You're right, it was pretty weak. I'm tired, too." Giving Travis her profile, she hit a couple buttons on the oven, opened the door, and then slid two of the plates onto the center rack. "So I performed at a birthday party this week. The youngest Miller kid?"

Travis went to the fridge to retrieve another beer. "No clue who that is."

"Really? The parents graduated your year, I think. He's a ginger. She smokes menthols and always insists she's quitting tomorrow."

A long-buried memory from high school trickled in—a group of seniors standing outside the homecoming dance passing around a brown bag with a forty-ounce inside. He could almost smell the cigarette smoke, mint coasting down his throat when he bummed a drag. Travis's mouth jumped at one end. "That actually rings a bell."

"I overheard them talking at the party. Ginger Dad is the school principal now, and they're hoping you'll come do a demonstration for the team. You know, for inspiration."

A weight dropped in Travis's stomach. "Oh yeah?" He pressed his tongue to the inside of his cheek until it hurt. "A bunch of kids? That's not exactly my kind of thing."

"Funny," she muttered. "That's precisely my thing."

"Right." He massaged his eyes. "The birthday parties."

"Not just birthday parties." Georgie shrugged. "I love kids. They're basically magic little balls of optimism that love you unconditionally. I can't wait for my own." As if realizing she'd been speaking out loud, Georgie hastily set a spoon down. "Um. Kids don't have to be your thing to run a baseball clinic."

Still a little stuck on Georgie's announcement that she wanted children, Travis asked, "Aren't you a little young to want kids so bad?"

"Some people dream about playing in the major leagues, others dream about finger paintings drying over the kitchen sink." She paused. "I want a career, too, but . . . yeah, I want a big, noisy, happy family. You've never wanted that at all?"

"No," Travis said without hesitation, wondering why the word dropped like an anvil between them. Frankly, the idea of being responsible for a child unnerved him. Already here he was, back in Port Jeff, his professional baseball career a thing of the past. Going nowhere. The similarities were too reminiscent of his father to think he wouldn't fuck up fatherhood, too. He tried to shake himself back to the topic at hand, but it took an effort.

Run a baseball clinic? Damn. He was surprised by how much he *didn't* want to pick up a bat. Jesus, he could barely fathom trying to play the sport he used to live for. Why make the effort when he'd lost too many steps to resemble a shadow of his former self?

"Your brother was just saying it's the busy season right

now." Feeling Georgie's searching eyes, he paced into the living room, snagging dirty socks as he went. "Everyone is remodeling before fall temperatures set in, and he's short a couple guys. I can't leave him high and dry."

"You could teach them more in an hour than they'd learn in months from someone else. It wouldn't have to be right away, either. There's plenty of time before the season starts." She smiled at him over her shoulder. "They love you. It would be like a dream come true."

"Drop it, Georgie."

Hurt danced across her features before she could turn away and hide it, and she continued to load his fridge with enough food for the next few nights. Travis leveled an inward curse at himself. Hadn't he *wanted* people to talk to him about baseball and stop walking on eggshells? This girl had done it twice without any prompting. Where did he get off snapping at her for poking a sore spot he hadn't even been aware of having?

They could be friends, him and Georgie. That's what was wrong. He didn't *want* one—especially her. She was too young, too positive, and too related to his best friend. For some reason, he couldn't stop himself from thanking her, though, in his own way. For thinking he was worth her attempts to wave away the gloom. "Listen . . ." She turned hopeful eyes on him and he frowned back. "Pick a day next week and I'll come take some measurements on that fireplace."

Her hands flew to her chest, flattening there. "*You're* going to redo my fireplace?"

"If you don't make me clean," Travis said, crossing his arms.

Georgie threw open the cabinet beneath his kitchen sink and started rooting through whatever cleaning supplies the last tenant had left behind, since he sure as shit hadn't bought any. "I'll clean this whole place top to bottom if I'm getting a fireplace out of the deal. Does Tuesday sound good for our appointment?"

"Tuesday, fine. But do you understand the ass kicking I'm inviting from your brother, having you cook and clean for me? Not happening."

She straightened, examining a bottle of Windex. "You seem to be suffering from the delusion that my brother cares how I spend my time. He just wants me out of the way."

None of his business. None. "He cares about you."

Her mouth moved into a little O, and Travis found himself staring at it longer than he should. Apparently this was what happened when he didn't get laid for months. The closest woman started to look good. That was the only reason his fingers were tingling to unsnap Georgie's overalls and get a good goddamn look at her. Relieved by that iron-clad reasoning—almost—Travis turned away.

"Fine, let's both clean this fucking place. That's the only way this doesn't bite me in the ass."

Georgie tilted her head. "You mean rats. It's the only way rats don't bite you—"

"Shut up, Georgie."

"Done."

She got started shoveling garbage and takeout containers

into a black garbage bag while Travis ate yet another round of her amazing cooking, not bothering to hide his exasperation when she snuck *A League of Their Own* into his DVD player. A few times, when she caught him watching the screen and lifted her chin in sarcastic reproof, Travis got the urge to tickle her. Or ruffle her hair. Things he never would have hesitated to do when they were younger. Something made him keep his hands to himself this time, though. Intuition told him an innocent touch could lead down a distinctly *not* innocent path—and he wouldn't be questioning that instinct or exploring it any further.

"Have you managed to avoid the dating competition?" Georgie asked while shoveling old magazines into a trash bag.

"Sort of," he droned, catcalls from the construction site echoing in his head. "Come to think of it, how do I know you're not a spy? Or worse, a contestant." When she came up sputtering, Travis winked to let her know he was joking. "What about your dating situation?"

Before he could berate himself for asking Georgie about something that was damn well none of his business, she laughed. "In a word? Dire. Most of the men I come into contact with are off-the-market fathers. Not a lot of young single men hanging out at princess parties." She picked up a petrified sock and tapped it against the wall, raising an eyebrow at him. He shrugged. "Maybe you should let the dating competition contestants take a tour of your place. Problem solved."

"If you're suggesting we stop cleaning, I'm in."

"You wish," she said, dropping the sock into her garbage

bag. "We soldier onward. Especially now that you've drawn attention to my lack of dates. I have to keep busy now or wallow in pity."

"Stop." Travis wiped an unknown substance off the coffee table. "I'd say the problem is everyone in town knows your brother and doesn't want to piss him off."

"Again, I assure you, my brother wouldn't even notice if I started dating."

Travis watched her work for a moment, remembering not only brunch but the conversation with Stephen in the minivan. "Is it that bad, Georgie?"

She straightened, looking so young and vulnerable that he wondered what was wrong with him, spending time alone with her. *Noticing* things about her. "Is what that bad?"

Why the hell was he involving himself in this? Travis didn't know, but he couldn't seem to stop himself. "You, uh . . . seem to get left out a lot. Or not considered as much as you should." He went back to cleaning the table. "Starting to think you weren't exaggerating."

When Georgie was silent for a few beats, he looked up to find her staring into space. "Remember when you were at my house the other day and you said it's no one's fault, you made yourself a joke?"

"Yeah," he rasped.

"It's a little like that for me, too. The family was already solid when I was old enough to be part of the conversation. Like all little kids, I got shushed a lot, so I had to be persistent and annoying to be heard. A pest." She shrugged. "I'm older now, but the dynamics are the same. I guess it's easier to let them remain than to try to change them. Because what if I failed? Or what if I really am a pest?"

Travis wanted to tell her she wasn't a pest, despite his own treatment of her. The words were right there on the tip of his tongue, but what if saying so made her comfortable around him? Made her rely on him or view him as a friend? He didn't want a friend right now, did he? Didn't want *anyone* too close. "Families are complicated," he said, even though it didn't sound good enough. Wasn't reassuring in the way her words had been for him. "They probably don't even know they're hurting your feelings, baby girl."

She sighed. "No, I think you're right about that."

"I've been on teams where one voice always seems to get passed over. When I played on the Hurricanes, they brought a guy up from the minors. A vet. I mean, this guy was in his forties and still grinding. He was dismissed by all the new talent, including me, as an old man. A guy who took decades to be relevant." He rolled his shoulders. "Right after the injury, I sat beside him in the dugout for several games, and I realized . . . this guy knew more about the game than all of us combined. Pointed out things I never would have seen on my own." Georgie watched him silently from across the room. "You shouldn't give up or stop demanding to be heard," he said, needing to leave her in a better place and having no idea why. "Maybe you just need a different way to make them listen."

Georgie gave a slow blink. "Thank you for that."

Refusing to acknowledge his relief that he'd apparently said something right, Travis grunted and went back to tidying. A couple hours later, the credits rolled on the movie to the sound of Madonna's voice, and Travis realized he'd been standing in the middle of his living room, broom forgotten in hand, for the last twenty minutes. The apartment was pretty damn close to spotless. Where was Georgie?

He found her sprawled facedown on the foot of his bed. Fast asleep.

Travis expected to be annoyed. Instead, he stood there noticing her lack of one sock, as if she'd kicked it off in her sleep. No toenail polish. Her face was pressed to the bedspread and turned to one side, smooshing her face into a pout. If he had any kind of functioning heart left in his chest, he might have found the whole picture she made kind of adorable. Since he didn't, though, he really needed to figure out how to get her the hell out of there. They had already spent way too much time together. Letting her stay the night at his place crossed a line—and no one on God's green earth would believe Two Bats had done nothing more with Georgie than clean.

"Hey." Swallowing a surge of guilt, Travis nudged her shoulder. "Georgie. Wake your ass up."

"Have you seen Dale?" Georgie muttered in her sleep, clearly nowhere near awake. "I need Dale."

"Who's Dale?"

Georgie's eyes flew open. Her legs scrambled, but she was too close to the edge of the bed, so her knee found no purchase. She flopped onto the floor before Travis could drop the broom and catch her. "Ouch."

All right. There might have been a dime-sized portion of heart left rattling around inside of him, because the sight of a sleepy, disoriented Georgie with half her ponytail loose had him kneeling before he could think better of it, one of his hands lifted to run over her hair. "You all right, baby girl?"

She yawned so big, he could see her tonsils. "Are we done cleaning?"

For the second time that night, he got the urge to laugh. "We're done."

"I should go."

He swallowed hard. "It's for the best."

Travis helped Georgie climb to her feet, having no choice but to grip her waist when she swayed. *Not speculating on what's under her overalls. No, sir, not me.* He was ready to insist on driving her home, but she reanimated by the time they reached the front door, like she'd never been asleep at all. It was kind of freaky, actually. Before she could walk out, she turned back and threw him a smile. "I saw you watching the movie."

"No, you didn't."

"Good night," she called, going down the stairs. "The rats should leave you alone now."

He sighed. "Thank you, Georgie."

"Me and my fireplace will see you Tuesday."

When Travis closed the door, he could feel the grudging smile trying to mar his face.

Shaking it off with a curse, he stalked off to bed.

Who the hell was Dale?

CHAPTER FIVE

Georgie circled a garment rack, browsing through hangers of old clothing. When she came to a gray T-shirt with the Port Jefferson High School logo, she tugged it out of the jam-packed row and held it up to face the woman behind the register.

"Hey, I think this used to be mine!"

She got a thumbs-up in return, before the thrift shop owner, Zelda, went back to reading her romance novel. Thus was their dynamic. Sometimes Georgie wondered if Zelda would rather have a completely empty store than have to deal with a customer interrupting her book. In a few minutes, the older woman would finish her chapter, dog-ear the page, and be ready to talk. That was just her process. Georgie was well used to it, considering Second Chance Zelda's was where she'd been buying her clothes for years.

Being the youngest of the Castle family meant Georgie's wardrobe growing up consisted of hand-me-downs, from Bethany *and* Stephen. She'd attended school in patched-up jeans, faded sweaters, and sneakers from five seasons ago. Not that her parents couldn't afford to buy her new clothes, but Morty Castle came from humble beginnings and didn't believe in fixing something that wasn't broken. His credo was what made him so successful in the house-flipping business. Making necessary changes only, focusing on curb appeal and sprucing existing features, had served him well.

Had that logic served Georgie well? Classmates had definitely poked fun at her oversized or unfashionable clothing more than once, but as with most small towns, the past popularity of her siblings had helped curb the bullying. It didn't hurt that local phenom Travis Ford was a close friend of the family. And finally one day, Georgie reached a point where there *were* no more hand-me-downs. They'd literally all been handed.

Almost five years had passed since she'd ridden shotgun in her mother's station wagon on the way to Zelda's for the first time. The back of the wagon was loaded with decades of Castle kid clothing, ready to be donated. They'd planned to venture to the mall afterward to finally buy Georgie some threads of her own choosing, but she got no farther than the overloaded racks of Zelda's. It was too late. Secondhand clothes had become her comfort zone. Soft, old camp T-shirts, flannel, discontinued jeans. What could be better?

Lately she'd begun to wonder this very thing. What *could* be better?

Georgie had two uniforms: a clown costume and thrift shop rejects. Was that part of the reason her family didn't take her seriously? Because she still dressed the same way she had in elementary school?

She ran her finger down the pleat of a floor-length skirt, letting it drop.

After chewing her lip for a minute, she slipped her cell out of the pocket of her jeans and pulled up her contacts, running her thumb over Bethany's name. Asking her effortlessly chic sister for fashion advice wasn't high on her to-do list, but she didn't have anyone else to call. After graduating from high school in Port Jefferson, people had two options: stick around and marry someone local, or leave for college, club your mate over the head, and drag them home. If you were Port Jeff born, you always ended up back on its shores. Unfortunately, both of Georgie's closest childhood friends hadn't quite managed to club an unsuspecting gentleman yet and were still living single in vastly different zip codes.

On the other hand, Bethany worked as a stager/decorator for Brick & Morty, meaning she got the bat signal only when a house was completed. Most of her time was spent ordering materials online or hunting down unique pieces at antique malls on Long Island. There was a good chance she'd be around.

Georgie bit the bullet and tapped Bethany's name.

G: Hey, can you meet me? I need help.

B: With what?

G: Clothes. For . . .

Georgie's thumbs paused on the screen. She should have had a better game plan. Her reason for wanting new clothes had more layers than a Super Bowl Sunday snack dip.

Most importantly, the clown business was waning. Those phone calls she'd returned last Saturday? She'd booked only two jobs out of them. Her birthday parties were top-notch, those eight noes had assured her, but they were looking for something . . . *bigger*. Georgie knew it would take a lot of hard work to turn a fledgling one-woman operation into something respectable. An actual business that advertised and made bids. As of now, she relied on word-of-mouth referrals and repeat customers who knew her, knew her reputation, and, in most cases, were friends of the Castle family.

The Castle family. They didn't take her seriously. How could she expect anyone else to?

She looked down at her faded 501 jeans that had probably belonged to a deceased lumberjack. Her scuffed boots peeked out under the frayed hems, taunting her. What did people see when they looked at her? Not a businesswoman.

Not a sexually desirable woman, either. And maybe, just maybe, when Travis came over to measure her fireplace on Tuesday, she wanted him to see one. Someone worth polishing the family jewels over. Georgie shot a cautious glance at Zelda, as if that inappropriate thought had occurred out loud. She'd been saying *a lot* of things out loud lately.

Have you seen Dale? I need Dale.

Had she really called for her vibrator in front of Travis Ford?

She buried her face in a fleece-lined jacket. Oh God, that had simultaneously been the best and worst night of her life. Her intentions had been pure. She'd only wanted to drop off some leftovers for the man who had no family left in town and had just watched his career burn to the dust. Even if she hadn't been nursing an infatuation with him for a long, long time, she would have done that.

Instead of doing the noble thing and leaving, she'd spent two hours watching a shirtless Travis Ford bend over to pick up trash and stretching to dust off high surfaces. There was no movement he could make where something didn't flex. There was nigh *constant flexing*. She'd meant to lie down for only a few seconds after changing his sheets, because who can resist freshly laundered sheets? Turned out all that athletic muscle observance had revved her subconscious, because she'd dropped right into a sex dream. As with all her naughtiest fantasies since time began, they starred Travis Ford. However, since most of her fantasies involved use of Dale—and *not* the real deal—she'd called her Day-Glo orange pal's name instead.

There had been a split second when she woke up where she swore Travis was looking at her with something like . . . tenderness. A figment of her imagination, obviously, but she continued to go back to it, replaying how warm it made her feel. How warm Travis made her feel in general. Not in the simple hot-for-jock kind of way, either. He'd let his guard down on accident a couple of times when they were alone and showed her someone different from the infallible superstar of her dreams. He was so utterly *human*. She should be worried that it did nothing to detract from her admiration of him. No, it only seemed to heighten it. Why?

Georgie's phone buzzed again.

B: You need help with what? Have you been kidnapped?

G: No. Never mind. I'm just looking for outfit advice.

B: I'd let you borrow something, but all my clown suits are at the cleaners.

There it is. Shouldn't have bothered. Georgie shoved her phone back into her pocket with a grimace. The dismissive texts from her siblings were nothing new. But this desire to prove to them she was a capable adult only grew stronger. And maybe, just maybe, it had something to do with Travis noticing her as more than his best friend's annoying little sister.

"I'll catch you next time, Zelda," Georgie said on her way out the door.

Zelda merely turned the page in response.

Travis sat down on the stoop of the four-bedroom Cape, smacking the demolition dust off his jeans. Trying his best to ignore the house across the street, he cracked open a ginger ale and drank deeply. When Stephen had told him the address of this renovation, why hadn't he declined? Out of anyone in Port Jefferson, Stephen would have understood. But it would have been admitting a weakness, and Travis had too many of those right now, didn't he? Still, living in this town meant being surrounded by his past. He didn't need to have it staring him in the face morning until night. No. He damn sure didn't need that.

Travis's father no longer lived in the ramshackle Colonial

across the road, but since it had never been sold, all the signs of neglect were still there. The eaves drooped like sad, sloping eyebrows over grime-covered windows. Once upon a time, the trees surrounding the home were tall and proud. They hadn't been trimmed in so long, though, they'd formed kind of a leafy green barrier around the house. A blessing, since it partially blocked everyone's view of the house from the street. A breeze blew past, smacking a shutter off to the side of his old bedroom, just like it used to when he slept inside, scaring the shit out of him in the middle of the night.

If he closed his eyes, he could remember his mother pulling up outside the house in her old white Ford Explorer, dropping him off for the weekend. She'd sigh and hesitate. He'd pray she would bring him home and not force him to endure his father's turn, custody agreement be damned. But she never caved, telling Travis to get out and go wait on the porch until his father returned home. Sometimes he'd sit there until the middle of the night, waiting.

A can cracked open behind Travis and he turned to find Stephen leaning against the wrought-iron rail, draining his own ginger ale, the work site drink of choice since they couldn't have beer. Not on Stephen's watch. "Got about another hour here before we head." He shook some dust from his hair. "I want to get that wall opened up in the dining room and see what kind of structural support we're dealing with. Could fuck up the open concept unless we want to knock it down and add a support beam."

"Ouch. A beam will cost you."

"Something always does." Stephen took a slow sip and

rolled it around in his mouth. "Been weird working this close to the old house?"

"That's putting it mildly." Travis stood and strode into the house. "Let's get back to work."

"Don't you own the place now? Why not knock it down?" Stephen said, following Travis into the renovation, where the third member of their crew, Dominic Vega, was repointing an exposed brick wall, his movements slow and methodical. Focused. "Might be cathartic."

Or it could enable the demons to run amok.

"We don't share the same definition of 'cathartic,'" Travis muttered.

"Are you referencing sex?" asked Stephen. "I drive a minivan part-time, so I need dirty jokes explained to me now."

"If I'm talking about sex, you'll know it."

Dominic set down his trowel and crossed his arms, his legs braced in a military stance that meant business. "What *are* we talking about?"

"Nothing," Travis answered, ignoring the impulse to look back out the window at the shrine to his childhood across the street. "The boss can't mind his own business."

Stephen sighed. "Having all the answers is a burden, but I press on."

Dom coughed into his fist, the blue tattoos on his knuckles covered in dirt and specks of mortar. "Why not sell the place? Make it someone else's problem?"

"Maybe being proactive with the house will prove he can still give a damn about something," Stephen said, punctuating his statement with a superior sniff. "God forbid."

Travis didn't care for the hollowness of his own laugh. There was no chance he was going to tell Stephen and Dominic that while he did own the house, his father's name was also still on the deed. And the last thing he needed was to bring that old fucker back into his life. He'd be keeping that to himself, though, because to an outsider it might seem like Travis was scared to confront his father. That wasn't the case. It wasn't that easy. The last time he'd seen his father, he'd beaten the odds and gotten scouted by Northwestern. He merely wanted to avoid hearing *I told you so* at all costs now that he'd failed.

"I don't give a damn about anything. You should both try it sometime," Travis finally responded. For some reason, Georgie's face popped into his mind. The odd timing propelled him into picking up a sledgehammer and burying it in the dining room wall. "Come on in, boys. The water's fine."

"No, thank you." Stephen inspected the wall through the hole. "I like the hot water Kristin is boiling me alive in. Keeps me young."

"Keeps you on the verge of a stroke, you mean."

"Maybe." Stephen almost smiled, but whatever he saw in the wall made him frown. "We're going to need to bring in a support beam."

Dom came up behind them. "Shit."

"Yeah." Stephen massaged the bridge of his nose. "But if I've got a post in the middle of Bethany's open concept, she'll have to change the whole design."

"And you'll have to replace the balls she's going to rip off," Dom muttered.

"If she hasn't changed since high school, that sounds about accurate." Travis dropped the sledgehammer and started to gather his tools, knowing it would be pointless to move on until they brought in a crew to bolster the structure. "You guys up for a beer?"

"I'm in," Dom said, taking off his work gloves and shoving them in his back pocket. "Rosie is taking some exercise class tonight, so I'm fending for myself. Again."

A deep trench formed between Dom's eyebrows. Growing up, Travis remembered those two being a solid couple who seemed to speak their own language, no one else in the room existing when they were together. They'd had each other's backs, named their future children, and were voted Most Likely to Get Married. After graduation, Dom made the yearbook prediction a reality and proposed to Rosie, right there in the center of the football field, both of them in caps and gowns. Months later, having parked a ring on Rosie's finger, he'd joined the marines and spent time overseas—but he'd come back quieter. More serious.

Travis didn't intend to diagnose Dom the way Stephen might, but there definitively appeared to be trouble in paradise where Dom and Rosie were concerned. Even Travis, who thought marriage was an unrealistic institution, didn't want to see the couple drift apart. Back in the day, everyone had been so positive they'd be the ones to beat the odds.

If Dom and Rosie were going to separate, Travis could only be grateful they didn't have children. He knew too well how divorce could turn a child into a pawn in an ugly game of chess. After all, he was standing across the street from the hell his own parents had created for him.

Yeah, definitely time for that beer.

They each took their own truck into town, parking in the lot behind Grumpy Tom's and piling in through the back door, reserved for regulars. Port Jefferson was a small town, but it had become an increasingly popular destination over the years. Most of the sightseers stayed near the water where the ferry let off or shopped on Main Street. Every once in a while, some of them wandered into Grumpy Tom's, but most of the bar's patrons were locals. Some blue collar, some white collar, and all with one goal: to watch the ball game and unwind. Tonight in particular that was exactly what Travis needed.

Before they could order drinks, a man slid in beside them at the bar, pounding a fist on the wood and drawing attention with a booming laugh. "There he is. I knew Two Bats would get back on the prowl if we just gave him time." The man scanned the bar. "Slim pickins tonight, but once the ladies hear you're around, it'll be standing room only. We all stand to benefit."

Having his sordid past glorified didn't sit right. Over the last year, he'd been traded to Chicago, San Diego, Miami. During nights out, or even in professional settings, men would approach him and ask for details of his exploits. Travis usually satisfied their curiosity without actually imparting any real information. The old *I never kiss and tell* routine. But even that felt wrong now. He wasn't up for it anymore. And the reminder of his reputation was bothering him more than usual tonight, having Stephen within earshot—the man whose little sister had fallen asleep on his bed last week.

Travis sent the patron a vague smile, hoping he'd take the hint and fuck off. "All right, man."

"The boys were saying you haven't picked up one skirt since coming home, and I said . . ." He paused to swig his beer. "I said you've probably been going into Manhattan for the high-quality pu—"

"Okay, buddy. I'm going to stop you there." Travis slid off the stool, avoiding Stephen's eyes. "Order me a beer. I'm going to make a phone call."

Stephen was eyeing the idiot with disgust. "Sure."

Travis didn't actually have a phone call to make; he just needed some air. Salt and humidity filled his lungs as he stepped out the back door of the bar. Wind kicked up from the distant water, blowing his hair around. Thankfully, the alleyway running behind Grumpy Tom's was empty so he could have a minute to himself. He tugged his cell out of the back pocket of his jeans to check the time, surprised to find a missed call from his agent.

Hope straightened his spine before he could stop it. Was it possible a shortstop position had opened up and he was being called to suit up? They'd exhausted all options weeks ago, his agent telling him playing professional ball again was hopeless. What if something had changed, though? Maybe an overseas option?

He hit the call back button, holding the phone to his ear as he paced in a circle.

His agent picked up on the second ring. "Ford. My man."

"Donny." He tried to shake off the hope and failed. "What's up?"

"First of all, it's not what you think. Sorry. Nothing has changed." Donny rambled right over the thick slowdown of Travis's pulse. "But I've got a line on something better."

Travis pressed his palm to the bridge of his nose. "Better than playing ball?"

"Fuck yes. Do I have to remind you about ice baths, road fatigue, and B12 shots in the ass? I know, I know. You're going to tell me that sounds like heaven. But what if I told you, Ford, you could sit in an air-conditioned box at the stadium in a suit and commentate?"

The idea was so out of left field, Travis could only shake his head. "What?"

"The New York Bombers are looking for a new voice. Fresh, young, easy on the eyes. They've got a short list of candidates and you're on it." He could hear his agent punching computer keys in the background. "It pays in the two-comma neighborhood and you only have to work home games. National television. Who knows where it could lead? Look, man. It's the next best thing to being on the field. You'll be at the field, talking about the game you love. What do you say?"

Travis found himself thinking about the old Colonial with sagging shutters. The echoes of voices from the past in the kitchen, the feel of the coarse wooden porch underneath him. The man who'd told him he'd come crawling back as a disappointment eventually. Travis might have failed to achieve the kind of career he'd dreamed about, but *this*? This could be a way to salvage it. Commentating had never even occurred to him. Now it was this bright, shiny thing that made the chance to prove himself attainable again.

"You said I'm on a list. How do I get to the top?"

Donny sighed. "You know how it goes. There's always a rub, my man." His agent stopped typing, probably adopting his all too familiar *let me level with you* pose. "This is network television. They want wholesome. They want someone who isn't going to show up hungover with panties hanging out of his pocket."

"That happened once."

"At a children's hospital charity event."

A jab of regret made Travis close his eyes. Just one of the many times he'd lived up to the Two Bats hype. "I'm not that guy anymore."

"Right now you're not—you're in a rut. But a leopard doesn't change its spots." A calculated beat passed. "We just need to make them think you did."

Travis shook his head. "How am I supposed to do that?"

"I'm working on getting you an invitation to dinner with the head of the network. Might be a couple weeks. Lie low until then. Or better yet, settle down and pop out a kid or two."

"Not even if the Bombers offered me a ten-year contract, Donny."

His agent snorted a laugh. "Worth a shot. Seriously, though. Find a way to prove some stability and we're a shoo-in. You're great on camera. Recognizable." Another phone went off in the background. "I have to take this. I'll keep you posted on that dinner invite."

"Yeah. Bye."

Feeling a little like a sleepwalker, Travis returned to the bar. It was too early in the game to tell Stephen and Dominic about the potential commentator job. He didn't want to jinx himself, so he slid back onto his stool and picked up his beer, glad to see their unwanted guest had returned to his side of the bar. Travis's mind should have been filled with the possibilities of getting a job involving baseball—something he'd stopped thinking of as an option over a month ago. Instead, something else was niggling at his subconscious. Like he'd shown up for a game without his favorite glove.

"Hey, what day is it?"

"Tuesday," Dominic replied.

Fuck.

The few sips of beer in Travis's stomach went sour.

He'd forgotten the fireplace appointment.

Poised to ask Stephen for Georgie's number so he could call and reschedule, Travis took the phone back out of his pocket . . . and stopped. *Let's recap. You're getting ready to ask your best friend for his little sister's phone number. Are you fucking insane?*

Yeah. He was. They never should have been spending time together in the first place. This was exactly what he needed—a wake-up call. If Stephen knew they'd been hanging out, he'd deck him. Travis would deserve it, too. He'd apologize for missing the appointment next time she showed up to pester him. Then he'd send Georgie on her way. For good this time. Still, when he put his phone back in his pocket, the guilt and unease refused to fade.

CHAPTER SIX

Georgie tightened her hoodie strings as she walked into the torture palace, also known as Fun 'n' Flirty Fitness. She'd been inside this place once before for an introductory yoga class—and that time had also been her sister-in-law's fault. Kristin couldn't seem to stop getting certified in things. Yoga. Zumba. Life coaching. Seriously. Pick a lane. In Stephen's ongoing quest to keep Kristin as happy as a frolicking bunny, he'd issued the demand for his sisters to make an appearance at Kristin's first official night as a Zumba instructor. The timing could not be *better.*

She signed in at the front desk and moped down the hallway, wishing she'd gotten lucky and contracted malaria. An infectious disease was the only way Stephen would let her off the hook, although he'd probably *still* be pissed about her canceling. The Castle family operated by a strict set of unspoken rules that must never be tested. One, their mother was a saint and must be treated thusly and obeyed in all things, lest the sky come crashing down. Two, when their mother wasn't around, Stephen was next in line to the throne. It had been that way since Georgie was a child, and even though she thought it was bullshit, following his directives was as deeply ingrained as the *Bob's Burgers* theme music.

Georgie stopped in front of the dark, empty aerobics room, wondering if she'd gotten the day mixed up. No, no. It was definitely Tuesday. The day Travis was supposed to come over and help her realize her dreams of fireplace glory.

The pressure in her chest had been growing stronger since this afternoon. By now, it felt like a pair of pliers was digging into her heart. *God, I'm such an idiot.*

She'd worn her hair down and everything. Made a cheese plate. Cleaned.

Just thinking about it made her want to die.

In a burst of much-needed movement, Georgie slapped on the light in the aerobics room, tossed her duffel near the stacked mats, and plopped cross-legged in the center of the floor. Maybe Zumba would be good for her. She could sweat out some of the shame.

She turned her head and caught her reflection in the mirrored wall, jolting when she saw the girl with tearstained cheeks. A girl who'd cried for an hour over a man who thought of her as a dumb little sister, just like everyone else.

Georgie had stuck her business degree diploma in a drawer and become a clown for a reason. Making people laugh and spreading joy made her happy. Especially when it came to children. Perhaps her youngest-sibling status made her relate to little kids more. They were talked down to and dictated to about their wide-eyed naivete, just like her. Whatever the reason for her unusual career path, Georgie adored children and dreamed of having her own someday. Performing at birthday parties and bat mitzvahs never failed to be the highlight of her week.

She adored being a clown. She didn't appreciate being made to feel like one, though, and it seemed to be happening more and more lately.

The twist in her chest intensified, just in time for Bethany to waltz into the room in a toss of blond hair and a flash of dazzling white teeth. "Hell? Party of two?" She dropped her black Chanel bag in a pile with Georgie's ancient gym duffel, falling into a perfect stretch beside her younger sister on the floor. Effortlessly glamorous. That was Bethany. "What's wrong?"

"Nothing."

"Are you sure? You seem even more depressed than this situation warrants."

"I said it's nothing." Georgie spread her legs in a V and crawled forward, enjoying the vicious tug in her hamstrings. "Shouldn't the instructor be here first?"

"Changing the subject. Noted." Bethany poked her in the side. "You have your period?"

"No."

"Me neither."

"Why even remark on it?"

Bethany shrugged. "Just making conversation until you tell me what's wrong. You blow-dried your hair. I know it wasn't for this shit show." Bethany leaned into Georgie's line of sight. "Tell me."

"Travis didn't show up to look at my fireplace today!"

Georgie exploded, pressing fingers to the ache in her chest. "I don't know why I expected him to remember. It's not like it was set in stone. But he remembered brunch when no one else did. I thought . . ."

"Wait. Whoa, whoa. Back up. Travis who? *Ford?*" Bethany did an exaggerated double take. "What is wrong with your chimney and why is that philandering asshole going anywhere near it?"

"It's my fireplace, not my chimney—and don't call him that."

"Why not? You didn't go to high school with him, Georgie. He plowed through half the senior class. *Before* midterms. What happened after graduation is well documented. He more than lived up to the title of philanderer." Bethany's love-hate relationship with men showed through in most instances, but apparently hate was edging out love in her post-breakup state of mind. "He's the one the assholes look up to. I know, because I've essentially dated all of his wannabes. It's going to get even worse now that he's back in town." Visibly calming herself, Bethany tilted her head at Georgie. "But I digress. Please tell me why *you're* fraternizing with Travis Ford."

Georgie might regret unburdening herself in front of ballsy ball-breaker Bethany in the morning. Right now, though, the humiliation wouldn't be contained. "I've been in love with him as far back as I can remember. Obviously there's no chance of him being interested in *me* like that. I'm not delusional, but he seemed like he needed a friend and so do I. We hung out a few times." She gave Bethany the sister death glare. "Nothing happened, so please don't tell Stephen any of this."

"Ugh. I knew you were going to say that." Bethany tapped her fingers on her knees. "Really, though. He shouldn't be sniffing around you in any capacity. Stephen would shit a Cadillac."

"Everyone seems to think so."

"Is this . . . Zumba?" asked a soft, hesitant voice from the doorway.

There stood Rosie, Dominic's wife, thus sealing Georgie's utter embarrassment. Especially in the face of Rosie's quiet but stunning beauty. In this garish light, Georgie was a paste monster, whereas the department store perfume girl glowed golden brown. She didn't even have to wear a sports bra, just one of those spaghetti-strap tanks with a built-in panel that Georgie had always been too self-conscious to try out. Rosie pulled off the abbreviated attire with ease, but as usual, she seemed a little uncomfortable in their company. Possibly because her husband was an employee of their family business. At the annual Brick & Morty picnic, Georgie had exchanged small talk with her—and God knows, rumors of her marriage being on the rocks had reached everyone—but they'd never really had an in-depth conversation. She'd always regretted that. Especially since Rosie seemed to lack confidantes, just like her.

"I could just . . ." Rosie tucked her loose black hair behind her ear and backed into the hallway, shoulders hunched. "No big. I can wait out here."

"No," Georgie called, desperately trying to dry her eyes

with the sleeves of her hoodie. "Come in, Rosie. How much did you hear?"

Every line of her body uncomfortable, Rosie came in and perched slowly on the stack of mats. "Oh. A little."

"All of it, huh?"

It took Georgie, distracted by their newcomer, a moment to realize Bethany had gone dead silent. She returned her attention to her sister to find Bethany frowning. "Is this why you wanted help picking clothes? Sounds like you might be hoping for a little more than friendship." Bethany shifted. "You should have told me the truth."

"I wouldn't exactly call us confidantes."

In a million years, Georgie never expected her sister to seem so devastated. Bethany swept through life without a hair out of place. Her role at Brick & Morty was to stage houses, and the final product never failed to elicit gasps from potential buyers. Books stacked according to color. Tasteful pendant lighting. A bowl of buttered croissants and a vase of fresh flowers on the table to make people feel at home. Georgie's sister never missed a beat, except when it came to choosing men. Right now, though, under the hellish glow of aerobics lighting, Bethany looked like she'd been struck dumb.

"You make a joke out of everything, Georgie. It's hard to tell sometimes whether you're genuinely upset or being sarcastic. But I'm your big sister." Her voice was just a touch uneven. "You're supposed to come to me with this shit, especially—but not limited to—unrequited love."

A wrench dropped in Georgie's stomach. "I'm sorry. But

it's not like you talk to me about your male-related fiascoes, either. I have to hear it from Mom."

Bethany stared. "I'm *embarrassed* by them. Every man I date either cheats or can't commit. Or is already way too committed to his mother. Or PlayStation. I might break up with them, but I'm still being rejected. It's not exactly something I want to talk about."

"I would love to hear about your embarrassment." She waved a hand when Bethany arched a blond brow. "You know what I mean."

Her older sister chewed her lip, appearing thoughtful. She laid a hand on Georgie's arm, leaned to the side, and nodded at Rosie. "If you're finished trying to sink into the exercise mats, you're welcome to join us, Rosie. Georgie only bites if you take the last strip of bacon."

"I was four years old," Georgie complained. "Let it go, already."

Rosie moved so quietly Georgie didn't know she'd decided to come closer until she dropped gracefully into a cross-legged position, putting the women in a triangle facing one another. "This seems like a private moment . . ." Rosie hedged.

Bethany waved her off. "Oh, stop. All three of us have man trouble. It's not a secret."

The rich brown of Rosie's skin deepened with red. "It's not?"

"No," Georgie muttered, shooting her sister a look. "No, it's not, but no one is going to force you into admitting it. We came to do Zumba, not group therapy."

"It's true." Rosie kept her attention on the ground, but her fingers were trembling where she kept them laced in her lap. "I'm married to a man I don't even know anymore. We sleep in the same bed—when he doesn't fall asleep on the couch—and he's a complete stranger."

Bethany and Georgie traded a look of surprise. Rosie usually kept herself detached when they were in a group setting together. To be fair, the Castles never shut the hell up long enough for someone new to speak. But this admission from Rosie was unusual to say the least.

"I'm sorry you're dealing with that," Bethany said. "Do you guys fight?"

Rosie barked a laugh, then slapped a hand over her mouth to cage the sound. "He's barely talked to me since he came back from Afghanistan," Rosie murmured, dropping her hand. "It's hard to find things to argue about in all that silence. We mostly avoid each other. It's easier."

"Easier than what?" Georgie asked.

"Finding out it's over, I guess." As if becoming aware of her surroundings, Rosie shifted on the floor. "I didn't mean to make this about me."

"It's about all of us," Bethany said slowly. During Rosie's admissions, Georgie had sensed her sister growing more and more fidgety. Now she seemed antsy enough to breakdance. "Look at us, ladies." Bethany jumped to her feet, jabbing a finger at Rosie and Georgie. "Three smart, hardworking women, moping on the floor all for the same reason. Men. They've failed us. But I'm willing to bet we're shouldering all the blame. God knows Travis and Dominic and my collection of shit sticks aren't sitting around, wondering where they went wrong. No, they're out having beers and consoling themselves with YouPorn."

Georgie raised a hand. "To be fair, that is also my preferred method of consolation."

Rosie snort-laughed into her wrist.

"What is your point, wise elder?"

"My point is . . ." Bethany dropped to her knees, taking each of them by the shoulder. "Fuck. Them. We should be out having beers and shrugging off *their* feelings. We should be the ones deciding what we want in our relationships, friendship or otherwise. Not waiting around for these bitch-asses to get over themselves and see what's in front of them."

When Bethany started this passionate tirade, Georgie had been all prepared to laugh. She couldn't deny a winded sensation in her chest now, though. Like she'd run far and fast and landed on this floor. The wry smile on her face had fled. Bethany was right. While Georgie had been crying into herbal tea and angrily sorting clown makeup earlier this evening, Travis hadn't been thinking about her at all. What was the freaking point of all this sadness? It didn't change the course of history or make a dent in Travis's man brain. It had no point.

Travis didn't owe her anything. Deep down, she knew that. But him blowing off their appointment was just another disappointment in a long line of them she'd learned to live with. From her family. Her friends who'd moved away and started calling less and less. The drop in business. She'd allowed everything to happen because she was afraid of proving that she was nothing more than the inconsequential last in line to the throne.

"Let's end this now," Bethany continued. "Right here, right now. Let's fucking liberate ourselves. Not only from brother-mandated Zumba, but from the dudes bringing us down. Let's start making decisions that don't land us in this state of mourning." She waggled her eyebrows through a dramatic pause. "It's time to fix ourselves up, ladies. Because look around. We're alone here. We're more alone with them in our lives than actually being alone."

"And since we're alone anyway, we might as well be alone and moving forward. Making ourselves happy." Georgie nodded. "No one else is going to do it."

"Yes." Bethany let out a slow breath and squeezed Georgie's forearm, reaching for Rosie's as well. "A club. I'm proposing a club for women, of which we're the founding fucking members. We all want things. Let's go get them together."

"I can't . . ." Rosie blurted out, shaking her head. "I agree with everything you're saying, but I'm not in the same position. He's my husband."

"You're right. You have a different situation." Bethany ducked into Rosie's line of sight and smiled. "But you can still be in the damn club. There must be something you want, Ro."

Rosie took a moment to answer, but her chest began rising and falling faster. "I've wanted my own restaurant. Argentinian. For my mother's side." She shook out a laugh. "I've never told anyone but Dominic and we haven't spoken about it in years. It's like he forgot."

"But you didn't forget," Georgie said.

"No. No, I think about it every day."

Close friends or not, Georgie couldn't stop herself from reaching over and taking Rosie's hand, relieved when the other woman didn't hesitate to cling. She didn't know a lot about Rosie's past, but she remembered the small Argentinian woman Rosie used to squire around town, along with her father—an African American man named Maurice who'd owned a local auto body shop. He'd since passed, too. Bethany took Rosie's free hand, linking the three women where they sat on the floor. "What about you, Bethany?" Rosie asked. "What do you want?"

"Me? I'm giving up on men. Full stop. I've been shafted for the last time." She wiggled her blond eyebrows. "I want to swing a sledgehammer."

That shocked a laugh out of Georgie. "What?"

Bethany sighed. "I'm tired of just making things pretty. Been sick of it for a while, actually, but our brother won't let me set foot into a project until it's ready to be staged." She snapped her teeth at an invisible Stephen. "We took over the business from Dad together. I've been doing this just as long. I want my own projects. If Stephen won't give them to me . . . I'll figure out another way to get them."

Georgie shook her head. "I had no idea. I thought you loved staging."

"There are a lot of things we don't know about each other. Let's fix that," Bethany told her softly. "Can you forgive me for having my head up my ass?"

"Yeah," Georgie managed, hope fluttering in her chest.

"If I can forgive you for the tie-dye hand-me-downs, I can forgive anything."

Bethany laughed. "Good." They traded a smile. "And I do love staging. But I want more. I want to look at a house and know its bones. If I'm ever going to do that, I have to build them myself." She nudged Georgie with her knee. "And you, little sis? What's your big dream?"

Moment of truth. "I like being a clown." Georgie shrugged, allowing her ideas to transform into actual words. Possibilities. Something she'd never done before, except for scribbles and drawings in a spiral notebook, never to be voiced aloud in case someone told her she was too young or too naive. Or just ignored her altogether. "But I turn away half my business. I'm either already booked or they want a balloon maker, too. Pony rides. If I want to stay viable . . . or work anywhere outside Port Jeff . . . I have to expand. Turn my one-woman show into a full-time entertainment company."

Bethany squeezed her hand. "What's stopping you?"

No one takes me seriously. I was afraid everyone would laugh. "Nothing, I guess," Georgie said instead, having made more progress tonight already than she thought possible. "So, when is our first meeting?"

"Let's not lose momentum." Bethany appeared to flip through a calendar in her head. "How about Friday night? Seven o'clock at my place. I'll have tequila on hand and we'll come up with a name, you know, just to make it official. But most importantly, we'll figure out a way to reach our goals. Together alone."

"Together alone," Georgie and Rosie echoed in a whisper.

They let go of their linked hands, stacking them like pancakes in the center of the triangle.

"I could save this until Friday night, but I'm very clever and I've already thought of a name," Georgie said, beaming at the other two women. "Just Us League on three. And let's hope DC Comics doesn't come after us for copyright infringement."

Rosie and Bethany laughed and they threw up their hands. "Just Us League."

"I'm sorry I'm late," Kristin squealed, rushing into the room. Georgie and Bethany's sister-in-law floated like an early Disney princess, humming to herself and catching the light with her diamond earrings. She was a ball of sunlight and southern gentility. Until you pissed her off or she didn't get her way. Hence Georgie attending her Zumba class even though she'd like to be sitting in front of the television with a nice cheese plate. If Georgie skipped the class, Stephen would suffer the consequences, and it was only a matter of time before the fallout trickled down. Once, Georgie declined a fresh-baked muffin from Kristin because it contained lemon zest. Which was gross.

Kristin put those little yellow rinds in everything for six months.

"Your brother is very handsy after a few beers," said Kristin. "I didn't make it through the kitchen before—"

Georgie groaned. "We don't need to know."

"Very well," Kristin said primly, hooking her iPod up to an adapter. She swiped across the screen and a Latin beat pumped into the room. "Who's ready to Zumba?"

The three of them rose to their feet like cranky zombies, but managed to get through the hour without taking a flying leap through the plateglass window onto the street to escape. Georgie couldn't help but feel . . . energized after class ended, though, and it had nothing to do with suggestive hip movements. Starting tomorrow, things were going to change.

First order of business? Fix her own damn fireplace.

And maybe get a new haircut in the name of symbolism.

CHAPTER SEVEN

Travis stared into his empty refrigerator and listened to his stomach growl.

He'd eat a muddy fucking boot about now, but none of the takeout menus in his drawer appealed to him. It pained him to admit it, but what he wanted was more of Georgie's leftovers. The chipotle meatloaf had ended up being his favorite, because Georgie had hidden peas underneath the mashed potatoes, so the little green balls ended up in every bite even though he couldn't see them. Like a sneaky way of making him eat vegetables.

Travis closed the refrigerator with a frown and leaned back against it. It had been two days since he'd missed their appointment and she hadn't shown up again. He'd half expected her to barge into the apartment by now and launch more lo mein at his head. Actually, with every day that passed, he kind of *wanted* her to arrive in a snit and bean him with noodles. It was worse wondering if he'd hurt her feelings. And Jesus, this was why he'd wanted her to leave him alone in the first place. Now he was staring at the blank wall in his goddamn kitchen, concerning himself with someone he shouldn't have been associating with in the first place.

An image of her opening the door with a messy apron, trying not to get emotional because no one had shown up for brunch, bombarded Travis's brain. He fell into that category now, didn't he?

His stomach gave an uncomfortable twist. The kitchen seemed really small and dark all of a sudden. "Shit," he muttered, shoving a hand through his hair.

The kicker of it all? He kind of wanted to tell Georgie about the possible commentator job. More than he wanted to tell Stephen or Dominic. What the fuck was up with that?

She would tell him the truth with none of the bullshit. That's what was up. He would get her honest reaction or nothing at all. Right now when nothing in his life made sense, that truthfulness was valuable. He'd had team managers smile to his face while preparing to blindside him with a trade. Had teammates clap him on the shoulder and tell him another opportunity would come, when they both knew damn well it wouldn't. To know with 100 percent certainty that Georgie would shoot straight with him . . . it made him itch to have her in front of him. Just for a little while.

If he had her phone number, he would have given her a call to reschedule the appointment. But he didn't have it. And he was not about to ask Stephen to slide him those little-sister digits. There was no doubt in Travis's mind that

Stephen would get the wrong idea. Travis didn't have any interest in Georgie beyond redoing the fireplace no one else seemed to have time for . . . and maybe confiding in her about things he didn't plan on telling another soul. Not a big deal.

"Christ. You need your head examined." He turned and threw open an overhead cabinet, looking for anything that resembled food. He wasn't totally useless in the kitchen. As a kid, he'd spent a lot of days and nights fending for himself. When his father was too depressed and drunk to cook, Travis scrambled his own eggs and made his own school lunches. Fried his own burgers. His meal choices had been made on the fly until he'd read an article in *Sports Illustrated* that outlined the daily protein intake of Sammy Sosa. Steaks, vegetables, fish, brown rice. All things he'd been missing.

Convinced he'd never make it to the pros without the proper diet, Travis started a paper route, just so he could buy the right groceries. His route was done on foot, since his parents couldn't afford a bike, but he'd gotten up earlier than the other paper route kids and made it work. After school, he'd go to the store himself and walk the half mile home, arms wrapped around two paper bags. Travis could still feel his father sneering at him from the kitchen archway while he tested the temperature of his first steak.

Someday you'll realize it was all a waste of time.

Swallowing the fist in his throat, Travis circled the kitchen table. Yeah. It wasn't so much that he couldn't make his own meals. Apart from his lost month after being cut from his last team—when he'd gone on a takeout-and-booze bender—he'd been pretty handy in the kitchen. He didn't necessarily need Georgie to fill his fridge with tasty goodness.

But it had been really nice opening the fridge and knowing someone cared. Travis never had that in his life. Sure, when he'd become friends with Stephen, the Castles invited him over for dinner at least twice a week. Those nights had been a godsend when his paper route money ran out, but in the later years, Vivian had started splitting duties with Dominic's mother. Who's going to feed the Ford boy tonight? Despite their best intentions, they'd inadvertently made him a charity case.

Nothing remained permanent. For those few nights when he'd had someone's leftovers in his fridge to come home to, though . . . for once, something had seemed constant. Tangible.

Travis didn't realize he'd moved into the bedroom until he started pulling on some sweatpants. He threw on a gray World Series champs shirt, leaving it untucked, and stuffed his feet back into his work boots. Trying to shake the inconvenient sense of dread, Travis plucked his tools and a legal pad from where he'd left them near the door and headed for the truck. It would take only ten minutes to measure Georgie's fireplace and then he could get back to enjoying his night alone.

Travis turned the corner onto Georgie's block and saw the small brick ranch-style house at the end of the cul-de-sac. The sun was setting, outlining it in a pink glow. He didn't know how much money Georgie pulled down from her clown gigs, but the Castle influence had probably gotten her the house for a steal. It wasn't the nicest house on the block, but it was the most colorful. Red and white and yellow flowers were planted along the walkway. Instead of a sprinkler head, she had a giant rotating frog plopped down in the center of her lawn. Flip-flops lay forgotten on the porch, lit up by the glow of the porch light. Homey. Bursting with character like the owner. Someday a bunch of kids would be playing tag in the yard.

It probably wouldn't happen for another decade, though. At least, right?

A honk jolted Travis and he found himself idling in the middle of the street. Trying to figure out why he'd gone from starving to zero appetite, he pulled forward and let the neighbor pass and turn into his own driveway. But where he would have parallel parked at the curb in front of Georgie's house, as he'd done at brunch, Travis was surprised to find another truck parked out front. One just like his.

Who did it belong to? A man?

Dale?

Travis's pulse started kicking at the base of his neck, but he didn't know why. Georgie had to have friends. Girls she'd gone to school with who still lived in town. The truck probably just belonged to one of them. Toolbox in hand, he passed behind the truck and spotted an I'D RATHER BE REELING IN A BASS bumper sticker and paused. Okay, probably not a girl.

Georgie didn't have a boyfriend—she'd lamented that very fact to his face. Had she met someone since then? Shouldn't a new guy have to go through some kind of vetting process? When Travis reached the door, he laughed when he realized he was bracing himself, shoulders squared. For what? Why the hell did he care if Georgie was in there hiding peas under mashed potatoes for someone else?

He blamed the humidity for the sweat popping up at his hairline.

Georgie answered the door . . . only she looked slightly different. As in not the same. As in the haphazard knot stuck through the back of a baseball cap was gone. Chocolate waves stopped just beyond her shoulders. Down. Her hair was down. And shorter, maybe? A big chunk of it had been cut right in front. Bangs. They were called bangs and they didn't hide her green eyes, like the hat tended to do. Nope, those eyes were right there in the open, big and questioning.

There was something more, though. Her surroundings were soft, the glowing light draping her from head to toe. She stood barefoot with a mug of tea in her hand. With bangs. And frayed jeans shorts with the pockets sticking out beneath the hem. This was not the baggy-jeans-wearing brat or flustered Saturday morning cook with flour in her hair. She was a relaxed and—might as well face it—sexy woman standing in the doorframe of her own home.

"Um. Travis?" She waved a hand in front of his face. "Have you received any blows to the head today? Should I call a doctor?"

What is going on with you? He shook himself. "I'm here to look at the fireplace."

She took a long sip of tea. "That's not necessary."

Damn. She was really pissed. "I forgot. I'm human. Whose truck is that?" He rolled his shoulder. "Is it Dale?"

Was it his imagination or did the blood just drain from her face? "No, Dale is . . . on vacation. It belongs to Pete. My fireplace guy."

Now it actually felt as if he'd received a blow to the head. For a few seconds, Travis even stopped breathing. Surely he'd heard her wrong. "Are you kidding me?"

"Nope." She stepped back into the house, as if preparing to close the door. "You're off the hook. And I need to get back—"

Travis surprised himself by sticking his boot in the opening. "I said I would be the one to do it."

"And *I* said I don't need you now."

Travis couldn't explain why it was so fucking imperative that he be the one to fix Georgie's fireplace, but it was. Fucking imperative. Some fisherman named Pete wasn't touching that brick monstrosity when he was perfectly capable of doing the job. The idea of letting her down made him queasy—and he had. Fine. Okay. He could admit this girl had done the impossible by getting him out of bed and out into the world again. She'd actually made him laugh. Filled his refrigerator. Now if she didn't let him show his gratitude, he was going to be good and pissed.

Admitting to himself that Georgie was responsible for him being in the land of the living again turned over something desperate in his stomach. Without stopping to acknowledge the bad idea, Travis pulled Georgie into a hug, frowning when she didn't even bother to wrap her free arm around him. Frowning as she fit against him perfectly. Lots of frowning in general. "Hey." He planted a kiss on the top of her head. "I'm sorry, all right? I should have come by sooner."

Georgie remained silent, so he squeezed her tighter, noticing she had kind of a smoky peach scent. Is this how she always smelled or was this new, too?

He hesitated for a second before tucking some strands of hair behind her left ear . . . and attempted to ignore the swelling that happened downstairs. Christ. Did his cock just get hard for Georgie? *Stephen's little sister,* Georgie? *Relax.* He'd gone months without sex. That's the only reason holding Georgie tucked against him was having an effect. Any other time, this kind of contact would be totally platonic. Travis swallowed. "I, uh . . . like your new haircut."

"Thank you." Georgie pushed out of his hold, her cheeks red. "You need to go. I have this covered."

Something akin to panic started to set in. "You're really serious, aren't you? You're not going to forgive me for missing the damn appointment."

"I forgive you, but I won't be accepting a rain check." She backed into the house. "If you're determined to stay, suit yourself. But I'm not canceling."

At that, she turned on a heel and vanished into the house. Travis followed, feeling dumbstruck over how this situation had become so important to him. And completely escaped his control. Upon entering the foyer, the first thing he noticed was a collage on the wall beside the coatrack. Georgie sitting in her tree in the Castle backyard, pale legs dangling like a snapshot from his memory. The Castle family crowded around a Thanksgiving turkey. Georgie in a midair leap, holding up the keys to her new house. He started to walk away, when something caught his eye. A picture of him? Yeah. There he was, in his baseball uniform, sitting at the top of the high school bleachers. Stephen sat right beside him, but he wasn't even looking at the camera, leaving Travis as the main focus.

He strode into the living room with something lodged in his throat.

It lodged even deeper when he saw Pete. He'd been expecting a salty old Long Island man. Instead it was some guy Travis's age, standing shoulder to shoulder with Georgie so they could look at a sample book. Bald by choice. A beard.

"Can I see your contractor's license, please?"

Georgie stomped her foot. "Travis."

"Her family owns a remodeling company. She knows at least four men that could do this work." He jerked a chin at Georgie. "This was just a little act of rebellion, but she's over it now."

Indignation rippled across Georgie's features. "I don't work for Brick & Morty. I'm a private citizen with my own house who knows how to find my own contractor—whose license I already checked, by the way." He didn't like the sharp rise in color on her neck. "You wouldn't even know I'd hired someone if you hadn't taken it upon yourself to show up. I'm an adult, Travis. I don't rebel for attention."

"All right. I *hear* you," he shouted back. Shouted? Yeah. There was something on the line here and he couldn't figure out what. All he knew was he'd considered this girl a pest a week ago and now he didn't like the idea of her not coming around anymore. He didn't like the idea of leaving her with this guy, either. At all. "Should you be alone with a strange man in the house?"

"He's not a strange man. I performed at his daughter's birthday party."

"Oh." Travis cleared his throat. "You're married."

Pete shook his head and held up an empty ring finger, as if to say, *Sorry, sucker.* "Single dad." He propped the clipboard on his hip. "And if it were my daughter, I'd be more worried about leaving her alone with Two Bats."

Hot acid bubbled up in Travis's stomach. "You sure you want to go there, pal?"

Pete took a step in his direction, but Georgie waylaid him with a hand on his arm. Since Travis could write a five-fucking-volume guide to sex, he easily recognized the rekindled interest in Bald Pete's eyes when Georgie touched him. "Could you excuse us, Travis?"

He crossed his arms. "I'm good right here."

Calculation danced across her face a second before she marched up to Travis, crooking her finger like she had a secret. Keeping his attention locked on Pete, Travis leaned down so she could whisper in his ear.

"Dale is my vibrator."

Travis choked. Had he heard that right? Her smug smile told him he had. The innocent memory of Georgie lying on his bed and mumbling that she needed Dale took on a whole new meaning. Before he could stop himself, his sick mind conjured those frayed shorts being tugged down her legs, her right hand guiding a shuddering device between her thighs. Her head tossing back, mouth forming an O. A little mewling sound left Imaginary Georgie's mouth . . . and his own hand took control of the shaking toy. "I'll be outside."

She dropped back on her heels. "That's what I thought."

He walked out of the house in a daze. Since when did a woman talking about sex in any capacity throw him off his game? Nothing caught him off guard when it came to the pleasures of the flesh. He'd seen, done, and heard it all. Not when it came to Georgie, though. She'd been frozen in time in his mind as a gangly preteen. That wasn't her now, obviously. And that image he'd held of her for so long was beginning to thaw. Rapidly. She was a woman now who . . . masturbated. A woman who didn't wait around for whatever scrap of attention her brother and his best friend decided to throw her. That message had come through loud and clear tonight.

A minute later, Travis climbed into his truck and watched Georgie and Pete through the front window of her house. Watched her slowly warm back up after their tiff and start to get excited about the design, nodding and beaming as Pete gestured to the old brick fireplace. Travis knew a man's body language when he was asking a woman out. Pete had it. In response, she shoved her hands in her pockets, probably stuttering through an answer.

Goddammit. This was none of his business. She didn't

want him here. Why couldn't he turn the key in the ignition and drive home?

Instead of doing the logical thing, he waited for Pete to leave the house, sharing prolonged eye contact with the man through his windshield. Had Georgie said yes to their date? The man betrayed nothing with his blank expression, except for surprise that Travis was still standing—or sitting, rather—guard outside the house.

Join the club.

CHAPTER EIGHT

In a testament to her unusual life choices, neither Bethany nor Rosie blinked when Georgie walked into their first Just Us League meeting in full clown makeup. There hadn't been time to change or wash her face after the seven-year-old's birthday party. Baby wipes might have been just the remedy, but frankly she didn't mind hiding behind the mask today.

Talk about a one-two punch.

The birthday party had started off fine. Wild squealing mayhem, sure, but that was par for the course. Toward the middle of the festivities, however, she'd started to *feel* like one of the kids. At one point, the hostess had patted her on the head and handed her punch in a Dixie cup. Georgie totally understood her being hired to entertain the kids, but lately she'd become so much more aware of the division between herself and the other adults. While they all stood off to one side sipping sangria and swapping handyman recommendations, she was relegated to eating half-slices of pizza at the kids' table. The parents didn't mean any harm—they were lovely people.

They just looked at her and saw a clown. Only a clown. Not a businesswoman.

Or even a fellow grown-up.

Right on the heels of Travis invading her fireplace appointment and needling her sorest sore spot, even the laughter of children hadn't soothed her troubled soul.

This was just a little act of rebellion, but she's over it now.

Teeth grinding, Georgie hopped up onto a stool beside Rosie. She wasn't sure she'd ever felt as helpless as Travis made her feel—and that was saying something. She'd been an idiot to think he could see her as a friend. An equal. Good thing she'd revealed Dale's true identity and given herself an excuse to avoid Travis until the day she died. *Oh my God.* Had she actually done that? Knowing Travis would prefer not to see his best friend's little sister as a sexual object, she'd thrown it in his face, banking on the awkwardness sending him running.

On second thought, maybe she'd revealed the secret so he would be *forced* to treat her like an adult. One who schedules her own fireplace work, dammit. Too bad she hadn't unmasked Dale *before* he'd made her feel the size of a thimble.

"You look pretty depressed for someone dressed like a clown," Bethany remarked from her lean against the kitchen island. "Did the party mother give out Super Soakers and pin a target to your back again?"

"No. And we don't talk about the Great Drenching of 2017."

"Right," Bethany drawled, pushing away from the kitchen island. She went to the freezer and took out a chilled bottle of tequila and three frosty little shot glasses, setting them down on the polished granite with a flourish. "I was going to propose we make it a tradition to open every Just Us League meeting with a shot of Patrón, but I didn't realize it would be so necessary. You both look like the bachelorette who didn't get a rose."

Georgie sent a glance in Rosie's direction, noting that the other woman did, in fact, seem kind of . . . frozen. Graceful though she was, Rosie's arms were crossed loosely at her middle, her shoulders in an uncharacteristic hunch. The only one of the three women who appeared upbeat was Bethany. Nothing new there, though. Bethany embodied the term "upbeat," whether discussing a five-hundred-dollar scratch-off win or a cheating ex-boyfriend. Positive or negative, her poise never slipped, especially in her element. And her sleek, sophisticated all-white kitchen was most definitely Bethany's element.

"I second this tequila proposal," Georgie mumbled. "Pour generously."

"But of course," Bethany said, uncapping the bottle and sliding golden liquid into the icy shot glasses. "Bottoms up, ladies of the league. We have much to discuss."

Rosie, Bethany, and Georgie clinked glasses, each having various reactions to the liquid bite as it went down. Bethany smiled, Georgie grimaced, and Rosie gave a hoarse cough.

"So," Rosie croaked. "What other traditions did you have in mind, Beth?"

A smile tickled the edge of Georgie's mouth. "You've got it all planned out already, don't you?"

"Only a loose framework." Bethany held up the bottle one more time and both women wordlessly slid the glasses back in her direction. "Let's start by sharing one good thing—and one bad thing—that happened to us this week. I'll start, since it's my brilliant idea." She shook back her blond hair. "Good thing: I finally told Stephen I want to head my own flip."

Rosie reached across the island and patted Bethany's hand. "Good for you."

"Bad thing: he told me no."

Georgie made a sad game-show noise. "I bet he didn't even give you a reason." She dropped her voice several octaves. "Reasons are beneath Stephen Castle."

"Not one fucking reason. Unless you count caveman grunts."

"I'm sorry." Rosie twisted her shot glass on the island. "What now?"

Bethany took her second drink. "Now I consider . . . pursuing my goal outside of the Brick & Morty fold."

Rosie's jaw dropped, mimicking Georgie's. "Competing against the family business?" She blew out a breath. "Everyone in town knows Brick & Morty rules the Port Jeff real estate scene. You're a brave woman."

"I think you mean crazy," Georgie said. "Beth. Are you really ready to look Dad in the eye and see the shock of betrayal? The business is everything to him. To the whole family. Quitting or pursuing another line of work is one thing, competing is another."

"Yeah, well." Bethany shrugged. "Maybe when they

dismiss me so easily, I feel betrayed." She shifted in her heels. "You know?"

"Yes," Georgie rushed to say, something hot twisting in her chest. "Actually I know exactly what you mean. I've been dismissed more times than a software update reminder."

Bethany didn't say anything for a moment. "You're right. I'm sorry."

Georgie was afraid if she dug deeper into that apology, she'd burst into tears, so she packed the moment away for later. "I've got your back with Dad. Together we will withstand the force of paternal disappointment. I mean, I'm a fucking clown, so I'm basically immune to disappointment at this point."

The three of them laughed—and Bethany poured another shot. Georgie had been only half joking about her father's disappointment. But the fact was . . . no one had ever asked Georgie to be a part of Brick & Morty. If she wanted a position, they would find one. No doubt about that. But every vital position seemed to be covered. The last thing she wanted was for them to humor her by inventing some glorified secretary role. Their mother did the bookkeeping, their father provided guidance even in retirement, Stephen managed the flips, Bethany staged. If they needed a clown to juggle on the curb to attract potential buyers, Georgie was their girl. For now, though, she was the odd woman out. The kid sister who'd always left the heavy lifting to the adults and big kids . . . and in their eyes always would.

"Rosie." Georgie used her knee to nudge the only married woman among them. "You're up, lady."

"Already?" Rosie's groan turned into a laugh. "I sound like a broken record. Nothing has changed. Nothing ever changes in my life. Nothing bad or good even stands out this week."

"Try," Bethany said, shuffling aside the empty shot glasses to lean across the island. "There had to be something."

"Mmm." Rosie closed her eyes and took a long breath. "Bad: I sprayed a customer in the eye with perfume during the early shift. They ducked at the wrong time and . . . *wham*. I'm lucky they recognized me from church or I could have been fired."

Bethany and Georgie traded a wince.

"Good . . ." Rosie trailed off for a few seconds, her hands bunching in her skirt. "I bought a newspaper and circled ads for vacant restaurant spaces."

"That's amazing!" Georgie shook Rosie gently. "Are there any good ones in town?"

"Yes, but . . ." Rosie rolled her eyes. "The amount of work I'd have to put in to make it what I envision is just overwhelming. And expensive."

"What about a lease?" Bethany asked.

"No." Rosie showed a rare flash of determination. "When I finally do this, I want the place to be mine." Her eyelids fluttered down, shielding her eyes. "We've got money saved, Dominic and I. He hasn't touched the money he earned while serving. And Brick & Morty pays so well." She smoothed her sleeve. "My parents left me some, too. Considering I hid the newspaper under the mattress so Dominic wouldn't see it, I'm a long way off from asking to use what we have saved, though."

Georgie frowned. "How would he react?"

Rosie started to answer, then closed her mouth. "I have no idea anymore. I think I'm afraid to tell him I want something. Anything. Or all the other things I want . . . that are missing . . . will come pouring out and I won't be able to take them back." As if alarmed she'd revealed too much, Rosie looked at Georgie with a silent plea. "Your turn."

Her problems seemed to pale in comparison to Rosie's. But as always, Georgie's impulse was to lighten the mood any way she could. "Good: I got asked out on a date."

Bethany smacked both hands down on the island. "What?"

"Thank you for acting like I just announced I'm joining the PGA Tour."

"Shut up. It's just that you haven't been on a date since . . . Have you ever been on a date? You know what? I'm digging a hole. Never mind." Her sister dragged the shot glasses back out to the forefront and started pouring. "Give us the details."

When she tried to conjure up the man who'd asked her out, she could only see Travis's face. *Ignore him.* Easier said than done, though. She'd been picturing him in conjunction with her every romantic impulse seemingly forever. "Um. His name is Pete. Midthirties, maybe? Single dad. He came to give me an estimate on fixing my fireplace."

Bethany made a low whistle. "You're one to talk about betraying the family business."

"If I hired Brick & Morty to do the work, they would see it as a favor. I don't want favors. And I don't want what Stephen and Dom and Travis think is best, which is exactly what would happen."

All three women fired back another shot.

"Anyway." Georgie swiped at her mouth with the back of her wrist, remembering too late she was still wearing clown makeup. Bethany lobbed Georgie a napkin and she cleaned the white-and-red residue from her costume sleeve, while continuing the story. "I didn't say yes or no to the date, but I promised to call with an answer. So I have to say no, right? I kind of thought the point of this club was to shun the menfolk."

"Not shun. Just . . . compartmentalize." Bethany pursed her lips. "The point of this club is to support and encourage each other. Yes, we're also taking a firm stand against the men in our lives being dicks and leaving them behind *if* necessary, but we have to give new men a chance to be dicks before we shun them."

Georgie gave a golf clap. "Somehow that made perfect sense."

"Go on your date, Georgie, but keep everything on your terms." Her sister jabbed the island with a square-tipped fingernail. "Maybe getting a sampling of what's out there will help you move past your Travis hang-up. Sounds like it's long overdue."

"Yeah. It is." Georgie twisted her lips. "Speaking of Travis . . ."

Rosie turned in her stool. "Ooh."

"Bad: Travis showed up with his tools while Pete was there, demanding I let him keep his word and fix the fireplace. It was a giant tool party in more than one sense of the word."

"Oh my God." Bethany threw back her head and cackled. "This is such a priceless gift."

"I'm glad you're enjoying it." Seeing the other women react with openmouthed shock made the reality of what Georgie had done caught up with her. "I kicked him out."

Her older sister took a twirling victory lap around the kitchen.

"They argued?" Rosie asked, her voice soft with concern.

"Yeah. They totally did the alpha male construction dance. *Me fix fireplace. You go home. Look. A hammer.*" Georgie sighed. "Travis got all weird about me being alone with Pete—"

Bethany fell forward over the island, chin on fists. "Oh, really?"

"Not like that," Georgie huffed. "Trust me, Travis Ford couldn't care less if I go on a date. For some reason, he decided to show up and make me feel like an incompetent child." Georgie swallowed hard. "And I'm really over people making me feel that way."

Her sister's triumph went flat. "I'm guilty of it, too, Georgie. It's hard to think of you as anything but my little sister sometimes." She nodded. "I'm going to try harder, okay?"

Georgie didn't know how to verbalize what it meant to her, just having those insecurities acknowledged, so she stayed quiet. Until Bethany showed up at her side and delivered a hip bump, almost knocking her off the stool.

"Text Pete. Do it now in front of us so you don't chicken out."

"What . . . *now*?"

Bethany raised an elegant eyebrow. Rosie leaned in, too,

as Georgie took out her phone and tapped out a brief text message. Her phone buzzed almost immediately with a response.

"Done," she breathed. "We're having lunch."

"Fabulous! Now tell me again how you kicked Travis out. Talk slowly. Leave nothing out." Bethany laughed when both women gave her disappointed looks. "Okay, fine. I'll just have to imagine it. And I will. In the meantime, though, let's talk Georgie's entertainment business and Rosie's restaurant . . ."

CHAPTER NINE

Georgie had never set foot inside the local girlie boutique. But she could tell from the outside that it was a far cry from Second Chance Zelda's. Yes, she was about to darken the doorway of Glitter Threads for the first time—which really shouldn't have been so daunting. Most of Georgie's outfits came in the form of used denim and unwanted sweaters, but clothes were clothes, right?

Still, she hesitated.

Time to play a round of What Would Bethany Do?

Georgie's sister would sweep in and walk straight into a changing room, rattling off her measurements without looking up from her phone. Clothes would be brought to her for approval. No perusing racks for Bethany Castle. Oh no. She didn't buy clothes. The clothes needed to be sold *to* her.

To be fair, Georgie could do things Bethany wasn't capable of. She could juggle five oranges, could make scarves come out of people's ears, and had the ability to stop a child's tears in under five seconds. Her other non-clown-related skills included making her own bath bombs, gardening, and reciting dialogue from the classic Tom Hanks movie *Splash*.

None of which gave her the push she needed into the shop. This should be easy. She'd even come bearing gifts.

Georgie looked down at the sea salt caramel mocha in her right hand, hoping Boutique Tracy wasn't lactose intolerant. That would really put a damper on her apology. And Georgie definitely owed her one. The Just Us League meeting had left her with such a good feeling. The support of two women had really dragged her out of her gloom. Now here she stood outside this intimidating, hyperfeminine environment, ready to pay it forward.

"I'm going to count to three," she whispered. "There will not be a four."

As soon as the countdown ended, Georgie propelled herself into the shop, coming to a halt when she realized Boutique Tracy had been watching her from the other side of the glass the whole time.

"Well." Georgie extended the coffee. "This is off to a great start."

Tracy eyed the to-go coffee cup like it contained slugs. "Can I help you?"

"I just came in to apologize." She turned in a circle, looking for a place to set down the coffee, deciding on a pretty shelf full of headband/scarf things and a fanned-out stack of the newest sex-themed issue of *Cosmopolitan* magazine. "You don't have to accept. But what I did was really mean. I shouldn't have lied and put you in an embarrassing situation. And I'm sorry about it."

Nothing from Tracy. Not the slightest twitch.

"Okay, well . . . that's a sea salt caramel mocha and it's

the shit. I'll take a sip if you want to make sure it isn't poisoned—"

"No need."

Silence fell again. "Gotcha. I'll be on my way."

Georgie barely made it to the door when Tracy snagged her elbow. "Wait." The other woman shifted on her feet. "I didn't mean what I said about you having short legs." She sniffed. "But you wear really unflattering pants. I can help you with that, though. Since you did bring me my favorite drink."

"It's so good, right?" Georgie whispered.

"Sinfully so."

And just like that, Georgie was being dragged to the dressing room and stuffed inside. This wasn't just your average dressing room with two hooks and a bench, though. An antique chair sat wedged in the corner beside a very flattering mirror. Her feet sunk into plush pastel carpeting. And the lighting. My God. This dressing room was an Instagram filter a girl could live inside. Woodsy potpourri smell emanated from all sides, but no matter how many times Georgie turned around, she couldn't figure out where it had been stuffed.

Overall, it was nice. Really nice. Just standing in the room made her feel important.

"All right, bitch." Tracy burst through the heavy velvet curtain with an armful of blouses, dresses, skirts, and those headband/scarf things. "Why are you still wearing clothes?"

Panic cut Georgie's excitement in half. "I didn't realize you'd have to see me naked. I'm wearing, like, the worst underwear you've ever seen."

Tracy sighed. "Jessica! Panties!"

Thus the transformation began. Over the course of the next hour, Georgie was divested of every piece of clothing on her person, including her basic cotton underpants, sports bra, ancient Skechers, jeans, and hoodie. Left behind in their place, she was fitted with a matching purple silk bra and panty set, a black pencil skirt, a bright blue sleeveless blouse, and sparkling silver pointed-toe flats. Every time a new piece of the ensemble was added, she stood a little straighter. It couldn't be this easy, could it? They let just *anyone* dress this fashionable? She looked . . . nice. Really nice.

"This is going to cost me big time, isn't it?" Georgie said, staring at the unrecognizable girl in the mirror.

Tracy picked some lint off Georgie's shoulder. "Don't think of the numbers. Think about how you feel."

"Easy for you to say, person who works on commission." Although Georgie couldn't help but admit . . . wow. Her legs didn't look the least bit shrimpy now. Had her body always been this shape, or did the mirror possess magic, transformative qualities? The skirt rounded at her hips, cinching at her waist. She had pretty damn decent boobs, too! Who knew? She definitely wouldn't get seated at the kids' table in this outfit. Still, she couldn't exactly dress this way at children's birthday parties. "Where would I even wear this?"

Tracy groaned. "Why do women believe they need an occasion to dress up? Dress up for life, goddammit!" Finished with her dramatics, Tracy eyeballed Georgie in the mirror. "Any dates coming up, maybe?"

"Yes, actually." It felt good being able to say that, even if she wasn't totally sold on Pete.

"Well. There you go." She circled around Georgie, tucking and smoothing. "And paired with a blazer, you could wear it for job interviews, business meetings . . . or just to make a certain someone jealous."

"Like who?"

Tracy's nonchalant sniff wasn't convincing. "You helped the man fake an imaginary doctor's appointment. I just thought there might be something there."

"Oh no." Georgie rushed to correct her, the tips of her ears heating. "No. He's just my brother's friend. The date is with someone else."

A slow, devious smile lit up Tracy's face. "Oh, really?"

Why did everyone seem to be in on a big secret except for Georgie? "Yeah." Georgie turned to the side, a little alarmed over the tight material presenting her butt like baked goods in a display case, but she could go with it. "I guess I haven't treated myself to nice clothes in . . . ever. I've *never* done this." She fashioned a dramatic wrist to her forehead. "Tell me the damage and let's get it over with."

"Not just yet." Tracy unzipped Georgie's skirt. "We have a lot more to try on."

"Aw, shit."

By the time Georgie walked out of Glitter Threads, her credit card was playing taps. A bag full of luxurious, very un-Georgie-like clothes weighed down each arm as she walked out onto Main Street in her original pencil skirt outfit. Was it just her or were people staring? No. Definitely just her. Right? Granted, she knew almost everyone in town and they'd never seen her in anything but oversized sweaters and discount jeans. But when a repeat client of Georgie's walked right past her on the sidewalk without saying hello, she was forced to wonder if she'd become unrecognizable. If so, wasn't that just a little exciting?

Not that people had to spruce themselves up with expensive clothing and frilly panties to be important. Or even to feel good. But she'd spent her whole life buried under clown makeup and garage sale treasures, so presenting a new, more exposed version of herself made the pulse in her wrists beat faster, made tingles race up and down her back. For the first time in maybe forever . . . Georgie felt pretty. On the heels of standing up for herself to Travis, she couldn't help but feel as if a new phase had begun.

Starting with today's lunch date.

As she turned toward the municipal parking lot, though, her excitement dimmed a little. Pete seemed like a nice guy. A man dedicated enough to his child to hire a clown for her birthday party and record the whole three-hour affair on his GoPro. But every time she imagined sitting down across from someone in her new outfit, a cocky, blue-eyed womanizer stared back at her. Dammit.

With Travis's likeness floating around in Georgie's head, it took her a minute to realize the man in question was actually coming toward her from fifty yards away, flanked by two women. Cell phone pressed to his ear, he was at a seven out of ten on the annoyance meter, but they continued talking to him anyway. Or *at* him, rather. She'd witnessed this scene many times in her youth. Travis being fawned over sent a swift kick to her stomach, sharper and uglier than it used to. And yeah. Holy crap. She must be unrecognizable, because as she drew even with Travis beside her parked car, he caught sight of her and glanced away, before his gaze came zipping back.

The hand holding his phone dropped to his side. *"Georgie?"*

Feeling like an impostor in her new clothes, while the women surrounding Travis made their fashion choices seem so effortless, she moved to unlock her car. She didn't *want* to watch him get fawned over. She just wanted to get the hell out of there. "Hey."

"Hey?"

Travis blocked her path to the trunk and tipped her chin up with a finger, narrowing her universe down to that single touch. The stubble on his cheeks and crispy aftershave. Damn him.

"Who are you and what did you do with Georgie Castle?"

"She's in here somewhere." Georgie backed away with a gulp, but the warmth of his finger remained imprinted on her skin. With Travis standing in front of her, it was impossible to pretend she was excited for her date with Pete. "I decided to send my overalls back to the nineties."

Behind him, the women sort of milled around for a moment, then scooted off in a jumble of harried whispers. He didn't seem to notice or care, sounding kind of dazed. "Why are you dressed like . . . like . . ."

The straps of the heavy bags were starting to leave indentations on her arms, so she set them down on the pavement. "Like what?"

"So pretty," he rasped.

Oh. This was why women carried travel vibrators. One smoky word out of Travis's mouth and her thighs went shaky. Moisture gathered on her brand-spanking-new panties—*Jesus, don't think about spanking.* Shoot. Too late. Travis's hands were so big. They would definitely leave a mark. *Jumping the gun much?* She hadn't so much as gotten naked with a man, let alone had one spank her. She might not even like it. But she was certainly thinking about it. Was it possible the fancy clothes were making her hornier than usual? Not the point. The point was Travis Ford had just referred to her as pretty and he'd sounded like he'd been holding back more. Was this real life?

"Thank you. It turns out they make clothes that actually fit a person's body. You learn something new every day." Why was she talking to Travis about her body? He was going to think she was purposefully calling his attention to it. As in flirting. She had no business flirting with a man who'd probably witnessed and participated in the finest flirting on God's green earth. "I have to go." She pressed a button on her key ring and popped the trunk, but Travis beat her to scooping up the shopping bags. "Can you just throw them in . . ."

Whatever he saw in the bag made his brow furrow. Georgie would put a hundred dollars on it being the panties with the golden rose pattern, because such was life. Honestly, he already knew about Dale, though, so what was a little more humiliation at this point? Instead of panties, he pulled out a copy of *Cosmopolitan* magazine instead, which she did *not* remember agreeing to buy. Boutique Tracy strikes again. Travis turned the glossy magazine around, the words "Have Sex Like a Porn Star" emblazoned across the top in bright neon pink.

"Doing a little studying?" He didn't give her a chance to answer, an unwelcome awareness seeming to creep over him. "Why are you dressed up? What's the occasion?"

"Why can't life be the occasion?" She quickly waved a hand. "Sorry. I've been in a potpourri-scented girl palace for an hour. I'm high on pheromones."

Travis, silent and frowning at her legs, was clearly still waiting for an answer. She most certainly did not owe him one, but it wouldn't hurt to walk away on friendly terms. "I went into Glitter Threads to apologize to Boutique Tracy, and she dressed me up in exchange for a sea salt caramel mocha, okay? And . . . I like it. She told me my legs aren't actually short, which I'm embarrassed to admit I've been kind of obsessing about."

"Didn't I tell you your legs were—"

"Normal. You said they were normal." She turned away from his deepening scowl and closed the trunk on her purchases. "I'm late for a date. See you around, Travis."

When she moved to open her driver's-side door, Travis's hand appeared above her head and smacked down to keep it closed. "Hold on there, baby girl. We're not done."

Georgie spun on Travis, surprised to find him so close. "Um. Wh-why is that?"

"Look. About the other night at your place. I acted like a dick." The sincerity in his eyes held her still. Still and trying not to swoon into the gutter, where she would eventually be carried away to the ocean. "I'm sorry, okay? You can stop punishing me for it now."

Confusion slipped in. "How am I punishing you?"

Travis pushed off the car and crossed his arms. "For a while there I couldn't walk two feet without tripping over you. Now nothing." A vein stood out on his temple. "What's this about a date?"

Georgie didn't know where to lend her focus. The fact that Travis actually *apologized* to her, or him noticing her absence and appearing to dislike it. Or his growly bear attitude. Him caring enough to question her at all seemed surreal. "You didn't seem to want me around."

"Is that how it seemed?" His cheek twitched. Twice. "Huh."

The alarm on her cell phone started to chime in her bag, signaling that she had only fifteen minutes before her lunch date with Pete. Truthfully, she was grateful for the escape. Life was not making sense right now. She had to be reading into Travis's apology the wrong way. He didn't miss her. *Stop dreaming, Georgie.* There was a perfectly nice gentleman waiting for her. One who'd never treated her like a rebellious child or disappointed her. Yes, she needed to douse the growing flame of excitement over Travis finally seeming to give a rat's behind about her and vamoose. Before she got any ideas about fanning it.

"I'm late." It took an effort to turn away from Travis's

scrutiny, but she managed to twist and open the driver's-side door. Unfortunately, Travis stepped closer to Georgie at that exact moment and the door rammed hard into his shoulder. He hissed a breath. Her heart stopped beating. She spun back around—and found Travis clutching his right shoulder. *The* shoulder. The one he'd torn the rotator cuff on, followed by multiple surgeries and eventually being cut from the Hurricanes.

"Oh my God." Had she just inadvertently hurt him all over again? "Oh . . . oh my God. Is it okay?" Her hands were shaking as she reached for his shoulder. "I'm sorry, I—I . . ."

Travis shook his head but didn't push her hands away. "It's fine. Just a twinge." He looked up, seeming to realize how upset she was. "This thing is pinned and screwed down in so many places, a wrecking ball couldn't break it. Just needs a little ice."

"You're supposed to ice an injury right away." She looked around. "Where's your truck?"

"I walked."

"Come on." She took his good elbow and guided him to the passenger side, opening the door. "It was my fault. I'll drive you."

"No, it wasn't . . ." He trailed off when her phone alarm went off again—*chime-chime-chime*—a crease forming between his brows. "You'll cancel the date?"

"Obviously." Impatient to fix the harm she'd done, Georgie poked Travis until he gave in and folded his big body into her passenger seat. "I'll never make it now." She whipped out her phone and fired off a quick apology to Pete. "Let's go."

Travis stretched his long legs and fastened the seat belt with a click. If Georgie didn't know better, she'd think the injury had *relaxed* him. He dispelled that notion with a long-suffering sigh. "If you insist, Georgie."

CHAPTER TEN

Under the guise of watching passing scenery, Travis couldn't stop himself from stealing glances at the reflection of Georgie's legs. Jesus Christ. Shit had definitely taken a turn. He'd thought Georgie making his dick hard the other night had been a fluke. Not anymore. This off-limits attraction was insanely real, and weirdly, it had gotten *worse* during their separation. What the hell kind of sense did that make? Out of sight was supposed to mean out of mind. Yet the other night, he'd been cooking a steak on the stove and caught himself staring into space, remembering the fringe of her jean shorts.

Okay, more like the skin he'd seen it touching.

Travis turned to study Georgie's profile under the pretense of adjusting the air conditioner. Had her upper lip always been so fucking full?

Think of her as an awkward kid. Think of her as an awkward kid.

Travis took a deep breath in through his nose and closed his eyes, searching through his memory bank for something that would remind him not to think of Stephen's little sister as a sexual being. Immediately, a moving image came to mind of Georgie at thirteen, waving at him from the bleachers, the light catching her braces, nachos balanced on her lap. All right. Braces and nachos definitely weren't sexy. But the memory didn't generate anything but . . . fondness. Comfort. It never occurred to him before now that she'd come to almost every single one of his games. Home *and* away. His own *parents* hadn't even come to the games.

Back then, she'd had a commitment to him, but he'd never returned it. He'd never returned a commitment to *anyone*. Hell, he didn't have the first clue how. His example had been two bitter adults who hadn't bothered to shield him from the ugliness of their divorce. What was he playing at, allowing Georgie to feel guilty enough to drive him home?

"Should I call Stephen and tell him you won't be back at work?"

Georgie's question stopped Travis from venturing any further into the past. "No work. It's an inspection day."

"Oh, okay." She paused, her fingers drumming on the steering wheel. "So it looked like you had quite a fan club back there."

It took him a moment to realize whom she meant. Right. The two women who'd asked him for autographs and refused to take his cues to end the conversation. When he'd given up and started walking away, they'd seemed more than happy to join him, even after he'd rudely answered a phone call from Donny. His agent had called to inform him a name on the short list for the commentator job had been nixed, thanks to an intoxicated rant outside a club that went viral. That left only Travis and two other candidates. And hell, it was kind of nice not being the one to have a public indiscretion for once. "Asked me to sign their balls—they thought that was pretty funny," he muttered. "Wasn't really helping my cause having them follow me like that."

"What cause?"

The kick of anticipation in his bones wasn't lost on Travis. He'd been keeping the news about the on-air position to himself for days. But there was no denying he wanted to tell Georgie. Get her take on it. He hadn't wanted that from anyone else. Combined with his definite noticing of her physical attributes and he was entering dangerous territory. "My agent has a line on a commentating job with the Bombers. For me."

The car swerved and Travis didn't think, he just threw an arm in front of Georgie to protect her. She squeaked. With the screech of tires, they swerved onto the shoulder, and there he was. With a handful of little-sister tit.

"Christ, Georgie." He let her go like she'd caught fire, but not before registering the fullness of her breast, the way it tucked into his palm like a sweet little peach, her nipple tightening on contact. "What are you doing?"

"I got excited." With a bright pink face, she stared straight out the windshield. "It's okay. I know it was an accident."

His cock didn't care about categorizing the touch. It only wanted to react to the shape and size of what Georgie kept inside her bra, blood rushing to fill the organ until it stiffened in his jeans. From one tiny grope? Who *was* he anymore? "You're goddamn right it was an accident."

Her throat worked with a swallow. "It's way too soon after I told you about Dale."

Travis dropped his head into his hands. "Jesus, don't bring that up now."

"I figured it might be better. You know. To address the five-hundred-pound vibrator in the room." Her voice dropped to a whisper. "It wasn't. It wasn't better."

"Just drive, Georgie."

"Good idea."

The car's engine revved gently, and they pulled back onto the thankfully empty road. He couldn't help but notice she continued to fidget in her seat, though. Why couldn't she just sit still? That skirt was fighting a losing battle to cover her thighs. Travis had to grip the seat to keep himself from reaching over and tugging the hem back down to her knees. At this rate, he wouldn't be able to climb out of the car in an upright position.

"Travis, this is huge."

No shit, Georgie.

"The *Bombers*. I mean, Garland is having the season of his life right now. Nunez has already thrown *two* no-hitters. *Everyone* is watching the games. Are you seriously telling me you'd get to do the play-by-play?"

"It's a possibility." Travis couldn't hide his amused smile. "I didn't realize you paid such close attention to the stats."

"I got into the habit of memorizing the numbers when you played for the Hurricanes," she said in an offhanded way, before snapping her mouth shut. "I mean, you couldn't go anywhere in town without seeing the games. They were on every screen."

"Yeah?" Thinking about how he'd taken that support for granted caused an uncomfortable tug in his chest, but he coughed his way through it. Honestly, he could have gone hours talking baseball with Georgie, enjoying the way she came to his defense and pulled no punches about the other players. It felt normal. *She* made him feel normal. But he didn't know how much time they had together, especially if he got the job. But that was still a big "if." "We both know I was on those television screens for a lot of different reasons. That's what might prevent me from getting the job."

He could feel Georgie's knowing look from the other side of the car. "But you're not interested in being that way anymore, right? Being . . . Two Bats. Unless you feel differently now—"

"I don't." They held each other's gazes for a heavy beat. "Anyway, they don't want their network associated with the guy who used to ask out reporters during press conferences." He shook his head at the cringe-worthy memory. "Family network, family image."

"I see." Georgie pulled up along the curb in front of his house. "How are you going to manage that?"

He blew out a breath. "Hell if I know. Maybe I'll get a cat."

"A cat would definitely help with your rat problem."

"I don't—" Travis cut himself off and pushed open the passenger door. "Never mind. See for yourself."

What was he doing? He didn't need to invite her upstairs.

He was perfectly capable of getting home by himself—the shoulder barely hurt anymore. But when he should have thanked her for the ride and urged her to leave, Travis guided Georgie into the building instead. All right. He'd simply prove he'd kept the apartment immaculate and send her away. They'd hang out for twenty, maybe thirty minutes tops. Just long enough so that she couldn't make her date with Pete.

You're a bastard. A bastard who had no business manipulating Georgie's social life. God, though. There was something about her on a date that didn't sit right. He couldn't explain it.

Oh no? His body's reaction to Georgie's ass in that skirt as she climbed the stairs was a pretty fucking effective explanation, now wasn't it? There was no sense pretending he wasn't hoping and praying for that seam running down the middle of her ass cheeks to rip. Fine. Georgie Castle was hot. With a side of cute. An ass built to curve against his lap . . . and freckles. If that combo wasn't a mind fuck, he didn't know what was. Where did she learn to walk like that? Or was she walking the same as usual and he was just noticing every tick-tock of her hips, every curve of her thighs and calves?

When they reached the top of the stairs, Travis withdrew the house keys from his pocket and searched for a way to take his mind off Georgie's butt. "So. A sea salt caramel mocha is the female version of an icebreaker?"

"Rosie, Beth, and I usually kick things off with tequila, but a mocha will do in a pinch."

Travis slipped his key into the door and nudged it open,

gesturing for Georgie to precede him. "Kick things off. Like what?"

"Oh, we're moonlighting as vigilantes now."

"Are you?" Travis followed after her, trying to see the apartment through her eyes. He wasn't lying when he said he'd kept it clean and organized, almost nervous she'd show up and be disappointed. Now, she turned in a circle and gave him a thumbs-up, causing a ripple of satisfaction to pass through him. Damn, he liked seeing her happy with him, especially after the fireplace shit show. He could only grunt in reply, however. "I hope you haven't been fighting crime at night in your clown costume, because that's just scary."

"You say 'scary,' I say 'effective.'"

She went to his freezer and started wrapping ice in a dish towel. Taking care of him in a way he'd always had to do for himself. In a way he'd always *wanted* to do for himself, abhorring the thought of depending on another person. Why didn't he mind when Georgie did these things?

"Anyway, clowns aren't scary. We live to make people laugh."

"You're right," he said hoarsely. "You could never be scary."

"How do you know?" She twisted the ice-filled towel, approached him, and carefully laid it on his shoulder, causing something to stick in his throat. "You've never seen me perform."

"I don't need to watch your act to know you can't pull off scary. You're nothing but a sweetheart."

Georgie's breath hitched at his unplanned words. "Are

you forgetting my lo mein fastball?" she murmured. "I'm not sweet."

Ignoring a mental warning to stop flirting with Georgie—*right now*—Travis tipped his head toward the makeshift ice pack. "Sure about that?"

She let the ice pack go as if it had bitten her, forcing Travis to catch it with his good arm.

"Okay, I'm going to take off." She stepped back with an unconvincing smirk, but Travis could still make out the concern in her eyes as she scrutinized his shoulder. "Make sure to ice on and—"

Panic caught him off guard. Over her leaving? A week ago, he couldn't get rid of her; now she was going to put burn marks on the floor running away. "Hold on. I want to hear more about this club."

"You do?" Visibly gathering her words, Georgie rubbed her hands down the sides of her skirt. "It's . . . a fight club," she said.

"Try again."

"We're starting our own line of organic hand sanitizer."

"Nope."

"Phone sex operators?"

"That's not funny." His chest was crowded by the urge to laugh for the first time in days. It seemed to be his permanent state around this girl. "Tell me. Or I'll pay a visit to your mother and ask her to get it out of you."

Her face transformed with feminine outrage. "That's cold. You know we can't lie to her."

"And she could never say no to me."

Georgie shook her head. "The old square-jawed smirk. It's a one-two punch." With an eye roll, she turned on a heel and stalked off down his hallway. "Where do you keep your Advil?"

"Nightstand. Bedroom." Travis followed Georgie in that direction, hitting an invisible wall in the doorway to his bedroom. Leaning forward over his nightstand, Georgie's shape took on a whole new meaning when silhouetted next to his bed. A wave of her hair fell off its perch on her shoulder, making her lips stand out against the dark backdrop. Last time she was in this room, he'd still considered her kind of a pest. Stephen's sleepy little sister. Now? She'd become the sexy temptation in his bedroom at an alarming rate. That curve of her ass pressed to the skirt zipper, leaving nothing to his imagination. He wanted to drag that zipper down and find out what her butt felt like in his hands. Against his tongue. Wanted to learn the secrets of her body and pleasure more personal ones out of her mouth. And this definitely marked the first time in history he'd been eager to get inside the head of a woman.

"Here." She straightened and offered him two Advil. "Take these. Promise you'll call the doctor if it still hurts in the morning."

He took the pills and tossed them back dry. "You're not getting out of telling me."

Georgie groaned up at the ceiling. "The Just Us League, okay? We started a club."

Travis absorbed that. "You came up with the name, didn't you? Clever."

"Right?" She beamed up at him. "I thought so."

"Seriously," he rasped, a pill obviously having gotten stuck in his throat. Right? That had to be the reason he sounded like a wrench scraping on concrete. "I love it."

They smiled at each other for a few seconds before Georgie shook herself. "We all have goals, you know?" Pink spread on her cheeks. "We're just helping each other reach them."

"What's your goal?"

"Why?"

"Maybe I can help."

She rolled her lips inward, leaving them twice as full when she freed them. *Goddamn.* "I want to expand my business from a one-woman operation to a full-fledged entertainment company. But first," she rushed to add, before he could respond, "before any of that is realistic, I need people to stop treating me like a child. If my own family—this town—can't take me seriously, I can't expect . . . I can't . . ."

Travis waited for Georgie to continue when she trailed off, but she seemed to be hypnotized by something over his shoulder. He raised an eyebrow. "You in there, baby girl?"

"I have a crazy idea," she whispered. "'Maybe you just need a different way to make them listen.' Isn't that what you told me?"

Yeah. He recalled the story he'd told her during their apartment cleaning session. He'd definitely said that. Apparently she'd taken it to heart. He didn't know whether to be touched or regretful.

"You need the television network to believe you've gone

family friendly. Travis, that's me. I'm so disgustingly non-threatening, I get noogies in the tampon aisle. Too much information, I know, but hear me out—"

"Georgie . . ." Caution crawled up his back. "Wherever this is going, it sounds like a no."

"If you pretended to date me—"

"No."

She clapped a hand over his mouth. "Just long enough for the network to think you're settling down and definitely not going to swagger out of Britney's hotel room—again. What would it be? A couple of weeks? Tops?" Excitement made her eyes a bright sea-glass green and he couldn't look away. "We'd be killing two birds with one stone. You get the commentator gig. My family—this whole *town*—would stop thinking of me as the pesky youngest Castle kid."

Travis grasped her wrist, tugging her palm away from his mouth, surprised to find his pulse racing, his breathing unsteady. "Absolutely not."

"Why?"

"Because, Georgie," he blurted out. "Your stock will go too far in the opposite direction. You won't get taken seriously. You'll be labeled as another one of Travis Ford's flings. People will be disappointed, thinking you had your head screwed on tighter than that." He jabbed a finger at her. "You want to look like a grown-up? You will. One that makes bad decisions."

"Wow," she whispered. "You have a pretty low opinion of yourself, don't you? Are you just worried about people thinking I've made a bad decision . . . or do you believe it?"

Whatever she saw on his face made her eyes go soft. A little sad. "And here I thought you were cocky."

He brought their faces close, listening to Georgie suck in a breath. "You don't know a lot of things."

"I could." A beat passed. "You could tell me."

With a concerted effort, Travis stepped away, swiping a frustrated hand along the back of his neck. When had this conversation gotten away from him? Suddenly this girl thought she could call him out? Attempt to examine him? No. Fuck that. He didn't even have the nerve to examine himself. Bottom line, this ruse she'd proposed wasn't happening. Not a chance.

"We wouldn't actually be . . . you know." She shifted. "*Doing* it. Obviously."

Travis scoffed. "You'd be the first to want to date Travis Ford without the perks."

Her eyelids fell to half-mast. "It didn't sound like you were offering them."

He moved into her personal space, his voice emerging harsh. "I'm not."

"Fine," she said, so low he almost didn't hear. "I wouldn't know how to take full advantage of them anyway."

Virgin. Alarm bells went off, but he stayed right where he was, listening to their rapid breaths. Reminding himself she was his best friend's little sister didn't help when she was this near, close enough to touch. To taste. He could no more move away from the approach of Georgie's lips than he could take on a thousand-man army. If he didn't kiss her, someone else would claim that first kiss. No. No, he didn't want that. *Fuck. That.*

Their mouths met.

Parted for two surprised beats.

And melded back together.

CHAPTER ELEVEN

Oh. Whoa.

Clearly Georgie had been drugged by Boutique Tracy and this was a hallucination. She'd been silly to think Tracy forgave her so easily. Her organs were probably being harvested while she dream-kissed Travis in his bedroom. Okay, but how to account for the texture of his mouth? Texture had never been a factor in her fantasies, unless one counted those few times she'd practiced on her own hand. But she hadn't done that since age thirteen.

Fine. Sixteen. Whatever.

In the past, she'd watched them kiss from an almost third-party standpoint, as if it played out on a movie screen. This? Right now? This was a drastic shift.

I'm kissing Travis Ford.

He tasted Georgie the way someone eats their first bite of tiramisu in a restaurant. A slow, savoring mouthful, followed by a gruff, appreciative groan. His head tipped to one side, eyes narrowing with suspicion as if maybe the kiss was a trick and *she* would harvest *his* organs if he gave in and enjoyed. But he gave in anyway, his eyes flickering with hunger. Surprise. He slid his fingers into her hair and took control of her head, angling it for himself. Their thighs pressed together . . . and he licked right in, stopping mid-taste to flick their tongues together . . . before sweeping his through her mouth like a sensually destructive force.

And it definitely had that effect. For sure. Her legs turned the consistency of water; a rash of heat wove in patterns all over her skin. God, he was a lot taller than her. She'd always known that but hadn't considered how it applied to the mechanics of kissing. Now Georgie knew his hair fell forward and mingled with her bangs, a soft intrusion in startling contrast to his mouth, which had started to move . . . faster. Oh God. Stop thinking and keep up.

Stop thinking about what the shudder in his chest meant. Or how he moved into her, until she had to balance on her toes to keep the kiss going, her head tilted all the way back, exposing her throat, making her so vulnerable. Vulnerable to the hand that left her hair and trailed down that exposed throat, a work-roughened thumb circling in the hollow—

God. That one little movement of his thumb set off fireworks below her waist. And he knew it, too, because he made an encouraging noise in his throat. One that said, *Let it happen, baby girl.* And she was. She was letting herself kiss Travis. How had she gotten here? Was he kissing her because he liked her? Or because she was the only one available? So many questions and all of them were being swallowed up by the sensations firing her blood, the give of Travis's lips and how his tongue seemed to know exactly where hers would be, so he could rub them together.

Travis broke the kiss, his harsh pants leaving condensation on her mouth. "Let's slow down some, baby girl. We didn't, uh . . . fuck." He sunk his teeth into his bottom lip and eyed her mouth, shaking his head. "I think there's supposed to be more buildup to what we just did."

"You think?" Sweet Lord, his body heat was like being wrapped in warmed cashmere in front of a roaring fire. "You're supposed to be the expert."

He puffed a humorless laugh. "Not on kissing."

In other words, his talents lay in the more serious sexual arts.

"Oh." Jealousy crackled in Georgie's belly, surprising her. She'd never been enough of a masochist to get jealous over Travis Ford. What was the point in living her life in constant flux between shades of green? This jab of unpleasantness was new but sharp. Real. Maybe it had something to do with how he looked at her, brow furrowed, a muscle bobbling in his throat. The lines of their relationship had just been irrevocably blurred, but Georgie hated the thought of him looking at someone else like that now that she'd been on the receiving end. There had been no reason to be jealous over a man who was basically an untouchable movie star to her. This man, though . . . he was just *her* star for now. No one else's.

Adding the stroke of envy to this morning's uptick in confidence . . . and Georgie found herself anxious to leave a mark. She could wake up from this dream at any moment. Or, let's face it, Travis could lose interest, reject her fake-dating proposal, and go after someone more like Tracy.

Chalk up the kiss to momentary insanity. Why shouldn't she reach out now and grasp this chance to achieve a fantasy she'd been playing out mentally since she hit puberty?

"Show me what you're an expert in."

Travis stopped breathing, his hands dropping to her elbows. Holding tightly, but not pushing her away. "Georgie." He expelled her name on a breath, but she saw something primal flare to life in his eyes. "I'll eat you alive. *No.*"

"You won't." She tugged her arms out of his grip and—saying a prayer to whichever saint bestowed courage—reached back and unzipped her skirt. "Oh." She frowned. "In my head, the skirt was going to drop and I was going to cock a seductive hip."

His lips parted. "How do you do that? Make me this hot and want to laugh at the same time."

"See, I'm teaching you something new." She was painfully aware of the vulnerability written in her every feature. "Your turn."

Hesitation battled with need in his expression, and it was so intoxicating up close, Georgie's knees wobbled. "Once we find out how this feels, though . . ." His hands stayed fisted in the air beside her hips, hesitating, clenching and unclenching, before finally settling on them. "We won't be able to forget."

"You're worried I'll never forget how bad you were. I understand."

His right eyebrow went sky-high. "Are you employing reverse psychology to get me into bed? I'm impressed."

Georgie shrugged a shoulder. "Not bad for a virgin."

"There it is." He dropped his head forward. "Christ. I had a feeling you were a virgin. But I wasn't positive."

"Glad I could clear it up. We don't have to—"

"We're *not*."

"Cool. But we are . . . ?"

"On-top-of-the-clothes stuff only."

"Do panties count as clothes?"

"I don't know. Yes."

"Sweet." Before she could lose her nerve, Georgie wiggled the skirt down over her hips and nudged it aside, feeling her face turn pink but staunchly ignoring it. "I'm ready."

The world tilted when Travis picked her up by the waist, tossing her into the center of the bed like she weighed less than a feather. He crawled slowly up her body. "No. You aren't."

"I lie corrected," she breathed.

"Stop being cute." Without breaking eye contact, he unbuttoned her blouse. The entire thing in seconds with quick wrist twists. "Your bra counts as clothes, too."

She gave a jerky nod. "You make the rules."

"That's right." He surged forward and growled against her lips. "I'm no one's entertainment anymore. You want to play? I decide how."

Those words cut through the waves of lust plowing through Georgie. That statement was so at odds with the Travis of her memory. The arrogant baseball player who'd strutted to the batter's box, doffing his hat to the crowd. Taking requests on which part of the outfield he should aim for. She wanted to explore the change he'd shown her now more than once.

His mouth dominated hers, leading the dance, giving no quarter. Almost as if he wanted to scare her off. His body said he needed her, though. To Georgie, inexperienced or not, Travis had all the classic signs of an aroused male. And Georgie was an expert now, because she'd thumbed through the issue of *Cosmo* today in between fittings at the boutique. Dilated pupils. Harsh breathing. Most importantly, a growing bulge behind his fly. *Oh my God. Travis is on top of me with a hard penis. This is happening.*

"Goddammit, Georgie. Don't zone out on me."

"I'm not. I'm zoning in. Way in."

His forehead fell into the crook of her neck. The feeling was so nice, her thighs seemed to lift automatically to wrap around his hips. Travis liked that. He gave a closed-mouthed moan and shifted between her legs. "I've got no fucking right to be between these legs."

"You do. I gave it to you." That last word ended in a gasp when Travis's teeth grazed her shoulder, his waist rolling into the cradle of her hips at the same exact moment. "Oh wow."

"Try to sound a little less innocent while I get you off," he rasped beside her ear, catching her lobe with his teeth. "How about that?"

"Yes, Travis."

This name she'd said thousands of times in her life sounded entirely different in a threadbare voice with the insides of her knees resting against his rib cage. Head to toe, she trembled, turned on by his expert abrasiveness, her belly hollowing on a long shudder, her toes curling, nipples peaking.

God help her, there was something kind of hot about Travis's self-directed anger. This man had a will of steel and the focus of a world-class athlete, but apparently he'd lost a battle with himself over her. *Her.* She couldn't turn off the excitement, no matter how hard she tried.

"Yes, Travis," he echoed, shifting his hips slowly. Making her squirm. "Why weren't you agreeable all those times I told you to go home?"

"I'm selectively agreeable."

That smart-ass comment earned her a rough punch of his hips. "Look where it got us. You had to keep reminding me how nicely you grew up. Now we're halfway to fucking."

Oh my God. Her head spun, Travis's face blurring into two, then fusing back together. Was she seriously supposed to have a conversation while this gorgeous, filth-spewing man rocked between her thighs? "I told you to go home once, too," she said in a rush. "I left you alone. This isn't all my fault."

She'd thought the hard kisses Travis was giving her were mind-blowing, but the slow one he laid on her just then had her seeing stars. "The quiet got too loud once you'd come and gone." Another long kiss that left her gasping. "How dare you."

Before she could address *that,* he reversed their positions. Her equilibrium spent a few seconds off kilter, her body yearning to be pressed down. Hard. And she might have said something to that effect out loud, because Travis cursed and closed his eyes, hands flexing on her hips.

"Move up a little, baby girl."

Baby girl. She loved when he called her that. Probably because he winced every single time, like he couldn't control the endearment. Her knees inched up the bed and she settled in again on Travis's lap—"Oh." She fell forward, catching herself on his shoulders. "Th-that's . . ."

"Mmm." He lifted her up with his hips, bouncing her once. "Feel my cock, Georgie?"

Uh, yeah. The giant appendage that made Georgie feel like she was sitting on a full aluminum foil roll? "Yes, I feel it."

His big hands smoothed down the cheeks of her backside, sending a crazy intense ripple down her middle, culminating at her sex. "Close your eyes and do what you want with it."

A whimper wrenched itself from her throat. "I don't know what I want to do with it."

"Yes, you do." His arm came up fast, his hand wrapping around the back of her neck to draw Georgie down for a slow, wet kiss. "Virgin or not, you've thought about riding this dick or you wouldn't have dropped your skirt for me. Tell me I'm right."

Oh, she'd thought of it only about four hundred thousand times. "Y-you're right."

He gave an openmouthed groan. "Then ride it so I forget touching you makes me a bastard." Travis's hands found her bottom again, fingers sliding under the edge of her new panties to get a good grip on her flesh. "Maybe you need a little help." Breath coming fast, he began rocking her up and back. And Lord. Lord. She'd consoled herself for years that her vibrator was as good as any man, but she'd been wrong. There was no substitute for feeling a man's arousal against her thin, wet panties. Or hearing him grit a curse when she angled back and pressed her clit to the denim fly of his jeans, rubbing shamelessly, as she was doing now.

She wanted to see more of him, so she dragged his T-shirt up to his neck and exposed his abdomen. The bunched pecs decorated with flat brown nipples. Why pretend not to appreciate the sight when it was obvious, by her pumping hips, that she appreciated his physique very much? Travis knew how his body affected her, too. It was there in the glazed eyes he locked on her. He dragged his tongue across his lower lip and flexed his stomach for her, making his pecs jump. Holy. Sweet. Jesus. Yeah, there was still some of the cocky man left behind and he was bananas hot. Her whole body felt fevered and alive, watching the ridges of his muscles dance just for her. But even as she gripped his huge shoulders and worked herself on his fly, the orgasm continued to hang in the distance. Just out of reach.

"Come on, baby girl," Travis gritted. "We're on the same team. We both want to get rid of our aches. Need to take care of yours first, but those little hips of yours have got me real fucking close."

Oh God. Oh wow. That admission almost did it. Almost teetered her over the edge. She was making Travis have an orgasm. And despite her inexperience, she'd seen enough of the internet to know men didn't usually climax with their pants on. That had to be good. Her thighs were trembling violently and the flesh between her legs clenched, clenched, but didn't give that final almighty spasm. Why? Why? She couldn't help but close her eyes and picture Travis above her, pressing her down. Demanding control of the situation. Of her.

"I see you," he rasped. "Dammit, Georgie. You had to be exactly what I need, didn't you?"

In a split second, she was on her back, with a big, horny man taking up her whole world. Filling every available inch of her vision. Caging her in. He jerked down the cups of her bra and sucked her left nipple into his mouth. Georgie cried out. A sticky, zapping ball of wicked energy gathered in Georgie's midsection, tightening, tightening. She couldn't breathe or think. Was that her whimpering Travis's name?

"You like me on top, don't you, baby girl?" Travis's hips rammed into the cradle of her thighs, his erection finding and pressing right where she needed, all while this man released an unforgivable and amazing stream of filth beside her ear. "Whining and shaking on top of me, showing me how hot you'd be to fuck, but baby girl can't seal the deal on her own. Can you? Need to be held down and told to come while I'm riding your pretty panties, don't you? Well, go on." Travis worked his hips in a rough figure eight, coming back to land on Georgie's most sensitive area. Eyes clenched shut, sweat dotting his brow, Travis powered through a quick string of thrusts, the movements so close together and rough, Georgie's teeth clacked together. "Telling me you don't know what to do with my cock. Maybe you don't. Maybe you need it *used* on you."

"Use it on me," she pushed through numb, trembling lips. "Need it."

Travis's moan hung in the air as he lunged for her neck, dragging his tongue up the side, pressing his teeth beneath her ear. Her wrists were jerked up over her head and pinned and it happened. An earthquake. Her orgasm obliterated her, twisting her loins like a pretzel and squeezing while her legs fought for purchase against the overwhelming nature of it.

"Christ, Georgie. Look at you. Feel you." Travis's mouth pushed into her hair, his lower body continuing its slow, insistent grind against hers. "Watching you come so sweet in my bed. What the fuck am I going to do now, huh?"

With her flesh seized up and pulsing through the most intense climax of her life, she was incapable of answering, but one train of thought plowed through like a piercing whistle. *Please him back. Please him back.* "Travis," she managed, dropping her legs open and circling her hips. "You need me."

Sexual pain slashed across his face, his body growing rigid. "Baby girl. I pump against this pussy one more time and I'm not coming anywhere but balls deep. Those panties are history. You hear me? You see how fucked up I am?"

"Yes . . ." Was this normal? Did his control always snap eventually? It was too much to hope for that it only happened with her, but she could pretend. She could pretend she was the only thing standing between Travis and insanity. "Find a way," she breathed.

If Georgie took one thing away from her first sexual encounter, it would be that she'd only scratched the surface of herself. Yes, her fantasies had always been rough in nature and she'd never been able to achieve an orgasm without imagining that gradual release of control, but when Travis sat back on his knees and flipped her over onto her stomach, the sensation of handing herself over to Travis robbed her of common sense. Her orgasm had ebbed, but this desire to please him seemed almost . . . mental. Like she could hear and answer his thoughts and needs with her body.

Georgie watched through tunnel vision as Travis leaned over her back and removed something from his nightstand. She'd never seen him like this. Jaw clenched, muscles bunched. Tense. So tense. His erection pushed against the fly of his jeans, looking painful. He'd fully removed his shirt and a light sheen of sweat covered his shoulders and stomach, turning her on all over again. *My God, he's almost too sexy.*

That was her final coherent thought before Travis moved behind her again. A tick of the clock passed. Two. And then his fingers slipped beneath the back panel of her silk high-cut bikini briefs, gathering the material together between her cheeks. Tugging. Some might call it a wedgie, but she'd had her fair share of those and this . . . was *not* like one of those. Just the knowledge that Travis was touching her underwear made Georgie grow damp all over again. Once the purple silk was gathered at the center of her backside, those rough hands moved to her flesh, molding it with a grunt.

"Christ Almighty. Where have you been hiding this ass?"

She wasn't given a chance to answer. There was a snap behind her, like a bottle opening, followed by a liquid sound.

With her heart going wild in her throat, Georgie waited, gasping into the comforter when a thick layer of moisture was smoothed over her bottom by skilled hands, some of the drops landing on the material gathered down the middle. "What is that?" Georgie whispered, her body moving on autopilot, hips tilting to offer herself to him more completely.

"You told me to find a way." Travis's voice rasped low at her ear, his body settling on top of her, his thick, flexing thighs on either side of her hips. "Can't keep working over that pussy without finding out how tight it really is. And the panties have to stay on—"

"That's your rule, not mine."

He clapped a hand over her mouth, releasing a low curse when it made her whimper, her lower body shifting excitedly on the bed. "I should send you home with your shiny, new orgasm, but I'm not that kind of man, Georgie." His right hand released her mouth and slid beneath her hips, massaging her sensitive flesh through her wet panties. "I'm the kind who's about to use your ass to get off and come on your back. I'm too hot to give a sweet fuck that you're my friend's little sister right now. And that should bother you."

"Shut up," she whispered, lust weaving up her spine, turning her from awkward girl to desirable woman. Her ass lifted of its own accord, writhing against the hard denim ridge. "I want everything you said. I'm saying yes. Please don't stop."

His body flattened hers. Hard. Breath whooshed from her lungs. It was difficult to hear Travis's zipper being yanked down over the rattling of her pulse, but she grasped the noise and savored what she'd actually managed to drive a man to. A sexually experienced man. Travis.

When his flesh slapped down between her cheeks, Georgie's mouth fell open, her hands twisting in the comforter. Hot air puffed from his mouth into the cradle of her neck, followed by a long groan as his hips began to roll. The movements started off as seeking, testing drives, but they didn't stay that way for long. Soon enough, Travis's hands sank into the bedclothes right alongside hers, his erection tunneling up and back through the split of her backside in rough grinds. Every drive of his hips was accompanied by a guttural sound that became Georgie's reason for living on the spot. She opened her thighs wide as she could and offered herself up like a sacrifice.

And Travis accepted it. Unapologetically.

They weren't having sex, but their bodies mimicked the act in the most desperate fashion, sweat building on their skin, their heavy breathing filling the room. God, what would it be like to have him pumping and snarling at her like this while his flesh actually filled her? Would she survive that? Her loins were beginning to tighten again, just from the slick friction of their lower bodies, aided by the liquid he'd applied, Travis's chest and stomach muscles roaming up and down her back, his pace picking up, up, up . . . until she had to hold on for dear life or get thrown off the bed.

"This what you like, baby girl? Flashing me this ass and making me hungry for it?"

"Yes," she whimpered, tilting her hips as far as they would go . . . and oh God. Travis adjusted his manhood and surged forward again, letting that thick arousal drag along the front of her panties, muttering for her to get her ass up. *Up.* When she complied, he tucked himself flush between her thighs and ground forward right on top of her clit. "Oh please, oh please."

His hand wrapped around the bunched material between her bottom cheeks, using it as leverage to keep her still while he bucked, the mattress springs squeaking beneath them. "Might be a virgin, but you've been dreaming about fucking for a while, haven't you?" His hips dropped down on top of Georgie's hard, his hand tucking back beneath her to rub her clit with rough circles, his lower body never ceasing in its powerful drives. "This is it, baby girl. Down and dirty like goddamn animals. Getting off however we can. That's all I know how to do."

"No," she managed, the onslaught of sensation making her voice seem distant. "Y-you can do anything."

Travis gave a hoarse groan into her neck and bore down on her clit with two stiff fingers, his hips starting to move in disjointed patterns. "Go on. Soak those panties one more time. I want you too messy to go back out in public. Straight home in that skirt, baby girl."

Was it the command that set her off? Or his touch? Georgie didn't know or care, could only scream into the mattress as her flesh pulled again and again in rhythmic waves. Hot fluid landed on the small of her back a moment later, the sound of Travis's broken growl echoing off the walls. Her orgasm lifted in intensity at the proof of his satisfaction, her pelvis grinding against the mattress, not a drop of shame to be found anywhere.

"Look at you," Travis said, voice unnatural. His hand came down and laid a resounding smack on Georgie's buttocks, starting a ringing in her head, sending bone-deep fulfillment coursing through her. "How dare you make me come this hard with your fucking panties on." He squeezed the spanked flesh, then gave it a final, lighter slap. "How am I ever going to look at you again, without knowing how bad you need this?"

Sensing they were done, Georgie waited for Travis to clean off her back with his discarded T-shirt, then flopped her boneless body down on the bed and rolled over. He was in an upright kneel, tucking his still impressive flesh into his jeans before zipping up. Exhaling. The trenches in his forehead made her nervous. When would he look at her? She needed to get a read on him after what they'd done. Travis was a notorious anti-commitment flag bearer, so she definitely wasn't expecting a declaration of . . . like . . . She didn't expect *anything*, did she?

His guarded expression told her to keep it light. If this never happened again, there was a slight possibility they could go back to how things were before. At least for Travis. As for her phony-relationship proposal, there was a good chance she'd just made it impossible. The plan had been to keep things platonic. None of the perks. But they'd just hard-core perked.

"So I thought porn-star sex had way more camera angles," she managed, blowing some hair out of her face. "I didn't even get to see the money shot."

That surprised a low laugh out of him. "Trust me, it was professional quality." He shook his head while looking her over. "Come here."

Her heart ramped up to a hundred miles per hour. "Why?"

"We don't have to get up *right* away—" He cut himself off with an impatient noise. "Quit asking questions and get over here."

There was no help for her enthusiasm. With the prospect of being held by Travis—both of them half naked—excitement sprung up inside her like a geyser. She sat up and threw her arms around him, toppling them sideways onto the pillows. Obviously, she'd caught him off guard, but he recovered with an exasperated sigh that ruffled her hair. Seeming at odds with himself, he eventually wrapped an arm around the small of Georgie's back, tugging her into the warmth of his chest.

"A few minutes won't hurt," he muttered, seemingly to himself.

She nuzzled into his chest hair to hide her smile.

At least ten minutes passed while they lay there. A clock ticked in the distance, matching the drum of Travis's heart against her ear. Every time he shifted, she thought the cuddling was over—and it seemed like Travis did, too. That he was surprised to find his fingertips trailing up and down her back, his chin dropping on top of her head. She'd thought of basking in Travis's strong arms millions of times, but the reality made those fantasies seem silly in comparison. This was a real-life man with complications. A past. A future taking shape.

I'm no one's entertainment anymore.

Was that how he'd been treated? Was that how *she'd* thought of him before he came home?

Acting on impulse, she laid a kiss in the center of his chest and felt his heartbeat falter. "Sometimes when I do parties, I try to start a conversation with one of the parents, but I can tell they just want me to go entertain the kids. It's like this really stiff smiling, nodding hint to get back to work. To doing what I'm good at."

"Why are you telling me this?"

"Do you think I'm more than a clown?" She swallowed. "Professionally and . . . figuratively."

He ran a hand down her hair. "Of course I do, Georgie."

Cool relief slipped beneath her skin. "See? People can be wrong. They can treat you one way when you deserve another, but it's their fault. Not yours." His frame was beginning to stiffen against her, so she rushed to finish. "I'm sorry if you were treated like less than you are."

For several heavy beats, he didn't move or breathe. "All right," he said finally, removing his arms from around Georgie and rolling onto his back. "That's enough."

Georgie banished the pinch of hurt. "Don't be so romantic."

He stacked his hands behind his head. "You've got the wrong man for that."

"I know." She sat up, perching on the edge of the mattress

with crossed legs. "I know you're not romance guy. I don't expect anything." She looked back at him over her shoulder. "That's why our arrangement will be perfect."

"Are you out of your mind, Georgie?" A harsh, humorless laugh left his mouth. "After what just happened, you think that's actually an option? No. Jesus, I'm trying to figure out how I'm going to look your brother in the eye again."

Irritation ripped through Georgie. Where before she'd been a tranquil pond, a stone had just been hurled right into the center of it. "Oh, you know what? *Forget* it." She lunged off the bed and pulled on her clothes, searching the floor of his bedroom for her shoes. "I just had the most adult experience of my life and I'm still just someone's little sister, aren't I? Get back to being a clown, Georgie. Screw that."

"Now hold on just a goddamn minute."

Travis climbed off the bed and Georgie backed up into the bedroom doorway, out of sheer self-preservation. Wearing nothing but jeans and bed head, he was a magnetic, sexual authority. If he asked her to get back in bed, she would forget her anger and do it in a second. No denying it.

"There are rules for this kind of thing and they would apply even if you were fucking forty, baby girl. Don't you dare get pissed at me."

"Too late." She left the bedroom, determined to be out the front door before Travis could follow. That turned out to be wishful thinking since he caught up with her two steps later. His hand curled around her elbow, whirling her around. Was that a flash of panic she'd seen in his eyes before he hid it?

"You want to fake date so everyone will stop thinking of you as a kid—"

"And you can get your job."

"Fine. Let's do it." Expression serious, he pointed back at the bedroom. "But that can't happen again. We're not going to confuse what this is. If we have sex, someone will get confused."

"Just admit it. You're talking about me."

"Yeah, fine. I'm talking about you." He stepped close enough that she could smell his light sweat, the musk of what they'd done. Along with his proximity, the smell was like a caress between her legs. And how annoying that he could turn her on even while being condescending. "I have no problem walking away from a few hookups and never looking back. You don't know yet if you're capable of that." His eyes closed. "Christ, I shouldn't even be considering this."

Maybe he was right. Georgie tried to imagine what it would be like, dating Travis in public *and* spending time in his bed. When he got the job and it all ended, it would hurt if—when—he dropped her. What if the real Travis she'd only begun to scratch the surface of . . . turned out to be equally as incredible as superstar shortstop Travis of her dreams? It was hard to admit, but maybe he was right.

She could get hurt if they slept together. Badly.

But wasn't it worth having respect for the rest of her life? Yes. A smidgen of pain now weighed against decades of her family, friends, and customers treating her like an adult. There was no contest. And she was a big girl. At the very least, *she* knew that. She could go into this arrangement with her eyes wide open and emerge mostly unscathed, couldn't she?

"Fine. Dating. No sex. We wouldn't want my lady brain to get confused by an orgasm. A wedding dress might magically stitch itself onto me." Travis stared down at her with a baleful expression. "See? Ridiculous. Are you in or out?"

He dragged a hand down his face, leaving his mouth covered a moment. Considering. "The only way dating you would help me land this job would be the press getting wind of us." Hand dropping away, his lips moved into a grim line. "I don't like the idea of cameras following you."

"I can handle it."

His jaw twitched. "You realize if we want to be realistic for those cameras, we'll have to get pretty close. It's not going to be real." The tone of his voice dropped. "It won't be real when I kiss you, Georgie. And we can't take it further. Will you remember that?"

A hole was punched in her stomach, but she garnered some bravery and stepped closer to Travis anyway. "Will you?"

It took him a moment to answer, his attention straying to her mouth. "Yes."

"Then we have a deal," she breathed, putting her hand out.

"Hold up. We need some fine print." Travis crossed his arms. "My agent is working on setting up a dinner with the head of the network in a couple of weeks. When it's over, I'll know whether or not I have the job. There'll be no reason to—"

"Keep this up. I understand." Georgie wet her lips. "That

should be more than enough time for everyone to reevaluate their opinion that I'm nothing more than a silly clown." She widened her eyes and prompted him again to shake her hand. "After the dinner we end it, no muss, no fuss."

After a few beats, his warm palm slid against hers and gripped, although his expression continued to be wary. "Deal."

CHAPTER TWELVE

I have a girlfriend. A fake *girlfriend.*

Travis flipped off the table saw and stepped back, pushing his safety goggles onto his head. He really shouldn't be operating heavy machinery while being so epically predisposed to getting a hard-on. There could be a serious tragedy. He'd have a new nickname: One Bat.

That scary possibility should have been enough to ease the thick pressure in Travis's cock, but as he'd learned last night after his third round of beating off, there was no relief. Every time he let his mind drift, it returned to Georgie's tight little ass cheeks. The dribble of lube on those smooth curves, the liquid trickling down the center to be absorbed by her silk panties. He'd had no finesse yesterday. No game. Once she offered herself up, he'd been incapable of hitting pause. Or catching his breath. Or doing anything but *getting there getting there getting there.*

What scared him the most was he'd gotten that way from kissing her.

As soon as their tongues touched, there had been this urgency crowding him. To take as much as he could. Taste every inch of her and hope his mouth didn't forget. Had anyone ever kissed him with so much trust? No. No one kissed or exposed themselves like her, honest and unrestrained. No one had ever pulled him in so deeply. He'd forgotten about work and responsibilities and vanity. Christ, he hadn't even minded holding her when it was over.

Oh, you didn't mind *it? Right.*

He was full of contradictions lately, wasn't he? Hook up with Georgie again? Nope. Bad idea. But he didn't want anyone else to lay a finger on her. Hell, he wasn't all that thrilled knowing about her vibrator, Dale. It made exactly zero sense to Travis.

This relationship was phony, so where was this possessive streak coming from? It was almost as if he was . . . jealous. Georgie was adorable and funny and date-worthy before that inconvenient makeover. Now she was walking around Port Jefferson looking like the girl next door had decided to fulfill every man's naughty librarian fantasy. At least that's how she'd looked yesterday. He'd seen inside the bags, though. There'd been all kinds of girlie shit in there. For all he knew, she was in the town square dressed in pasties and a tutu while he sucked sawdust.

Pull back, man. Listen to yourself.

Travis removed the goggles from his head and tossed them on the workbench. Massaging the bridge of his nose, he attempted to center himself the way he used to do in the locker room before a big game. Think. Release the negativity. Embrace the focus.

He was attracted to Georgie. Couldn't-keep-his-dick-*down*

attracted. But he'd get over that part. They hadn't engaged in the main event, so he probably just had some extreme form of blue balls. If it meant spraining his fucking wrist, he'd handle the problem sooner or later. It would not be solved, however, by touching her again. What he'd said yesterday wasn't arrogance talking—it was simply more common for women to get attached when sex was part of the equation. Basic science, right? The idea of hurting Georgie made him feel like the buzz saw was spinning in his stomach, so he wouldn't go there.

Associating himself with her could go a long way in getting him the commentator job. Her family was prominent in Port Jefferson. She was the epitome of wholesome. Until he got her on her back, apparently. Nothing wholesome about how she came.

His dick pushed against the front of his fly and he cursed.

He was dating Georgie to help secure the job. That needed to be the *only* reason for this arrangement. When he was a kid, the ballpark was the only place he'd ever felt truly at home. At peace. It embraced him when no one inside the four walls of his home ever bothered to. Hesitantly, he let himself smell the freshly cut grass, dirt, sweat, spilled beer, and tobacco. That familiarity had been moved outside his grasp, and it still stung. If he couldn't still be the best, why bother? This sport he'd loved had become a tool of disappointment in himself. But in a way, commentating was his way back onto the field, without having to get too close and feel that failure again. He *needed* this. He needed this to save him from being a has-been at twenty-eight, the way his father assumed he would.

Fake dating Georgie could not have anything to do with getting her sexy curves underneath him again. And it certainly couldn't have shit to do with wanting to simply be around her. Or with the fact that letting his guard down around her gave him the same sense of peace as the ballpark.

Temporary. It would only *ever* be temporary. Baseball was forever.

At the sound of gravel crunching, Travis turned and looked out the window to find Stephen arriving in his god-awful minivan. His baby-brained friend hopped out of the van with a tray of coffees, stopping to talk to Dominic. Energy snapped in Travis's shoulders the way it hadn't in months. That drive that had been missing was back, breathing oxygen into his body, which had felt flat and sluggish since getting cut from the league. The catalyst for the change had to be the possibility of a new job. A new purpose. *That's* where he needed to put his focus. Getting his name to the top of the short list.

He'd been given a way. Taking it sure as hell wasn't going to be easy.

A moment later, Travis stepped off the new porch, his work boots landing in a mixture of dirt and construction debris. Stephen nodded in greeting, a smile breaking across his face. Travis could only grimace in return as he went to join the men, guilt slithering like a serpent in his belly. There had been a lot of truth to Georgie's complaint yesterday. She *was* more than someone's little sister. A lot more. That didn't change the fact that Travis had stepped over a clearly drawn line. There would be consequences.

"Brought you one," Stephen said. "Black, right?"

"Yeah. Thanks."

His best friend tugged the collar of his shirt. "I was just telling Dominic my theory."

Travis raised an eyebrow. "What theory?"

"There's been a shift in the universe." Stephen shook his head. "Kristin is keeping a secret. Gossiping with my mother on the phone." He dropped his voice to a dramatic stage whisper. "There's something up with the womenfolk."

Dominic got a far-off look on his face. "Rosie has been stuffing newspapers under the mattress. Does that bolster your theory?"

"Maybe." Stephen frowned. "Why's she doing that?"

Dominic's answer was to shrug and light a cigarette, blowing smoke into the afternoon haze.

Of course, Travis knew what that was about. The Just Us League. Any other time, he would have kept the intelligence to himself, but today was not the day to lie to Stephen. Not when he already had so much shit piled on his head. "They started a club. Far as I know, it's only Rosie and your sisters. I don't think it was formed to fuck with your heads, though, boys. More like . . . an adult sorority."

"My wife is in a club," Dominic muttered, his jaw flexing. "Women only, you said?"

Travis nodded and Dominic relaxed.

Stephen, however, was tense and staring at Travis, probably wondering how Travis knew about the club. Knowing the confession couldn't be put off any longer, Travis addressed Dominic without looking at him. "Would you excuse us for a minute, man?"

He felt Dominic shift a glance between them. "Sure."

"Might want to take the hot coffee."

That gave both men pause, but Stephen seemed to shake off whatever suspicions he'd racked up. "What's going on with you?" he asked, setting the tray of coffees on the roof of his minivan instead of handing it to Dominic. "You haven't looked this nervous since you broke my bike axle trying to jump that trench in seventh grade."

"I made it eventually." Travis waited until Dominic walked away but noticed he didn't seem inclined to go too far. Smart man. "Stephen, something happened with Georgie."

His friend's face turned white. "What do you mean? Is she okay?"

"Yes," Travis rushed to say, realizing he'd phrased that statement in the worst way possible. "Christ. Yes, she's fine." His own heart was up in his throat at the imaginary scenario where Georgie was hurt or worse. So much so that it took him a minute to continue. Even then, his pulse continued to hammer from worry. "At least, she was fine when she left my place yesterday."

"What?" Stephen asked quietly, his voice taking on a dangerous quality. "You better be joking."

"I'm not joking. She gave me a ride home from town and . . ." He dragged a hand down his face so he wouldn't have to see the betrayal etched in Stephen's features. "It didn't go as far as it could have, but that's no excuse. I take full responsibility."

When he opened his eyes again, Stephen was pacing in a

circle. "What the fuck, Travis? Why? It's open season on you in this fucking town and you pick Georgie? You could have anyone else."

"She's not like anyone else."

Stephen put his hands up. "Whoa."

Travis shook his head. "I didn't mean that how it sounded." He hadn't, right? "That came out wrong. I just meant to say, I'm not interested in anyone. Especially not the women hunting me for sport. Georgie and I . . . we became friends. And trust me, I'm as fucking surprised by that as you are." A memory of Georgie sliding into his apartment with groceries and a smile forced Travis to pause. "One thing led to another. I didn't see it coming."

Was he talking about their friendship or the hookup?

Or something else entirely?

"Goddammit, Travis."

"I know." Shaking off the wayward thought, he squared his shoulders. "Take a good, hard swing, just miss my face. I'm in line for a commentating job on a wholesome television network and they'll never let me on camera if they think I'm going to show up with busted eyes."

His friend showed a spark of reluctant interest. "Commentating job?"

Travis nodded, grateful the guy was still talking to him at all. "Voice of the Bombers' home games. I've got a few guys to beat out. I'm working on it."

Right here, right now, he could confide everything in Stephen. Maybe even solve Georgie's problem in one fell swoop. *You don't treat her like an independent, grown-up woman. No one does.* It would save her having to go through the ruse of dating him. Telling Stephen Georgie's reasons for proposing the arrangement felt like a betrayal of her trust, though. He physically couldn't make himself do it.

No. Georgie's family was her main problem. If Travis implored Stephen to start treating Georgie with more respect, it could backfire. Maybe even earn her more of that famous Castle ridicule. He would not be responsible for that. In fact, the very prospect of *anyone* giving her shit made his blood rise several degrees. The only way to keep Georgie's confidence was to let her family believe the ruse, too. No way around it. No way to assuage the guilt of lying to his best friend, either. "We're seeing each other. It's casual." He fixed Stephen with a look. "She understands I'm not looking for anything serious."

Stephen's mouth fell open. "Travis, are you really this fucking stupid? My little sister has been in love with you since she hit middle school."

Light streaked across his vision. He was dropped into a vacuum of no sound, as if he'd fallen into a lake. But he kicked to the surface as fast as possible, because surely he'd misheard. "No, she's not." His voice sounded funny. Hoarse. "Georgie? You're full of shit."

"She stole my yearbook so many times to pledge her undying love to your senior picture, I finally just let her have the damn thing." He grabbed a coffee off the roof of his van and drained half of it. "Had your rookie year poster on her ceiling and everything. And don't get me started on game day. If anyone talked while you were up to bat, she'd bite their head off."

That image of Georgie sitting in the bleachers with nachos in her lap came back through a totally different filter, accompanied by dawning understanding. Oh yeah. She'd had a thing for him back then. No doubt about it. How could he have missed it? Or maybe he was so used to being the center of attention back then, he'd acknowledged it as his due and kept moving.

He almost wanted to cancel the whole arrangement, right then and there. No way was he going to be this girl's boyfriend, fake or not, if she was in love with him.

But Georgie wasn't in love with him. The notion was ridiculous. She'd had a *crush* on the superstar, a childish infatuation. He was no longer that superstar. Far from it. And she was no longer a middle schooler with awkward limbs, either. If he treated Georgie like she was still that young girl with braces, he was no better than everyone she wanted to prove wrong. They were both adults. Different people from whom they'd been when she stared up at that poster. Hell, he'd fallen *way* too far to earn that kind of hero worship from anyone, let alone Georgie. She'd probably laugh at that old torch she used to carry. Before she found him facedown in a hangover and tempting the rat population.

He chose to ignore the thorn in his throat when thinking of Georgie laughing off the past infatuation. "Listen, I don't do serious. And I've been up front with your sister about that. If she chooses to ignore the warning, that's on her. But I don't think you're giving her enough credit. She's old enough to listen."

"And if she doesn't?"

Restless and agitated, Travis cut him off. "Are you going to hit me or not?"

Stephen looked like he wanted to say more, but shrugged and set his coffee down on the roof of the van instead. "I think you know I have to." He put up his fists, rolled his neck. "This is going to hurt me more than it hurts you."

"Fuck's sake. Just do it already."

His friend stared at him for so long, Travis wondered what the hell he was seeing. Finally, Stephen let his hands drop. "Nah, I'm going to pass. I think you're headed for something even more painful."

Travis was left standing beside the minivan feeling like he'd been sucker punched anyway.

CHAPTER THIRTEEN

Georgie rolled on her back in the grass, laughing as half a dozen five-year-olds dog-piled on top of her. The impact of the children knocked her red wig off, sending hair spilling out in every direction, covering half her face and nearly dislodging her spongy red nose. A dog joined the party, licking her face and sending kids and parents alike into fits of amusement. This was the part she loved most about birthday parties. The sugar high. When kids turned totally loopy and stopped being shy. Yes, the second half of a party was always the best. It was also the portion of the show where physical injury became a real possibility, but that was just splitting hairs.

Speaking of splitting hairs, it had been forty-six hours since she'd seen Travis. They'd made a deal to be in a fake relationship and shook on it, but it seemed they were waiting for the other to make the first move. If they remained true to form, Georgie would be the one to show up and foist her presence upon him. Doing so never gave her pause before. Was it so bad that she wanted him to make the first fake move this time?

What did it say about her personality that she'd had to create distractions to keep herself from dropping in on him? That she was proactive? Thankfully those distractions had been super productive. Over the last couple days, she'd contacted a designer about a new website for the business and placed an advertisement for freelance employees. She didn't have the money to bring anyone on full-time yet, but she would get there. Having a plan filled her with confidence and a sense of accomplishment.

A feather-like feeling tickled the back of Georgie's neck and she looked around, assuming one of the parents was trying to get her attention. But nope. They were all congregated around the snack table gossiping. So why did her skin continue to prickle?

Georgie looked toward the gate and found Travis watching her over the painted white posts, a smirk on his ruggedly beautiful face. Every inch of her body started to buzz, her mouth going dry. Holy shit. She'd imagined him into reality.

Travis was making the first move.

"This is what your future looks like, Georgette Castle," one of the mothers called while walking past the clown-kid dog-pile in the grass, a pizza box in her arms. "Follow me, party animals."

Travis's smirk faded fast. He lifted a hand to remove his sunglasses and there were his eyes. So intense. They beamed down at her like she was a thousand-piece puzzle, stirring up chaos inside her rib cage.

"Travis?" Georgie murmured, sitting up to adjust her wig

as the children abandoned her to follow the scent of pizza. "What are you doing here?"

"I saw your car," he said, sounding gruff.

When he didn't elaborate, she noticed the building discomfort in his frame and laughed to split the tension. "You look like a live childbirth just went by in your Facebook feed."

The joke did nothing to make his shoulders relax. Not that she was pulling off casual, either. At least not internally. Her heart was spasming like a dying fish. The last time she'd seen Travis, they were half naked and giving each other orgasms, so some nerves could be expected, right?

God, he looked mouthwatering. His heather-gray T-shirt molded to his ripped stomach, his face boasting the sprouting of a beard and tired eyes. He looked so out of place in the suburban setting—like one of those charity commercials where a famous athlete visits a fan on their doorstep. All broad shoulders and corded forearms. That was Travis Ford. A gorgeous, talented bachelor meant for a bigger, flashier life, but sent to live with normal mortals instead.

And she was sprawled on her ass in a clown suit.

Their sweaty hookup must have been a dream.

But she'd dreamed enough about Travis to be able to separate fantasy and reality. The reality was way more hands-on. And not her own hands, either, like usual.

It was definitely Reality Travis towering above her now, because Fantasy Travis never had tired eyes or seemed unsure. This man did, though. And he was the one she'd been missing.

She'd missed her fake boyfriend.

Was she crazy to embark on this mission?

There'd never been any fear of Fantasy Travis hurting her. She could just conjure up another dream, couldn't she? A better one that ended in him kissing her under the shower of ticker tape during a World Series champions parade. But the more she got to know Reality Travis, the more Fantasy Travis started to fade, leaving this real, breathing, complicated man in his place. He appealed to her even more.

So much more.

Travis seemed to be angling his body to block something behind him, making Georgie purse her lips. "What's going on? More autograph seekers?"

"There's a photographer following me." He raised an eyebrow at her dropped jaw. "It's now or never, baby girl."

God, he just had to go and call her that. Thank God she was wearing her clown suit, because the nickname sent goose bumps coursing down her arms. "A photographer? As in paparazzi? That was fast."

"Yeah." He cleared his throat, no longer looking at her. "The network announced their short list of candidates for the new voice of the Bombers last night." His expression was kind of perplexed. "I'm . . . still on it."

"Travis, that's amazing!" Georgie lunged to her feet, joy making her want to open the gate and throw her arms around him. When she saw the raised camera, she squeaked and hid behind Travis's impressive form instead. "Wow. They don't even ask."

"Nope, we're fair game." His blue eyes strayed to her

mouth and seemed to darken, his right hand lifting to cradle her jaw over the gate. "But out in the open like this, we can decide what they see."

"Oh," she whispered, inhaling his masculine scent. "That's nice."

"Nice? Maybe." His tongue dragged temptingly along his full lower lip. "We know I can be a little mean." Georgie was positive he was about to kiss her, but his forehead knitted together. "So does everyone in town know you want a bunch of kids?"

What did that have to do with kissing her? "Not everyone," she answered honestly, looking up into unreadable eyes. "Just everyone who sees me around them. Which happens a lot, because, hello, clown."

"Yeah," he said quietly. "You kind of come alive around them, don't you? Even more than usual." She wanted to bask in the compliment, but something was bothering him. That much was obvious. "Associating with me could mess that up for you, Georgie. Might be hard to find a nice guy after being with me. Even if it's just for the cameras."

Just for the cameras. That's right. Why was it so hard to remember that when he was standing so close, looking at her with something akin to tenderness? His visible concern made it almost impossible to swallow. "If a man held something like that against me, he wouldn't be a nice guy. Definitely not someone I'd . . ."

"Make a family with," he said quietly.

"Right."

They continued to scrutinize each other over the gate,

drawing closer ever so subtly. Because of the photographer? Or because she physically couldn't stop herself from gravitating in his direction?

"Travis Ford?" The spell he'd effortlessly wrapped around her was broken when the father of the birthday boy shouldered past her with an outstretched hand, holding it out to Travis. "No one told me the local legend was invited."

"I wasn't," Travis answered, shaking the man's hand but still looking at Georgie. "My girlfriend here is the entertainment and I've never gotten a chance to watch her perform. Mind if I . . . ?"

"Of course." The father swung open the gate. "Come on in. We'll get you a beer."

Travis sent her a wink. "Perfect. Thank you."

Georgie watched with a mouth poised to catch flies as Travis waltzed into a children's birthday party, parting the crowd of parents like a pop star through a packed arena. Just like when Travis walked through town, the reaction to his presence was mixed. Men either greeted him with man-crush vibes—overdoing the handshake and widening their stance, as if preparing to bro down over some baseball talk—or edged toward their wives and tried not to look insecure. A couple of the women pretended he didn't exist, probably not wanting to give Travis the satisfaction of knowing he could sell a million copies of *ESPN The Magazine*'s Body Issue. And yet another contingency of women did their smiling, head-tilting best to dazzle him.

And then there was Georgie, standing in the middle of

the yard with her trap wide open, watching Travis smoothly make himself at home. She was blown back to reality when a little girl tugged on her polyester sleeve. "Can we do the bubble party now?"

"Yes!"

A trio of kids behind her started cheering.

"Everyone get their best bubble-catching hands ready! I'll just go fire up my nifty bubble factory . . ."

Five minutes later, Georgie was racing from one end of the backyard to the other, a bubble maker held high above her head and leaving a trail of translucent bubbles behind her. Ten five-year-olds laughed and followed along, although one of them dropped out to dance to the Kidz Bop song that blared from the radio. There was always one.

"Okay," Georgie gasped, planting her hands on her knees. "Who wants to get their face painted? I can do dragons or ballet slippers—"

"My mom says it'll leave a rash and I can't do it!"

A little girl with curly red hair stuck out her lower lip. "I don't want a rash."

"Me either," said a boy, edging away from the pack.

Well used to the domino effect, Georgie smiled and knelt, getting down on their level. "How about I test the paint on your hands, so you can see it won't give you a rash."

"Test it on my mom!"

"Don't test it on my mom. My dad says she's too sensitive!"

Georgie sent an amused look over at the observing parents, her breath catching when she noticed Travis watching her with an unreadable expression, arms crossed over his chest. "Um. How about I paint one of the adults' whole face? Would that make you feel less scared?"

As she'd known they would be, all the children were in unanimous agreement. "Yeah!"

Before she could think better of it, Georgie waved at Travis. "Mr. Ford would love to be our volunteer. Everyone say hello to Mr. Ford."

A chorus of greetings filled the backyard, mingling with Travis's low chuckle.

He set down his beer and swaggered his way over to the grass. Earlier, Georgie had set up a face-painting station, complete with card table and stool. Travis eyed the child-sized stool now with a dubious look. "You don't expect me to sit on that, do you?"

Georgie blinked. "But you must. It's the face-painting stool."

"Right." He scratched his jaw and Georgie's belly flipped at the rasping sound, knowing exactly how that stubble felt rubbing in the crook of her neck. Travis caught her eye as he sat, lips twisting as if he could read her thoughts. "You've got me where you want me." How dare he make sitting on a kiddie stool look cool? "Do I get to pick my design?"

She gestured to the riveted group of children. "We should really let the birthday boy pick."

Travis's mouth twitched. "Sounds dangerous."

Never in her life had she worked a party where the parents stopped talking and paid such close attention. You could hear a pin drop in the backyard. Inviting Travis up to have his face painted was a bad idea. Terrible. She could feel her every action being scrutinized. Why did Travis have to pick now to reveal his playful side?

Attempting to disguise her nerves, Georgie turned to the birthday boy. "Carter? What do you think? Should we give him a butterfly? Or maybe a Minion—"

"A dog!"

Travis sighed. "I've been typecast."

Georgie bit back a laugh. "A dog it is."

Trying her best to ignore Travis's eyes, which seemed to be hooked on her every movement, Georgie dipped the paintbrush into the black paint, intending to start with his nose. The brush hovered for long seconds, refusing to move, despite what her brain commanded it to do. Probably because of his warm breath on her wrist. And the way his knee rested against hers, those big baseball player hands at the ready. As if they were going to pull her down on his lap if given the slightest encouragement. Or was she imagining that? It was totally possible Travis was suffering through this while she had a full hormonal breakdown.

"I have a dog! Her name is Lola."

"My cousin's dog bit someone."

Thank you, little ones. The voices getting her back on track, Georgie smoothed the brush along Travis's nose in an upside-down triangle. "Mr. Ford is more of a nibbler." She snapped her mouth shut. "I—I mean . . ."

Travis threw back his head and laughed, along with several of the parents.

"Shut up," she whispered, face flaming. "Help me backpedal."

His gaze dropped to her neck. "Should I tell them how you found out?"

Oh Lord. This wasn't happening. She was an aroused clown. Her nipples had turned into these awful, painful little spikes and the sound of Travis's sex voice filled her mind. *Virgin or not, you've thought about riding this dick or you wouldn't have dropped your skirt for me. Tell me I'm right.* A drop of sweat slid down her spine, absorbed by the bike shorts she wore under her costume. This was what happened when a girl remained a virgin well into adulthood, got a taste of Travis, then went back to depriving herself. She exploded. They wouldn't need a piñata at this party—they could just collect little pieces of her off the ground.

Finally, Travis seemed to realize her predicament, because his smile slowly melted away. "Hey." He licked his lips, his eyes a little unfocused. "Think about the time you spent an hour making the perfect hopscotch before Stephen and I sprayed it away with the hose."

When that reminder did nothing to cool her lust, Georgie knew she was in big trouble, but she did her best to pretend his method had worked like a charm. "You're right. I'm making you a really ugly dog," she murmured. "With a gas problem."

"That's the spirit. Although I'm not sure how you can translate that on canvas."

"Where there's a will . . ."

Turned out, Georgie's will was pretty strong, because she made Travis ugly as sin for the first time in his life. Through the magic of art, she made his cheeks look like heavy jowls, his nose stumpy. His flinch when he looked in the mirror sent the parents and children alike into a riot of laughter, providing her with no small amount of satisfaction. But nothing stopped the raw, physical draw she felt pulling her toward Travis. Not even the dog face. She'd always found him the most attractive man on the planet, but now she knew he walked the walk. Knew he could fulfill hungers inside of her she hadn't even been aware of.

Even though it was against their one, single rule, her body wanted to go another round.

Her body wasn't her biggest worry, though. It was her heart. She was a smart girl capable of objectivity, right? Now if she could only maintain that objectivity while Travis stared at her like a meal, she'd be golden. Was he the only man alive who could get to her like this? Watching him as they packed her party gear in silence, she couldn't even conjure a decent memory of Pete's face. Although Pete would no longer be an option as soon as word spread that she was seeing Travis, would he?

She waited for the regret, but it never surfaced.

"Hey," Travis said, shouldering her carrying case and falling into step with her as they left the backyard. "I'm glad I crashed the party. I knew you were good, but I didn't realize you ran the whole show like that. It's a lot of work."

"Thanks." Wings of surprised pleasure beat in her chest. "It wasn't always so organized. My first year of clowning was more like a series of mutinies. I'm still scarred."

"Kids are no joke." A beat passed. "This job hasn't put you off having your own?"

"No way," she said without hesitation, a smile curling her lips. "It makes me want them more. That look on their face when the cake comes out and everyone sings happy birthday. It's like you can see a memory forming in their head. It's magical."

She could feel Travis watching her closely. Why the sudden interest? "Your mother made me a cake for my thirteenth birthday," he said. "Only one I'd ever had."

Georgie stopped walking, a fist taking hold of her throat. "She did that?" She barely checked the urge to bury her face in his chest and sob. "What color was the icing?"

He laughed without humor and glanced away. "Yellow. With white writing."

Travis's body language told her not to press any deeper. That he'd already given her more than enough for now. But God she wanted to. She wanted to relive all her earliest memories of Travis, but know what he'd been thinking this time around. "You see? Magic memories."

"Yeah." With a swallow that lifted his Adam's apple, he set the carrying case down behind the trunk of her car. "How do I get this paint off my face?"

"You don't. I switched to permanent lacquer when your back was turned. Good luck commentating with a dog face."

"Very funny."

"I have questions about our plan."

"Wow, you really just jumped in feetfirst." He stepped closer. "Fire away."

Georgie pressed a hand to her fluttering stomach. "We're going to be doing a lot of canoodling, so to speak, for the cameras," she said quietly, in deference to the man not so discreetly snapping shots of them beside his blue Honda about forty yards away. "Let's say you drive me home and someone is following us. They're going to expect you to come inside. And . . . what if *s-e-x* just *happens*—"

"You did not just spell out the word 'sex.'"

"Sorry, still in birthday party mode." She straightened her spine. "If sex happens—"

A parent cleared his throat behind her. Scarlet-faced, Georgie turned around.

"We were just hoping for a business card," said a man in a Giants cap who wouldn't meet her eyes. "You know, uh . . . for the future."

"Yes, of course," Georgie croaked, handing him one from her pocket. "We have specials running through Christmas. I look forward to your call." A moment later, she was alone again with Travis, who was definitely battling a laugh behind his fist. "It's not funny."

"Please stop. You know it's funny."

"I'm trying to have a serious conversation with you."

"You're dressed like a clown and my face is painted like a dog, baby girl. It ain't happening." Travis took the car keys from her hand, popped the trunk, and stowed her gear. Once it was put away, he rounded the car with the box of baby wipes she kept in the trunk. "Come here."

"I can . . ." *Clean off my own face.* But of course, she wouldn't be doing that, because it was far too incredible having Travis tilt up her chin and smooth the cool, wet wipes over her mouth, getting rid of her wide red clown smile. Then down her cheeks and over her T-zone, careful as he cleaned around her eyes. All in all, it probably took him a single minute, but it lasted forever, because her brain moved in slow motion, counting eyelashes and wondering if he'd been born with the freckle under his right eye, or if it had popped up one summer as a child . . . and none of these thoughts was productive. Neither was the electricity snapping and humming between them, garnering power from the phone lines and nearby houses, building and building until Georgie had to push Travis away or risk public indecency. "O-okay, I can get the rest."

Why was he staring at her mouth like that all of a sudden? Like a wolf who'd spotted a lamb. Had he been as affected by what they'd done as she had? It didn't seem possible when he'd been with so many women. Women who actually knew what they were doing. The subtle sound of a camera snap reminded Georgie this was all for show. Travis wanted a job on a family-friendly network and she wanted adult respectability. She needed to remember that.

Travis cleared his throat. "You're good." He tugged out a few wipes and returned the box to her trunk. While he used his reflection in the back windshield to help him clean off his own face, he cut a glance in her direction. "You were saying?"

"Oh. Right." Her courage to have this conversation had been ferried away on a lust gondola, but she begged it to come back. "Um. Okay, so you heard what I said before."

"About us having sex." His jaw popped. "Yeah. I heard."

"Well, you're not going to be able to see anyone else for

real. While this is going on." Oh God, what was she doing? Stop. Nope. She kept going. "Won't you need some kind of . . . action?"

"Yes, Georgie. My very survival depends on it."

"Are you making fun of me?"

"Yes."

She barely resisted sticking her tongue out at him. "I'm only pointing out that we're pretty compatible in the adult arts and you could probably teach me a lot. About art. While we're killing time."

"Christ. So much to unpack there." Laughing without humor, he swiped a hand down his face. "My mind hasn't changed. It's not happening again. We do this, we keep it black and white." His jaw bunched as he looked her over. "It doesn't matter if there's something of an . . . attraction here. We're keeping this platonic. That going to work for you?"

She was relieved and disappointed at the same time. Without the magic of his touch, she had a much better chance of keeping her heart intact. Why had she pushed the issue in the first place? Probably because he'd looked at her like she was the last woman on earth that afternoon in his bed—and she couldn't stop thinking about it.

Okay, fine. Keeping things platonic was necessary for her self-preservation.

For the next little while, she was Travis Ford's pretend girlfriend. *Pretend.* As long as she could remember that, she would walk away from this arrangement with the reputation of a woman of the world. Her heart wouldn't be a crumbled mess, either. As long as she held this part of herself back.

"Why do you look relieved about the no-sex thing?" He massaged the center of his forehead. "Jesus Christ, Georgie, you are confusing."

"How do you want me to react?"

"I don't have a fucking clue," he muttered, almost to himself. "Let's go get a drink."

"What? *Now?*"

"Yeah." After the smallest hesitation, he leaned in and kissed her forehead, his audible swallow echoing her own. "We've got a camera following us. No better time than the present."

"Oh, right." She forced a flirtatious smile but never felt it reach her eyes. "There. I'm smitten."

"Great," he said drily. "I'll meet you at the Waterfront."

"Ooh." She twisted side to side. "Fancy, fancy—"

"Too much."

She scowled at him.

His mouth twitched. "Not enough."

"Oh, get out of here," she grumbled, shoving him away.

"Just right," Travis called on the way to his truck, throwing a smile back over his shoulder that almost melted her into the pavement. "Drive safe, baby girl."

CHAPTER FOURTEEN

Travis had an ulterior motive for asking Georgie to get a drink while she was still wearing her clown suit: it would be a lot easier to keep his hands off her in a shapeless polyester tent. Unfortunately, she'd texted him that she'd gone home to change, so he'd been waiting in the restaurant parking lot for twenty minutes with a mounting sense of doom, wondering if she'd show up wearing the skirt again. The one she'd wiggled out of in his bedroom before he'd thrown her down and humped her to an orgasm. He'd been thinking about sliding his hands beneath that skirt way too often lately.

Including right now.

Had the camera given him an excuse to get a little closer to Georgie than he should? Probably. Without that safety net sitting fifty yards away, he *probably* wouldn't have risked tipping her chin up so he could clean the makeup off her face. Not kissing her had been a battle, camera or not. He'd found himself wanting to lean in and demand to know what was inside her head.

Was she over the crush?

Yes. The answer was obviously yes. He'd been around plenty of women with an affinity for him and none of them called him on his bullshit like Georgie. None of them challenged or motivated him. When a woman wanted a man, she flirted, right? There was a dance involved. She sure as hell didn't come right out and propose he teach her about the adult arts. Didn't that imply she would use those lessons . . . elsewhere at some point?

Travis realized his hands were strangling the steering wheel and forced himself to let go.

Yeah. There was nothing to worry about in terms of Georgie's past crush. He was not the boy she'd watched from the bleachers. Or the man she'd watched hit home runs from her living room floor. He was a three-dimensional asshole and completely wrong for her—a girl who aspired to start a family and make magic memories.

He was completely wrong for anyone.

Travis tipped his head back, resting it against the driver's seat. He was walking a dangerous line here by pretending to date Georgie. They needed to make it convincing in public, but *not* in private. He could not compromise on that, no matter how much he was tempted to do otherwise. And fuck, he was tempted. Might as well admit it. She could turn him on in a goddamn clown suit. As if that wasn't enough to scare him, since being reintroduced to Georgie the adult, he'd run the gamut of feeling protective, possessive, and straight-up missing her.

But there was a game plan. He just needed to stick to it. Most importantly: to not sleep with her if they ended up alone. In fact, he needed to avoid being alone with her at all costs. No reason to tempt temptation itself. If he could keep his pants zipped for a couple weeks—tops—he'd be Mr. Wholesome and land himself the commentator position. And he could walk away without worrying that Georgie had grown attached.

Done.

Travis swallowed a lump in his throat and checked his mirror. The reporter in his blue Honda lay in wait a few parking spaces away, most likely thumbing through the pictures he'd already captured of Travis and Georgie. They were in it now. No turning back. If they hadn't already set every tongue in town wagging after the birthday party, they would as soon as they walked into the restaurant together. He'd intentionally chosen the Waterfront because it was the busiest spot in Port Jefferson and had been since his youth. With an eatery in back and a bustling bar in front, it catered to young and old. With the sun setting on Saturday night, everyone would be meeting at the Waterfront for a quick dinner and a few drinks, before pub-crawling their way to a Sunday hangover—a Long Island tradition.

Headlights bounced off the interior of Travis's truck. Georgie's car.

Travis opened the driver's-side door and climbed out, turning to lean up against it. By Georgie's third attempt to back into a parking space, Travis was shaking his head.

He was prepared to question why she didn't simply pull in headfirst, but the words died on Travis's lips when Georgie came into view. No skirt this time, but he felt that low stirring in his belly regardless. Maybe even stronger this time around. She'd traded her clown suit for a loose summer dress and sandals that crisscrossed up her legs and tied below the knee. Hair that she'd hidden beneath an orange wig earlier was in a braid that sat on one shoulder. As she drew closer, he noticed a light sheen on her lips that made him think of bites taken from fresh fruit.

Every inch the sweet girl next door . . . until he let himself notice her tits. *Kill me now.* They'd been pushed up and separated and put on display in the V of her dress. Why couldn't he look at her body and remain objective? He'd never had this problem before. Much of his life had been spent crossing paths with gorgeous women, but this one made him feel like his clothes fit wrong.

A young guy walking past her in the parking lot did a double take. After tugging an earphone out of his ear, he said hello. As in hel-*lo.*

"Hi," she said back, slowing to a stop and looking at the man with an oblivious expression. "Did you need something?"

Clearly shocked that his skeevy hello had earned him a positive response, the guy backed up like a dog who'd spotted a stray treat. "Now that you mention it—"

"No, he doesn't *need* anything. Christ." Travis inserted himself between Georgie and the idiot, pulling her up against his side. His irritation plummeted when he saw Georgie was genuinely confused. "He thinks you are attractive, Georgie. He just did a shit job of letting you know it."

"Ohhh." Travis watched Georgie clock the reporter sta-

tioned a few spots down. "And . . ." She gave him a conspiratorial nudge. "What would be the right way?"

They weren't even inside the restaurant yet and the danger line was blurring. It was enough to walk into the establishment holding Georgie's hand. Buy her drinks. Put an arm around her shoulders. People inside would get the hint and so would anyone who saw the resulting pictures. He didn't need to lean in as he was doing now, his palm sliding down her bare arm to twine their fingers together. He didn't need to draw those fingers to his mouth and kiss them. Twice. Slow. "You look fucking beautiful."

"You're right," she breathed, staring at the knuckles he was still holding. "That is definitely the right way."

With the taste of her on his lips, taunting him for his lack of control, Travis turned and dragged her toward the restaurant. "Now you know."

"Wait." She still sounded breathless. "Shouldn't we, like . . . reconnoiter?"

He stopped and faced her. "What?"

"*Reconnoiter.* You know . . ." She spoke in a hush out of the side of her mouth. "Perform recon. See who's in there. Form a game plan."

"I have a game plan."

She widened her eyes at him. "Care to share? I'm one-half of this team."

A flash went off over Georgie's shoulder. "We look like we're having an argument."

"Trouble in paradise. Today on TMZ." She crossed her eyes at Travis and he found himself fighting a smile. "We will be having an argument if you don't clue me in. I've never had a real boyfriend, let alone a fake one."

"You didn't need to remind me."

"Harsh."

Travis lost his smile. "I didn't mean it to sound harsh, Georgie. Only that I'm aware how much more experience I have than you."

She gave a dainty tug of her earlobe. "And *you've* had an official girlfriend?"

Knowing he'd been bested, he narrowed his eyes at her. "Point taken. I still know how to convince whoever is watching that you're mine."

Did he imagine her shiver? "How?"

His body's response to that single word was chemical. This woman whose body called to him on an insane level wanted to know, in explicit terms, how he planned to put a claim on her. How he would lead everyone to believe they were regularly sweating up the sheets. It was curiosity on Georgie's part, but his blood couldn't help heating at the perceived challenge. Couldn't help heating at all of her. The inquisitive eyes and secret smile that, dammit, really made him feel like they were on a team. Her tits. God, yes, her tits. The glow of the streetlamps on either side of the entrance made them look soft and touchable. It didn't help knowing she'd never had her nipples sucked before him and had gasped and squirmed the first time it happened. Maybe he couldn't be the one to suck them the next time, but letting everyone think he had would have to suffice.

"Come here."

This time she definitely shivered in reaction to his change in tone. She stepped forward, fingering the end of her braid, and Travis stayed right where he was, head tilted, waiting until a sliver of paper couldn't fit between their bodies. Her heat rolled into his belly and journeyed lower, waking up hunger he needed to be ashamed about, but couldn't seem to stop when they were face-to-face. His arm moved on its own, snaking around the small of her back and tugging her tight against his body. "You want to know how I'm going to let everyone know you're mine, huh?"

Georgie pushed against his chest and backed up. "No."

Denial crammed his belly full. "No?"

She gave him a meaningful look. "Did you already forget this position you want is at a family-friendly network?" Her eyelids fluttered. "You shouldn't be looking at me like that."

Fuck. How did he continue to lose his common sense around this girl? Why couldn't he look at Georgie and see all the logical reasons that being in a physical relationship with her would be bad?

Not to mention, she was right. Being caught making out with yet another woman on camera was a good way to get his name crossed off the short list.

Yet another woman.

He didn't want to admit to himself that Georgie felt like anything but.

Travis gave a tight nod and led her into the Waterfront, camera flashes going off in their wake. Apart from the music pumping over the loudspeaker in the bar area, the room slowly turned dead silent. No one spoke or moved as Travis guided Georgie to the closest open stools. He could feel the eyes on them—knew she must, too—but she didn't take her attention off him once. It set the organ in his chest to pounding, and by the time he boosted her sideways onto the stool, the conversation they'd been having completely eluded him. "Uh." He swallowed. "What do you drink?"

"I'm rusty on ordering drinks. Most of the parties I'm invited to only serve Capri Suns." She licked her lips in slow motion. At least that's how it happened in his head. "My go-to in college was vodka and lemonade."

"Cute."

"Don't call me cute in my gladiator sandals." She gave him a solemn look. "I'm battling a lion later tonight—you should come."

Warmth invaded his chest. "He doesn't stand a chance."

He tore his eyes away from her pleased smile and gave their order to the bartender. That's when Georgie finally seemed to notice that every eye in the place was trained on them. She sucked in a breath and he stepped closer on reflex, curving a palm to her shoulder. "You're really good at this," she whispered.

"What?" He looked down to find himself crowding her, his fingers playing with the tip of her braid. "Oh. Yeah, lots of practice," he lied smoothly, abundantly aware he'd never been this affectionate in his life. Cursing himself for the way her eyes dimmed in response, Travis rushed to make it better. "Tell me more about your club." The bartender set down their drinks and Travis handed Georgie hers. "The Just Us League. Do you have a motto yet?"

"All for one. And one for Paul. Paul is the stripper we hire for meetings."

Travis broke off halfway through a chuckle. "That's a joke, right?"

"Of course. A stripper named Paul would never get hired. He'd have to call himself Daddy Manroot or something." She broke off with a laugh. "Your face right now."

"It's the face of anyone who hears the term 'Daddy Manroot.'"

"Sorry." She smiled around her straw as she took her first sip. "I really shouldn't be telling you top secret club information. Can we keep everything between us?"

There it was again. That same team feeling. He . . . liked having it with her. "I'm a vault, baby girl."

She made a wishy-washy sound. "I don't feel too terrible discussing my sister, since she used to steal my Halloween candy, but Rosie's situation is a different story."

"Does it have to do with the newspapers Dom keeps finding stuffed under the mattress?"

"He knows about them and hasn't said anything?" She took in that information and recentered herself with visible effort. "In other news, did you know Bethany wants to run her own project?"

Travis raised an eyebrow. "Really? I thought she liked staging."

"She does, but she wants to make decisions on layout and swing a sledgehammer, too."

Hell, he could relate to that. Demo day was like heaven on earth for a construction crew. Letting loose on a wall or breaking up concrete was goddamn therapeutic. It couldn't be so different for a woman wanting to blow off steam. "Has she talked to Stephen?"

Her nose wrinkled. "He turned down the idea."

"Stephen not wanting to break from tradition?" Travis snorted. "I don't believe you."

"No? He already bought the stick-figure family for his minivan window." A few seconds passed. "Traditionalist or not, he should give Bethany a chance."

"What if he won't?"

"She's going to take it somewhere else. And we're going to help her." She circled the rim of her glass with a finger. "That's the point of the club."

"And Paul."

"Always Paul."

They shared a smile. And then it faded and they went right on looking at each other. For too long. Until alarm started to build in Travis's gut. Nothing about this felt even remotely fake. On the upside, they were definitely succeeding in being branded a couple. His hands couldn't seem to stay off her. Without a formal command from his brain, Travis's thumb continued to brush her neck, his thigh pressing to her knee. Their heads were leaned in so they could hear each other talk over the music, but he was so close, he could hear a whisper. Fuck, she smelled incredible.

"What about you, Georgie? You make any progress planning the entertainment company?"

Her whole face lit up, just inches away from his, giving him an up-close view of her shifting freckles, the stretch of her mouth. "I lucked out, actually. I put an ad on an employment website and found some freelance performers. The owner of their company moved to Vegas and they're looking for a new home. I'm meeting with them next week." Her shoulders bounced. "If we click and they're as good as their references say, I can start booking twice the number of parties."

"That's amazing," he rasped. "Good job."

Looking down at his hand on her knee, she seemed to lose her train of thought. "Yeah. Um . . . and I'm working with a designer on a new website . . . and I'm taking a webinar on advertising. So basically I'm Michael Douglas from *Wall Street* now."

This was how cute she could be on dates. Any man with the commitment gene and half a brain would propose before the dessert course. And it was really bad how much he wanted to kiss her, thanks to the jealousy that spawned. "Michael Douglas wouldn't look anywhere near as sexy in that dress," he said, his upper brain clearly not in command.

"I'd have to take it off so he could try it on," she whispered, seeming to slow down the action of the bar around them. "Just to know for sure."

A hungry pulse started in his balls. "Should I be worried that I'm getting turned on while you're talking about Michael Douglas in a dress?"

"No." He heard her swallow. "Because you're thinking about *me* naked, not Mr. Zeta-Jones."

I definitely am now, baby girl. Thinking of her in that little golden thong he'd seen in one of her shopping bags, how it would look between her ass cheeks. How she'd been on her way to a date with another man with those shopping bags. Jealousy trickled into his gut again—an emotion he was neither used to nor adept at handling. Not by a long shot. The fact that he could get jealous over this girl at all was bad news.

With a warning echoing in his head, Travis stepped back from Georgie and took a long sip of his beer, forcing himself to stop staring at her and pay attention to the bar instead. As he'd expected, the photographer had followed them inside and was now taking "discreet" cell phone pictures on the other side of the room. Several patrons were watching them, some he even recognized from the past or since he'd returned to Port Jeff. There was some head shaking going on, but mostly gleeful curiosity.

"Two Bats." A hand clapped down on his shoulder, turning him around to face a man around his age he didn't recognize. He was accompanied by a red-faced woman who was trying to hide behind her drink, a tourist map open in front of her on the bar. "I'm Mike, this is Cheryl." He scrubbed a hand down his face. "Told her I wouldn't say anything, but you've always been my wife's hall pass."

A hole opened in Travis's stomach. Why hadn't he taken this possibility into consideration? Of his persona catching up with him in public. The fact that Georgie was bearing witness made it so much worse than ever before. "That so?" He forced a tight smile. "I'm honored."

Laughing, the man turned to face Travis fully, and he instantly regretted that he hadn't shut the interaction down harder. The cameraman had already scented blood and was moving closer, within earshot of the conversation. "You can fit her into your busy schedule, can't you?" Mike jerked a thumb over his shoulder. "I'd finally get a night of peace and quiet."

Travis nodded stiffly, shame bubbling to the surface. He wanted to throw Georgie over his shoulder and make for the exit. "Schedule is full tonight, pal," he rasped, apologizing to Georgie with his eyes.

Mike was clearly not ready to let the running joke drop. "Tomorrow, then. You should be ready for someone new by then, right? That's Two Bats's style. Hit her and quit her—"

Travis's anger erupted. Just blew like Mount St. Helens down deep in his gut. The joke being played at his expense made him queasy, but as soon as the man suggested he'd hit and quit Georgie, a switch flipped and he saw bright fucking red. *This is what people think of me.* His fist slammed the bar and he turned, crowding Mike. "You want to disrespect me? Be my guest. But don't you ever—*ever*—speak about her like that, motherfucker," he said for the man's ears alone. "Or the only thing I'll be fitting into my schedule is your full-time ass kicking. You hearing me?"

Mike's hands came up in surrender, but Georgie stepped in between them. Travis couldn't see her face, but the tension in her body told him she was furious. On *his* behalf? "How dare you talk to him like that? Like he exists for your entertainment. You don't know him. He's not like that. Not anymore," Georgie said, jolting back against Travis's chest when the camera erupted in a series of shots.

His arm automatically went around her waist protectively, the need to get her out of the restaurant eating him alive. "Baby girl, come on—"

"Apologize . . . to my boyfriend. *Now,* please."

"Yeah," Mike muttered, chin tucking into his chest. "Sorry, I was out of line."

"Thank you," Georgie huffed.

With his fucking heart in his mouth, Travis watched his best friend's little sister turned take-no-shit woman drain her drink and smack it back down on the bar, turning to him with a dazed expression.

"Want to go?"

"Yeah," he rasped, throwing some money on the bar and guiding her around Mike and Cheryl to the exit. He moved in a trance, barely aware of the cameraman following them, although the man was on his cell phone now, speaking in a low, rushed tone. What the hell had just happened? One minute he'd been sinking into a mire of shame; now he might as well be watching a grand slam sail out of the park.

Even after agreeing to this charade with Georgie, he'd never really expected to shed his image as a lothario. What was the point of trying to change the public's mind when it was already made up? Had he been selling himself short? Would Georgie defend him with such conviction otherwise?

They hit the parking lot and moved in tacit agreement toward Georgie's car. *"Well,"* she breathed. "Tonight wasn't a very compelling argument for you to stop getting takeout delivered every night, huh?"

"Georgie," Travis growled, yanking her to a stop at the

driver's side. Her head fell back, calling attention to the strands of hair that had slipped loose from her braid, the streetlight catching the sheen of her mouth. *Gorgeous.* Outraged, too. All for him. "Thank you." He couldn't keep the disbelief out of his voice. "No one's ever done that for me."

"Done what?"

He cupped the back of her head, allowing his fingers to weave through her hair. Damn, touching her felt incredible. Especially when she sighed a little and leaned into his palm. "Defend me."

She scrutinized him for a few beats. "How long have people been speaking to you like that?"

"A while," he whispered, a hot pulse pounding in his temples.

"They shouldn't. You deserve better," she returned, going up on her toes and laying a soft kiss on his lips—just as a flurry of flashes went off, making her eyes go round. She rocked back on her heels, dislodging his hand. "I . . . This thing between us . . . will make it stop, won't it?"

This thing. This *thing*. Their arrangement, which would end when they were both satisfied with the results.

That's why you're here.

"Yeah," he managed, needing like hell to pin her to the car and tongue fuck her into a stupor, the family-friendly persona he was trying to achieve be damned. God help him, he couldn't keep his neck from craning, breathing once, twice, against her mouth. "That's what this is all about, right?" He said it mostly to remind himself that their relationship wasn't real. But when Georgie took the hint and eased away, climbing into her car and driving out of the parking lot, he couldn't keep the regret at bay.

Striding past the gleeful cameraman to his truck, Travis could only hope tonight had done the trick. Because this fake relationship was either going to kill him before he got the job . . . or start to feel far too real before it was over.

CHAPTER FIFTEEN

Georgie woke up from a nap with thirty-one text messages and fourteen missed calls.

There was also a half-eaten granola bar stuck to her forehead, but that was beside the point.

She jerked into an upright position and picked a mini chocolate chip from where it had been embedded above her eyebrow, shrugging and popping it into her mouth.

She'd had a midmorning birthday party for a one-year-old, which should have been easy peasy, but both of the organizer's sisters had come down with a cold, leaving no one to help decorate and serve food, so Georgie had pulled double duty. Made a nice tip out of the whole thing, too, though it had been unnecessary. She'd been far more grateful for the woman's candor as they'd plated apple slices and ransacked the house for matches to light the birthday candles. They'd been in it together, as opposed to being employer and employee.

It had almost felt like her dating experiment with Travis was already working, but that couldn't be right. Barely enough time had passed for people to find out—

Fully conscious now, she snatched up her phone again. Oh, this was it.

The Travis was out of the bag.

Leave it to her friends who hadn't bothered to pick up a phone in months to be texting her now. They'd each messaged her five times.

> You're dating Travis Ford?
> Have you . . . you know . . . met the second bat??
> You've been holding out on us!

Georgie frowned down at her phone. Those kinds of questions weren't out of the ordinary between her and her friends. But reading them made her feel hollow. There was no excitement to text them back and overshare, like they used to do about their boyfriends before time and distance caused a strain. It was all a hoax, so obviously there wasn't that typical feminine urge to squeal to her friends.

It was more than that, though. Reading the messages, she could only think about the couple in the bar last night. How they'd treated Travis like a punch line and how he'd allowed it to happen—to a point—as if it were his due. Her irritation renewed, Georgie rose from the bed, continued to scroll through her plethora of messages and missed calls. Most of them were from her mother and she'd be taking the coward's way out on that one. For now. Vivian Castle didn't like to be left in the dark, so there would be a wave of passive aggression headed in Georgie's direction. She'd cross that bridge when she came to it.

Bethany had called several times. No Stephen. Huh. She couldn't decide if she was surprised or not by that. On the one hand, Stephen never bothered himself with her social life. On the other, Georgie was dating his best friend. At least that's how it would appear. Had Travis told Stephen they were seeing each other? For some reason, the possibility of Travis taking that initiative gave Georgie butterflies.

Great, big, whopping ones. Which was stupid.

Although, maybe he'd told Stephen it was fake.

Those butterfly wings stopped flapping. Maybe *that's* why Stephen wasn't calling. He was just shaking his head in private over Georgie's latest antics.

There was no time to think about it now. Tonight was the Just Us League meeting and there was no time like the present to face the firing squad, also known as her sister. She'd promised to be more forthcoming with Bethany, but would it be so bad to keep this secret to herself for now? To let everyone really believe she and Travis were an item?

Resolving to make the decision on the road, Georgie sped through a shower, threw on one of her new pairs of leggings and a loose V-neck. She shoved her feet into a pair of flats on the way out the door and made it to Bethany's in record time. Before she walked through the front door, she took a deep breath and prepared for a barrage of questions. She got a sniff from her sister instead and an *uh-oh* look from Rosie.

"Uh, hey."

That set off Bethany. Her sister pinched the bridge of her nose and paced the length of her kitchen. "Uh, hey? A photo of you kissing Travis Ford in the parking lot of the Waterfront goes fucking viral and you just stop answering your phone?"

In her nap haze and rush to get out of the house, she'd completely neglected to research how everyone had found out about her and Travis. "Which photo is this?"

"Take your pick! There's like . . ." Bethany snatched an iPad off the marble countertop and swiped across the screen with a furious finger. "Eleven. *Twelve—*"

Oh no. This is bigger than I thought it would be. Georgie's stomach pitched as she crossed the room. "Let me see." One glance at the screen and she was rolling her eyes. "This isn't viral. This is the *Port Times Record.*"

"It's viral for Port Jefferson," Bethany shot back. "And the picture where you're telling off that man in the bar made *SportsCenter,* so it's not contained to the local news. It was on Plays of the Week, Georgie. Mom said Dad almost choked on a chicken bone."

Georgie hopped up onto a kitchen stool, marveling over the face staring back at her from the glass screen. Was that her looking so fiercely passionate? Yes, it was. And she couldn't find it in her to regret defending Travis. Not for a second. Her belly couldn't help but flip at the kissing picture, even though she knew the sentiment behind it was contrived. Their affection was all for the camera. Her heart started pounding nonetheless when she landed on the final picture. Travis staring after her in the parking lot with an expression she'd never seen on his gorgeous face before. Maybe it was the camera angle. Travis would never be wistful for her. Not in this lifetime. "Um," she rasped. "So Dad choked on a chicken bone?"

Bethany slapped her hands on the counter. "What is going on?"

"We went on a date." Looking for an ally, Georgie turned to Rosie, who feigned fascination with an untouched shot glass of tequila. "We decided that was allowed."

"It is. But him, Georgie? *Travis?*"

"Yes. Travis." Indignation rose up in her swift and furious. It wasn't just the couple in the bar. It was everyone, wasn't it? The whole world thought of him as some brainless sex symbol. So much so that he had to date the town's dopey birthday party clown so people would . . . take him seriously. They both wanted the exact same thing, didn't they? That did it. She wouldn't tell a single soul their relationship wasn't real. She'd be out and proud about her fake boyfriend. "You haven't spent time with him since he came back. He's done being thought of as a player."

"Yeah, but is he done *being* one?" Bethany gave a long exhale. Georgie could tell she was dying to put in another two cents, but she managed to refrain. "I'm guessing you haven't spoken to Mom. She has dibs on this kind of information and ESPN scooped her. You're going to get Guilt Face at Sunday dinner next weekend."

Georgie started. Their family was close, but with everyone so busy, their dinners were more of the spontaneous variety. Georgie would pop in for lunch or Stephen would bring bagels by and fill their father's need for business talk. Formal dinners with everyone in attendance occurred only when someone organized a summit. "Sunday dinner? Who called it?"

"Me. I'm breaking the news to everyone that I'm striking out on my own." Bethany sent Georgie a look down her nose. "If you'd been here on time, you'd know that."

"Sorry. I'll be there. Solidarity and all that. Yada yada."

"Are you bringing Travis?"

Her skin flushed. Bring Travis to a family dinner? Why not just hang herself in a museum so everyone could walk by and pick her apart? "I'll ask him."

Rosie rubbed a circle into her back. "Did you go on your date with the fireplace guy?"

"No. Something came up," she hedged. And looking over at Rosie and her soft, encouraging expression, Georgie encountered a swift kick of guilt. "Rosie, I have to tell you something. I really have no excuse for not calling you sooner . . . I've just been so distracted. But you can punch me in the stomach afterward, if you need to."

Rosie drew back her hand slowly. "What is it?"

"Dominic knows about the newspapers under the mattress. He mentioned it to Travis." She gave her friend an apologetic look. "You need to find a new hiding spot."

Two spots of color appeared on Rosie's cheeks. "Oh."

"I'm sorry."

"Why should you be sorry?" Rosie gestured to the bottle of tequila with the international symbol for "pour." "I mean, you're not the grown man ignoring his wife, instead of just asking her questions and having a normal conversation. That would be too much to ask for. Stupid . . . jackass."

Rosie slapped a hand over her mouth.

After pouring a round of shots, Bethany picked up a pen and scratched some notes on a nearby legal pad. "We're going to have to meet twice this week. No way we can cover cock talk and get important things done—"

"Bethany?" Georgie said.

"What?"

"Lose the agenda."

Her older sister primly set aside the work pad. "Might I suggest, Rosie, that instead of hiding newspapers under the mattress, tomorrow you leave a dead rat in their place?"

"I was thinking more along the lines of my vibrator. It's capable of more affection than Dominic lately." Rosie split a look between them. "Tequila makes me overshare."

"We're here to overshare. It's encouraged," Georgie murmured, sympathy for Rosie's obvious relationship troubles swimming in her stomach. "Did you find a commercial space for the restaurant yet?"

"There's one," Rosie whispered. "There's one I like. But I'm not ready to . . ." She shook her head. "I'm not ready yet. I'm good with my newspapers for now."

The front door of Bethany's house blew open, Kristin breezing in with a basket full of muffins. "Hello, ladies," she twanged in her Georgia accent. "I heard y'all were having a meeting tonight and I came by to join the club."

Bethany narrowed her eyes at their sister-in-law, who was making herself busy at the kitchen bar, putting muffins on plates. "How did you know about the club?"

"Stephen found out from your mama."

"Shit," Bethany muttered. "Why do we tell that woman anything? She's like a colander and yet we continue to pour in information."

"So this is about thumbing our nose at men, right?" Kristin trilled excitedly, sliding onto a stool at the island in one graceful motion while balancing three plates of muffins. "If so, count me in. I'm leaving your brother. He's really done it this time."

Georgie bit her bottom lip to keep from laughing. "What did Stephen do?"

Kristin huffed. "I made him lunch to bring to work this morning. Pecan chicken, fresh-baked rolls, and a cucumber salad. Do you know he left it in the fridge?" She set down the plates with a clatter, balled up her fists, and perched them on her knees. "I would have forgiven him, only he came home from work tonight and didn't say anything about it. Nothing about how he suffered without my chicken or how terrible his fast-food replacement lunch was. Not a darn thing. So I waited until he got in the shower and I left. I won't be underappreciated."

"Kristin," Rosie started. "Maybe he just had that tired work brain. He probably would have opened the fridge sooner or later and remembered he forgot to take your chicken."

"Also," Bethany chimed in with mock sincerity, "we're literally talking about chicken here, so—"

"Pecan chicken," Georgie cut in smoothly, patting Kristin's arm and trying not to show how ridiculous she found the complaint. "One of his favorites, right, Kristin?"

"I don't know." She looked up at the ceiling. "I just don't know anymore."

Across the circle, Bethany mouthed a silent countdown. *Three, two . . .*

Outside the house, a vehicle screeched to a halt, followed by a door slamming and angry boot steps storming up the walkway. The door to Bethany's house opened without preamble and in stormed their brother in flannel pajama pants and a sweatshirt, his hair still wet from the shower. "Get in the truck, Kristin."

His wife stood her ground—or sat it, rather—refusing to turn and look at him. "You've done it this time," she called dramatically. "Enjoy your life of deep-fried potatoes and fake meat."

Stephen pointed at Bethany. "This is your fault. Putting ideas into her head."

"You're the one that forgot her pecan chicken!" Bethany burst out. "That shit is important."

"Oh, now she thinks so," Georgie drawled, reaching for the tequila.

"You're one to talk, Georgie. This"—he waved an angry hand around—"girls' club has taken away your common sense."

Georgie ignored the twinge of pain in her chest, keeping her features schooled as she filled the glasses. "I'm guessing you saw the pictures."

"Don't remind me. I saw them coming and I still want to blind myself."

Hope replaced the discomfort in her chest, floating up like a dozen balloons. "You saw them coming? How?"

"Travis told me you were seeing each other a couple of days ago." He continued on as if he hadn't made his sister capable of floating up to the moon. "It was only a matter of time before everyone took an interest. You're not exactly a likely pair. For good reason."

Bethany muscled up to her side, shooting a glare in Stephen's direction. "Don't take that line of thought any further. She's heard enough for tonight."

A flicker of nerves—maybe even sympathy—passed across her brother's face. "He's going to chew you up and spit you out, Georgie."

"That's my problem, Stephen. Not yours," Georgie returned, her voice vibrating. And damn, it felt good to not only stand up to her brother, but to have him reevaluate her with a look. *That's right. I'm not just your dopey little sister.*

"Fine," Stephen finally grumbled. "I've got my own problems to deal with right now."

Kristin shot to her feet. "Oh, I'm a problem now?"

"No. No, honey, I . . ." Stephen shoved a hand through his wet hair. "Can we talk about this at home?"

His wife crossed her arms and waited.

Their brother shifted in his boots. "I missed your chicken like hell, Kristin. I was going to tell you all about how leaving it behind ruined my day, but then I got to looking at the calendar. You know, the one that says when you're . . ." He cleared his throat loudly. "It says when you're, you know, ovulating. So I was trying to get the day cleaned off as fast as I could, so we could . . . uh. I wanted to—"

"I think we're good here," Georgie said, raising her hand. "I'm pretty clear on what happened and don't need any more details. Who's with me?"

Everyone's hand went up besides Kristin's and Stephen's.

"You may take me home now, Stephen Castle," Kristin said, lifting her chin. "Girls, you can keep the muffins."

She'd barely finished her sentence before Stephen scooped up his wife and left the way he'd come, kicking the door shut and leaving the room awash in silence. Georgie's pulse was still pounding a thousand miles an hour in her ears, though. Travis hadn't told Stephen anything about their plan. Her brother couldn't lie for shit, so that much was obvious. He'd kept their secret. He'd respected her feelings without her having to ask. It made Georgie all the more determined to rock her end of the bargain. To validate Travis's hopes the way he was doing for her. To be on his team. In order to do that, she needed to know more about him. The things she'd missed through the lens of youth.

"You guys were in Travis's grade, so you remember what happened with his parents. I was younger, so the details are a little blurry." She laughed without humor as something occurred to her. "Actually, it might be the one thing we haven't spoken about."

Bethany winced. "It was a pretty nasty divorce. I remember overhearing Mom and Dad talking about it."

"Nasty how?"

"There was a custody battle. Neither parent was happy

with the decision, so they kind of used him to piss each other off." Bethany frowned. "Ugh, this is making me feel bad for being mean to him. Subject change soon, okay?"

"I was so wrapped up in Dominic back then, everything else is a blur," Rosie said. "But I do remember him always needing a ride to school. He'd show up on foot some days, on the bus others. Sometimes your mother brought him. Rarely his own parents."

"He got passed around a lot," Bethany added. "There was no real . . . stability."

"Passed around," Georgie echoed quietly, her pulse slowing along with time, thudding in a morose pattern. "That's awful."

You've always been my wife's hall pass. Those remembered words from the night before brought back a whole host of memories. Travis pictured with another woman every day of the week in the newspapers, during those early days of his career. Until he simply wasn't anymore. Around the same time, he'd started getting passed between teams faster than he could probably decorate his locker.

Passed around.

I'm no one's entertainment anymore.

Had Travis ever had a stable relationship in his life? Did he know what one looked like?

Had anyone ever made him feel worthy of a lasting one?

She'd always held to the truth that Travis was her soul mate. That was before she knew him, though. Those beliefs were founded on a childhood crush. What she'd begun feeling for Travis since he returned home? That wasn't in the same league. That had depth and . . . fears attached.

Georgie didn't hold any illusions that she could be Travis's one. But she couldn't deny an odd sense of responsibility to prove to Travis he was worthy of finding and keeping his one. Even if it wasn't her. When no one else had been up to the task of forcibly removing Travis from his downward spiral, she'd thrown lo mein at his head. Did she have the courage to take one more step?

They might be in a fake relationship. What if she could make it feel real?

Real enough that Travis realized what he was capable of.

"Georgie, are you okay?"

"Yeah." Georgie tapped her lip. "Um . . . what's next on your infamous agenda?"

But as Bethany perked up and started to read from her clipboard, Georgie was forming her own.

CHAPTER SIXTEEN

Georgie slicked paste onto the final cutout for her zombie birthday party vision board, placing the green slime recipe just below a scene involving dry ice and a strobe light. Hello, next-level birthday party. She could see it now. Kids draped in medical gauze and fake guts walking in slow motion through the backyard, trying to complete the apocalypse scavenger hunt before time ran out. Until now, she'd been entertaining the five and below set, but it occurred to Georgie she was missing out on the older kids. They wouldn't scare as easily, and zombies never went out of style. She couldn't wait to put this option on the website.

The doorbell rang and Georgie leaped from her position on the living room floor into a battle stance, a scream lodged in her throat.

So much for the *under fives* being the scaredy-cats.

Gathering her composure, Georgie made her way to the door and opened it. There was no one on the other side, but whoever had rung the bell had left something behind. Even after she stooped down to pick the object up, it took her a minute to realize what it was.

A trophy had been left on her front porch. It was cheap and garish, with a little plaque on the bottom that read WINNER, TRAVIS FORD DATING CONTEST. Upper lip curled in disgust, she searched her cul-de-sac for whoever had left the unwanted object and spotted no one. With a sniff of indignation, she slammed the front door of her house, entered the kitchen, and shoved the trophy as deep as it would go in the garbage, burying it beneath coffee grounds and eggshells.

When the deed was done, Georgie paced her kitchen. The trophy made her even more determined to show Travis his worth—and she needed to act. Now.

Unplugging her phone from the charger, she meandered her way into the living room, plopping down into a cross-legged position on the floor. Georgie had texted boys before—she wasn't a *total* newbie. Having always been the type to get friend-zoned, she'd never phone flirted, though. But if she was going to clue Travis in to his own potential, she'd reasoned it was better to dip in a digital toe, instead of diving right into the deep end.

Georgie rubbed the phone against her lips, trying to conjure the perfect, easy breezy text message. She couldn't make her ulterior motives obvious, but she wanted him to talk to her like . . . a boyfriend. A real one. The key would be for her to remember their relationship was all for show and nothing more. She frowned as she dropped the phone into her lap, her fingers moving over the screen.

G: Heyyy youuu.

Deleted.

G: Hey, did you call me? Sorry I missed it. While I already have you . . . wanna talk flavored lube?

Nope.

G: I hear sea salt caramel mochas put people in a good mood. If you're free, I'll let you put me in one.

"Dude, that's pretty bleeping good," she murmured, her finger hovering over the send button. "Dare I send this perfectly crafted text message, or do I chicken out?"

She tipped her face up toward the ceiling and breathed deeply through her nose, dropping her thumb to the blue icon. Sent. There, it was done. She'd invited Travis for an afternoon coffee date and he could very well say no—

Georgie's phone vibrated and she snatched it up off the floor.

T: What was that?

G: What was what?

T: A very flirtatious tone, Miss Castle. Don't think I missed it.

G: Are you going to put me in a good mood? Or do I have to do it myself?

Wait. Was that flirty or sexual? Flirty. Probably. No, definitely flirty. As soon as she sent the message, Georgie fell back onto her area rug and closed-mouthed squealed. *Oh my God.* This was why her friends in college had walked around in a hormonal haze. There was something exhilarating about making yourself vulnerable to the opposite sex. And the anticipation of their reaction? It was like a free fall. A little voice in the back of Georgie's mind told her it wouldn't feel like this with just anyone, but she ignored it and lifted her phone as it buzzed again.

> **T:** Your good mood is better when I'm the one giving it to you. Grinders in 20.

"Twenty minutes?" Georgie was off the floor like a shot, stumbling on her way to the bedroom and pulling out the first outfit she spied upon opening her dresser drawer. A jean skirt and a blue tank top. She stripped off her yoga pants and T-shirt, shoving her body into the new clothes, ripping off the tags as she kicked open her closet in a search for shoes. A moment later, she jogged down the hallway, her sandals slapping off the hardwood floor—and out the house she went.

It wasn't until she parked at Grinders did she remember a bra.

Or remember she'd forgotten to wear one, rather.

If there wasn't a camera on Travis's tail again today, he wouldn't have agreed to the coffee date. At least that's what he continued to tell himself as he parked outside Grinders and watched the white Escalade pull along the curb across the street. He wasn't here simply to get his Georgie fix. Or because she'd given him a hard-on via text. This was about business. His agent was excited about his chances of getting the job. Hell, he was calling more than he had while Travis was in the league. He was in the position to be their top pick. But he needed her to make it happen.

He scanned the street for Georgie. Despite his eagerness to lay eyes on her, he nursed a dose of guilt. This plan of theirs felt like it was benefiting him far more than her. Sure, everyone in town—and beyond—was buzzing about how she'd defended him in the Waterfront the other night. Most of the headlines ran along the lines of "Don't Mess with Two Bats's New Girlfriend." A lot of men might have felt like their masculinity was being challenged by having a woman come to their rescue, but goddamn, Travis felt the exact opposite. This warm glow wouldn't dissipate, no matter how much time passed.

He needed to give something back to Georgie, to make fake dating him worth her while. Her family was the main reason she'd struck her end of the bargain, wasn't it? When would he get to return the favor she'd done for him the other night? Simply taking her out for drinks or coffee didn't seem adequate.

The fingers he'd been tapping on his thigh stilled when he spied Georgie crossing the street. Christ Almighty, she looked sexy as hell for a midweek coffee date. That skirt was pure sin wrapped around her hips and ass—but why was she wearing a scarf?

Travis pushed out of the truck with an eyebrow cocked. "You realize it's summer, right?"

"Yes," she returned quickly, stopping on the other side of the vehicle's door, which was open between them. "I'm cold."

Concern trickled in. "Are you getting sick?"

She visibly latched onto that. "Probably. That's probably it."

Again, the need to do *more* for her prodded Travis. His rule about avoiding being alone with her went right out the window in the face of her needing help. Needing *him*. "Let me take you home, then. I've got a smoothie recipe that'll help ward it off. Used to make them before games when I felt myself getting a travel bug." Before he could stop himself, he reached over the top of the door and twisted a piece of her hair around his finger. "Sound good, baby girl?"

Georgie swayed a little but seemed to catch herself. "Is there a camera?"

"A what?" It took a moment for her meaning to penetrate. "Oh. Yes. White Escalade."

Did he imagine the spark dimming in her eyes? Her head dipped before Travis could make a judgment, Georgie coming around the open door of the truck and wrapping her arms around his waist. The perfect melding of her curves to his planes almost took the wind out of him. All he could do was focus on keeping his breathing even as he dropped his mouth to leave a kiss on the crown of her head. She snuggled closer—no, he *pulled* her closer. When had he started hugging her so tightly?

"I lied about getting sick," she said, her words muffled by his chest.

Relieved and confused at the same time, Travis laid his

cheek on top of her head, telling himself it was all for the pictures. "Why?"

Georgie pulled back a couple of inches, casting a glance over his shoulder at the photographer. "I'm wearing a scarf because I forgot to put on a bra."

Before he could guess her intentions, she unknotted the scarf and tugged it open. Travis groaned, low and heavy, his dick bulging in his jeans. Taller than Georgie as he was, he could see way more than the swell of her tits. Way more than the outline of her tight nipples where they strained against the light blue cotton of her tank top. He could see straight down the middle of her cleavage to the flat stomach beneath. "Jesus, put the scarf back on. You might as well be naked."

Pink stained her cheeks as she covered herself again. "You should give a woman more than twenty minutes to get ready."

Travis let his exasperation show. "*You* texted *me,* Georgie."

"I didn't expect you to want to put me in a good mood right then and there."

"Stop telling me to put you in a good mood," he growled, backing her against the still-open door. "Or I'm going to do it."

"Family network," she breathed, pushing at his shoulder.

Nice to meet you, blue balls. Travis stepped back and dragged a hand down his face. "Let's go inside."

"Good idea."

He watched Georgie put a smile on her face with visible effort, moving out of the way so he could close the door. Once he'd locked the door, she reached out for his hand, leaning into his shoulder as he took it, the whole boyfriend-girlfriend dynamic feeling far too real. He held the door as she passed him into Grinders, which was mostly empty in the post-lunch, predinner no-man's-land. With no one there to witness them together, the realness of *them* hit home even more, but he found himself distracted from that worry by Georgie's pursed lips as she read the posted menu. The way she shifted around and licked her lips, waiting for the girl to take their order, so fresh and sweet looking he couldn't help speculating on how her neck would taste. Or the inside of her wrist.

A few minutes later, they were sitting across from each other at a table.

"Do you want to see my boobs again?"

Travis almost spit out the first sip of his sea salt caramel mocha. "What?"

She laughed into her own sip. "I'm just kidding. You look all tense."

"I'm not."

"Okay," she returned, mimicking his deep voice. "Would you really have taken me home and preemptively nursed me back to health?"

"I would have made you a smoothie," he corrected her.

"That's nursing. You would have nursed."

He was caught between laughing and shaking his head. "I have no idea what being nursed back to health is like. Not unless it includes physical therapy or an ice bath."

Here he was again, telling Georgie things he never expected to hear outside of his own mind. She didn't make him regret it, though. She only looked back at him in a solemn way, as if taking it in. Taking him in. Being in the moment together without expectations or disappointment that he wasn't the famous athlete she'd seen on television.

"Have you spoken to your parents since you came back to Port Jeff?"

"No." Leaning back in his chair, he crossed his arms over his chest, as if to hide the sudden rattle taking place in his rib cage. "Actually, I haven't talked to them since I left for college."

"Almost a decade?" she whispered, looking stricken. "I was younger and kind of oblivious during the divorce and after. I'm sorry things never got better between them and you."

"I'm not."

Now that he'd made it uncomfortable, he waited for her to drop the subject, but she didn't. "Did you ever wonder in the middle of a game if they were watching?"

Travis chewed on the inside of his cheek. "Yeah," he finally heard himself admit. Out loud. It hadn't been just once, either. "Every game."

He heard Georgie swallow from across the table. "They should have. They should have been watching like proud parents. They should be proud of you right now, Travis. It's not easy to start over."

This was where he was supposed to thank her or find something else to talk about, but he had the urge to confide in her. Wanted to hand her a piece of himself, because he knew she would take care of it. "It's him, mostly. My father." He pressed his tongue to the inside of his cheek. "My mother was young. She got trapped in a bad marriage and didn't know how to cope. If he played the same head games with her that he played with me, I don't fault her for wanting to be anywhere else."

Georgie wanted to argue, but he winked to let her know he was fine, and she relaxed.

"It's my dad who got to me," he said after a moment. "Who . . . gets to me. He made sure I would hear his voice in my head long past the point I should."

"What does it say?"

He exhaled. "That I'm not as good as I think I am. That I'm a fake."

She pressed her lips together until they turned white, then let them fill with pink again. "There was nothing fake about the way you slid into home and knocked that ball out of Ted Church's glove to win the second game of the Series. You're a part of history. Some people just can't stand knowing they're not even a footnote."

Warmth spread in his stomach. How did she know exactly what he needed to hear? Not some tired platitude, but a real, tangible thing he could recall in his memory and reinterpret through her eyes. "Thank you."

"Do you think I'm silly and selfish for wanting more from my pretty amazing and semifunctional family when you got nothing from yours?"

"No." He reached across the table and twined their fingers together without thinking. "No, baby girl. I don't. You have to fight for what you deserve. What you want is no more or less important than what anyone else wants."

Georgie studied him for a moment. "When I walked into your apartment that first day, you told me coming back here as a supposed failure made you just like your father." She shook her head. "You not only tell me but make me *feel* important . . . How can you think you don't have the potential to be a hero, on or off the field?"

This time Travis did change the subject. He'd heard a lot of empty idioms throughout his career in sports. The kind of motivation that ends up on a poster in a high school locker room. What she'd said, though, made him think. He might have left his hovel and rejoined society, but part of him had remained in the dark. Every moment spent with Georgie brought him a little further into the light, however.

They talked long after their coffees dwindled, Georgie telling him about plans for a new advertising campaign for her business and a new zombie birthday party theme she was considering. In turn, Travis told her about the time in college his team's bus had broken down on the way to a game and they'd had their engine serviced by cult members. It felt good to make her laugh. Felt good to laugh *with* her. By the time he walked her to the exit an hour had passed and he was overdue back at work.

Out in the sunlight, she smiled up at him in a sort of breathless way, a hand restless at her throat. And for the first time since Stephen told Travis that Georgie was in love with him, he actually wondered if it could be true. *Did Georgie love him?* If so, he should *not* be spending this kind of time with her. He'd hurt her when they'd both gotten what they wanted—and hurting this girl would kill him.

Travis opened his mouth, intending to tell Georgie what Stephen had told him, praying she would deny it. Right? He didn't want her in love with him. At all.

"Do I look smitten enough?" Georgie said with a cocked eyebrow, before he could speak. "Our friend is snapping away across the street."

"Oh. Yeah." *Idiot.* Of course she wasn't in love with him. It was just for the camera, same as it had been since their arrangement started. "I, uh . . . wasn't sure he'd waited."

A beat passed. "Are you going to kiss me?"

He wanted to. Her mouth looked ripe and incredible, and she would taste like caramel and Georgie. Why did it suddenly feel wrong to kiss her so it would be immortalized in a picture? "Yeah," he rasped, leaning down and pausing the barest distance above her lips. "Yeah."

Georgie's forehead wrinkled in confusion, cutting a sidelong glance along the street. "Travis?"

Finally, he dropped his mouth to hers and inhaled, pulling deeply on her mouth, barely stopping himself from giving her his tongue. Claiming her. With a serious effort, he eased back, steadying Georgie on her feet. "When am I going to see you again?"

"Um . . ." She blinked. "Will you come to family dinner on Sunday?"

Remembering the vow he'd made to himself to do more to help Georgie, Travis nodded. "I'll be there."

She smiled up at him and he bit down on his tongue to keep from kissing her again. "What about you? Any more progress with the network?"

It was proof that his relationship with Georgie was bordering on dangerous that he'd completely forgotten to tell her about the latest call from his agent. He'd totally lost sight of why they were fake dating in the first place. "The head of the network, Kelvin, invited us to dinner at his house. Next week, in Old Westbury." He watched her face transform with cautious excitement. "That probably means I'm the top candidate—"

"Oh my God, Travis. And this could be the final test." Her wide eyes turned unreadable. "Things are changing for me already. For the better. If you get the job . . . we wouldn't have to do this anymore."

"Have to." His nod was jerky. "Yeah." Christ, he needed to get his head together. This dread churning in his stomach was not a good sign. "I'll let you know the details about dinner," he said, laying a final peck on her cheek and backing away. "Bye, Georgie."

"Bye, Travis," she called over her shoulder as she sailed across the street, scarf clutched to her chest. "You did it, by the way!" she said—a little too brightly?—giving him one final look before turning to leave. "I'm in a great mood!"

That made one of them.

CHAPTER SEVENTEEN

Well, *this* was fucking awkward.

Stephen frowned at Travis from across the Castle family living room, bottle of beer in a white-knuckled grip. They'd worked together a handful of times on the flip since news outlets had started splashing pictures of him and Georgie across their pages, but they'd avoided conversation that didn't involve building materials or floor plans. Grunts, pointing, and manly throat clearing had become their communication method of choice. Which worked on a noisy construction site, but not so well in a quiet living room.

Restless, Travis started to pace in front of the fireplace. Where was she?

The front door opened and Travis's muscles tightened, but Bethany breezed into the house instead of her sister. Travis hadn't seen Bethany since high school, although he remembered her well. And he wasn't fooled for a second by her bright smile. She hated his guts. If he recalled correctly, she'd written *You'll get yours, playboy scum* in his yearbook.

"So good to see you, Travis," Bethany enthused. "Thank

you for taking a break from your busy schedule of ruining the lives of women to be here."

"Please." Ignoring the hollowness in his stomach, Travis saluted his beer. "It's the least I can do."

She clasped her hands beneath her chin. "Selfless as always."

Kristin bounced out of the kitchen and stopped in front of Stephen, popping a canapé into his mouth. Chewing, he grumbled, "If anyone should be taking shots at him, it should be me."

"Teamwork is key in this family." Bethany set her purse down and dusted off the arms of her blouse. "While we have you to ourselves, I should tell you I am completely fine with you dating Georgie."

Travis raised a skeptical eyebrow. "Oh, I can tell."

"She's smart. Funny. Selfless." Bethany ticked Georgie's merits off on her fingers. "And she's taken charge of her sexuality."

Stephen interjected a loud sigh. "Gross."

"As soon as this whole business is finished, she'll be wading through options." Another brush of her sleeve. "I'm looking forward to it."

Travis's stomach pitched. In the kitchen, pots and pans banged together loudly, mingling with the Castles' signature bickering. Sights and sounds from his youth, and he was grateful for them now, because they distracted him from his seasickness. Georgie dating other men. Recognizing the best thing to ever happen to them, they would lock her down in a heartbeat. Travis would be nothing more than a stepping-stone. In the past. Before Bethany could rain down another blow, the front door opened again.

In the split second before he saw Georgie, he was hit with anticipation and . . . joy. Yeah, joy. Everything would be fine now. She was here with her wit and funny facial expressions and that way she looked at him. Like she understood his every thought without him even opening his mouth. That was before he saw her.

Holy motherfucking shit, Georgie, are you trying to murder me?

She looked so good it hurt. As in his dick. Hurt.

Why? The long-sleeved dress wasn't even revealing. The V-neck showed off the swell of her tits, but the buttons came up high enough that you couldn't classify what was showing as cleavage. No, it was the high hem at the bottom that made his mouth water. The yellow dress was loose around her thighs, but it showed so damn much of them, he wanted to cry. He was scared of her turning around. Didn't even want to know where that hem hit her ass. Were her legs always so shiny—

Wait a minute. Wait a damn minute. They'd been waxed.

These were lounging-poolside-at-a-resort-in-Vegas legs. Which led him to a seriously disconcerting question. What else had she gotten waxed?

"Georgie," Kristin said, clapping her hands together. "Look at you."

Bethany put two fingers in her mouth and whistled. "Hide your sons, Port Jefferson," she drawled, sending Travis a wink. "A fashionably late entrance and everything. The student has become the master."

"More like I got caught talking to Mrs. Casey about a party for her triplets." Georgie set down the bottle of wine she'd carried in, her eyes briefly landing on Travis. A red blush overtook her face and, goddamn, that uncalculated reaction increased his hunger tenfold. This girl could make a man crawl and had no idea. "She wants an underwater theme, so apparently I'll be wearing a snorkel and flippers."

"Do they make clown bathing suits?" Bethany said on a laugh.

"No," Travis growled. "They don't."

Everyone stared at him, including Georgie. He liked having her undivided attention. Putting himself in this awkward situation was worth it just to have her look at him, ground him, show him that rare, honest quality he couldn't get anywhere else. Yeah, he was staring, too, so he was grateful when Vivian and Morty ambled out of the kitchen with yet another cheese plate.

"I'll carry it," Vivian said out of the side of her mouth. "That way you'll stop eating olives before everyone has a chance to see my masterpiece."

"It's food," Morty pointed out, patting his pocket for his eyeglasses. "Food is supposed to be eaten, not styled."

Vivian skidded to a halt and thrust the cheese plate at her husband. "Georgie! Is that a dress? Are you wearing a dress?"

"Is that what this is?" Georgie looked down. "I must have worn it by mistake."

"No! No mistake." Vivian circled around the back of her daughter. "Oh, excuse me. Someone's got a pair of pins.

And not the kind that go in your hair. What do you think, Travis?"

"Don't answer that," Stephen called, draining his beer.

"Mom," Georgie groaned. "You're pretty much ensuring I never wear another dress again in this house."

"My lips are zipped." Vivian patted her hair and grabbed the cheese plate from Morty, just in time to thwart his olive stealing. "I just think it's nice, Georgie bringing a date to Sunday dinner. I don't mind the short notice at all. About the extra place setting *or* the actual relationship. I find out things when I find them out, I guess. That's a mother's lot in life."

Travis almost laughed as all three siblings traded a wince.

"Dinner is almost ready," Vivian said breezily. "Everyone have a glass of wine and relax, okay? This is so nice. All our kids in one place."

The Castles disappeared back into the kitchen.

"Stephen," Kristin said, tugging on her husband's arm. "I have some cupcakes out in the car. Can you help me carry them in? I made enough to feed two armies."

Stephen eyed Travis and Georgie, obviously dubious about leaving them alone. "Sure, honey."

"Nope, I'm not going to be the third wheel. I'll go make a call," Bethany muttered, sliding the glass door open and dipping into the backyard. And that was how Travis and Georgie ended up alone in the space of minutes. The turn of events sent his pulse thrumming, made his blood heat. Not helpful. Nothing could come of it. There would be no relief. Their objective was to convince the outside world they were dating, not to satisfy each other with touches. Or kisses.

There was an attraction here, but he wouldn't act on it. Not when moving on was inevitable.

Travis couldn't make himself issue any of these warnings out loud, though, as Georgie crossed the living room in his direction, her legs giving a sexy little flex beneath that fluttery hemline. Had he once actually referred to her legs as normal? *I was a fucking idiot.* They were petite and lithe and the color of warm sand. He wanted to . . .

Georgie stopped in front of him, hijacking his thoughts. Pretty. So pretty with her chewed-on lips and sun-kissed nose. Had she been outside? Maybe it was the way she only reached his shoulder that sent protectiveness surging up to his jugular, while somehow—at the very same time—he wanted to seek refuge in her.

Nothing made sense anymore.

Georgie whispered something to herself that Travis couldn't hear and shifted side to side. Before he could ask her to repeat it, she touched him. Georgie touched him and there wasn't a single camera around. She placed her flattened palms on his pecs and . . . her lips parting on a nervous breath . . . she slid them up and around his neck, bringing their bodies flush.

"What are you doing?" Travis said hoarsely, the impact of her unexpected touch making him unsteady on his feet. "Georgie—"

She'd gone up on her tiptoes in order to get her arms around his neck. When she wobbled a little, Travis could do nothing but wrap a protective arm around her back. The other followed, tugging her tight against him. His mouth found its way into her hair, exhaling, every inch of him reacting to having her body molded to his hard planes so securely. The chaos that had been churning inside him all week settled, while a different kind of commotion took shape. She parted her lips against his neck and his groin tightened to the point of pain.

Oh my God.

"What is this?"

"We're hugging," Georgie whispered, her lips brushing his skin again. "That's all."

"Don't do that. Don't talk to me in that innocent voice. Not when all your sweetest parts are pressed up against me in that cock-tease dress." Trying and failing to maintain an awareness of their surroundings, Travis angled his hips and listened to her breath stutter. "You're turning me on and you're very aware of it."

"Am I?" Georgie leaned back just enough to study his mouth for one beat, two. "I'm trying to be authentic. Isn't this how a girlfriend greets her boyfriend?"

A low thudding began and spread throughout Travis. In his heart, testicles. Hell, both. Simultaneously. They both hurt like a son of a bitch, so all Travis could manage was a gruff "How would I know?"

Georgie ran her hands up his shoulders, cupping the sides of his face. "I'm glad you're here. I like having you around."

With those words hanging in the air, Georgie shifted out of his hold and left the living room, sauntering into the dining room like a certified seductress. The pulse in Travis's ears hammered nine times for every one of her steps, his hands bereft without the privilege of touching her. What in the ever-loving hell had just taken place? He'd been prepared for an uneasy dinner, considering her siblings wanted to lop his head off with an ax. Instead, she'd walked in here and completely thrown him off-balance.

As if in a trance, Travis joined Georgie in the dining room. As a young man, he'd always sat between Stephen and Morty, but the seat beside Georgie had been left open this time. They traded a look as he sat down, more of that sweet blush darkening her skin and making his tongue feel heavy. They should talk, shouldn't they? Unfortunately, they weren't alone for more than a couple seconds. Morty and Vivian came in shoulder to shoulder, bumping off each other like tethered planets, both of them trying to carry the platter holding a roast. Bethany slunk in and fell into her seat across from Georgie—but Travis was focused on Georgie and therefore saw only the look of concern she sent her older sister, followed by a bolstering smile. Something was up.

"All right." Stephen stomped into the dining room and sat to the right of Morty, Kristin floating to the chair beside her husband and perching with a beaming grin. "Bethany, you called this dinner. What's your gripe?"

"Who says there has to be a gripe?" Vivian protested from the opposite head of the table, wineglass poised in midair. "Can we not exchange pleasantries first? Your sister wore a dress, Stephen—tell her she looks nice."

Georgie hid her face behind a napkin. "Oh God. Mom."

Stephen sighed. "You look nice, Georgie. Yellow suits you."

"Well, it's no clown suit . . ." Morty started, laughing at his own sarcasm.

The rosy glow faded from Georgie's cheeks and Travis frowned. Before he could say something in her defense—what, he didn't know—Stephen spoke up again. "Is it this women's club that's got you dressing up? Or him?"

"It's not a women's club." Bethany drilled her brother with a look. "We don't meet to do makeovers, you moron. We're not twelve."

"I'm just saying, Georgie, you were fine in the overalls and the . . ." Stephen wiggled his fingers above his head, making reference to Georgie's missing messy bun. "Seems like someone should like you for yourself, not how you look."

Travis fixed Stephen with a look. "I liked her in the overalls just fine."

Several beats passed. "Why am I not in this club?" Vivian said brightly, breaking the tension. "Am I too old?"

Morty cut into the roast with gusto, sawing off slivers of meat. "You're not too old. You're too happy."

Bethany centered herself with a long breath. "We're not doing makeovers and we're not throwing darts at pictures of male genitalia—"

Vivian laugh-snorted. "Bethany Castle."

"Actually, I just signed up me, Rosie, and Georgie for a Tough Mudder."

"Ooh, what's that?" Kristin piped up. "I want to go."

Stephen grunted and started the passing of the side dishes. "Explain."

Bethany sat up straighter. "It's a five-mile run, including an obstacle course. A team-building exercise. In the mud."

Georgie paled. "We barely made it through Zumba, you complete lunatic."

"Eh, we'll be fine." Bethany lifted her wineglass. "Next Friday in Bethpage. You're all welcome to come and cheer us on."

"I'll be there," Travis said automatically. If Georgie was going to run five miles and jump over walls in the summer heat, she could get hurt. Or dehydrated. Thinking about it almost turned his appetite. When he glanced up from spooning potatoes onto his plate, he found Stephen and Morty glowering at him. "What? She could twist an ankle or . . ." The room fell silent, knives and forks ceasing their clacking against plates. *Jesus. Pull it together, man.* He passed the bowl in his hand and dug into the now massive mountain of potatoes that he'd apparently been piling on for a full minute. "You never know what kind of a medical setup they have at these things," he finished gruffly.

"You're not doing it," Stephen grunted at Kristin, before softening his tone. "Please."

Kristin firmed her chin. "We'll see."

"Discord," Morty droned. "Bethany, your club is creating discord."

"It's not just her club," Georgie said. "We started it together."

"You're going to follow what your older siblings do, though. It's up to them to set a good example for the youngest."

"She's twenty-three," Bethany pointed out. "If this

were Victorian England, she would be classified as an old maid."

Georgie's laugh lacked its usual sparkle. "You could have left that part out."

Travis was caught between bites, listening to the conversation unfold around him. It had been years since he'd been in the midst of the Castle banter, but their dismissive attitude toward Georgie was more meaningful to him now that he knew how it affected her. She had changed. Grown up. Why the hell didn't they notice?

Frowning, Travis stabbed his fork back into his potatoes.

"Now that all the delicacies have been passed and plated . . ." Bethany cleared her throat. "Let's talk about the reason we're all here. I want to preface this by saying no one is going to like it. Just strap in—we'll get through it."

Georgie set down her fork and crossed her legs, drawing Travis's attention. The yellow hem of her dress crept up, almost to her hip, the muscle of her thigh flexing . . . and his mouth went dry. But her body language said she was preparing for battle on her sister's behalf and that realization let loose a stream of chemicals into his bloodstream. Georgie getting ready for an argument put him on alert, because they'd become teammates. Hadn't they?

"Is this about heading up your own flip?" Stephen drawled.

"Yes."

"What?" Morty bowed his head. "God give me strength."

"I've asked Stephen several times for a chance to run my own renovation, start to finish, and he has declined. So I've decided to purchase my own property and proceed outside the confines of Brick & Morty."

The utter betrayal on Morty's face was hard to witness. He slowly set down his fork and leaned back in his chair, folding his hands on the table.

"You stage, Bethany," Vivian said softly. "You chose that role yourself."

"I know I did, but now I want to try more."

"Maybe it was a mistake, leaving the business to my children," Morty said. "Is that what you're saying? I've only been retired a handful of years and already you're dismantling the company."

"Bethany wants a more active role. That's the opposite of dismantling, Dad. That's—"

Morty held up a hand. "Let the adults talk, Georgie."

Travis's fist slammed on the table so fast, everyone jumped. He hadn't planned it. But anger went ripping through him so fast, his hand moved on its own. That single action hadn't taken the air out of his ire, either. Not even a speck. "I have a lot of respect for you, Mr. Castle. More respect than I have for my own father. But I can't sit here and listen to you treat Georgie like her voice doesn't count for something. You're better than that. And she's damn sure too important to be cut off or spoken to like a child."

Everyone had a different reaction to his outburst. Stephen stared at him, surprised and thoughtful. Bethany appeared ready to cheer, Morty properly chastised. But Travis couldn't get his damn eyes off Georgie long enough to acknowledge much of it. He got even angrier, actually, because this girl who'd forced him to climb out of his hole all those weeks ago looked so grateful when she should have *expected* someone to come to her defense. She deserved that and more.

"Travis is right," Morty said, his expression contrite. "Georgie, I apologize. Please finish what you were going to say."

Georgie and Travis had been staring at each other since the Great Fist-Pounding Incident. Christ, he liked being on her side. Liked the idea of her counting on it way too much. He also liked those pretty parted lips. Remembering how they felt against his sent blood rushing to his cock. There he was, with a hard-on for the youngest daughter at the Castle family dinner. No help for it. Her dress had scooted up so fucking high on her leg—enough to see the shadow between her thighs. A few inches above that would be her panties. Her wet pussy.

I know you're wet, baby girl.

"I, um . . ." Georgie cleared the rust from her voice. "I was just going to say, Dad, that, uh . . ." Bethany snickered into her napkin and Georgie shot her a look. "Bethany loves Brick & Morty and she's one of the main reasons it's so successful. She wants to help it expand. If Stephen takes the time to guide her on a flip, they could double the number of projects the company takes on. She's never failed at anything, relationships notwithstanding—"

"Thanks, sis."

"Beth deserves a shot." Georgie turned her attention to Stephen. "You hate change and need control. We all get it. But this isn't like the rope swing at the lake when we were kids—and yeah, I'm still salty you made us go through a sign-up sheet to take a turn. It was a rope swing, dude. But we're adults now and we shouldn't hold each other back in the name of tradition. Compromise, Stephen."

"I'll think about it," their brother said after a moment, tucking back into his meal. "That'll have to be good enough for now."

"Fine," Bethany responded with a curt nod.

"Fine," echoed everyone at the table, save Travis.

A few ticks of silence passed.

"Where is Coco?" Vivian said, looking around the room. "Did we bring the dog in from the backyard, Morty?" She didn't wait for an answer. "Georgie, would you mind going out and having a look for Coco? God forbid she ate those toadstools—"

"Sure, Mom."

Georgie was already up from the table, heading in the direction of the living room. Unable to stop himself from following her progress, Travis nonetheless caught Vivian's gaze.

She winked at him.

Caught between laughter and keeling over from shock, Travis tossed his napkin on the table. "I'll go help her."

CHAPTER EIGHTEEN

Oh my God.

Georgie floated into the backyard, calling Coco's name in a croak. Her knees had the consistency of vapor; her heart rapped loudly in her rib cage. If her mother hadn't sent her outside, she would have burst into flames. Need concentrated itself between her legs, pulsing and tugging and relentless. How was she going to handle the rest of this dinner, Travis sitting so close by, acting like a hero?

"Coco?" she called, tugging her neckline away from her skin and blowing cold air down into her cleavage. Oh, cool. Look at that—her nipples were rocks. "Come here, girl."

Nothing. No jingling of the dog's collar.

She walked farther into the backyard, hooking a left and heading down the small slope toward the pool. Walking past the tall oak tree she used to climb in her youth brought back so many memories. The only ones she could conjure at that moment involved Travis. How she'd had the beginnings of a sexual awakening perched in that tree as a preteen, wistfully wishing she had boobs.

The culmination of her feverish daydreams had veered

into more adult territory one afternoon when Georgie had been tapped to clean out her parents' attic. She'd found a box of old VHS tapes, among them a tape labeled FEAR. Since her parents were gone for the day, she'd fired up the ancient VCR in the den, which Morty and Vivian never used anymore but still hadn't thrown away. Stephen wasn't the only member of the family who hated change. She'd been pleasantly surprised to find out the movie starred Mark Wahlberg and Reese Witherspoon and decided the tape probably belonged to Bethany—but around the one-hour mark, the scene happened.

The one on the roller coaster when Mark uses his finger on Reese.

Until that moment in her parents' den, Georgie hadn't even known the meaning of the word "horny." And, oh Lord, the guilt. Wahlberg played the worst kind of abusive sociopath in the movie, but Georgie got turned on so badly, she'd replayed the scene nine times. She'd finally closed her eyes, flopped over on her back, and imagined Travis reenacting the scene with her. In his Hurricanes uniform. Hands down her jeans, she'd had the first orgasm of her life on the floor of her parents' den to a VHS tape, while an internet full of free porn sat mere feet away.

Why couldn't she ever do things the easy way?

Instead of running far and fast from an unavailable man, she'd decided to show him that being available wasn't so bad. Between inviting him out for coffee and bringing him to dinner tonight, she'd intended to prove to Travis he didn't have to spend his life being passed around. But she'd been hoping to hold at least a small part of herself back in the process. To lessen the blow when he eventually walked. Or found someone else. Or realized definitively relationships weren't his jam, insecurities or not. But hold herself back from the guy who'd almost broken the good china standing up for her?

Not going to be so easy.

Every time she was with Travis, he revealed something else. A piece of the past, a hope for the future, a tender side. Tonight he'd proved he cared. He'd shown up for her. She'd thought herself in love with the swaggering baseball phenom, but she was dangerously close to falling for this newer, more complicated man. Deeper than she ever could have gotten with her youthful ideal of Travis.

Behind her, Georgie heard the sliding glass door open and close. She stopped and turned, her pulse rocketing into another stratosphere when Travis strode down the slope after her. The hunger on his face made Georgie take a step backward. Oh. Apparently she had this seduction thing in the bag. It had already stuck. Go, team.

As soon as Travis was even with Georgie, he stooped down and threw her over his shoulder. "Where?"

She tried and failed to ignore the new view of his butt. "Wh-where is the dog?"

"The dog is closed in the back bedroom," he responded in a patient but concise tone. "She's not in the backyard."

"Then why did my mom send me out here?"

Travis didn't say anything.

"Oh." Georgie drew out the word. "Ladies and gentlemen, my mother the wingman."

"Pool house or garage, Georgie?"

There was no question as to why Travis was seeking a private location, and it made her blood burn hotter. Although, since she was upside down, a lot of that hot blood raced to her head and made her dizzy. So be it. She'd just voiced her opinion at a family gathering and now Travis wanted to kiss her. If that wasn't cause for a head rush, she didn't know what was. "I, um—pool house, I guess?"

They crossed the threshold of the tiny changing hut a few seconds later. The door smacked shut behind them and they were enclosed in darkness. And move over, Mark and Reese, because she'd never been so poised to combust in her life. Travis was breathing heavy as he dragged Georgie off his shoulder, her legs cinching around his waist on the way down. Soft flesh settled on hard to the soundtrack of a groan, a whimper. A slow grind of those ready parts, followed by all-out panting. Growling. He lunged and rammed her backward into the wall, and their mouths locked in a feverish battle.

Georgie's mind could barely function around the passion of it. The intensity. Her senses turned to blank slates that knew nothing of touch and taste. They waited eagerly for Travis to teach them new ways—and he did. His mouth moved with sensual intention, giving her quality, not quantity. He dragged out and relished every dance of their tongues, every re-angling glide of their lips. Every breath they broke apart to take. Savoring, pushing their foreheads together, sipping at her mouth, his breath stuttering, throat working. Making her feel like the first and last woman to ever be kissed in all of history. And all the while, his rough hands climbed her thighs, eagerly rounding her hips to clutch her bottom. Molding it to the shape of his fingers and palms.

"Open your eyes and look at me, Georgette Castle." Travis's voice rasped at her in the near darkness, leaving no room for nonsense. She'd never seen him like that, focused and determined. Serious. Maybe a touch nervous. "Look at me."

"I'm looking," she whispered, wondering if he was aware that his erection was pressing hard into the silk of her panties—and if he also realized it wasn't really an opportune time for a conversation. "I'm here. I'm looking," she breathed anyway.

"Good." He kissed her once—hard—then went back to having a serious face. "I can't do it. I can't stop myself from taking you." He groaned against her mouth, using his grip on her bottom to drag her higher on his lap. "I need to be inside this so fucking bad."

Sparks shot around in her brain, like someone had thrown coffee on the control panel that kept her rooted in reality. "You do?"

Travis pushed up hard between her thighs, locking her against the wall with his hips. "Don't ask me that again when I clearly want to fuck you into next Christmas."

"Do it," she gasped. "Oh my God."

"I will. When I can take my time." He lifted an eyebrow and gave her a meaningful look. "Virgin."

"Right. I forgot."

"I didn't." He rolled his hips in a slow circle, grinding

their lower bodies together. "Been thinking about it almost exclusively."

Georgie's thighs started to tremble, along with her insides. "That's . . . hmm. Good?"

"Good." His mouth lifted in a cocky grin. "Sure, baby girl."

In other words, as soon as Travis had the opportunity, he was going to turn her into a babbling puddle of limbs and organs. Noted. "What am I supposed to do until then?"

Travis eased his hips back, allowing her legs to drop, but kept her back flush to the wall. "You need a little something?" His fingertips traveled up the inside of her thigh. "I'll rub my fingers in the right spot while we figure some stuff out."

"Like—" She sucked in a breath as his fingers invaded her panties, the middle one sliding right down the wet split of her sex. "L-like what?"

He hummed against her ear. "You. Tempting me to give in and fuck you."

Georgie's inner thighs threw a spasm party. "*Yes.*"

"Consider it done. I'm going to give in like a motherfucker. *I have to.*" He panted for a few beats. "But our original deal . . . it still has to stand." A line formed between his brows. "Georgie, I want you to understand, even if this is only going to last until the network dinner, it'll be the longest I've ever been like this with someone."

"Like what?"

"It'll be more than a fling." She heard him swallow. "Our futures look different, Georgie. I don't have the family gene, and you . . . that tradition runs in your blood. I can't be that for you, but I'll be damned before you regret this. Us. Letting me into your bed. While this lasts, tell me what you need to feel . . . important."

You. Just you. Every single part. "Being on my side during a family discussion," she whispered. "That was a really good start."

A dismissive sound left his throat. "Don't give me any credit for that, Georgie. It needed to be done. What else?"

The pad of his middle finger prodded her entrance, slicking moisture up to her clit and polishing it in easy circles. "Uhhhh." A bolt twisted deep in Georgie's belly and her neck started to lose power. "Uh. I don't know. Romantic gestures? Is that a thing?"

"Yeah." He didn't sound 100 percent certain. "Flowers and whatnot, right?"

Georgie giggled. "The blind leading the blind."

Travis's mouth cut off her laughter. He moved her lips wide, leaving them there for several breaths, before flicking their tongues together. Just once. A rebuke. A promise. Without his body wedging her against the wall, she would have dropped from the pure, uncut sexuality of it. "I've got two more questions. And one selfish demand. You ready?"

"Yes." His middle finger picked up the pace on her clit, giving deep, thorough love to all sides, the middle, occasionally giving it a gentle pinch. Honest to God, Travis seemed so focused on what came out of her mouth, she couldn't figure out how he multitasked so effectively. Sex God. Her fake boyfriend really was a Sex God. "Really yes."

"Question one. You wax this pussy for me?"

She looked up at him through her lashes. "Uh-huh."

He let out a shaky exhale. "Correct answer." His index finger inched inside her in a slow, long glide, a growl kindling in his throat. "I'm going to worship this thing next time we're together."

"See? Romantic gestures," she breathed. "You're already a pro."

Travis's laugh was winded. "I'm a rookie at virgins and *fuck,* while we're on the subject, you're closed up around my finger so tight, I'm probably never going to look your father in the eye again." He exhaled hard. "How have you been . . . imagining your first time?"

The eagerness in Travis's tone caused a pang in Georgie's chest. How could anyone write this man off? Whether or not they were in a real, committed relationship, he wanted to make her first time count. She couldn't exactly tell him the truth, however. That she'd been envisioning her first time with him since she'd hit puberty. Although the moment called for a certain measure of truth, so she did her best. "Don't laugh, but I've always pictured it happening on the couch. Like, two people who can't control themselves and touching gets out of control . . ."

"You want to Netflix and chill your virginity away."

"Don't judge me."

"I'm not." His mouth lifted at one end as he leaned in slowly to kiss her, working their lips together in a thorough, mind-spinning dance. "I just want to give the millennial what she wants. Until she's a naked little mess underneath me."

"Oh." Georgie's flesh clenched around his finger, the low, insistent throb growing heavier, heavier, until it became necessary to shift her thighs closer together. She knew the warning signs of an orgasm well, but she'd never been required to speak through one. Or had another human being keep her perched on the edge, as if the objective was enjoyment instead of getting there as fast as possible. "A-and your selfish demand?"

His tongue traveled along the curve of her lower lip. "I'm asking you very nicely to let me refinish your fireplace, Georgie," he said. "Cancel the single dad."

Travis's heart rapped violently in his chest, sending vibrations into her body. This was so important to him? Really? "Yes. I will," she whispered, her curiosity deepening when he took a relieved exhale. "Um. Okay, my turn," she murmured. "I don't, um . . . I mean, just while this is going on. If you could . . . and I'm not being, like, *jealous*—"

"What?" Intense blue eyes bored into hers. "Just say it."

Gather some bravery, girl. "Can it be just me—for you—for right now?"

Travis narrowed his gaze at Georgie, that *rap-rap-rap* echoing louder, carrying from his body to hers. "No one puts their fucking hands on either one of us until we decide different." He slipped a second finger inside her and pumped firmly—holding—ripping a gasp from her mouth. "That work for you?"

"It does," Georgie managed, her hips beginning to move up and back, seeking friction. "F-feels so good. *Travis.*"

He laid his mouth on top of hers, his thick thumb beginning

to brush back and forth across her sensitive clitoris. "Make my hand wet."

"Oh . . . yes." Her stomach hollowed, loins twisting. "Yes, okay."

"You're so goddamn tight, baby girl," Travis groaned, angling his fingertips to brush a glorious spot inside her. One that turned every cell in her body into an unlocked fire hydrant in the summertime, opening the floodgates to new sensations. "You better pick a boring movie, because you're not going to see a minute of it. Soon as we get on that couch tomorrow, I'm going to ride you straight through the credits."

"Right." She grasped for an ounce of concentration and missed. "*Cold Mountain* is free on Netflix. That should work."

Her last word emerged choked. A shivering glaze moved up and over her head, exhilarating and scary at the same time. Travis seemed to sense Georgie reaching her peak, because he nipped at her jaw, then let his open mouth travel down her neck, all while his fingers continued a slow thrust into her heat, his thumb tormenting her clit. "Let it happen, baby girl." He scraped his teeth along the base of her neck—right on top of her pulse. "When we go back inside, I'll know you're sitting at your parents' dinner table, still dripping a little in your silk panties."

Travis gently sank his teeth into her.

Georgie's flesh contracted with so much intensity, tears sprang to her eyes, the power to stand evaporating. Travis held her up with a strong arm around her waist, while the wave of ecstasy rolled over her like a force of nature. As with last time, there was an innate instinct in her to please Travis, so she groped blindly for his erection, frowning when he snagged her wrist, tugging it away. "No, no," he taunted beside her ear. "You're not getting away with jerking me off. I want it *all* next time. Want you flat on your back and taking me deep."

If she'd been coherent, she might have even been embarrassed by how soaked she left Travis's massaging hand and pumping fingers, but he seemed to crave it. The proof was in every lick of his tongue inside her mouth, every rushed exhale into her hair. "Oh my God. I—y-you . . . Did that so . . . Wow."

He snapped his teeth down on her earlobe. "Cancel the single dad."

"Done," she whimpered. "No single dads allowed."

"Good girl."

Long, dizzy moments later, Travis straightened out her panties, using a towel from a nearby shelf to dry the insides of her thighs. He even ran his thumbs over Georgie's face to fix her makeup. Finger-combed her hair. And he walked her back to the house, with a hand settled possessively on her butt. His smile was so self-assured and comforting, she must have imagined the slight tremor in his fingertips.

CHAPTER NINETEEN

A new doubt popped up every time the realtor's high heels clicked on the hardwood floor.

She couldn't do this. Paying rent for an office space would be too much pressure. She was a clown, for the love of everything holy. Clowns didn't have offices.

But successful entertainment company owners did. That's what she wanted, wasn't it? To give her eventual full-time employees a reputable place where they could report for duty, have meetings, store equipment. A place where she could greet clients and go over options for their child's birthday party—and beyond. As of this morning's series of interviews, she now had a juggler, a magician, and two Disney princess impersonators working on a pay-as-we-go basis. There was no rule that said they needed to stop at birthday parties. The possibilities were endless.

Still, there wasn't even a scrap of furniture in the two-room space above the bagel shop. She would be putting Ikea furniture together until she was fluent in Swedish. There would be pressure. If she had a slow month, sacrifices would need to be made. If an employee couldn't hold up their end of the contract, firing them would fall on her shoulders. This was the big time.

Georgie realized the realtor was watching her from across the sunlit room, Main Street spread out behind her in the two identical windows.

"Um." Georgie turned in a circle. "How many square feet did you say?"

"Eleven hundred." The realtor tapped a few buttons on her phone. "Kind of cozy, but you'll be grateful for that in the winter."

"Right."

God, she felt out of her element. She'd worn a loose summer dress and styled her hair, hoping a put-together appearance would give her a boost of confidence, but she still felt a little intimidated by the polished realtor. The woman wasn't even making eye contact with Georgie. It was on the tip of her tongue to thank the realtor for her time and promise to call with a decision later, but it was an excuse to run. To sidestep making a decision. This place was perfect for her needs; she just needed to make the leap.

Georgie paced to the window and looked out over the town she knew so well. It blurred until she could see only her reflection in it. How much she'd changed on the outside. Had she changed on the inside, too?

She took a deep breath and closed her eyes, searching for something—anything—that might lead her to believe she was capable of renting this space and turning her small business into a thriving one.

In her mind, Travis's fist came down on her family dinner table.

She's damn sure too important to be cut off or spoken to like a child.

A shiver snaked down Georgie's back. Travis's blue eyes did look at her like she was important, didn't they? Like he was not only interested in her thoughts, but . . . *needed* to know them. She'd set out on a sneaky mission to make Travis believe in himself, but he'd slowly been doing the same for her. They'd been doing it for each other, hadn't they?

She turned from the window, still not sure if she could pull the trigger. The realtor looked up with an inquisitive expression, and Georgie started to panic, but was brought up short when she heard high heels tapping up the building staircase. A couple seconds later, her sister breezed into the office space. "Hey, Georgie." She flashed her teeth at the realtor. "Hello."

The other woman stood up straighter. "Did you have an appointment?"

"She's my sister," Georgie answered, lowering her voice for Bethany's ears alone. "What are you doing here?"

"Just in the neighborhood." Bethany made a show of removing her oversized sunglasses, taking in the whole office space in one spin of her heel. "What are they asking for rent?"

Georgie named the figure and Bethany pursed her lips, throwing an arm around Georgie's shoulders and turning them away from the realtor. "That's a decent price, but we can do better."

"Not in town, we can't."

"No. You're paying to be on Main Street. I get it." She bumped their hips together. "You haven't really been involved in the turnover aspect of Brick & Morty, but no one ever agrees to the starting price. Not even when I've staged it to look like the cover of *Home and Garden*."

Georgie glanced over. "But this is a rental."

"Rules were made to be bent."

Had Bethany ever taken the time to teach her something without a direct order from their mother? Georgie didn't think so. This wasn't forced at all, though. They were just two women talking, working toward a common goal. Bethany had shown up to help her because she wanted to, and that alone made Georgie feel worthy. Validated. Like she had every right to be there, making the decision to rent a commercial space and strike out into uncharted territory.

The boost of confidence gave Georgie an idea.

Standing taller than before, she turned toward the realtor. "Brick & Morty is our family company. If you can convince the owners of this building to knock ten percent off the rental price, I'll talk to my brother, Stephen, about throwing you an upcoming listing."

The realtor's lips parted. "You're Georgie Castle. I . . ." She was already dialing her phone. "I didn't put it together. Let me see what I can do."

Bethany gave a low whistle. "Damn, girl. I was going to suggest a five percent discount by offering to pay cash." She squeezed Georgie. "You do me proud."

Georgie blinked back the moisture in her eyes. "Thanks."

Romantic gestures.

Right.

Travis knew as much about romantic gestures as he knew about spring fashion trends. But he'd given up the impossible battle of keeping his hands off Georgie. This was what she claimed to need to make it feel right. So here he was. At her house. Breaking and entering.

He twirled the key ring around his index finger and contemplated the cheerful red front door. Fake boyfriends were allowed to come over unannounced, weren't they? She wouldn't mind. Probably.

And it wasn't as if he'd come here to roll around in her sheets or steal her panties while she wasn't home. He had a mission. The contents of his truck bed were proof enough of that. He'd woken up bright and early this morning and knocked on the Castles' front door, relieved when Vivian answered—he hadn't been lying to Georgie about needing some time before looking her father in the eye. Then again, maybe doing so would always be a little difficult, since he planned to do all manner of ungodly things to Georgie. Starting whenever she arrived home from the birthday party she was working.

But he wanted to make some progress before then.

Travis slipped the key into the lock and twisted, letting himself into the house. He walked through the silent interior, smiling as he stepped over a pair of clown shoes, and continued through the rear entrance into the backyard. After propping open the side gate, he started carting materials from his truck, setting up his table saw and belt sander on the back lawn. Carrying the final item on his own was something of a task, because it was difficult to navigate turns with a tree branch on your shoulder, but he managed.

Hours later, he'd sawed the tree branch into equal pieces of lumber and started the process of sanding the rough grain, making it smooth to the touch. He took one water break, only to realize he didn't have any water. There'd been no choice but to track a little sawdust and dirt into Georgie's kitchen to retrieve a bottle of cool refreshment. While he stood in the tiny kitchen with vintage fixtures and a sign over the stove that said OH, FOR FORK'S SAKE, Travis got an idea. After making a phone call to a local restaurant, he went back out and commenced sanding once again.

Romantic gestures. This had to be one, right?

He hadn't witnessed too many of them in his life. Once, during his first season with the Hurricanes, a teammate had proposed to his girlfriend before getting on the bus. He'd gotten down on one knee, right there in front of the friends who proceeded to tease him ruthlessly for the entire ride to the airport. The proposer hadn't given a flying shit, though. He'd just been happy to get a yes, damn the consequences. At the time, Travis couldn't believe any man would voluntarily tie himself down. He'd thought the guy was a sucker.

He still did. But he could admit to himself that he wouldn't mind seeing Georgie that happy. In fact, he craved it. And that scared the shit out of him.

Travis switched off the belt sander and took a slug of water, swiping the wrist of his work glove across his forehead. A large, thick plank lay on its side in the grass, knots and age rings visible in every gorgeous inch—that piece would serve as the mantel. One day, Georgie would put framed pictures of her children on it. She'd start a fire in the wintertime, run her fingers along the glossy texture. Would she think of him?

He'd taken his shirt off in deference to the heat, but the sudden cold made him wish for it now. He paced away from the machinery, tapping his water bottle on his thigh. No longer seeing the shade-dappled backyard around him. Once upon a time, Travis's father had probably made romantic overtures to his mother. Probably brought her flowers and squired her on dates.

Then Travis had come along and put an end to all of that, hadn't he? Not only had any semblance of romance ceased, all-out warfare had started. A memory resurfaced, not so different from countless others knocking around in his head. After the initial separation, his mother and father both wanted to go out with friends on the same night.

"You take him."

"Not tonight. I need this."

"I need to get away, too. I've had him for four nights straight!"

"Oh, wow, four whole nights. It's called fatherhood!"

"You're preaching to me? What kind of a mother doesn't want to care for her son?"

"Maybe a mother who wants her life back. How about that?"

A familiar hand settled on Travis's shoulder and he spun around, breathing like he'd just run up the side of a mountain. Georgie stared back at him, hand still poised in the air. Travis swallowed hard, battling back the urge to scoop her up and bury his face in whatever part of her was closest. She had that fresh-scrubbed look, as if she'd just wiped off her clown makeup. The little flyaway hairs around her face were damp, eyelashes in clumps, lips pink and parted. Fading sunlight lit her up and drenched her exposed legs, highlighting the concern in her eyes.

"Hey," she murmured. "You're here."

Travis cleared his throat but didn't get rid of the rust. "Yeah." She was watching him curiously, seeing too much, and he didn't have the stomach to explain what had shaken him up. So he forced a smile before she could ask. "I'm here."

Her attention traveled down his chest and belly, color rising in her cheeks. "You're here."

"You already said that."

She squeezed her eyes closed. "I . . . was just confirming."

It was unbelievable. One minute around Georgie and warmth crept back into his blood, making him feel normal. Balanced. "Aren't you going to ask about the construction taking place in your backyard?"

"What?" She jolted, clearly seeing the machinery and lumber for the first time. "Oh! Are you? No. Is this my fireplace you're working on?"

Travis nodded once. "Recognize the wood?"

Her gaze flicked to his lap. "Wait . . . what?"

"The wood for the fireplace, baby girl." A laugh snuck out. "Christ, we better punch that V card before you have a nervous breakdown."

She threw up her hands. "Well, I can't help it! You turned my perfectly innocent backyard into construction worker porn. All we need is some light jazz."

"Yikes. What kind of porn are you watching?"

"The respectable-lady kind."

"Liar."

Georgie gave an exaggerated toss of her hair. "No, I don't recognize the wood. Where did you get it?"

Travis took a step in her direction, very aware of the fact that they hadn't touched enough for his liking. Distracted by exactly how much he needed their skin pressed together, he didn't guard his words. "I've been thinking about you constantly."

"Thank you," she whispered, swaying to the right. "I've been thinking about you, too."

He caught Georgie, keeping her upright. "Remember those summers you spent in that tree in your parents' backyard? You sat up there, legs dangling, reading those books . . . What books were they?"

"Those were *Seventeen* magazines I stole from Bethany and hid inside books. I took the personality quizzes over and over until I got the answer I wanted."

Caught by surprise, he laughed. "You wouldn't come down out of the tree until Vivian threatened to give your dinner to the dog."

A line formed between Georgie's brows, her gaze moving to the mantel he'd been sanding. "Travis Ford." She pressed a hand between her breasts. "What did you do?"

"Convincing Vivian to let me saw down the branch took

some effort, but I pointed out she has about fifteen trees in the backyard, so she caved."

Georgie's face landed smack between his sweaty pecs, her arms motionless at her sides. "Oh no. I hate crying." Her exhale coasted down his belly. "Oh God, it's coming. I can't stop it."

Relief settled over Travis and he pulled her close, because if she didn't care about his manual labor smell, neither did he. "You love it?"

"I love it. I worship it. Thank you."

The moisture of her tears slipped down his skin and time seemed to slow down. So slow, he could hear every tick of his pulse, could count every thread of hair on her crown. "You forgive me for missing the appointment?"

Her words were muffled. "I already forgave you."

"Yeah, but you really mean it now. It's not grudging."

"You make it sound like I was sulking."

He tried to stop himself from kissing her forehead. It was too intimate a gesture, and he was very aware of the lack of cameras present. It was just the two of them. But he didn't stand a chance against his impulses when she looked so soft. His lips pressed to the spot below her hairline and lingered, his arms gathering her closer. "You were pouting a little."

Georgie poked him in the ribs. "You're just trying to make me stop crying."

"Guilty."

Travis tilted Georgie's head back and brought their mouths together, licking away the salt from her lips. Stealing it off her tongue. Jesus, he couldn't close his eyes, because her happily tearstained expression was too invigorating. He'd done that? They stood for long minutes in the dimming backyard, wood debris at their feet, Georgie letting him master her with the kind of kissing he'd never participated in before. He kissed her like he was . . . taking care of her. Soothing her. Letting her know he'd stand guard while she wept. And the responsibility made him feel like more of a man than he ever had in his life.

His cock stiffened like a son of a bitch, but when he would have jerked her hips close in the name of friction, Travis let himself ache. Let his flesh beg and fill out his jeans, while he focused on the girl in front of him. The girl offering her mouth in a way that made him feel . . . worthy.

He was almost too dizzy on the sensation to realize Georgie had pulled back. "Travis?" Her thumbs traced his jawline. "What were you thinking about when I came home?"

Telling Georgie about the monsters that lurked in the deepest corners of his mind didn't scare him. Not anymore. But he didn't want her sympathy tonight. Tonight was about her. So he kissed her soft mouth again, taking the contact deeper until she gasped into his mouth. "I'm going to take a shower, all right?" He ran his fingers along the curve of her shoulder, pressing a thumb to the side of her neck and massaging. "I'm going to feed you before I introduce you to God."

CHAPTER TWENTY

What was the deal with panties?

A girl buys a grip of freaking underwear, and within a week, half the silky little mofos have been abducted by aliens or sucked up into some washing machine purgatory.

Where did they all go?

Georgie rifled through her sock drawer, hoping a pair of her overly expensive panties had gone rogue, but no dice. They were all in the bottom of her laundry basket, where they definitely weren't going to help her get laid.

You don't need help getting laid. It's a done deal.

"Right."

Still, though. Instead of wearing them all immediately, she could have saved them for special occasions. There had been no need to clean her house in an organza thong, although she *had* felt pretty fancy while scrubbing the toilet. Georgie took a deep breath through her nose and headed for the closet, trying not to peer through the crack in her en suite bathroom door. Travis was naked on the other side, rubbing her soap up and down his disgustingly hot body, getting ready to sex her up. No big deal, right?

She opened the closet door and scanned the contents. A dress would be trying too hard for a night on the couch. Jeans would be too hard to get off—and since she didn't have any panties to wear, they'd rub her the wrong way. Literally. In her Netflix and chill fantasies, she'd been cool and casual in an oversized, off-the-shoulder sweater and leggings. Easy and effortless. She didn't own anything like that. Dammit, Boutique Tracy.

The shower spray cut off.

Georgie snapped an oversized T-shirt off a hanger in a panic—maneuvering her boobs to maximum boobiness within the confines of her lace bra—and dropped the shirt over her head. Perfect, right? Her shoulder peeked out. Just like in her fever dreams . . .

Hurricanes. It was the Hurricanes jersey with Travis's name and number on the back. Oh no. No, wearing his clothing would be way too on the nose. If he saw the loving care she'd put into ironing and hanging the jersey up in her closet, he'd probably deduce she'd spent her teens and early twenties infatuated with him, which absolutely could not happen. She could see his face now—just sheer horror, his eyes scoping for the nearest exit. She'd never be able to look him in the face again, let alone be his casual, just-for-now hookup.

Who was she kidding? This relationship was the furthest thing from casual. For her. Travis returning her new, decidedly adult feelings was one giant, unrealistic hope that needed to be squashed early. He couldn't be making it any more difficult to heed that warning. Fashioning her fireplace out of her favorite childhood tree. Kissing her with so much . . . passion. Yeah, passion. It was a real thing, turned out. Her intention had been to show Travis he was worth a commitment. That he was worthy, period. How far was she willing to go, when every second together deepened the love she'd always felt?

Georgie almost had the shirt off when the floor creaked just beyond the bathroom door. She yanked the blue cotton back down, her heart flying to her throat. Caught. She was totally caught. This would go down as the moment Travis ran for the hills.

The door opened.

Georgie spun around. "So. Funny story . . ."

Steam billowed out around Travis and his wet head. Wet, curling chest hair. Just wet. In all the places. The towel around his waist was so low, she could almost see where the happy trail led. The happy forest, that's where. An amused smile transformed his face as he walked out of the steam. "Is that my jersey?"

Georgie shook herself. "I, um . . . only bought it because they didn't have Nunez."

He stopped in front of Georgie, lifting her chin with his index finger. Because she'd definitely been laser focused on the dick print tunneling to one side on the front of his towel. "Liar." His fingers traced down to her shoulder, running along the seam of the shirt. "You wear it often?"

"No," she said too quickly.

A line formed between Travis's brows. Something she couldn't name passed behind his eyes, like an awareness.

Or guilt? But that couldn't be right. "I like seeing you in it." He leaned down and engaged her mouth in a slow, erotic kiss that went straight to her toes, pinging every erogenous zone on the way down. "Just not tonight."

His head dipped for another kiss, dark intent making his irises seem black. Their mouths met and his hands found the hem of her—his?—their shirt, yanking it up—

The doorbell rang.

Travis's forehead fell to hers, his humorless laugh pelting her mouth with heat. "Jesus Christ. This is karma, isn't it? She's out to get me."

She waded through the lust clouding her brain. "Who is that?"

He turned his head to check her bedside table clock. "That's the dinner I ordered, in all my infinite wisdom."

"Lo mein?"

Travis laughed and pulled her close, turning them ninety degrees and guiding her from the bedroom, kissing Georgie as he walked her backward, their steps matching. "If I don't fuck you soon, Georgie, I'm going to need a straitjacket."

Heat stained her cheeks. "I prefer you in a towel."

"Yeah, I kind of noticed, you pervert."

They reached the front door and Travis pinned her up against it, fully ignoring the deliveryman outlined in the glass. He kissed her hard, angling his hips against hers, making her gasp at what she felt there.

"Talk. We have to talk. This is a good thing." His thumb found her bottom lip, tracing it, before sliding into her mouth. "Food first," he rasped. "Man, I hate food right now."

The doorbell rang again. "You can't answer the door like that," Georgie whispered.

One of Travis's eyebrows went up. "I ordered chicken parm from Marciano's."

Her pulse stuttered. "How did you know my favorite?"

He shrugged. "Vivian might have mentioned it."

No, he'd asked. She could tell by the way he tried to play it off. Oh, she was in deep trouble if this was Travis's version of casual. "Why haven't you opened the door yet?"

Travis kissed her forehead with smiling lips and reached past her to open the door, using it to block the man's view of her. Georgie couldn't resist turning to watch through the glass, though, as the deliveryman gaped at the former major league baseball player in a girl-sized towel.

"Uh. Delivery for Ford." He shifted, clearing his throat. "Travis Ford, right? I thought you lived in that three-family on Caroline Avenue."

"I do." Travis took the bag and handed it to Georgie with a wink. "This is my . . . girlfriend's house."

Knowing he'd called her the title for show didn't stop Georgie from almost levitating.

"Right. Girlfriend." The guy laughed as if they were in on a joke, but he sobered when Travis stared at him in stony silence. "Listen, I've been kind of hoping you would call for a delivery at some point. I play for the high school, and we would freaking die if you came to run a fall clinic or something. Maybe just pass on some of your tricks, you know?"

"Not this time around." Travis's smile was tight, and

Georgie could tell he didn't enjoy letting the kid down. "Maybe when my work schedule loosens up."

Even though Georgie couldn't see the delivery boy's face clearly, his disappointment was palpable. "Yeah. Hey—do you think I could get a picture?"

"I'm in a towel, kid."

"Yeah, no one is going to believe this."

Georgie was laughing into her wrist when Travis gave her a thoughtful look. "Sure, take your picture." The kid turned around and held up his phone for a selfie. Travis held up his right biceps and flexed. "Make sure you get the address in the picture."

"Sure, Mr. Ford."

A moment later, Travis closed the door. Obviously deciding to ignore the suspicious look on Georgie's face, he stooped down and threw her over his shoulder. "What?"

"What?" Georgie fumbled to keep the sacred chicken parm upright. "I thought we were supposed to be courting the family-friendly crowd. There's nothing family friendly about your . . ."

"My what?"

Georgie felt her face heat. "The towel hides nothing."

Her world righted itself as Travis set her down on the cool counter, stepping between her legs with a wicked smile. "Are we talking about my dick?"

"The one and only." God, he was so *close* with that flirting smile and he smelled like her soap. Was this man really in her kitchen, planning to feed her and deflower her? All on the same night? "I—I mean, you can't exactly hide it."

"Nah." He tucked his tongue into his cheek. "It doesn't hide well."

Oh, mama. "Right. But, I guess, as long as the network thinks I'm the only one seeing it, you're fine."

A shadow crossed his eyes. "That's right."

Georgie wished she hadn't just reminded him their relationship was based on reaching a goal. Wanting to bring them back to the comfortable place they'd been, she lifted her hands to settle them on his chest, but got cold feet and left them suspended.

"What's that?" Travis frowned at her hands. "You seem hesitant to touch me. Like you're not sure I want it."

I've been dreaming about touching you for so long, having the opportunity seems surreal. "No, I—"

"That hug you gave me yesterday in your parents' living room?" His palms skimmed up her thighs, setting off a low tug in her belly. "I've been jerking off thinking about it. Jerking off to a hug, Georgie. Your hands need to report for duty."

She slowly settled her palms on his pecs, her fingertips sifting through now-dry hair. "Yes, Travis."

A ripple moved down his muscled chest and stomach. "Keep them there." Giving her a dark look, he reached to the side and opened the takeout bag, removing the contents with jerky movements. She heard the clacking of plastic forks and knives, but couldn't look away from Travis's flexing triceps long enough to deduce what he was doing. Until he held a bite of saucy, cheesy chicken to her mouth. "Eat. I'm at the end of my rope."

Georgie accepted the bite, humming as she swallowed. "I have to tell you something."

"Yeah?"

"I signed a lease on an office today." His movements stilled, pride lighting up his eyes. It was breathtaking. She wanted to cuddle that reaction to her breasts and never let it go. It made her want to have the same pride in him. To give it back.

"Damn. Congratulations, baby girl."

She wrestled with a smile. "The realtor was really put together and had that whole air-of-indifference thing happening, you know? When I was trying to get the courage to tell her I wanted the space, I thought of you standing up for me at dinner."

He searched her face. "You did?"

"Yeah. It gave me a push." She surrendered to the impulse to throw her arms around Travis's neck, wincing when a bite of chicken got squashed between them. But when she tried to pull back, Travis dropped the plastic fork and wrapped his arms around her. "So I'm returning the favor now," she whispered. "Just a quick reminder that you're more than just baseball. It can still be something you love. Something you play and enjoy. And then you can return to you. You're enough without it."

His breath gusted into her neck. "Am I?"

"You bought my favorite dinner and turned my climbing tree into a fireplace." She stroked her fingers over the hair curling at his neck. "You're batting a thousand in the gestures department, Ford."

Travis lifted his head, his serious expression slowly turning to amusement. "Was that an intentional baseball reference?"

"I was trying to stay on theme."

Georgie squealed when Travis dragged her off the counter, urging her thighs around his hips. Her neck lost power and his tongue immediately took advantage, finding and exploiting her sensitive skin. Carrying her into the living room, Travis's lips curved in her hair. "We're just about done being fucking cute for tonight, Georgie, so I hope you got it out of your system."

"Are we?"

"Yes." His eyes turned serious as he lowered her onto the couch, his mouth hovering a mere inch above hers. "We are."

She couldn't squeeze her legs together with Travis's hips in the way, but God she needed to. Needed to put pressure on the ache he'd tempted to life. The charming man with vulnerabilities to spare was fading out, leaving a famished, sexual being in his place, licking his lips and looking at her top to bottom. "What are we going to be instead?"

"Bad." He produced the condom he'd tucked into the waistband of his towel, then snapped it off, dropping the white terry cloth beside the couch. "Really bad, baby girl."

CHAPTER TWENTY-ONE

As Travis flattened Georgie underneath him on the couch, the weight of hundreds of one-night stands pressed down on his back, catching him off guard. They dropped in to haunt him because nothing—*no one*—had ever felt like her. And with the taste of her mouth turning him into a hungering animal, he wondered what inferior high he'd been chasing when this one was out there.

Jesus, his fucking hands were shaking. Yeah, obviously he was horny as all get-out, considering he'd been lusting after Georgie since . . . when? Had it really only been a matter of weeks? The timing seemed impossible when his body corresponded to her shape like a fist pressing into clay. Just, *Ahh. I'm here. I made it. I don't want to come up for air.*

Or it might feel that comfortable if his cock wasn't swearing like a sailor at him, demanding to know why he kept almost fucking Georgie, then stopping. *This isn't like us, man!* it seemed to shout inside Travis's mind, growing fuller and aching harder by the second. Especially when he settled that suffering bulk on her pussy and let his hips sink down, catching her shaky gasp with his mouth as a reward.

His dick was right. He wasn't used to waiting. But thank God he had. If he'd gobbled her up in one bite, he'd have missed this chance to savor—something he'd never given a shit about before. Now? His senses seemed to wake up and beg. For the clean smell of her skin, the tentative brushes of her tongue, her fingertips skating up his sides. Their breaths were loud in the quiet room, along with the sounds of their bodies shifting on soft leather, the couch springs sighing.

"Netflix," he rasped, breaking the kiss, then immediately diving at her neck for a taste. "We were supposed to, uh . . . *Cold Mountain*?"

"No." She writhed beneath him, the insides of her knees smoothing along his hips. "Just, um . . . definitely forget the movie."

He rocked against her pussy, making them both groan. "I want to do this right, Georgie. Exactly how you wanted it to be."

"If this went according to the plan, I would be wearing a slinky off-the-shoulder number and serving a signature cocktail, so . . . out with the bathwater, okay?"

Only this human being could make him laugh when his balls were on the verge of mutiny. One second, laughter kindled in his throat, and the next, it was tight. Just tight. Because flushed and looking up at him with her bright green eyes, Georgette Castle was the most beautiful thing on the planet. He wanted to give her pleasure. Wanted to protect her. And fuck the consequences, he wanted to turn himself into her addiction. Next time he walked through the front door of this house, she wouldn't be able to keep her hands off him. Or her sexy mouth. No more hesitations.

"Slinky off-the-shoulder number, huh?" Travis murmured, going in for a kiss, but detouring down the center of her body, before they could connect. While sliding lower on the couch, he dragged his open mouth down the front of her T-shirt and drew up the hem. "Maybe next time. Right now, I want you bare."

Georgie's stomach shuddered under his regard. "Oh, I'm pretty close to—"

"Where are your panties?" The last word of Travis's question came out as a growl, thanks to the smooth, delicious-looking pussy now level with his mouth. When he'd had his hips wedged between Georgie's thighs, there'd been a layer of T-shirt between them, so he didn't know she'd been going commando. No getting past it now, though. Or the distinct shade of pink along the center crease—a crease his tongue wanted to slide apart in a long lick. "Forget I asked. You should never keep this covered when it's just you and me. Ask me why."

She gave an audible swallow. "Why?"

Travis lowered his mouth, planting a firm kiss on the split of her sex. "Because if I'm not licking it, I'm going to be figuring out a way to spread your thighs so I can." He used his fingers to separate her flesh, then greeted what he'd uncovered, rubbing her with the flat of his tongue. Goddamn, so sweet. So fucking sweet. "The wet tells me that's exactly what you want, Georgie."

"Please." She seemed almost embarrassed by the lift of her hips, as if she wanted to play it cool but her body wouldn't allow it. "Please."

"I like the word 'please.'" He twisted his middle finger into her opening, his head dropping forward with a curse at the reminder she was so damn tight. "'More.' 'Harder.' 'Faster.' 'Deeper.' Those work, too."

Georgie's eyes rolled back in her head, her thighs falling open a couple inches. So trusting for a virgin. Because she trusted him?

Yeah, he thought so. Needed it more than was wise.

Travis eased his middle finger in and out of Georgie's opening, watching his handiwork up close. The way her inner thighs trembled, her belly hollowing. The way her clit became more prominent, as if requesting his tongue. Tempting it. Starved for the full experience of her scent, her texture, her taste, Travis had no choice but to bring his mouth lower, tucking a tongue alongside his finger in her entrance, listening to her breathing go shallow, before drawing it back out. Sliding it higher. With his finger driving in and out—faster now—preparing her, the sexy sounds of her growing slickness making his mouth work harder, his tongue curling around her clit. Absorbing her shiver.

"Travis."

"Tell me if you're going to—"

"How do I know? This isn't h-how it feels when I . . ."

He pushed his finger deep and jiggled it against her G-spot, giving a pained smile when she cried out, her hips jerking on the couch. "You'll know."

Georgie's back arched. "Oh . . . I think?" Her fingernails clawed at his shoulders. "Maybe now. Yeah. Now."

Beating back the reluctance, Travis took his tongue away and found the condom he'd left beside the couch. He quickly covered himself in stretched latex and prowled up her body, quieting her requests to hurry with a hard kiss. "Next time, I'll let you come all over my mouth, baby girl," he said, words muffled by her lips. "I'll lick it up like ice cream. But this first time you're going to go off while I'm sunk so deep in that pussy it never forgets who broke it in."

He didn't mean to give such a vicious first thrust, but there was no help for it. No option to go slow when his dominant position above Georgie turned her flushed and panting. A corresponding part of Travis recognized what she wanted—needed—and his body gave it in no uncertain terms. That first drive of his cock drew a scream from her throat, but it wasn't made up entirely of pain. It was relief. He could actually *feel* her relief at being filled. Knowing Georgie had lived with an unfilled need made him wild to fill it. To blow those expectations out of the water.

"Again," she whispered into his shoulder, her eyes unfocused. "Don't stop."

Travis reared back and bucked, the possessive streak she'd brought to his life buzzing and snapping to run free. "Look at me while I'm teaching you how to fuck."

"Yes," she sobbed, shifting underneath him, making him grind his teeth. "Please."

I want to own her. Make her say his name in that breathless way until he heard it in his sleep. It was an urge that rippled through Travis's muscles, rife with hunger so thick he couldn't saw through it. He'd just taken her virginity, and the responsibility of that made him want more. *More.* She felt better than anything he could ever imagine on his own. Hot and tight and needy, but her eyes looked up at him . . . and knew him. Nothing better in the fucking world. God, there was nothing that compared.

When Georgie made a choked sound, Travis realized his hips were bearing down hard, circling, grinding into her pussy. Making his mark. Her eyes left his, ticking down to where their bodies joined, and she bit her lip, some of the fever clearing from her expression. Here was proof that Georgie had gotten under his skin—into his head—because he could sense her thoughts changing direction.

"Hey." He dropped forward and captured her mouth in a seeking kiss. "Talk."

She shook her head, her words emerging choppy. "No, it feels so good . . ."

Another kiss. Another longer one with tongue. "And?"

Travis reversed the circle of his hips and a shudder passed through her. "I guess . . . I'm worried about whether it's feeling this good for you, too."

This girl who'd shown up and shouted him back into existence, brought him leftovers and bravely poked his sore spots? He had her number. She was a giver in all things. Right now, he had to convince her to *take. He* needed to be the giver. For her. Just . . . her. "I've never had my head in this before, Georgie. I'm usually a million miles away." Heart rapping against his ribs, he skated his open lips over her temple. "I'm right here. I can feel every fucking squeeze of your pussy and breath out of your mouth. Feels so good, I'm already trying to figure out how to get back inside you again. You're worried it doesn't feel good? I'm trying not to bust too early like a chump."

If eyes could actually take the shape of hearts, Georgie's probably would have in that moment. Her palms cupped his face and he leaned into her, letting her sigh wash over his face. "Really?"

"Yes. Christ, the things I'm going to do to you . . ." He pressed his face into the crook of her neck and pumped his hips harder, groaning over the perfect give of soft, wet flesh between Georgie's thighs. "No more worrying about me. When I do something you love, tell me."

Her fingernails grazed his back lightly on the way down to his ass, which she gripped hesitantly, then with more confidence. "I love when you teach me."

Travis held his breath as heat threatened to erupt from his balls. Fuck. Fuck. He hadn't beat off enough thinking about Georgie lately to last even a good half hour? *Fight it back. Make it perfect for her.* "You're not hurting?"

One breath against his neck. Two. "I don't mind it. I think I . . . like it."

Travis's hips were rolling harder and harder of their own volition at this point, his hunger strengthening with every smack of flesh, every whimper from Georgie. Jesus, she was sweet between the legs, so snug and hot. He'd never wanted this bad. Never felt wanted this much. A tightening started at the back of his neck and continued down his spine, curling at the base. *Get her there.* "You want me to teach you how to get off with my cock?"

Her eyelids fluttered, the muscles of her pussy contracting. "Yes."

He nipped at her mouth. "Use your fingers. Go find that little clit I licked so right." Breath coming faster, Georgie did as he asked, fingers wedging in between their hips, farther and farther until she gasped. "Good girl. Use your fingers to keep it from hiding. We want my cock to rub it all over, don't we?"

Georgie's nod was vigorous, her legs restless on either side of his body. "Yes, please. Rubbing."

Travis slid his forearm beneath Georgie's neck to anchor himself, loosely locking their lips together. "Tell me when I'm hitting it good, baby girl," he rasped, flicking their tongues together. "You want to learn, you open your thighs and let your man grind. Let me swell that pretty clit up good."

Using her fingers for guidance, Travis rode up the slippery pathway of Georgie's pussy, putting easy pressure on her clit, twisting his hips—then starting again. The first few times he performed the movement, Georgie's eyes went blind, the breath seizing in her throat, but it came out in a sobbing rush now, urging Travis to go faster, twist harder, his every movement bringing the base of his cock into hot, damp, desperate contact with her clit.

"Fuck, Georgie," he growled. "Open your thighs for more. You're getting more."

Georgie's back arched, her right knee extended out from the couch, giving him extra room to bear down, to angle his hips, and they descended into what felt like madness. Georgie whined and lifted her hips to meet his drives, her inner walls beginning a slow, tight milking of his cock. Travis almost couldn't even look at her, worried the unchained sexuality breaking free beneath him might ruin everything, might make him come before her. In the end, though, keeping his eyes off her, keeping his skin off her, proved impossible. He was coming. Soon. Now. It was happening.

Finesse went out the window and Travis fell on Georgie, grunting, sucking in shuddering gulps of oxygen, pushing her thighs open as he thrust, thrust, thrust, listening to her cries of his name, treasuring the husky awe of them in his ears. All around him.

Their mouths met and gorged, Georgie's hands slapping down on his ass to yank him deeper, urge him faster, and he didn't have to think, didn't have any option but to dip his head. Drop his panting mouth over her bouncing tits. Suction his mouth around her right nipple with a groan as come blazed a path up his throbbing dick, filling Georgie up as he continued to pump like a fiend.

"Shit. Too soon. *No,* no . . . baby—"

Her body went still, before quaking violently underneath him in climax—*thank God*—her pussy squeezing so tight, he shouted his victory into the crook of her neck, yanking her legs up and fucking into the storm for everything he was worth. His insides were razed, mind blown, but every cell in his body continued to gravitate toward Georgie until they were wrapped together on the couch, arms and legs entwined, mouths mashed together, hips slowing little by little.

Oh my God. Best everything of his life. Nothing came close.

But his chest ached. Hard. His mouth was dry, hands coasting and memorizing her skin. After sex came relief, right? What the hell was wrong with him?

When sex was over, it usually—always—meant parting ways after the sweat cooled. He'd never been anything but fine with that outcome, because he barely knew the women to begin with. Panic niggled at him now, though, refusing to give up. If Georgie tried to leave or make him leave right now, he wouldn't like it at all. No, he would hate it.

She wouldn't leave him, would she?

"Whoa," she whispered at his ear, her fingers threading through his hair. "Porn sucks."

His fear eased, a smile beckoning at the corners of his mouth. There was some insecurity in Georgie's expression, probably thanks to his silent panic attack. So he framed her beautiful face in his hands and kissed it right off her mouth. "Nah. We're just that good." He dropped his forehead to hers. "How do you feel?"

Her catlike yawn made his throat hurt. "Like that." She smiled, somewhat shyly. "But I also feel spoiled because that was better than . . . wow. Than I ever expected. And smug because you look spoiled, too. Are . . . you? You know, spoiled?"

"I can barely feel my fucking legs."

The smile bloomed, spreading to her cheeks, eyes. Gorgeous. "We brought it."

Could she hear his heart hammering? "Damn right we

did," he managed through the notch in his throat. "Come on, let's get you to bed."

"Me?" She pursed her lips. "You're visibly worn out."

Travis stood with a groan and scooped Georgie into his arms. "One time and you're already cocky, huh?"

She laid her head on his shoulder. "The student has become the teacher."

"We'll see about that." He yawned and pretended to stagger. "Tomorrow."

They laughed quietly, their mouths meeting for a thorough kiss. When he pulled back, she was watching him through her eyelashes. "Are you staying?"

Tension crept into his shoulders, but he didn't know where it stemmed from anymore. The worry that she might get the wrong idea and expect a commitment? Or worry that commitment didn't seem like such a ridiculous notion when it meant getting to carry this girl to bed regularly? "For a while."

Travis carried Georgie into her bedroom and lay down beside her, their bodies molding front to back like spoons, grounding him in the moment. His jumbled thoughts were almost forgotten in the warmth of her skin, the evenness of her breathing.

He wasn't keeping her. He couldn't. But what if he'd been wrong and this girl who owned his jersey and trusted him . . . did harbor real, lasting feelings for him? Then he was fooling himself that she wouldn't get hurt. He was a selfish bastard, plain and simple.

I need to tell her what Stephen told me. Give her a chance to confess or tell him her brother was wrong. Which one did Travis want to hear most? It didn't matter. He owed her full honesty, even if it meant their whole arrangement came crumbling to the ground. But as she turned in his arms and wedged her head beneath his chin, the words wouldn't come.

CHAPTER TWENTY-TWO

Travis had spent the night. In her house. In her bed.

Probably, definitely by accident, but the fact remained. He'd lost consciousness with his arms wrapped around her and he was *still there.* They might not have eaten much of the chicken parm, but it was a heavy meal. That had to be the explanation for him passing out curved around her so protectively. So big and beautiful and male . . .

A sigh slipped out of Georgie's mouth, but she gobbled it back up. She was not going to lose sight of reality here. As far as Travis knew, she was nothing more than a consenting adult engaging in a temporary sexual relationship with someone of equal mind. No sticky feelings or thoughts of white picket fences to be found. She'd been so confident in her ability to remain realistic. To know this situation was going to run its course. But she hadn't counted on him rising to the occasion quite so fast. And spectacularly.

Georgie closed her mouth tight around the toothbrush, trying to keep the scrubbing noise from waking him up. Damn, the man could sleep. He was facedown, legs and arms sprawled in four directions, his taut, naked ass a sight for sore eyes among the sheets.

This view. She could charge admission.

There was a fuzzy koala doing somersaults in her stomach, tickling her ribs and pressing down on her unmentionable parts. Although Travis had surely made mention of them last night on the couch. So many times. Each time better than the last. Who knew she was such a sucker for a filthy mouth?

Who knew you were such a sucker, period?

She was beginning to feel like she'd set herself up for one epic fall. What if she succeeded in making him believe he was worthy of a healthy relationship . . . and he went and found a different one? With someone else who wanted a future filled with fewer rug rats? After all, he *had* been the one to insist their fake-dating plan remain in motion even while they slept together. After being with her like this, could he really foresee ending it so easily?

What would she do then?

Unable to shake the encroaching gloom, Georgie dipped back into the bathroom to rinse out her mouth, stowing her toothbrush in the medicine cabinet. She'd already laid out a packaged spare on the sink for Travis when he finally woke up. Hopefully that wouldn't freak him out, having his own toothbrush. Maybe she should put it away and suggest he brush with his finger. That's what a cool, casual chick would do, right? Not present her Costco contraband after night one.

There was a low groan from the bedroom, followed by

the creaking of bedsprings. Georgie's sex clenched, causing a twinge of minor soreness. She'd expected her first time to be more painful—especially after seeing Travis's erect penis. But she'd been so worked up and . . . damp . . . there had only been urgency. To be pushed down and filled. To please. To get pleasure herself. Mission accomplished.

Georgie turned to fix her ponytail in the mirror and found her face bright red. She fanned her cheeks, commanding herself not to be awkward. So he spent the night. Didn't change anything.

There was a knock on the bathroom door. "Georgie?"

Her nipples turned to points at Travis's gruff, post-sleep rasp. "Yeah?"

Travis's pitch dropped. "You mind getting back in bed?"

Oh wow. She'd been worried he'd wake up like a cornered male, realizing he'd spent the night. Turned out, she'd been way off. With a calming breath, she toed open the bathroom door, coming face-to-face with a fully nude male marvel. "Good morning." Nerves jangling in her limbs, she busied her fingers stuffing a stray hair into her ponytail. "I would ask how it's hanging, but I can see for myself."

Completely unconcerned about the erection jostling around between them, he backed her into the bathroom. "Why are you dressed?"

As she reached the sink, she remembered the packaged toothbrush and oh-so-casually shoved it into the wastebasket. "I promised myself I would start training for the Tough Mudder today. I don't want to disgrace the family name."

Without missing a beat, Travis leaned past her and took

the toothbrush out of the trash. He popped it open, sliding the red object into his hands, tossing it from one to the other. "I've got sneakers in my truck. Give me a few minutes. I'll come with you."

"Sure, sure."

Travis applied toothpaste to the brush, ran it under the water, and stuck it in his mouth. "You're doing that thing again where you don't touch me. Which is funnier than usual seeing as how we spent the whole night plastered together."

"Did we?"

"Yeah." He scrubbed his teeth and spat. Like a damn baseball player. "Is that why you're acting weird? Because I forgot to leave?"

"Am I acting weird?"

He gave her a look of pure male exasperation. "You've got until I finish brushing my teeth to stop freaking out on me. Otherwise . . ." Dramatic pause. "We're going down to tickle town."

A tingle of alarm ran down her spine. "You wouldn't."

"I would." *Brush, brush.* "Bottoms of the feet, right?"

"We're adults now." Trying to be inconspicuous, she sidestepped toward the bathroom door. "You can't use a weakness against me you learned when I was a child. That's unethical."

He rinsed and spit, nestling his toothbrush alongside hers in the cabinet. *Thunk-thunk-thunk* went her heart, waiting for him to respond. "I gave my best friend's sister her first time on the couch last night. Didn't go easy on her, either." His attention dropped to the apex of her thighs, his jaw flexing. "Trust me, I didn't think of ethics once."

"Good," she said in a shaky whisper. "I'm more than the youngest Castle sibling."

"You're telling me."

Oh God. Her knees wanted to collapse. "All of this is irrelevant, because I'm not freaking out anymore. No need for tickling."

He sauntered toward her like a rangy-hipped cowboy. With a chub. "Why did you throw the toothbrush away?"

Her laughter was hysterical. "I think the court will agree that was an accident."

Travis stopped and crossed his arms. His big, buff arms with shadowed cuts and mouthwatering valleys. Boy, this bathroom had seriously great lighting. "You still haven't touched me. I'm starting to get annoyed."

"You can be aroused and annoyed at the same time?" She shifted on the balls of her feet, preparing to run. "There's one for the résumé, right?"

Her words were still hanging in the air when Travis lunged and threw her over his shoulder. Disoriented, she somehow managed to deduce where they were going—the bed—and she yelped on the way down, landing on her back. "Don't do it!"

"You had your chance." Travis shook his head, planting a hand on her chest and easily holding her down while he pried off a running shoe. "I didn't want to visit tickle town, but you left me no choice."

"Stop calling it that." Georgie half laughed, half squealed, attempting and failing to twist onto her belly. "Oh my God. A naked man is tickling me by force. I never want to hear clowns are scary again."

She peeked up to find his fingers poised above the arch of her right foot. "This hurts me more than it hurts you."

"Travis, *please*."

The gorgeous jerk had the nerve to wink. "There's that word I love so much again."

Her skin was on high alert, waiting for the dreaded sensation. "The anticipation is the worst part," she wailed. "Just do it or don't."

"There's only one escape."

Hope caused her to jackknife, but Travis pushed her back down. "What is it?"

"I want a proper good morning from you, and I'm not even sure what one looks like. Just know I wanted you lying there when I opened my eyes." His mouth was in a smirk, but his eyes were deadly serious. Dark. Her thighs turned watery in response. "I want your hands all over me. Your mouth on mine. And next time you get out of bed without giving me both, I'm going to find you, pull your pants down, and backhand that little tush you had tucked up in my lap all night. We clear?"

Georgie's pulse thundered in her ears, her intimate muscles searching for their counterpart, wanting to clamp down. Wanting friction. "Yes."

Travis watched her from under hooded lids for another second, then freed her foot. He sunk back on the bed in a kneeling position and waited while Georgie scrambled up. Intuition told her a single hesitation would earn her a one-way ticket onto her back again, so she didn't wait. She climbed him. She locked her thighs around Travis's waist and ran her palms up his shoulders, stopping when they were framing his face. And they fell into a groaning kiss, his hard flesh lifting and prodding the seam of her yoga pants. His hands slipped beneath her shirt, gripping her waist on each side, calling attention to their size difference.

Mint and male assaulted her senses, sending a rush of moisture between her legs. She scooted closer on Travis's lap and he broke the kiss to watch her—intently—as she writhed on his erection. As she moved, he gripped the nape of her neck and looked down, watching her. Watching their lower bodies slide and grind together.

"I say we skip the run," she gasped, as Travis captured her earlobe with his teeth.

"We're going." He slid his hand down to her ass and squeezed, thrusting his hips up into her at the same time. "Now you've got an incentive."

Denial seeped in. "But—"

Travis cut her off with a drugging kiss, but it was mixed with something else. Yes, there was lust, but she knew this man. And she was starting to think she'd hurt his feelings. Or made him worry. "I'm not used to waking up with other people, either, Georgie."

"I know."

He searched her eyes. "If it's too much, I won't do it next time."

In that moment, she couldn't think of anything but banishing the insecurities she'd caused. "Don't tell my siblings or I'll kill you, but . . . I always check under my bed for serial killers before I turn out the light and go to sleep. It didn't even occur to me to check for the ghost of Ted Bundy last night." She tilted her head. "I didn't worry about a thing with you snoring in my face."

A laugh boomed out of him. "Way to tarnish the moment." He studied her. "You really felt safer with me here?"

"Safe as houses."

He looked satisfied as he brushed her bangs back. "I like knowing that."

Georgie's heart was in her eyes. She could feel it. How much she showed him in that moment. Ten years of nursing an all-consuming crush she'd assumed was love, when she'd had no idea that this was what love felt like. This. This was it. So heavy at times it couldn't be lifted, so light at others it made you capable of floating. *Protect yourself,* a voice whispered in the back of her head. *He doesn't love you back. Then or now.* With a tight smile, Georgie was off his lap. She hit the ground running, her voice unnatural when she called over her shoulder. "We leave in five minutes. Think you can keep up?"

The route she took on their run brought them past the high school. Honestly, Georgie didn't plan it. But after that, it seemed only natural to cross over through the baseball field. Since the season wouldn't start for months, the expansive green sat deserted beneath a cloudy gray morning sky, automatic sprinklers ticking and spraying in the distance. Without looking at Travis, she could feel the tension creeping into his frame—his reluctance to go toward the diamond.

He'd started talking to her more about baseball, especially since he'd started gunning for the commentating job with the Bombers. But the idea of actively playing the sport again seemed to make him uncomfortable. As if he wouldn't allow himself full enjoyment of baseball unless he could be the best at it. Sadness settled over her. Made loss spread in her belly. She could blink and see him in his starched gray Port Jefferson uniform, standing at home plate and tapping the metal bat off his cleats. Trash-talking the catcher. Absorbing love and excitement from the crowd—especially her. He'd so obviously been the best, no one ever questioned his superiority. They celebrated it. Add to that the fact that Travis Ford practically glowed while holding a bat, and Georgie couldn't help but miss watching him play. The sport was a part of him.

Jogging beside him through the outfield and remembering the deafening cheers from the crowd, Georgie's gut told her not to stop pushing him. It could be something he loved, even if he couldn't make millions of dollars playing. More importantly, like she'd told him last night, he didn't have to be the best baseball player to be the best Travis.

With these thoughts dancing in Georgie's head, it couldn't have been a coincidence that the gray light happened to glint off a bat that someone must have left propped against the dugout. No. Coincidences that perfect didn't exist.

She veered right, praying she was doing the right thing.

"Where are you . . ." Travis stopped following her around second base. "Georgie."

She didn't let his warning tone deter her. "I'm just going to grab this bat. I'll drop it off at the lost and found later."

"Someone will probably be back to look for it before then." God, he looked so uncomfortable, rolling his shoulders in that stressed-out manner he broke out only when truly out of his comfort zone. "You should leave it."

Georgie hummed. "Okay." She started to return the bat to its original position, but swung it up onto her shoulder instead, bending her knees in a pitiful stance. "Too bad we don't have a ball."

"You don't have a hope in hell of hitting a ball standing like that." He made an absent gesture that wasn't really absent. His eyes were zoned in on her. "Choke up, Georgie. If you swing like that, you're going to knock yourself out."

"This is how Stephen taught me," she returned with a frown.

"Stephen was always better at hockey." Travis took a few steps into the diamond and sighed. "Bend your knees, weight on the back leg."

She locked her knees and leaned forward.

Travis groaned up at the sky. "You're killing me, baby girl."

When he stomped toward her, crossing over the pitcher's mound and looking like the cover of *Sports Illustrated*, Georgie took a bracing breath. But she could do nothing to stop the flood of excitement that pooled in her stomach. "What?"

"I know what you're doing." He leaned down and

growled into her neck. "Come here, anyway. You're mocking the baseball gods."

His front curved to her back in such a delicious fashion, Georgie had to close her eyes. His strong, capable arms bracketed her, the scent of male sweat and mint toothpaste giving her no choice but to sway. "Um. Who are the baseball gods?"

"Ruth, DiMaggio, and Gehrig. No question."

Georgie dropped her voice to a whisper. "Are they watching us right now?"

"They're too busy spinning in their graves. Slide your hands up, grip tight—and try not to make a sexual innuendo about it."

She giggled like an honest-to-God middle school girl but somehow managed to follow the dictate, even with pheromones having a rave in her bloodstream. "Like this?"

"Good girl," he said huskily against her ear, bringing his flexing thighs up against hers, securing her backside tightly in his lap. "Now drop that beautiful ass a little. Weight on your back leg." He groaned as she complied, thanks to her bottom dragging right over the swell of his manhood. "God yeah, just like that."

Oh boy.

It was safe to say the situation was getting away from Georgie. She'd chanced picking up the bat in an attempt to draw Travis back into his happy place. But the longer this went on, the greater the chance they would end up in an entirely different venue of happiness. She couldn't let this opportunity pass, though. Who knew when she'd have another chance like this?

When his hand traveled beneath the front of her shirt to massage her breast, his lips leaving an openmouthed kiss on her neck, it was now or never. "I think I got it," she said in a tremulous voice. "But could you show me, just so I'm sure?"

Travis's breath sighed out onto her neck. Above them, the sky darkened further, blurring their shadows on the ground, releasing a hint of salt into the air. "I think we've done enough for one day."

Knowing she played dirty, Georgie gave Travis an innocent yet beseeching look over her shoulder. "Please?"

A muscle twitched in his jaw. "Why is this important to you?"

It was so hard to keep the love hidden. This morning in bed. Now. Every time they reached this point where her heart ached to come clean, she drew back, afraid he might catch on. Right now, though, with something so vital on the line, she pushed through the nerves. "I used to sit in the bleachers and watch your games." She turned and eased away, casting a look at the seating area in question. "By the time they were over, I'd have little moon-shaped nail marks on my palms . . . and they wouldn't fade for hours. That's how exciting you were to watch." She rolled her lips together. "Not because of your batting average. Just because you made everyone want to love something as much as you loved baseball. To feel what you felt."

Travis seemed frozen. Or maybe they both were, because she couldn't attempt movement until he gave some sort of reaction. Finally, his chest lifted and fell on a heavy shudder. "When I used to play, we always kept a stash of balls in the eaves of the dugout. There's probably a ball or two." He sniffed and took the bat from Georgie, weighing it in his hands. "Better hit a few before the sky opens up."

She had already turned and was walking at a fast clip to the dugout, a cheer going up in her mind. It was happening. She'd done it. Her foot skidded on some loose dirt as she rounded the corner onto the dugout steps, breathing a sigh of relief when she saw the row of balls. Using her T-shirt as a carrying device, she gathered as many balls as she could and waddled back under the weight, probably resembling a harried duck. "What should I do?"

Travis took a practice swing, tension riddling his shoulders, and Georgie had a moment of panic. What if pushing him backfired?

Instead of answering, he held up his hand.

Georgie tossed him the first ball. He caught it with ease, staring at it a moment. His narrowed gaze eventually drifted out to the fences, his sturdy frame expanding. Preparing. "Stand back, baby girl."

She looked down to find herself mere inches from the batter's box. "Oh." Quickly, she scooted back. "Right."

Holding her breath, she watched as Travis tossed the ball up in the air. It had been months since he'd swung a bat, yet his body fell right into the familiar motion. His stabilizing leg bent, his arms carrying the bat back, his tongue tucking into his cheek. Muscle memory. And oh my God. Legs twisting, arms and torso flexing, he was magnificent. The ball cracked off the bat and went soaring, up toward the rapidly darkening clouds, and dropped way out in the outfield, rebounding off the fence with a *ping*.

Georgie could no more stop her loud whoop of pure joy than she could stop the rain that started to fall in gentle drips around them. Travis turned to her with stunned optimism, and she didn't hesitate to throw him the next ball. And the next. One by one, they dropped into the outfield or roared down the third base line, every *thwack* of the ball meeting metal making Georgie's heart sing louder. The rain grew heavier, soaking their clothes and hair, but they didn't stop until all the balls were gone from her T-shirt. If she had a million more, she would have stood there tossing balls to Travis until the sun went down, watching him grow more confident with every swing, but she couldn't have been any more victorious when he dropped the bat.

Tears blurred in her eyes as he strode toward her, lifting her into a bear hug. She laughed without restraint as he spun her in a circle around home plate, her arms clinging to his neck. "Show-off," she breathed into his ear. "How did that feel?"

"Good." He shook his head. "No. Great."

She held him tighter, sensing them walking but uncaring of where they ended up as long as he kept her wrapped in his arms. Remembering their morning conversation about wanting her touch, a dam inside Georgie split down the middle and burst open. She licked a stream of rain off his neck. Her thighs itched to climb higher on Travis's hips, so she let them and then twisted her fingers into his shirt collar to keep him in place for a kiss.

"Goddammit, Georgie."

"What?"

"Thank you." His eyes ran laps over her face, his fingers stroking the side. "How do you do that? You . . . accept me. Exactly as I am. But you still change me for the better."

I love you. That's how. She couldn't say it out loud, so she leaned in for a kiss instead.

When their mouths joined, it wasn't just a kiss. It was gratitude and adrenaline. Excitement and support and love. And it was frantic, rain-soaked glory. Georgie sank so deep into the kiss, she didn't realize they were in the dugout until Travis fell onto the bench, her legs still fashioned around his waist, their faces a mere centimeter apart. Breathing heavy. The change in position brought her aching center down on Travis's erection, catapulting her into a deep abyss of lust. She clung to his wide shoulders and worked herself up and back on the rigid flesh, encouraged by his biting curse.

"Please. Please, baby girl. Don't grind that little thing on me unless your pants are off," he growled against her mouth. "I need inside that pussy."

"You can have whatever you want," she whispered brokenly, drifting into that mind space that made her the hottest. Let Travis put his needs on display so she could be the one who took care of them. And after last night, she knew giving led to Travis worshipping her in return. Giving until his body couldn't anymore. The promise of that made her all the more eager to match his hunger *now.* "Tell me what you want."

Travis's energy shifted and he lifted her off his lap with

a harsh expletive, yanking down her yoga pants and practical white bikini underwear. Revealing her flushed sex. With a groan, he lowered the front waistband of his shorts, taking out his thick arousal, stroking it once in that big hand—never taking his eyes off her. "Get on your knees and suck this cock."

Georgie dipped, her legs losing their ability to keep her upright. She caught herself on two powerful, hair-covered thighs, her face level with Travis's lap. His scent was earthy and masculine, musky from their run—and hell if that didn't turn her on more. The filth of it. Having her bare knees in the dirt, perspiration still cooling on their skin, while a curtain of rain sealed them tight in the darkness. It was wrong and forbidden, and she craved it.

Travis reached out, riding his thumb along the crease of her lips. "Give me somewhere sweet to put this."

She'd imagined this scenario so many times. Driving Travis to the point of pain with her mouth, then relieving him. Such power in being on her knees. Her stance widened in the dirt, her hips tilting in a need to draw his eyes. After a breath for courage, she wrapped her hands around the ruddy base of his erection, her mouth closing over the head in a drawn-out pull, her grip twisting like a locking mechanism, the way she'd seen women do in videos.

"Oh. Fuck," Travis gritted out, his thighs jerking, feet lifting and landing back in the dirt. "Go easy, Georgie baby. Jesus. You've got a fucking mouth on you."

Go easy? Easier said than done. The taste of him, salty and raw, hit the back of her throat and she couldn't get enough.

His hair tickled her wrists and cheeks as she delved in for another hard suck, her right hand pumping busily. A spurt of liquid landed on her tongue and she moaned, taking him deeper, seeking more.

"Hot, wet little mouth. You're killing me with it." Travis came to his feet with a shout, one hand on the back of her head, the other wrapped around a dugout rafter. His thighs crowded either side of her face, half of his smooth bulk buried in her mouth. He rolled his hips back, bringing all but the tip of his arousal out of her mouth, before pumping back in slowly, deeply, her lips stretching around his flesh. "That your limit, baby girl?"

Georgie saw the underlying concern in Travis's gaze and nodded, nuzzling her cheek in the hair on his thighs. Encouraging him to thrust into her mouth again—and Lord, he did. With a guttural sound, he fisted the hair at the back of her head and started a soft pound, never going past the line they'd drawn, but taking filthy advantage of everything leading to that point. His hips punched, filling her mouth with sex, and every inch of Georgie—inside and out—reacted to the perfection of it. With her head tipped back, knees in the dirt, a man using her mouth, she'd never felt more like a woman. The more his fist tightened in her hair, the more she took of him, letting him invade her throat. Listening to him bark dirty words, the force of them echoing in the dugout. "Need" was a pitiful word for the state she entered and became immersed in, her thighs shaking, belly hollowing.

"Up," Travis shouted, jerking Georgie to her feet. He

ripped the shirt over her head, desperate hands shoving the sports bra up to her neck. Their panting mouths met and molded as he fell onto the bench, ripping a condom from his sagging pocket and rolling it down his arousal. He grabbed Georgie's bottom and urged her onto his lap, shooting forward to take one of her nipples into his mouth. "Fuck me. Ride me." His right hand came down and delivered a mean slap to her backside. "Do it now."

His hand moved between them, and Georgie sobbed when the thick head of Travis's erection found her entrance, wedging inside. She was a little swollen from last night's first time, the intensity of it, but she worked her hips and took Travis's full length, sinking down and down until her backside hit his thighs. "Oh God. So big."

"That's right. I got big . . ." Eyes glazed, he licked at her mouth. "And you got tight. That's why you're going to spend a lot of time with your panties hanging off one ankle."

Out of necessity, Georgie shifted to find a comfortable position, gasping at the zing of friction on her clit. She rubbed herself against his hard flesh again, her mouth open and moaning on Travis's shoulder. The movement naturally rode her up and down on Travis's pulsing erection, and his enjoyment was on full display, his head tipped back, eyes blind. Something didn't quite allow Georgie to drop into the moment, though. Just like that time in Travis's bedroom, she ached for the thrill of being pinned.

"I don't know if I can . . ." She broke off in a whimper when Travis began kneading her bottom, coaxing her into a slick, erotic rhythm, her sex riding up and down his length.

God, it felt so good, the give and take of soaked flesh, their shallow breaths mingling with the pelting rain, his chest hair abrading her nipples. But her mind wouldn't turn off the way it did when Travis was on top. She wanted him to hold the reins. "I don't think I can . . . like this."

"The hell you can't." Travis sat up straight, yanking her hips closer. He took her face in his hands, breathing heavy against her mouth. "You might be on top, but I'm still in charge, aren't I?" He kissed her long and hard while those words sunk in. "If I wanted to flip you onto your back on this bench and break you off, I wouldn't ask permission."

While he spoke, Georgie's hips began to move of their own accord. Out of pure necessity. Her thighs flexed, bringing her up, body rolling, ears dying to hear more. Because he was right. She wasn't running the show. On top or not, her pleasure was Travis's to give.

"Hey." He caught her chin in a firm hand, tilted his hips with a groan—wicked intention in the set of his jaw, the curl of his lips. "My dick aches so bad. Make it stop."

There was no hesitation after that. Only deep, wild lust. This was the part she needed so desperately to play. The embodiment of relief. The only one who could make him erupt. Georgie closed her eyes, using her index and middle fingers to toy with her nipples, all the while lifting and twisting back down on Travis's thickness. His choked sounds, the chafing of his hungry, calloused hands on her thighs and bottom, all turned her desire up to the highest decibel. He grew larger inside her with every stroke of their joined bodies, his groans turning to punctuated grunts—and already she knew that signaled the end of his tether.

And that's what broke her, along with the mind-blowing friction, the pressure in her nipples and clit—Travis giving in to the inevitable. Not being able to stand the pleasure. His arms flew wide to grip the bench, his teeth clamping down hard on his full lower lip. "Can't hold it in. Can't hold it in. Fuck, you're working my cock so good, baby girl. Spoiling me."

Georgie pressed her naked breasts to Travis's heaving chest, letting her mouth linger a breath away from his. Lapping at him once. "I want to make you come so hard."

"Motherfuck." Travis's grip returned to her backside, supporting it as he lunged to his feet—and he proceeded to bounce her like a puppet with no strings on his rigid arousal. Sweat slid down one side of his face, their lower bodies slapping together while the rain hammered home on top of the dugout. "You make me so fucking crazy. I can't take it. My *God.*"

Those gruff words pitched Georgie over the side of the precipice, her sex seizing with enough intensity to make her scream, the sound swallowed by Travis's fevered mouth. It bit at her and exploited her tongue while her knots untied, tension draining out of her in hard, trembling degrees, her thighs shaking around Travis's hips. *"Travis, Travis, Travis."*

"Coming," he rasped mid-kiss, his groan filling her open mouth. In this position, there was no way to escape the quaking aftermath of what she'd done to him. He stumbled to the right, jaw dropping, his manhood jerking inside of her, leaving a flood of moisture behind. The sight and sounds stitched themselves onto her memory, where they would remain for all time. Travis silhouetted by the concrete dugout, rain falling in her periphery, his male growl of pleasure filling the air. And eventually his comforting, calming kiss, the stroke of his reverent hands as he sat back down, cradling her against his chest. "Sweet girl. So beautiful."

She'd splintered apart at her peak, but those pieces drew back together now, stronger than before, glowing with contentment. "Sweet man," she whispered, cheek resting on his shoulder. "So strong."

Travis's pulse was already galloping, but it stuttered at her words, his arms wrapping around her in an unbreakable hold. "You make me believe that."

Georgie lifted her head to find Travis watching her with a thoughtful frown, and something passed between them. Something she didn't know enough to name and was too afraid to explore. Contentment spread like jam on bread in her belly, though, which made it twice as frustrating when her phone started ringing, tangled in her yoga pants somewhere on the dugout floor. "I should get that. Just in case something's wrong."

He gave her a final kiss and nodded, letting her stand and keeping his attention on her as she answered. "Hello?"

"Georgie. I need you at my house like yesterday."

She glanced down at her naked-in-a-dugout body. "I'm

kind of busy." Travis grunted his agreement, tugging her closer to nibble on her hip. "What's all that noise?"

"Oh, you noticed?" Bethany's sarcasm pierced Georgie's afterglow. "Our sister-in-law told the whole town about the Just Us League. And now every woman in Port Jefferson is in my kitchen, demanding to join."

"Shut up."

"Just . . . help."

Georgie sent Travis a regretful look. "I'll be right there."

Travis hovered in her periphery as they both got dressed. "The dinner with the network exec is tomorrow night."

That contentment she'd been feeling nose-dived. "Right." Along with the reminder of the end of the line came a need to protect herself as much as possible when she was in love with the man standing five feet away. "Actually I was thinking of heading over to Westbury early. There's a wholesale furniture shop in town I want to check out. For the new office." She shot him a smile. "Meet you there?"

His jaw twitched. "You want to arrive separately at this dinner when we're supposed to convince the network we're together?"

"Never mind," she whispered. "I don't know what I was thinking."

Travis's stony gaze told Georgie he knew exactly what she'd been attempting to do. Distance herself, even though she wanted to dive into him feetfirst. She tucked some haphazard strands of hair into her ponytail and backed toward the stairs, grateful the rain was letting up.

"Dinner is at seven, right? I'll be ready to go at six." Her smile felt stiff. "See you then?"

"My truck is at your place, Georgie. We're running back together."

"Oh. Yeah."

After what felt like an endless staring contest, they jogged back in silence.

CHAPTER TWENTY-THREE

Georgie gaped as she stepped out of her car.

Chaos reigned inside Bethany's house. Women spilled out the front door onto the porch, shielding their heads from the rain with umbrellas and newspapers. A deliveryman with a stack of pizzas pushed through the throng, holding up the bill like a white flag of surrender. Among the women, Georgie recognized her ninth-grade physics teacher, Boutique Tracy, and several other familiar Port Jefferson faces. Including her mother.

"Mom?"

"Georgie." Vivian paused mid-conversation to wave her closer. "Will you pay for these pizzas? I don't have any cash."

Right. It was well known that Vivian carried everything she owned in her pocketbook, but couldn't manage to slide out cash or credit cards, thanks to her acrylic nails. "Who ordered them?" Georgie called, leafing through her wallet as she reached the front yard. "Where is Bethany?"

"Inside, talking about stuff." Her mother shooed some women aside so Georgie could tunnel through. "Come on, move. Make way for the founder."

"I'm not the . . ." Georgie shook her head. "I just came up with the name."

"Founder! Founder!" Vivian chanted. No one joined. "What took you so long to get here? You weren't home on a weekday morning?"

Suddenly, everyone on the porch seemed interested in their conversation. "I was out for a run with Travis," she said, cheeks burning. "I had to shower and change."

"Must have been some shower," Vivian remarked, juggling her eyebrows.

"Yeah." Georgie cleared her throat. "Um. So everyone is here to join the Just Us League?"

A cheer went up around her, followed by a single shout of "Fuck them all!"

Once the clapping and whistling stopped, Georgie said, drily, "We'll see what we can do about that," handing some twenties to the pizza man and pausing on the threshold of the house to take in the scene.

It was standing room only in the living room and everyone was talking at once. Bethany was perched on the fireplace and seemed hell-bent on bringing order to a conversation, and thus she didn't notice Georgie's arrival. In the kitchen, Rosie shot like a gorgeous Ping-Pong ball between the oven and the marble island, dishing what looked like empanadas onto serving trays. Bottles of champagne and orange juice were everywhere. It was brunch meets insane asylum.

"Where should I put these pizzas?"

Wordlessly, Georgie took the stack of pies from the pizza

man and ambled toward the kitchen. "Rosie, you need some help?" Georgie called over the noise. "Where's Kristin?"

"I'm here!" singsonged her sister-in-law on her way down the stairs, a bright smile on her face. "Isn't this fabulous?"

"That remains to be seen."

"I'm good in here," Rosie finally answered, sliding the tray of empanadas in her direction. "Just . . . will you try one?"

When Georgie's stomach roared, she realized she was starving. Although she found it pretty difficult to regret skipping cereal in favor of orgasmic stand-up sex with Travis. Yeah. That was definitely her preferred method of sustenance, even though her reservations crowded in afterward. What did it say about Georgie that she was beginning to need Travis's touch, whether it was emotionally healthy for her or not?

Unable to dwell on her current predicament, Georgie shooed the rain cloud above her head away. "Sure." She snagged a meat-filled pastry off the tray and took a small bite, blowing at the steam before taking another. Flavor exploded in her mouth. It was the single best thing she'd ever tasted. In her life. There was richness and spice and texture, all surrounded by perfectly crisped dough. "Oh my God, Rosie. You made these? From scratch?"

"Yeah." The other woman smiled into her wrist. "Bethany said there was a crowd and she didn't have any food in the house, so I made a quick pit stop at the store."

"I could live off these. I want to live off these." Maybe it was the clarity that came from the best sleep of her life, followed by the best sex of anyone's life, but Georgie was gripped by a sudden idea to push her friend's dream a little closer to reality. "Rosie, can you whip up some more?"

She moved around some plastic bags on the counter. "I have enough ingredients to make three more batches."

"Do it." Georgie turned to her sister-in-law. "Kristin. You're responsible for this mess. You can redeem yourself by making sure everyone in this room puts one of these empanadas in their mouth."

Kristin sputtered a little, then relented with a chin lift. "Fine."

Rosie caught her eye across the island. "What are you thinking?"

"I'm thinking once everyone tastes what you can do . . . and wants more?" Georgie shrugged one shoulder. "Maybe we can crowdsource enough funds to open the restaurant."

A hand clapped down on Georgie's shoulder, forcing her to look away from Rosie's stunned yet hopeful expression. "Where the hell have you been?" Bethany whined, shaking her. "Our church choir director just mooned the pizza guy through the living room window. My neighbors are going to call the cops."

"Sorry, I was showering. I'll get everyone under control."

"Just showering?" Bethany narrowed her gaze. "I call bullshit."

Their mother waded in between them. "Girls. This is about uniting us ladies, isn't it?" She clucked her tongue. "Bickering sends the wrong message."

"Mom, our meetings are ninety percent bickering."

"It's how we communicate," Bethany agreed.

Vivian shook her head. "Sad."

More women swelled in from the porch, squashing everyone closer together. Above their heads, Georgie could see the white serving tray coming back empty. Kristin appeared a moment later, looking out of breath. "Well, those went over like a house on fire, Miss Rosie! They're hankering for more." A glint of steel flashed in her eyes. "Meanwhile, no one has even touched my corn muffins."

Bethany swiped a hand through their huddle. "Look, I'm glad so many women are interested in joining the club, but we have to whittle down the pack. We can't accommodate this many people effectively."

"On it," Georgie said, climbing onto a stool and giving a two-finger whistle. When every head whipped in her direction, self-consciousness tried to nudge her back down. A few weeks ago, she would have been terrified to stand up in front of all these women. But then she thought of all the progress she'd made with her entertainment company. Thought of how she'd spoken up at family dinner and made her opinion matter. Lastly, she thought of Travis and how they'd formed a team. It might not be forever, but right now she could feel his presence at her back. "First of all, thank you, everyone, for your interest in joining the Just Us League."

"Fuck them all!" someone yelled from the back of the room.

Georgie gestured to her mother to make her a mimosa. "This is going to be tough to hear, but I need everyone to be honest." She paused. "I'm not sure how Kristin lured you here. But if you're here for the free food, please take a slice of pizza or an empanada and go about your day. No lookie-loos."

Half the room headed for the door, slices in hand.

"Thank you for your honesty."

Her sister gave a sigh of relief, giving a lazy spin in the newly vacated space around her. Vivian appeared disgusted as she handed Georgie a glass of champagne and orange juice.

"The Just Us League was formed by Rosie, Bethany, and I because we wanted to accomplish something. Individually and together. We have goals. If you can relate . . . if you need help doing the same—and are willing to actively support other club members—we'd love for you to stay."

"I thought this was about saying sayonara to the men-folk!"

Georgie was pretty sure the woman who yelled that statement was one and the same with *fuck them all* lady. "That's not all it's about . . ."

"Careful . . ." Vivian murmured out of the side of her mouth.

"I mean, certainly, if there is a negative influence in your life, you should, um"—Georgie took a long sip of her mimosa—"examine that."

A hand went up in the living room. She looked familiar to Georgie, but she couldn't quite place her. Still, she smiled, encouraging her to proceed. "Kristin told us all that this club is about empowering ourselves. But she also confirmed the rumor that you're dating Travis Ford. He was at a family dinner and everything." She crossed her arms. "It's no secret Travis goes through women like water. How are we supposed to listen to your advice when you can't even follow it yourself?"

A murmur went up around the room.

Bethany took a position in front of Georgie. "Bad form calling her out in front of—"

"No," Georgie said, patting her sister's shoulder. "It's okay. She's right. But seriously, Kristin, you're, like, two seconds away from getting voted off the island."

Kristin slumped against the kitchen wall and stuffed an empanada into her mouth. "Oh," she sniffed. "These are so much better than my corn muffins."

No sooner had Kristin taken her second bite of the empanada than Stephen came striding into the house—once again with wet hair. He said nothing as he hustled his wife out the door. And his scowl ensured that nobody tried to stop him.

With the interruption over, Georgie faced the room again. Yes, the plan had been to convince the town, her family, and the press that she was dating Travis. She'd engaged in deception with open eyes. But standing in front of this room of women who were looking to *her* for guidance? She couldn't find it in her to lie anymore. So she told the truth. "He cut down a branch from the tree I used to climb as a child. And when I got home yesterday, he was in my backyard sawing and sanding. Turning it into a new fireplace mantel for me."

Gasps went up around the room.

"I know, right? So . . . people make mistakes. Like organizing a dating competition when the prize has no interest in being won," she said, giving some of the offenders a pointed look. "Sometimes when you don't know a person, it's hard to understand why they do things, right?" The pounding started in her chest. "I'm not asking you to change your opinion of Travis, but I'm asking you not to let someone make it for you. That is the purpose of this club. We're not about cutting people out of our lives. We're about refusing to accept anything less than what we deserve. About realizing that we're all important here despite mistakes or bad relationships or lackluster careers. Even someone with the nickname Two Bats. *No one* ask me if it's accurate." She refocused on the woman in the crowd. "To answer your original question, I'm not asking anyone to follow my advice. We're all here to learn and grow. Starting now. Who is with us?"

Georgie almost fell off the stool when everyone started clapping. They were with her, Georgie Castle. Could it mean they viewed her not only as an equal, but as a mature voice of reason? She'd been fake dating Travis in order to force everyone to view her through a different lens, but she'd ended up doing it on her own without even realizing it, hadn't she? She'd found a new way to make people listen.

She climbed off the stool, only to be wrapped in a bear hug by Bethany. "All right," her sister shouted over her head. "Who's ready to kick ass and take names?"

Everyone converged on them, champagne glasses lifted in a salute.

"If you're serious about being a member," Bethany continued, "you can all start by signing up for the Tough Mudder on Friday."

Another dozen women blew out the front door.

Travis stared across the street at his childhood home.

The rain had let up, but it still tapped from the roof of the rusted detached garage, probably due to a leak. Beer cans littered the yard, courtesy of local kids. A tree root came up through the walkway, cracking the concrete in half.

He wasn't sure how he'd gotten there. Only that he'd been restless as soon as Georgie left him this morning. So he'd gotten in his truck and driven there. To the scene of his nightmares.

Upon pulling up, his first thought had been a wish that he'd waited and brought Georgie along. His stomach would still be tied up in knots, but they wouldn't be nearly as tight. She would say the exact right thing. Would read his mood and know when to push, to pull, to do nothing.

With a growl of irritation, he crossed the street and walked into his yard for the first time since he'd left for Northwestern. Since he'd walked out with a suitcase full of the essentials and never looked back. His boots kicked through the gravel, rain landing on his shoulders. Again, he wished for Georgie's presence. But overall, it wasn't so bad. Those nights he'd sat outside waiting for his father to get home—or for his mother to pick him up—the yard had seemed so huge and dark. Now? Now everything looked smaller than his memories. Like the set of a bad play.

Even though his name was on the deed, he didn't have

a key. Opening the door was no problem, though, since the hinges were disintegrating with rust. One kick of his boot and the thing swung open. A cat went streaking out through his legs, issuing a loud yowl. Travis took a few seconds to center himself and stepped inside.

The house layout never made sense to him—and still didn't. There was no entryway or hall. The house simply began with the kitchen. All the furniture was gone, but the terrible green floral wallpaper had stood the test of time, and the floor was yellow with age. The house remained silent, except for the patter of rain on the roof, and Travis half expected to hear the tinny cackle of a television studio audience coming from his father's room down the hall. That's where the old man always stayed, leaving Travis to his own devices. Occasionally, they would cross paths on the way to the bathroom, and he swore the frown lines on his father's face deepened every time, the bitter cascading off him in waves.

"Could I do better than this?"

A mental image of his wretched apartment before Georgie helped him clean made Travis doubtful. Something was prodding him, though. A need he'd never felt before to put down roots, without the visage of his youth haunting him and telling him it wasn't possible. Why now? Why was he suddenly anxious to shed this final piece of his past so he could start building something new?

Georgie's smile danced in his head, but he laughed it off. No, a lasting commitment to another person was next level. Wasn't it? It was enough for now that he wanted stability. To win this job on the network and build a life he could be proud of. A lump built in his throat as he continued to think of Georgie. How she'd felt in his arms this morning. How natural and . . . *perfect* it felt to start the day with her. And it was impossible to pretend he was at his childhood home for any other reason than making progress within himself. To be better for her. To what end, he didn't know yet . . . but with the deadline of their agreement fast approaching, the idea of letting her go threatened his sanity.

Forcing himself to focus on the task at hand, Travis snatched the cell phone out of his pocket, tapping the number he'd programmed into his favorites years ago. He didn't get an answer, but the cheerful recording told him to leave a message.

"Hi. Yeah, my name is Travis Ford. I want to speak with someone about a property appraisal."

CHAPTER TWENTY-FOUR

He'd decided to pick Georgie up in a limo at the last second.

It wasn't a power play or a show of influence. No, if he was honest with himself, the eleventh-hour call he'd made to the limousine company stemmed from his need to soak up as much Georgie as possible. No more lying to himself. Since he wouldn't be able to read her expressions—and, fuck it, touch her—with two hands on the steering wheel, he'd just pulled up in front of her house in a black stretch. Half the neighborhood was out on their lawns by the time he made it up the path. Tonight had a lot of the same merits as prom night. Travis was wearing a tuxedo, he was picking his date up at the door, and tonight was definitely supposed to signal the end of something.

That reminder caused a baseball to get stuck in his throat.

Travis wasn't ready for this thing with Georgie to end.

In fact, calling it a "thing" was starting to get on his goddamn nerves. He was closer to Georgie than anyone else in his life. There had been a moment yesterday on the high school baseball field when Travis had dropped every pretense and just let her see everything inside of him. His love for baseball, his sadness over losing the ability to play. He'd forgotten to mask those always-present insecurities and laid them bare . . . and he was still standing. Better than still standing, actually. He felt unburdened. Stronger. Like a better version of himself.

All because of this girl.

Now he was supposed to parade Georgie in front of some corporate assholes and say good-bye to her at the end of the night? A *permanent* good-bye?

Panic made Travis's arm too heavy to lift and knock. Why had he decided to put a time limit on this . . . dammit, this *thing* with Georgie? Being alone had worked very well for him in the past. Answering to no one, keeping every short-lived relationship on his own terms. What he had with Georgie felt outside of his control, though. A flame that fed itself—and he had no fire extinguisher.

The front door of the house opened and Travis's jaw almost hit the porch. This was not the girl who'd woken him from his self-induced mental coma all those weeks ago. Except for in the eyes. Yeah, she may be dressed to induce fantasies, but that classic Georgie authenticity shone back at him from a pair of green eyes. Unbelievable that her eyes were demanding his focus when she looked insanely hot. Her shoulders were completely bare in the dress, a skirt flaring out around her thighs. Thighs that seemed to stretch forever thanks to the high heels. She was sexy and guileless and there was no one like her.

"Oh, wow," she breathed. "You, um . . . look very handsome. In that tux."

Travis's lower body responded so intensely to the husky quality of her voice, the proof she was attracted to him, that he could only stand there and breathe through it.

"You don't like the dress," she said, running her hands down the front of the dress. "I know I'm supposed to be the innocent small-town girl that has saved you from a life of debauchery, but they don't really make nice enough dresses for that."

"Georgie."

"I tried one with a higher neckline, but I didn't have the right bra, so the straps kept peeking out the sides and—"

"You look fucking perfect. *You* are perfect."

The worry in her eyes melted away. "Thank you, Travis." Her mouth popped open. "Is that a limo?"

"Yeah." Travis stepped over the threshold and backed Georgie into the house, kicking the door shut behind him. He didn't stop walking until her ass bumped the entry table, rattling knickknacks and making her gasp. "Listen up," he rasped against her mouth. "You stick by me all night."

Her fingers curled in his jacket as if they couldn't help it and he wished she would just rip it off and climb him, damn the dinner party. "What's wrong?" She laid a tentative kiss on his chin. "Are you nervous?"

"No." Travis turned his head and caught her mouth with a kiss. It was only meant to be a brief one, but her head fell back and he dove in, pressuring open her lips and rubbing their tongues together. "No, I'm just not sure what I was thinking. This plan. This . . . showing you off in order to get a job." His thumbs stroked the hollows of her cheekbones. "I don't like it. I didn't think this far ahead."

She was breathing with her eyes closed. "People do this kind of thing all the time."

"Believe me, I know. That's why it feels wrong with you."

Those green eyes popped open. "I don't understand."

Travis searched for the right words. Ones that wouldn't reveal this struggle he was having over tonight being the end. Georgie's mouth distracted him, though, and all that would come out was the truth. "I don't want you on display. I don't want . . . us on display."

The pulse in her neck visibly jumped. "Us?"

On the other side of the door, the limousine driver honked. Just a light tap, intended to let him know if they didn't leave now, they wouldn't make it on time. And thank God for that honk, right? He'd been about to tell Georgie he wanted their relationship to last beyond tonight. That he wanted it to be real. Wanted the right to kiss her, take her out, sit beside her at family dinners. Fuck her into the next stratosphere, take her jogging, show up when she performed at birthday parties, and, most importantly, tell other men to stay the hell away. Wanted the right to do it any time, any day of the week.

Ridiculous.

He didn't know the first thing about being someone's boyfriend. Jesus, though. "Boyfriend" sounded so much more accurate than "thing." With her sweet body pressed up against him, possessiveness flowing in his blood, they were so far beyond a thing, he almost laughed. Almost. He was too unnerved by the ultimatum he was giving himself. He couldn't just be her indefinite hookup—she deserved better than that. The prospect of letting her go made him feel submerged in quicksand, but she deserved someone who had a healthy outlook on commitment. Marriage. He was not that man. He would never, ever be that man.

Say good-bye tonight or ask Georgie for more. Those were his only two options.

"Travis?"

Taking one final sniff of her hair, he stepped away. "We should go."

Georgie scrutinized him for a moment and nodded, letting him open the door so they could step onto the porch, before she turned and locked up. Despite reminding himself he and Georgie couldn't be together, he found himself taking hold of her hand on the walk to the limo, cataloging her blush, her silent *Oh God, oh God* when she realized the neighbors were staring. A gust of summer wind blew a strand of hair across her mouth and he almost tripped off the sidewalk where it ended.

God, she was gorgeous.

Despite Travis's inability to stop staring at her, there was a definite strain between them on the ride to Old Westbury. He continued to hold her hand nonetheless, as if letting it go would make time go faster. They remained silent, facing forward in the rear seat, humming down the Northern State Parkway for half an hour before Travis couldn't take the distance anymore and dragged Georgie sideways onto his lap. She went without protest, tucking her head underneath his chin with a wince.

The weight of her in his lap caused his eyelids to droop. "What was that about?"

"I did lunges this morning. A whole lap around the high school track."

"More Tough Mudder training?"

She nodded, bumping his chin. "We have thirty-one new members and they seem to have made me their unofficial leader. I have no idea why. But now I feel compelled to set an example."

Travis's hand slipped under her skirt and ran a thumb along the outside of her right thigh. He decided not to be offended that her reaction was more rapturous than it was during orgasms. "First of all, thirty-one new members?"

"Yes," she moaned, shifting in his lap to give him better access to her sore muscles. "My sister-in-law led them to believe we were starting a manless utopia. You should all be seriously alarmed how many women showed up."

He applied more pressure to the spot just above her knee, laughing quietly when she went boneless, moaning without shame. "Yeah? I better release a man memo."

Her eyes sparkled up at him. They were almost enough to make him forget the growing bulge between his legs. Almost. "A man memo? Is that just cave drawings on a napkin?"

"It's a foolproof code. You'll never break it." He slid the hem of her dress higher and began massaging the inside of her thigh. "I take that back. You're pretty good at making me break codes, aren't you?"

"I assume you're talking about the best-friend's-sister code," she said breathily.

"The very one," he murmured, dragging a knuckle down the center of her black panties.

"Do you regret it?"

Travis's throat felt tight. All of him did. "No."

He'd never been in this place. Torn between aching to fuck and needing to talk. To just . . . hold her. Doing all of those things at the same time seemed like too much. Like they would rip him wide open. So he continued to run his hands over her roughly and breathed. Memorizing the smoothness of her thighs, the dip of her belly, the curve of her hip. He didn't know how long the touching went on, but eventually Georgie straightened up and stilled his hands with her own. She brought their mouths together for a long, torturous kiss. A slow one. His cock grew thick and pressed up into her backside, but neither of them seemed inclined to give in to the hunger. There was a need inside Travis to prolong the night, to hold time at bay—and the kiss succeeded in doing that. It was wet and endless and left them both shaking by the time they arrived at the sweeping Tudor-style mansion.

Georgie pulled away first, breathing heavily against his lips. "I—I meant to go over everything with you. Who exactly I'm meeting . . . anything I should talk about—"

"We're having dinner with Kelvin Fisher. His father used to run the network before he retired, and Kelvin has stepped in and started making changes. I've never met him. My agent is meeting us here and that windbag never shuts up, but he's a good buffer." His hand moved on its own, stroking her hair, her cheek. "There's nothing to be nervous about. Just be yourself." Nothing could stop him from leaning in again and giving her some tongue, deepening the kiss until her ass started to flex in his lap. "Thanks for being here with me, Georgie."

She nodded, her expression dazed as Travis lifted her off his lap. They both watched as he adjusted his hard dick and took some centering breaths.

"That's not very family friendly."

"No, it's not," Travis muttered. "Don't look so proud of yourself."

The limo driver opened the door and extended a hand for Georgie to take. "Oh, but I am," she threw over her shoulder with a wink. "Take your time."

Travis shook his head and climbed out after Georgie. At the entrance to the sprawling residence, a man waited with hands clasped behind his back to guide them inside. Travis had been to some incredible homes in the last few years, some belonging to coaches and teammates, but he could say without reservation that this one took the cake. It wasn't flashy or decked out with fish and flat screens. It was old money. Understated and tasteful.

Polished marble floors gleamed in the entryway, which spread into a foyer on one side, a wine cellar on the other. A staircase lay just beyond, curving around to the hidden second floor. It was huge and airy and lit by sconces. Low music drifted in, mingling with the sound of an unseen water fixture.

"Mr. Fisher is just showing your agent the grounds," said the butler. "Please wait here and I'll let them know you've arrived."

The man left the room, leaving Georgie and Travis alone.

"Whoa," Georgie whispered. "It's like we stepped into an Italian piazza or something. Probably. I've never been to Italy."

"Do you want to go to Italy?"

"Of course I do." She turned in an awed circle, heels clicking on the floor, her lips parted. "Who doesn't want to travel?"

Travis took a step closer to Georgie, unsure if he was going to kiss her again or demand to know everything she'd ever wanted in her life. To what end, he didn't know. But she was beautiful in the muted light and blown away by this mansion. It made him highly aware of the fact that they'd gone out only on a couple of impromptu dates. Is that what she would remember about their time together? "Georgie—"

"Welcome." Kelvin Fisher strode into the room the way a king might, but less aloof. His smile was hearty and genuine as he shook Travis's hand. The head of the network was younger than Travis thought, midway through his thirties and radiating energy. "Travis Ford," Kelvin said. "I'm a huge fan."

Travis nodded. "Thank you." He lifted an arm and Georgie slid under it like she belonged there. Fuck. It felt like she did. "This is Georgie Castle." Travis stopped short of calling her his girlfriend and wished like hell he'd staked that claim when Kelvin kissed her hand, smiling over it while she blushed.

"I've seen you in the papers. Have to say we all enjoyed reading the reporter's account of you swooping in to shut down that man in the bar. Well done." He tilted his head. "I'm not sure I've ever met a professional clown. Do you have any tricks up your sleeve for tonight?"

Georgie gave a ladylike shrug, taking her hand back so she could make a coin appear from behind Kelvin's ear. "It's not my best work, but you caught me on a night off."

Kelvin's laugh echoed off the many marble surfaces in the entry. Georgie grinned back.

Travis wished he'd kissed her one more time in the limo. "Let me guess. Donny is off somewhere taking an important call."

"Sports agents," Kelvin said, finally managing to drag his attention away from Georgie. "Can't live with 'em . . ."

"Can't sign a deal worth a damn without them," Donny said, swaggering into the room in a cream-colored suit. "Let's see if we can manage it tonight, huh, boys?"

Travis was forced to let go of Georgie to give Donny a back-slapping hug, but he really didn't want to. As soon as it was over, he urged her back up against his side as they followed Kelvin through the living room to the terrace. "We'll be dining alfresco tonight. I hope that's okay," Kelvin said, nodding to two women in aprons who immediately disappeared from sight. "I spent last summer on the Amalfi Coast and now I'm subjecting everyone in my life to Italian culture."

"There are definitely worse things," Georgie said, once again starry-eyed over their surroundings. And yeah, once again, Travis had to admit the atmosphere was pretty amazing. Evening was fading from the sky and candles were lit and flickering on every available surface. A low chandelier hung over an ornate antique table decorated with white and yellow flowers.

"Georgie," Kelvin said smoothly, signaling yet another member of his staff. "Can I offer you a glass of wine?"

"Sure, I—"

A small female child burst out through the back door onto the patio, throwing herself at Kelvin's legs. "Dada! I'm not tired."

Obviously not expecting the intrusion, Kelvin twisted awkwardly, trying to see the girl wrapped around his legs. "You have to be tired. We rode bikes. Built a fort. Everything we did today was designed to make you tired." He gave an awkward laugh. "We talked about this. I have a meeting tonight. Tomorrow morning, I'm all yours."

"It's cold in my room."

"We can adjust the temperature."

She peeked through his legs. "Who are they?"

Instead of answering, Kelvin turned to the woman pouring wine and communicated *Help me* with his eyes. The woman stopped what she was doing and rushed over, wrapping an arm around the little girl's middle and attempting to lift her. Which of course made the child scream.

Kelvin massaged the center of his forehead and offered them an apologetic smile. "It wasn't supposed to be my week, but something came up for my ex." His smile dropped as his daughter started to wail in earnest. "Bedtime is always an adventure."

Georgie moved away from Travis, skirting past the ornate

table to kneel in front of the child. "Hi. I'm Georgie. What's your name?"

The girl scrubbed at her eye with a chubby fist. "Madison."

"Do you want to see something cool?"

No hesitation. "Yes."

Travis watched spellbound as Georgie snagged three lemons from the centerpiece and started juggling them. "Okay, Madison. You have to help me. Clap your hands so I don't drop them."

The girl slid out from behind her father slowly, tears beginning to dry.

"I can't keep it up . . . my arms are getting weak . . ."

Kelvin crouched down next to Madison and clapped, finally giving the girl the push she needed to join in. Within seconds, the little girl was laughing, her eyes wide as Georgie picked up speed.

Christ. Travis didn't know what to make of the fiery sensation in his chest. It didn't take a huge leap of imagination to paint Georgie, Kelvin, and the child as a family. One that loved each other so much, they couldn't help but break into spontaneous acts of cuteness wherever they went. The dumbstruck way the other man was looking at Georgie made Travis want to knock him on his ass, even though he fully understood. Who wouldn't look at her like she was a fucking angel? That's exactly what she was in that moment. Every moment. A being sent straight from the clouds.

God, he was cold. Felt like a beggar watching a family eat

Thanksgiving dinner through a picture window. It was all so wholesome. Exactly what Georgie deserved. Exactly what she wanted.

Exactly what he could never give her. Someone else would, though.

Travis was so focused on the chaos in his stomach, he didn't notice Kelvin stand and make his way over. "Georgie is magnificent. You're a lucky man."

"Thank you," Travis managed, some honesty slipping free without his permission. "I don't know what the hell she's doing with me."

Kelvin chuckled, but his expression was thoughtful. "I didn't believe my team when they suggested you'd changed, but part of my success comes from being a good judge of character. I don't think a woman like her could be wrong about someone." He paused. "Still, I can't make an assessment on that alone. Why do you want this job, Travis?"

The last couple weeks came back to him in a rush of color and sound. Georgie was front and center of every memory. Throwing food at his head, tossing him baseballs in the middle of a rainstorm, sitting on her kitchen counter and telling him he was more than the sport. Somewhere along the line, he'd started to believe her, hadn't he?

"If you'd asked me that a month ago, I'm not sure what I would have told you. The truth would have been that I wanted the job so I wouldn't be a failure. I grew up surrounded by doubt and I didn't want to fulfill it. When the league dropped me, I thought I'd earned that doubt. Become someone who deserved it." He locked eyes with Georgie and her presence invaded him, rocked him full of confidence. "It's different now. I want the job because I love baseball and I would work damn hard. I would never take the opportunity for granted. But whether you see fit to make me the voice of the Bombers or not, I'm not a failure. I wouldn't fail you, either."

The men stood in silence for long moments before Kelvin finally spoke. "I don't think you will." They shook hands. "Welcome to the Bombers, Travis Ford."

CHAPTER TWENTY-FIVE

Travis wrapped his arms around her and they stumbled into the limousine, landing in a tangle of limbs on the plush leather backseat. "You got the job, Travis," Georgie squealed, laying kisses all over his face. "You did it."

"No," he said, taking her mouth in a kiss that tasted like lust, wonder. "We did it."

Georgie pulled back to study him, running her fingers through his hair, down his cheeks, completely incapable of keeping her heart out of her eyes. As thrilled as she was over Travis winning the contract, she didn't want to think in terms of the end yet. Panic crept into her now, reality raining down on her head. In a roundabout way, she'd found the place she wanted among her family and peers. Now Travis was the new voice of the Bombers and there was nothing stopping them from disembarking this ride they'd gone on together.

An intense need to delay the inevitable stole over her. "I want you," she whispered, scrubbing her hands down his stomach, fingers curling in his waistband. Their exhales tumbled out and collided. The hand Travis wrapped around the back of her neck was just the right amount of tight. Close as they were, she was surrounded in the scent she craved. Travis's aftershave traveled toward her on the cool air-conditioning and landed on her tongue. "I need you."

With a groan, Travis undid his belt and let the buckle sag, knowing without looking down that his rock-hard cock was on display, plumping the waistband of his briefs. "This what you want?"

Georgie shivered. "Yes."

"Cold, baby girl?"

Even in the dark interior of the limousine, it was impossible to miss the concern in his eyes. Not just for her comfort, but . . . something else. Was it too much to hope that the worry on his face was over tonight being the end?

"Get the dress off. I'll keep you warm." He loosened his tie and discarded it on the floor. Starting on his shirt buttons, his expression turning hungry. A little wild. "I said get it off."

Georgie remained frozen in the headlights of his intensity. His sudden urgency. And her need turned wild to match Travis's as he pulled her to the floor, turning her to face the leather backseat on her knees. "You want to leave it on? Fine. Bend forward for me," he rasped at the top of her head. "Now."

Heat dropped in her belly, loosening her limbs, electricity climbing lazily up her back to cradle her skull. Georgie flattened her hands on the wide seat, gasping when Travis shoved her knees apart with a guttural sound. She felt him lean back and peruse her, making Georgie's neck heat, moisture gathering at the juncture of her thighs. The skirt of her dress was lifted inch by slow, painstaking inch, where it remained settled around her waist. *Oh my God.* Oh yeah, this was . . . different. Anticipation crackled. More was coming. More than usual. Without a discussion, she knew they wanted to make this last time between them count. *Don't think about it being over.*

"Baby girl wore this tight dress for me." He groaned, a single finger sliding into the back waistband of her panties to tug them down, down, until they eventually caught at her knees. Leaving her bare bottom on display. "What are we going to do about this pretty ass of yours, huh? Rode all the way here with it so sweet and tight in my lap." Without warning, her hips were jerked high onto Travis's thighs, his erection huge where it prodded the split of her backside. "Look at what it did." He yanked Georgie's hips higher in his lap, swiping her earlobe with a flick of his tongue. "Look at what you did. You're not the least bit sorry about it, either, are you? If you are, it's not stopping you from pressing back on that dick you tortured. Rubbing on it like a hungry little cat."

"Sorry," Georgie breathed, ceasing the movements she hadn't even been aware of.

The apology was only halfway out of her mouth when Travis wrapped her hair in a skilled fist, easing her head back. All the way back until their eyes locked. "I didn't say to stop."

Writhing her hips in that position—back arched, face tilted toward the ceiling—started as awkward, but the slight contortion made her thighs slide together differently, thrust her breasts out, and put her womanhood at an angle and holy shit. Ten seconds of circling her naked backside on Travis's lap turned her into a needy mess. Hard eyes watched her from above, growing smokier with every swish of her bottom.

"That's right. Apologize for being a cock tease by teasing it even more."

"You feel so good," Georgie whimpered. "I can't stop."

The fist in Georgie's hair tilted her head sideways, Travis's tongue licking a warm, wet path up the side of her neck. "Good. Never stop." He moved close—so close—his body flush with her back, fingers busy on the side zip of her dress. Cool air kissed her skin as he pulled the garment off over her head, then settled her ass in his lap once again, inching her knees wider and thrusting himself against her body. Soft nudity on hard, clothed male. The contrast was so devastatingly hot, she moaned long and loud. "Tease me any time you want, because we both know your dirty little secret. You don't know how to tease me without giving it up. You want my cock and you want it deep."

Was it possible to have an orgasm from words alone? Because God, she was close. Her clitoris felt swollen and sensitive from her legs rubbing together. Her throat hurt from taking shallow, rasping breaths. *Hot, I'm so, so hot.* Georgie was so overwhelmed, she could only press the side of her face to the leather seat, Travis guiding her there with a firm hand. Could only hear the jingle and clunk of his belt hitting the ground in the distance, her backside lifting in an involuntary move. *Just have me. Have me.*

"Never banged you like this, have I?" Travis ground out, lightly slapping her butt cheeks with his erection. The way she'd seen men do on the internet—and why it came across so hot and animalistic to Georgie? A mystery. Travis spanking her with his arousal was enough to make her desperate, her fingers turning to claws on the seat. She heard the rip of a condom wrapper, and finally, the head of his manhood nudged her entrance. Georgie held her breath, whimpering when he grazed her neck with his teeth. "You know why I haven't put my dick inside you from behind yet?"

She let out a shaking breath against the leather, her heart hammering. "Why?"

Travis rammed himself home and Georgie's scream filled the limousine. "Because I wasn't sure I'd be able to control myself once I got you on hands and knees. With your ass smacking off my belly, I worried I'd cross that line into disrespectful—and some part of me still thought of you as my friend's little sister." He made a choked sound, falling on top of her, thrusting with a groan. "Not anymore. You're all mine now. I'll take you how I want."

With that pronouncement, his teeth grazed her shoulder, enough to make her jerk at the pleasure and pain. His hips never stopped thrusting, the ridges of his abdomen riding over the curve of her backside, their skin slapping together. And then those teeth left her shoulder, finding the back of her neck, dragging up and down, kicking off a wild surge of satisfaction in Georgie. Her back arched, thighs widening on the floor, becoming this man's pleasure tool. With her open mouth pressed to the seat, she could only whimper his name in a litany, glorying in the repeated driving of hard flesh into the giving entrance of her body, Travis grunting and cursing between love bites of her neck, shoulders, upper back.

"Mine," he rasped. Then more insistent: "Mine."

Georgie's fevered mind had only just picked up on the change in Travis's tone when his strong arms banded around her, holding tight. So tight. His hips continued to pound her from behind, but his breathing had turned erratic. Unnaturally so, even in their worked-up state. With his face buried in the crook of Georgie's neck, she only had to turn her head to search Travis's face—and she found his eyes squeezed shut, her name on his lips. "Travis," she croaked, kissing the forearms locked around her. "Look at me."

Tortured blue eyes found her and alarm flared in Georgie's chest. She twisted in the circle of his arms, giving him no choice but to slip from her body. He fell on Georgie, wrapping her in a bear hug, their sides pressed up against the seat. "Fuck."

"What's wrong?" She stroked a hand down the back of his hair. "Talk to me."

A muscle slid up and down in his throat. "Georgie, I can't do this."

Pain singed her lungs. "Are you . . . ending this thing between us now? I know it was only supposed to last through tonight—"

Travis clapped a hand over her mouth, his breathing harsh. "First of all, let's stop calling it a thing."

"Okay," she mumbled slowly into his palm.

"What you've done for me, baby girl . . . bringing me out of the dark? It's a miracle. Not a thing. *You're* a miracle." He closed his eyes, missing the awe that crossed her face. "You make me *better*, and I wish—I fucking wish I could do the same for you, but all I can offer is me. Other men can offer you the things you want. Family. Kids. I don't know how to give you those." His arms tightened around her. "But I don't think I can let you go, either."

Georgie felt like she was breathing through a straw. "Are you saying you want to be with me?"

"Want? No." Travis brushed their mouths together, letting the tips of their tongues touch. "I'm saying I *need* you. I'm saying no to ending this tonight. I was an idiot to think that was possible."

Georgie was shaken. Did he really just say those beautiful things? Was she in the middle of a dream? No. No, the warm male body pressed to hers was real, as was the emotion packed into every one of his words. *I need you.* Did he have any idea how much she needed him back? This man who'd blown her perception of him out of the water and replaced it with someone real and caring and magnetic.

Thank God. Thank God this wouldn't be over in a matter of hours. It almost eluded Georgie that she'd succeeded in her plan to cure Travis of his relationship phobia, she was so relieved this man wanted more. They both did. Georgie slipped her fingers into his hair, her thighs lifting to circle his waist. Between them, his thick erection continued to pulse, and her body was now weeping for its almost-orgasm. "Where do I even start?" Georgie said quietly, dragging her fingernails along Travis's scalp and watching his eyes glaze over. "Travis, I . . ."

Not the time, Georgie. They'd just decided to stop calling their relationship a thing. Declarations of love were a long way off. Maybe they'd never even get there. Bottom line, she needed to start small. Even though her chest felt like it might burst wide open from all the overstocked feelings.

A line formed between his brows. "What were you going to say?"

Georgie raked her nails lightly down his nape. "I was going to say I'm twenty-three, Travis. I don't want kids right now. Or a husband. There's all the time in the world." The words sounded hollow to her own ears and Travis was still frowning, but she pushed through, getting to the part that was nothing but the truth. "Right now, I—I just want—"

"A boyfriend?" His chest lifted and fell. "If that's enough for now, let me be yours."

For now. Did that make them temporary all over again? Maybe. But the prospect of being with Travis without an imminent expiration date proved too tempting. "Where do I sign?"

Travis still looked troubled about her claim that the future could wait, but after a small hesitation, his mouth settled over hers again. And their lips moving together reignited the heat between them like two pieces of flint. Georgie spread her legs, looking up at the sexiest man alive through her lashes. And Travis took the bait like a dying man. He reached down with shaking hands and guided himself back between her legs, thrusting deep with a moan. "I need to come inside you so bad, baby girl. Deep." He laid her down on the limousine floor. "I want it to stay there all fucking night."

She let him lock her wrists above her head, a buzz humming in her blood. So full of love, she wondered if her chest might explode. "Give it to me."

It was fast and rough, Travis's forehead pressed to hers, eyes locked on each other as he pummeled her body. He moved at a merciless pace, slapping their hips together, teeth baring every time she squeezed him with her inner walls. They groaned words that made sense only to their ears, called each other's name, and kissed as if frantic to memorize taste, texture, movement, breathing patterns. Travis freed Georgie's wrists in favor of pressing her knees open, the pace of his hips turning punishing but, as always, mindful of where she needed to be touched, the engorged base of his shaft hitting its mark and turning Georgie into a clawing, writhing creature, her fingernails buried in her boyfriend's ass. Urging him to buck, to use, to overpower. And he did. He did until tears leaked down her temples, the back-to-back orgasms blanketing her mind, narrowing her universe down to where their bodies joined.

"Goddamn," he muttered into her neck, voice sounding pained. "I need to blow so bad, but you're too beautiful when you come. Knock it off."

"Who, me?" Georgie said breathlessly, putting mock innocence—her favorite tool—to use, because she couldn't stand Travis in pain and it happened to be his kryptonite, too. She unsnapped the front of her strapless bra, bowing her back to present her bare breasts to Travis.

"Motherfucker," he breathed, his hips snapping in a rapid rhythm, jostling her breasts. "No. No, no, no . . . I want to watch you one more time."

She played with her nipples, pinching and rolling them between her middle finger and thumb. "But it feels so good when you fill me up."

"Georgie."

"Do it." She gasped as Travis closed his teeth around her chin, growling. "You can go harder, can't you? You don't have to hold back because I'm so tight."

He came with a roar that lasted for long moments, hanging in the air, that final pump of his stiffness telling her all about his desperation. And the expression of male rapture on his gorgeous face, the sticky, wet grind of their lower bodies, pushed Georgie into one final climax, a slow, all-encompassing one that made her shake violently. It made Travis's head come up, his eyes molten as he witnessed it. "Beautiful," he gritted. "You're so fucking beautiful."

They collapsed in a tangle of arms and legs, Travis tucking Georgie's head beneath his chin, his unbreakable hold surrounding her. No place in the world she'd rather be than listening to Travis's heart wail against his rib cage, throat rattling as it pulled in oxygen.

As they rumbled down the highway, she let the engine and Travis's heartbeat lull her, refusing to be sad over the three words that remained trapped in her throat.

CHAPTER TWENTY-SIX

Travis flipped up his collar against the wind on his walk through the parking lot. The first of fall had begun to roll in, bringing a brisk breeze off the water. Soon the leaves would begin to change, and everyone would break out their sweaters. It wouldn't be long before he was dodging kids in Halloween costumes as they trick-or-treated on Main Street. For the first time, he was actually looking forward to October for something other than the World Series. He was looking forward to everything right now.

He'd picked up the supplies he needed to put the finishing touches on Georgie's fireplace and he could already see her laid out in front of it. Last night, after the limousine dropped them back at her house, there had been no question he was staying the night. That's what boyfriends did, wasn't it? And it turned out his girlfriend often slept in these tiny flannel shorts that went straight up her ass—he'd found them in the back of her sock drawer while digging for something to keep her feet warm. He'd coaxed her into modeling them and now he was borderline obsessed. When he imagined Georgie in front of the fireplace he was building, she wore nothing but those booty huggers and a smile, her skin lit up from the flames.

You don't have to hold back because I'm so tight.

"Christ," he muttered, slowing his gait out of necessity. Wouldn't be a good idea to walk into Grumpy Tom's with a boner, especially because he was meeting Stephen for a beer. Unfortunately, that was how he'd spent most of the day. Hard—or about to get hard—thanks to Georgie.

Had he always liked sex? Sure. Every man did. But he'd been having a vague, watered-down version of it his whole life. Being inside Georgie? His body got high. And so did his mind. Their bodies moving together meant being attuned to fifty things at once. Her pulse, the swell of her clit, the peaks of her nipples, the quickening of her pussy, the waning focus in her eyes, her words, her breath, the softness of her skin, the roughness of her nails. The affection she radiated at him. Being aware of all of those incredible things at once, tending to them, while being completely absorbed by a warm, blanketing sense of belonging.

Damn. He hadn't seen Georgie coming. It was a great irony that the most selfless person in the world was inspiring him to be selfish. That's exactly what he was being. He *coveted* this girl. Wanted her all to himself, even though her goodness was meant to shine in other places. Watching her sleep this morning, he hadn't been able to stop his mind from projecting her onto a different time and place, where kids ran into the room and leaped onto her sleepy form. How long could Travis keep her to himself when he knew her dream was to have a family?

Travis's gut tied itself into knots as he pushed into the buzzing bar, the sound of the ball game and classic rock meeting his ears. No matter what happened down the road, he needed to be honest with Stephen now. About his phony relationship with Georgie and why it started in the first place. About how incredibly real his feelings were for her now. Lying to Stephen had never sat right and the guy was obviously worried about his sister. He needed to know Travis would do everything in his power to make her happy. As long as she let him. Which was why he'd called Georgie's brother this afternoon and asked to meet him for a beer at seven. Tomorrow morning, the girls were participating in the Tough Mudder. Her siblings would be present and he didn't want any more deception. He wanted them to see their sister with a man who'd die to make her happy, no questions asked—and not doing it for show this time.

Although as Travis scanned the room, he didn't see Stephen yet—

A familiar face at the bar made his blood go ice cold.

His father?

His father was here in Port Jefferson?

Travis watched in horror as Mark Ford teetered to the left on his stool. It was a scene right out of Travis's nightmares. And memories. Those visions in his mind updated themselves now, adding new details, like the extra weight around his father's waist, the hairline that had receded and thinned. How many times as a child had he snuck in through the back door of this bar, trying to pry his father away from the bottle? The sensation of hunger and shame crept up on Travis now, as if over a decade hadn't passed.

"Well, now." Mark slapped the bar with an open hand, turning on the stool. "There's my son. Knew you'd turn up here sooner or later. Always did."

Acutely aware of the attention on them, Travis cleared his throat and eliminated the distance between them. "What the hell are you doing back here?"

Mark laughed, lines fanning out at the edges of his eyes. "That's no kind of welcome."

"You're not welcome," Travis enunciated. "There's nothing for you here."

"Not true." Mark took a sloppy pull from his drink. A beer. But several empty shot glasses sat in front of him, like little sparkling badges of honor. "Got a call from the real estate agent letting me know you were selling the house."

An invisible slap landed across Travis's face. Of course. The deed was in both of their names. The real estate agent probably had no choice but to alert him of the appraisal. Travis's goal was to begin burying the past, but he'd dragged it out into the light instead. Dragged a bitter, foul-breathed reminder right back into the present.

"Took a ride by the house this afternoon," Mark continued, loudly. Loudly on purpose. Another one of the ways he'd humiliated Travis as a child. Needling him in public about a bad game, his eating habits, his mother, and laughing about it while everyone watched in uncomfortable silence. "You really let the place go to shit. Not that it was any great shakes back in the day, right? You always walked around like you deserved a fucking palace."

He spat the last word, and Travis closed his eyes, praying for patience. A way to make this end faster. End period. He still couldn't actually believe it was happening. "You want your cut of the sale? No problem. You didn't have to come all the way to Port Jeff to get it."

Mark jerked in his chair, a sneer shaping his mouth. "Don't talk to me like I'm some kind of beggar, boy. I have an interest here and I came to see to it. I have every right."

The bartender edged closer in Travis's periphery. "Everything okay, gentlemen?"

Travis nodded at the man without taking his eyes off his father. "Yes, sir. I'm taking care of it." His father started in with another angry outburst, but Travis cut him off. "I'll write you a check for half the appraisal amount. No need to stick around and deal with all the annoying paperwork, right?"

Mark let out a long breath through his nose. "You've just got enough money lying around to front me? Just like that?"

"That's right. More than enough."

His father took a cocktail straw off the bar and popped it into his mouth, chewing on the red plastic. "Real out of the blue, isn't it? Why are you selling the house now?" Mark pointed the straw at Travis. "It's a woman, isn't it?"

The volume of his father's voice had steadily risen to the point where it could be heard by everyone, even over the music and ball game. It would be a cold day in hell before Travis voluntarily said Georgie's name to this man who blackened everything he touched, though, so he remained silent.

"I won't play dumb. Saw in the papers you're dating that Castle girl," said his father, setting off a sour bomb in Travis's stomach. "Bet you fit right in with a family that thinks their shit doesn't stink."

Anger hit him hard. "Shut your fucking mouth, old man," Travis snapped, his fingers stretching and curling in his palms. "They've been better to me than my own family."

A spark of regret lit Mark's eyes, but it was gone as soon as it appeared. "And you're going to repay them by tarnishing the reputation of one of their daughters?" Mark laughed and it was an ugly sound. "Yeah, everyone knows how you carry on. You're a whore like your mother."

When Travis walked into the bar, he'd been Travis Ford the man. The man who'd had some bad runs of luck in a career he loved, but had managed to come through with perspective. He did an honest day's work with his hands, had good friends. He was about to embark on a new career path that scared him a little, but he had the confidence to throw his all into it. Most importantly, he'd landed a girl who made him so happy he couldn't see straight. But in one fell swoop, he was transported back to the boy who'd sat shivering on the porch until the middle of the night, feeling unworthy of anything but doubt. And that boy slowly became the man who'd been slapped like a Ping-Pong ball between teams until he stopped memorizing the names of his teammates, because what was the point, when he'd be gone before the ink dried on his contract?

Travis could only listen numbly as his father continued. "You should do that girl a favor and cut her loose before she gets her hopes up that you're actually a decent person."

"You honestly think I'd change for a girl?" As soon as the words were out of Travis's mouth, he hated himself. Acid rolled to a boil in his stomach, on his tongue. But he didn't want this man who poisoned everything to focus on Georgie another fucking second. His girlfriend was the best thing in his life, and he'd fight to keep the worst part away from her. Travis wouldn't put it past his father to find a way to hurt them, if he knew how important Georgie was to him. That was how Mark Ford operated. "She's a kid with a kid's crush," Travis rasped, the lies razing his throat. "All I did was use it to my advantage. You're looking at the new voice of the Bombers."

"Knew it. A leopard doesn't change its spots. Let's hope you do better behind a microphone than you did behind the plate." Mark laughed into his drink. "I'll leave my address with the real estate agent. Looking forward to that nice check."

"Enjoy," Travis rasped. "It's the last thing you'll ever get from me."

Disgusted with himself for betraying Georgie, Travis turned to leave—

And ran straight into Stephen. With an uncapped beer in front of him on the bar, he'd clearly been there long enough to hear everything.

Travis couldn't move. Couldn't breathe as Georgie's brother gave him a look of pure revulsion, his eyes running the length of Travis, before he vanished from the bar.

CHAPTER TWENTY-SEVEN

"Can you believe him, Georgie?" Bethany cried, screeching to a stop at a red light. "My own brother. Warning the other realtors in town not to sell me a property. You know what I think? I think he's afraid I'll do a better flip."

In hindsight, driving to the Tough Mudder with Bethany might have been a mistake. Her sister was hyped up and not in a good way. And honestly, her sister had every right to be pissed. But Georgie's head—and stomach—just wasn't into the bitch session today.

Travis never came over last night. He'd texted her around eight o'clock to say he couldn't make it. No excuse or reason. Just *I can't make it, baby girl.* She'd been half tempted to drive over to his apartment with a few cartons of lo mein but stopped herself. She was definitely new at this couple thing, but they weren't required to spend every waking moment together. Maybe he'd just felt like watching baseball and scratching in places he couldn't scratch in her company. No big deal, right?

Only she couldn't shake the intuition something was wrong. Had he changed his mind about them? Maybe those declarations he'd made in the limousine were simply made in the heat of the moment. In the light of day, it was possible Travis realized he'd jumped the gun and made a mistake.

Would he even show up today?

"Wait, hold on." Georgie lowered the sun visor and flipped open the mirror, so she could tie her hair into an even ponytail. "You made an offer on a property in town, but they wouldn't sell, because Stephen warned them not to?"

"I can't even get an appointment!" Bethany floored it through the intersection. "You really don't listen at all. If you weren't my sister, I'd probably date you."

"You took that one step too far," Georgie murmured, securing the hair on top of her head. "So they admitted this to you? Seems like that kind of treatment is illegal." Georgie smacked the visor back into place. "Maybe it's a misunderstanding. Is Stephen coming today?"

Bethany snorted. "Do you think Kristin would miss a chance to give him a heart attack? She's doing the Tough Mudder with us."

"Shut up." Georgie gave in to her first laugh of the day. "Well, maybe you'll get lucky and he'll keel over. You can have all the houses after that."

"Fingers crossed," Bethany muttered, taking a turn off the avenue and bringing them onto an uneven road, trees hanging low on either side. "This is ominous."

They bumped down the road for a few minutes, bright orange sign markers guiding their way, before finally reaching the clearing. Tents were set up, advertisements splashed across their canvas tops. Music boomed through loudspeakers. A starting line loomed in the distance. Nerves started to jangle in Georgie's belly as they parked the car and headed for the check-in. She'd bought new running shoes for the occasion and spent the week breaking them in, and even though they were destined to be ruined with mud, she was grateful to have them upon seeing the other decked-out participants. People took this shit seriously.

Trying not to be obvious about it, Georgie turned in a circle while waiting in the check-in line, scanning the observation bleachers for Travis. Not there. She already knew he wasn't there, because her senses weren't tingling, the way they always did in his presence.

Don't panic. He'll be here.

"There's Rosie," Bethany said, nudging Georgie in the ribs. "Oh my God, she looks so cute. She should never wear any color but lavender." She cupped her hands around her mouth. "Hey, queen!"

Rosie closed the passenger door of Dominic's truck and waved. But she didn't come join them right away. She lingered at the fender as Dominic, dressed in jeans and a fitted white shirt that showed off his heavily inked skin, sauntered around the front end of the truck . . . and whoa. Whoa. Animosity spiked in the air between husband and wife, but there was way more than just irritation there. Dominic looked Rosie top to bottom, sucking his bottom lip through his teeth. She tossed her hair a little, as if enduring the perusal, but even from a distance, Georgie could see the deepening glow of her brown skin.

Dominic stepped into his wife's space and tipped her chin

up with a jerk of his own, as if they had an invisible string connecting their movements. He leaned in for a kiss—but their lips didn't quite connect, and both of their sides heaved once, twice, before Rosie pivoted and left Dominic standing alone. His fist pounded the hood of the truck.

"Jesus," Bethany breathed. "I need to get laid after that."

Georgie nodded. "Same. And I'm getting laid now regularly."

"Braggart," her sister scolded. "When am I getting sordid sex details, by the way?"

"I don't know if that should be a thing."

"Sorry, it's a new club rule. All sexual exploits are to be discussed in great detail. Added it to the agenda this morning."

"You're out of control."

Rosie reached them, the flush still painting her cheeks and neck. "Good morning." She looked everywhere but their faces. "I need this today."

"You need something," Bethany muttered.

Georgie hip checked her sister. "Bethany."

"What? I'm just supposed to pretend I didn't witness them air fucking?"

"Ma'am," prompted an exasperated voice to their right. "If you're checking in, I need to see some identification."

Red-faced, Bethany unzipped the pocket of her running pants and handed over her driver's license. Rosie and Georgie followed suit, trying not to die of mortification in the process. When all three of them were checked in and had been handed their official paper badges, they scooted off to the side to wait for the rest of the Just Us League members to do the same.

"Sorry about before, Rosie," Bethany said, using the safety pins to affix the number to the front of her shirt. "I have boundary issues."

"No, don't apologize." Rosie shook her head. "I've known for a long time something is off with Dominic and me. Like really off. But seeing your reactions only confirms it." She narrowed her gaze on something over Georgie's shoulder. Georgie turned to find Dominic watching his wife from the edge of the crowd, a cigarette tucked between his fingers. The hunger in his expression was nothing short of ferocious. "If you want to know the truth . . ."

Bethany and Georgie waited.

"The truth is we don't talk. We avoid each other. He's angry. I'm getting angrier by the day. But the attraction . . . it's a monster. Sometimes the buildup goes on for weeks until we finally give in. We're just about there now." Rosie let out a shaky puff of air. "Obviously." With a shrug, she broke eye contact with her husband. "And then the vicious cycle starts again."

"Hey." Georgie squeezed Rosie's hand. "You have a long history with Dominic and no one knows your relationship better than you. But we're here if you want help. Or just to talk."

"I know. Thank you." Rosie jogged in place, the redness beginning to fade from her skin. "Without your help, I never would have launched my Kickstarter last night. Help fund Rosie's Empanada Factory. I already passed the thousand-dollar mark this morning." She was practically trembling with excitement. "If you hadn't put my empanadas on a tray at the meeting, Georgie, I probably wouldn't have had the balls."

In disbelief, Georgie released a rush of breath, feeling Bethany's hand rubbing circles onto her back. "Who needs balls when you have flaky dough filled with meat?"

"Indeed." Rosie's lips spread into a smile, more optimistic than Georgie had ever seen it. "Right now, I just want to kick ass and take names."

Bethany threw back her head and whooped. "We got that covered!"

By mile two, they wanted to burrow beneath the mud and let the earth reclaim their bodies as compost.

"Oh my God," Georgie wheezed, trotting over yet another mound. So many mounds. She hadn't trained for mounds. "Whose idea was this?"

Bethany made a strangled sound. "It was a collective—"

"No. No, it was you." Georgie splattered through a deep pit of mud. "You owe me new shoes and two hours of my life back."

"It's not so bad," Rosie panted, threading through the sisters on a spurt of momentum, then immediately slowing down. "Okay, it's that bad. But we're going to hit our second wind soon. I read about it."

They all screeched to a halt when a blond ball of light sped past them. "Hey, ladies. Sorry I'm late!" Kristin turned and jogged backward, somehow navigating the uneven terrain without looking. "Isn't it a beautiful day? Strawberry tarts at the finish line!"

"I'm going to kill her," Georgie growled. "Who's with me?"

Both women raised their hands, then doubled over from the physical effort.

"That's it. That's our motivation for finishing the race." Georgie took Bethany's and Rosie's arms and tugged them along. "We're going to murder my sister-in-law. Just keep repeating it to yourself like a mantra."

Somehow Bethany, Georgie, and Rosie made it through three miles of running. Ah, but then came the obstacle course. Several of the Just Us League members had caught up to them by that time. The desire to help each and every one of the women over the climbing wall and through the army crawl distracted Georgie from the pain of exertion. She'd expected a feeling of accomplishment. Satisfaction. But straddling her high school physics teacher and bodily dragging her through a mud pit while both of them laughed? It bonded them. Crossing the monkey bars, then jogging back to help Bethany prop up Rosie as she did the same? She wasn't just part of a team, she was *leading* it.

Georgie wasn't sure what made her turn and look at the row of spectators lining the makeshift fence. Maybe it was the sparkle at the back of her neck. But when she glanced over, Travis stood there in a ball cap, his beloved face softened with a smile. And it was too much. The explosion of camaraderie. Her boyfriend's support. The love she'd been keeping locked up inside herself for so long. The glue holding her together started to evaporate.

I'm going to tell him. I have to tell him everything. It won't stay inside.

"You came."

A frown marred his forehead. "Of course I came." Something was wrong, though. She could see it. Dark circles cradled his eyes, tension riding along his shoulders. "You're doing great, baby girl. I'll be waiting at the finish line."

Georgie nodded, relieved to have a better motivation than murdering Kristin. Taking one more worried look at Travis's face, she turned and rejoined the women, doing her best to give them her whole focus. They deserved it. Once they'd completed all ten obstacles, they all crossed the finish line together and were immediately handed . . . beer? Bethany, Rosie, and Georgie shrugged and clinked plastic cups.

"We look like we just crawled out of a swamp," Rosie said, laughing.

Bethany guzzled down half her beer. "We did."

"But we did it." Georgie's laugh turned into a sob, the earlier rise of emotions catching her around the throat again. "You guys, I'll be back. I have to do something."

They gave her a mud-covered hug and sent Georgie on her way. Picking through the celebrating crowd on her own, the magnitude of what she was about to do hit. How would Travis react? Would he panic? Would it make him happy?

Either way, she couldn't look him in the face anymore and water down her feelings. Every time she kept the words crammed down inside, it hurt. And there was a bone-deep knowledge inside Georgie telling her Travis wouldn't want her to hurt.

The crowd parted and there he was. God, so absurdly good-looking in jeans and a navy-blue sweatshirt rolled up to his elbows. He was looking for her, too, and when he found her, relief etched itself on every line of his strong body. Georgie didn't care that she looked like Swamp Thing; she could only gravitate toward Travis, and when he opened his arms up, she ran and leaped into them like they were the gates of heaven. To her, they were.

"You were amazing out there," he said into her neck. "They got tired and you motivated them. You were the leader."

Her heart lifted. "I promised them they could help me kill Kristin." Travis's laugh was so genuine, she wondered if she'd imagined how tired he looked. "Will you kiss me even though I'm covered in mud of questionable origin?"

His mouth found hers, gave it a teasing nuzzle. "I've never seen you more beautiful," he rasped. "The way you smiled out there. The way you're smiling now . . ."

The decision to come clean, the lack of the burden. It had to be showing on her face. "Travis, I have to talk to you."

"I have to talk to you, too, Georgie." The worry was back around his eyes, making her stomach clench, but his mouth continued to sample hers with distracting kisses. "Can we go somewhere—"

"Travis." Stephen's voice broke through the personalized fog surrounding them. "How about you put my sister down?"

Travis's jaw bunched tight. "Not now. Please don't do this now."

"You haven't given me a choice."

"I can clear this up," he said, throwing her brother a look. "Just let me talk to her first." Travis faced her once again, pushing their foreheads together. "Ah, baby girl. I fucked up. This is going to get bad. Just promise you'll give me a chance to explain."

Georgie's breath started to come faster, scraping along her eardrums. This seemed bad. Needing to get some distance from the comforting feel of him so she could be objective, Georgie eased herself to the ground, staving off Travis when he tried to tug her back into the cradle of his body. "Explain what?" Keeping her chin up, she transferred her attention to a glowering Stephen. "What's going on?"

Stephen's demeanor turned nervous—and that's when Georgie started to become truly terrified. She'd rarely seen her brother look anything but self-assured, especially since they'd entered adulthood. "When Travis stood up for you at dinner, he was right. You deserve better. I realized I haven't been treating you the way I should and I'm really sorry. And I just want to do right by you now. I wish that didn't mean hurting you," Stephen finished in a gruff voice. "I just thought . . . when he came to me about your relationship, I thought I saw a change in him."

Bethany bounded up beside Georgie. "What's the serious-face summit about?"

Concreted to the ground, Georgie ignored her sister. "Keep going."

Her brother gave a deep sigh. "It was all fake for him. He was dating you to help land himself the commentator job. None of it was real."

Relief landed on Georgie's head like cement. "Oh God. Okay, Stephen. We have a lot to talk about. Now isn't the time, but Travis and I both had our reasons for dating. At first." She squeezed Travis's hand. "It's super complicated, but please trust me when I say this is real."

Stephen's frown didn't relent. "I heard what I heard, Georgie. He called you a kid last night. Said he's been using you to his advantage. I'm as surprised as you are."

"Georgie, look at me," Travis implored her. "I was full of shit when I said that."

Georgie couldn't tear her eyes off her brother. There was more coming. Foreboding made her hands and feet feel like they'd fallen asleep, made her lips numb.

"When Travis told me you two were dating, I told him to back off so you wouldn't get hurt," Stephen said, dragging a hand down his face. "I thought he'd leave you alone if I told him you'd been in love with him since you were a kid. But he didn't. He . . . I can't believe this, but he used it. He called you a kid with a kid's crush."

The blood drained straight out of her. She couldn't breathe.

"What the fuck, Stephen?" Bethany muttered.

For some reason, Travis calling her a kid landed the hardest blow. How many times had he demonstrated the opposite with his words and actions? Something about the revelation didn't sit exactly right, but she was too bogged down in mortification to examine what it was.

"A kid with a crush. So you knew how I felt the whole time?" Georgie whispered. "Poor little Georgie. God, you must have felt so bad for me."

Her mind cluttered up with images of the last couple weeks. Travis above her, his mouth open on a moan. Travis opening a takeout carton in a towel, winking at her across the kitchen. The morning on the baseball field when he picked up a bat again. Was any of that real? Her stomach pitched, sharp jabs of pain penetrating her rib cage. Finding their mark.

"No. No, I didn't feel bad for you. I knew . . ." Travis rocked back on his heels, a hand plowing into his hair. "The kind of love Stephen told me about wasn't real. It was just . . ."

"What?"

"A young girl's crush," he answered quietly, his jaw flexing. "Hero worship."

The oxygen vacated her lungs. "You made that judgment without even asking me, didn't you?" A punch of misery hit her in the stomach. "Do you have any idea how stupid I feel? Knowing you were aware of how I felt the whole time? Silly clown with her silly, meaningless crush. I guess you never took me seriously, either. Not me and not our friendship," she managed, moisture gathering in her eyes. "The love didn't pass, Travis. It just became so much more. I still loved the guy who hit the home runs and showed off for the crowd. I also loved the imperfect man."

"Don't say 'loved.' Say 'love.'" Travis made a rough sound. "And Jesus, don't cry. Please don't cry." He tried to come toward her, but Stephen grabbed his arm, holding him off. "Let go of me. My girlfriend is crying."

"She's not your girlfriend."

Georgie couldn't even be sure who said those words. Her

head spun too fast to keep up. She only knew it was true. He'd thought of her as a stupid kid, didn't take her seriously, just like everyone else. He was aware of her feelings and sloughed them off like they weren't real. They were. So real that her heart was capsizing under the rupturing pressure.

"Georgie, I'm sorry. I'm *sorry.*"

Dominic joined Stephen to pull a struggling Travis farther away. It was a losing battle until security joined them, herding a belligerent Travis toward the parking lot.

"Get off of me. *Fuck.* Just let me talk to her."

Despite all the doubt paralyzing Georgie, her heart shouted at her to run to Travis, making her cry all the harder. But in the end, she let her sister and friends close ranks around her, shielding her from the crowd as she absorbed reality. Shielding her from the man who'd broken her heart.

CHAPTER TWENTY-EIGHT

Travis lay on the couch in the darkness facing the door. Staring at the hinges and knob, willing them to move. But they wouldn't. They wouldn't move.

He'd lost the one person who busted down his door.

As he'd done time and time again over the last several days, he turned onto his stomach and searched for her scent in the pillow he'd brought from his bed. It, too, was gone. He'd sucked it all up on day one. Absorbed it into his bloodstream, along with countless swigs of whiskey and no food.

His first night on the air was in a matter of days, yet the muddy clothes he'd worn to the Tough Mudder were stuck to his unwashed skin, a bristling beard overtaking his cheeks. Getting up to take a shower or make himself a sandwich sounded more difficult than training to be a fucking astronaut. Nothing could get him off the couch when he ached head to toe. Inside and out.

He kept his face buried in the softness anyway, wondering if he could die from carbon dioxide poisoning this way. Worth a shot.

Out of nowhere, the memory of Georgie crying slammed

into his consciousness again and he let loose a bellow into the pillow, forcing himself to remember every nuance as penance. How she'd shrunk into herself, going from confident to unsure right in front of his eyes. How she'd trembled and cupped her elbows. Almost immediately, the mental torture became too much, so his hand dropped to the floor, searching for a bottle of whiskey with something left inside of it.

"Come on." He barely recognized the hollow voice emerging from his own mouth. "Come on."

Travis's hand closed around the neck of a bottle and he sat up, wincing as his brain performed a somersault. *Please, God, let there be enough whiskey in this bottle to numb the memory of hurting Georgie.* Because fuck, he'd hurt her so bad.

Travis unscrewed the top of the bottle, but when he tipped it toward his lips, he stared down into the golden contents instead. Was this where he was at? Drinking himself into a stupor over losing a woman? That's exactly what his father had done. Or what he'd used as an excuse to drink himself into an oblivion anyway. Maybe he and Mark Ford weren't so different after all. Travis started to lift the bottle again and paused.

A voice drifted out of the darkness. One he knew as well as his own. It was Georgie's. Words she'd spoken the last time he'd been in this state.

You're only him if you lie down and play the victim. You're better than this.

"I'm not better. I lost you," he rasped into the silent living room.

Sweet man. Strong man.

His head tipped back on a miserable groan. The alcohol in his hand was so close, but he couldn't bring himself to drink it with Georgie's voice in his head. In his heart.

"Christ, I love you, Georgette Castle." He set down the bottle, filling his hands with his pounding head instead. "I'm in love with you."

No answer. Of course not. She wasn't really there to hear him realizing, far too late, that he'd started falling in love with her the day she'd barged into his apartment throwing food.

No, she wasn't there. At least not in a physical way. But in every other way that counted, she took up every corner and surface in his house. *A League of Their Own* sat in its case on Travis's television stand. Her Tupperware was still tucked in his cabinets. Her voice echoed off the walls. Exactly as it should be. Their things were meant to be in the same house. Their lives were meant to be twisted up and twined together forever. For so long, committing to forever had been unrealistic. A surefire path to bitterness and failure.

Well, he'd been wrong. This. *This* was failure. Having the very thing he needed more than breath and squandering it. Georgie had been the one person in his life to remain committed to him for better or worse, even when he was too young and oblivious to realize it. She'd loved him all along. Now that he wanted—needed—forever with Georgie, it wasn't an option.

You're only him if you lie down and play the victim.

"I heard you, baby girl," he croaked. "But you hate me now. You should."

The man Georgie deserved wouldn't wallow in self-pity, though, would he? No, he'd get his ass up and find a way to make her understand. A way to make her forgive. Was he that man?

Because if he won Georgie back, it would be with the intention of giving her everything she wanted in this life. A home, a future. Children.

Travis closed his eyes, imagining himself as a father for the first time in his life. He went back to the night of their dinner in Old Westbury and replaced Kelvin with himself. Squatting beside a little girl with Georgie's eyes and smile, clapping as Georgie juggled. He thought of finger paintings drying over the sink, just as Georgie had described weeks ago, only now it was a vision of heaven instead of hell. Because he could see himself there. With her. With the lives they created. He was a good man capable of more than he'd ever known. Georgie thought so and he would damn well believe her.

Such a huge wave of contentment—and responsibility—crashed into Travis's chest that he had to struggle through several breaths. And then he was off the couch, stumbling toward the bathroom, wrestling with his clothes and wrenching on the shower faucet. As he cleaned himself off as fast as he possibly could with a monster hangover, the vision grew stronger.

Someday he would swear to Georgie he'd seen the future in that shower.

She would tell him he'd still been drunk, but she'd smile and get misty-eyed.

No, forget that part. His Georgie would never cry again. Not the sad kind of tears, anyway. She would cry when he finished the fireplace. On their wedding day. When their children were born. When those same children graduated from college. Good tears. He'd give her good tears for the rest of her life. He was capable of it. He was this man—not some man who'd come before. If she believed in him once, she could do it again. This time it would be different, because he believed in himself. That he could make her happy. Forever.

First he had to win her back.

But it wouldn't be easy.

Travis was clearly the last person Bethany expected to find on her doorstep.

"You've got to be kidding me." She propped a shoulder against the doorjamb and hauled in a long sip of white wine. "My sister isn't here. Even if she was, I would rather exfoliate with sandpaper than let you see her for even a second."

Keep it together. Keep. It. Together. Don't beg to know where Georgie is. What she's doing. If she's okay. That wasn't his purpose there. And he didn't have the right to know yet. In lieu of words, he took a key out of his pocket, extending it toward Bethany to take.

"What is that?"

"It's the key to my house. The one I grew up in." Voice rusty from disuse, he didn't bother trying to make himself sound normal. It was taking all of his effort to stand there and not ask for news about Georgie. Something. Anything.

"Flip it however you want and keep the profit. It's yours. Free and clear."

Bethany straightened slowly. "You're giving me the house? Why?"

"It's important to her. You succeeding. All of you succeeding. She's good in that way. She's so fucking good, you know?"

"The best."

Travis took a necessary moment to breathe. "And I need her—I need her to know—the past is over. I'm done living there." Not wanting to give her room to refuse, he put the key in Bethany's free hand, closing her fingers around it. "But I'm going to ask for something in return. Because I'm fucking desperate."

"You'd have to be to ask me for help. I'm only giving you the time of day because . . ." The barest hint of sympathy crept into her expression. "You really do look like hell," she grumbled into her wineglass. "Why am I not enjoying this as much as I should?"

"You know I'm in love with her. That's why." Saying it out loud seemed to make it that much more true. Voicing the truth written on his soul felt so incredible, he couldn't wait to say it over and over again for the rest of his life. To Georgie. To anyone who would listen. Unless, of course, Georgie wouldn't take him back, in which case he'd be saying it to the business end of a pillow for the foreseeable future. "I love that girl in every way it's possible to love someone. And maybe a few ways that don't even have a name. I'm just asking you to help me prove it to her."

Bethany blinked away the moisture in her eyes. "You did a number on her."

The pain that ripped through him was so intense, Travis had to prop a hand on the house for support. "If she decides she'll be happier without me, so be it." He swallowed a fistful of nails. "Maybe that's true. But I'm not losing her lying down."

He could feel Georgie's sister studying him. Couldn't lift his head to confirm it, though. "What do I have to do?"

Hope sparked to life. Just enough to make his neck work, so he could look at Bethany. "Please. I have things I need to say to Georgie. Just get her to listen."

"Tell me your plan and I'll think about it."

When Travis finished, she swirled her wine in her glass and tossed it back. "Fine. I'll help. But afterward, her decision is final. You have to respect it." Just before shutting the door, she tossed up the key and caught it. "Thanks for the house."

Travis walked down the porch, zero spring in his step. No, it was way too early for that.

At least now he had a plan.

The promise of that alone would be enough to make it one more day, when he would fight for his damn life. *Their* life together.

CHAPTER TWENTY-NINE

From the neck down, Georgie looked like dynamite. Everything above that?

Not so much.

She'd been saving the little black dress for a special occasion. The one-week anniversary of the world's most traumatic breakup seemed special enough, right? Granted, no one besides the Just Us League ladies would see her wearing it, but the fitted silk material made her feel better. For, like, a full five seconds. Her longest streak yet!

Oh God. She shut down the camera app she'd been using as a mirror and dropped the cell into her lap. Through the windshield, she watched Bethany and Rosie flit back and forth in front of the living room window, preparing the house for the meeting. Georgie should have been in there helping them, but her sister and Rosie would take one look at her gaunt cheeks and sunken eyes and know she'd been a sobbing insomniac, despite her reassuring texts to the contrary. Plus, it would take so much energy to get out of the car and walk all the way to the front door. She'd have to fill chip bowls and uncork wine . . .

Georgie dropped her head back against the seat and groaned.

It was unbelievable how much she missed Travis even after everything. By sheer force of will, she'd gotten out of bed every morning, returned client phone calls, and booked an exciting number of parties, for both herself and the new entertainers. She might have sunk to the lowest pit of despair, but the new, improved Georgie wouldn't wallow there. People were counting on her. And yeah, pride was a huge motivator, too. She'd stood in front of these women and defended Travis, but that zeal had been misplaced—a mistake she would walk in and own. If she didn't own it now, she'd hide forever.

The temptation to do exactly that was so strong, though. God. What an absolute fool she'd been. She'd been blind, no idea that her secrets weren't secrets. That the person who'd been encouraging her didn't think she was smart enough to know her own heart.

How could he hold her in his arms so tightly through the night, knowing her feelings far exceeded his own? How dare he. How dare he give her some illusion he never intended to keep up.

Despite all of this, she needed him. Half of her soul felt torn away.

For what seemed like the millionth time, she closed her eyes tight and remembered the kisses, the hugs, the laughing, playing baseball in the rain. The way she'd felt about Travis had been right there all along, plain as day. Georgie might have tried to play it cool, but it was an inherent part of her. Every moment of their time together, she'd been expressing that love. Dropping off leftovers, encouraging him, throwing food at his head. Her heart had created an extra chamber for loving Travis Ford. The fact that he'd borne witness to it and continued to doubt made those feelings seem invalid.

Georgie's body moved with an awful lethargy as she climbed out of the car, careful not to trip over her own feet on the brick path. High heels hadn't been the best idea, considering her legs weren't working right. Just like the rest of Georgie, her limbs moved at a sluggish pace. Her hand lifted to the doorknob like it was submerged in a jar of Vaseline.

The door swung open before she was halfway through the process, and Georgie lost her balance, sending her pitching forward. Bethany and Rosie caught her, the simple human contact sending a shock wave of sorrow through her.

"I'm not good."

"I know, honey," Bethany said, helping her straighten and pulling her back into a hug. But not before she got a decent look at Georgie's face. "Oh shit. No worries. I've got a bottle of concealer upstairs that could hide the spots on a fucking cow."

Rosie rubbed a circle on her back. "How about a drink?"

"No, thanks. It'll only make things worse." She pulled away from her sister. "Maybe just, like, a half a glass of literally anything?"

"I'll grab some glasses and a bottle and meet you guys upstairs," Bethany said, giving her shoulder a final squeeze. "We've got more than enough time before everyone arrives."

Georgie and Rosie made their way upstairs, going straight for Bethany's en suite bathroom. She sat on the edge of the bathtub, instantly comforted by the luxurious cream-striped wallpaper and matching fluffy towels. The little notches in the wall where candles flickered gave off a glow and the scent of pears and freesia. Growing up, Bethany had always bemoaned sharing a bathroom with her siblings, vowing to have her own private bathing palace one day. Mission accomplished. Throw in a minifridge and it would be livable.

"I know your mind is all over the place right now," Rosie said in a soft voice, dropping into an elegant lean against the wall. "But . . . Georgie, I can't thank you enough. We hit the donation goal early this morning. For the restaurant."

"What?" Georgie gasped, the storm clouds parting. "No way. Oh my God, Rosie. That's fantastic." She shot off the tub, throwing both arms around her friend. "Of course you hit the goal once word of mouth got around."

"I can't believe it," Rosie whispered. "I can't believe that many want to come to my restaurant. Bad enough to put money where their mouth is."

"I can believe it," Georgie said, easing away. "Lots of work ahead."

Rosie blew out a breath. "Yes."

"We'll help you," Bethany said with a radiant smile as she walked into the bathroom, balancing a tray of champagne and three glasses. "It'll make me feel less guilty when I put you two in hard hats for demo day." With a twist of her wrist, she popped the cork. "I've got myself a house."

Georgie spun toward her sister. "You—how?" With too many emotions to compute in one day, her laughter was watery, but her pleasure was genuine. "Did Stephen cave?"

"No." Bethany pushed Georgie back down onto the lip of

the bathtub and handed her a glass of champagne. "Travis Ford handed me the key to his childhood house. Gave me permission to flip and sell it, free and clear."

Hearing his name out loud was a one-two punch to the sternum. All she could do was sit there and breathe in, out, in, out. He'd done what? "I don't understand," she finally whispered. "Why would he do that?"

Bethany rolled her eyes. "He said it was important to you that I succeed. Or something. I wasn't really listening." She set down her champagne glass and dragged over a designer makeup bag. "Let's get to work on those dark circles, shall we—"

"Wait a second." Georgie couldn't even feel the glass between her fingers. "He just came here and . . . Was he . . . Did he . . ."

Georgie's sister squirted some beige foundation onto the back of her hand and ran a silver-tipped brush through it, applying the cool liquid to Georgie's face. "Like I said, I was kind of half listening. He'd interrupted *Drag Race,* which is a cardinal sin in my house." She tilted her head, swiping the brush in a neat line between Georgie's brows. "Hopefully someone is doing *his* concealer, because he looked like *S-H-I-T.*" Georgie wanted to sink back into the empty bathtub and curl into a ball hearing that. "Honestly, it was all so sappy. Georgie this, Georgie that. Georgie is so good. I'm done living in the past. Et cetera."

"Et cetera?"

"Yeah. Et cetera." Done with the brush, Bethany stowed it back in the makeup bag and drew out a gray stick, the function of which Georgie did not know. But she sat there gaping as Bethany swiped it beneath her cheekbones and started to rub it in. "When I pulled the deed, I realized his father's name is listed on it, too. Turns out Mark Ford was back in town for a few days to make sure he got a cut. There were words exchanged at Grumpy Tom's."

"Travis's father was back?" Georgie sputtered. "Why didn't anyone tell me?"

Was this the part of the equation that had been missing? She'd been so mired in heartache, she hadn't stopped to think about why Travis would have called her a kid with a crush. Maybe there was a reasonable explanation. He'd still left her in the dark about what Stephen told him, but shouldn't she have given Travis a chance to explain? With his father in town, he would have been in a tailspin. And he *had* canceled their date the night before the Tough Mudder . . .

"I mean, it's all just noise at this point, right?" Bethany said breezily. "He messed up too big. It's done."

Georgie threw Rosie a look that said, *Help me.* "Um." Rosie nodded at her in the universal sign for *I got you.* "What else did he say? It's totally common to want a play-by-play when a guy talks about you. There had to be more."

"Nope, that was it. He looked like garbage and gave me a house." She applied some mascara to Georgie's lashes. "Oh, and Georgie this, Georgie that."

"Be more specific!" Georgie screeched.

"Drag Race *was on,*" Bethany said defensively. "Okay, look in the mirror."

Fully intending to ignore the command and strangle her

sister instead, Georgie nonetheless caught sight of her reflection and did a double take. "Oh, that's—wow."

"Not bad, right?"

"How did you—"

"Contouring. Georgie, meet your cheekbones."

"Hi, cheekbones," she murmured, then snapped back to reality. "Bethany—"

Downstairs, the doorbell rang. Even through the bathroom window, Georgie could hear the excited voices of the women outside. Her sister shrugged and pranced from the bathroom, leaving the candles to flicker in her wake.

"Can you believe that?" Georgie asked Rosie in a high-pitched voice. "I'm supposed to just be satisfied with 'this and that'?"

Before Rosie could answer, raised voices from downstairs captured their attention. The sound of a cheering crowd ripped its way up to the second floor, but it had the force of thousands behind it and surely wasn't coming from the arriving guests. Georgie thought she caught the corner of Rosie's mouth tilting into a smile, but it vanished so fast, she must have been mistaken.

"What is that?"

Rosie gave her a bland look. "Go find out."

Moments later, Georgie descended the stairs into the rapidly filling living room, finding everyone crowded around the television, also known as the source of the cheering. Able to recognize the sounds of a baseball game in her sleep, Georgie stopped short. How could she have forgotten? Today was a home game for the Bombers—and Travis's official start as their new voice. Her pulse tripped all over itself as she waded through the throng of women, each of them watching her pass on the way to a front-row seat.

There he was. Her fake ex-boyfriend. His sinfully good-looking face filled the screen with an expression more somber than usual. At least more somber than he'd been during their phony relationship. Or was that just wishful thinking that he'd been happy? No. No, it wasn't. But now a strain played around his eyes and the corners of his mouth, even as he responded to questions from the cohost welcoming him.

"I speak on behalf of the Bombers organization when I say we missed seeing your face on television and we're looking forward to seeing a lot more of it."

"Thank you," Travis said, clearing the rasp from his voice. "Honored to be here."

"I understand you brought someone along with you today."

"Yes, I did." The camera panned out to reveal a dozen awestruck faces of teenage boys in uniforms, one of whom Georgie recognized as the kid who'd delivered their chicken parm. "Doing the play-by-play for the Bombers isn't my only job. This is the Port Jefferson High School baseball team, and I'm going to be working with them in the off-season. I didn't think they'd mind watching the game from the booth today."

Resounding agreements went up from the students, making the cohost laugh. "Something tells me you're right." He shifted in his seat, visibly changing gears with a jocular smile. "Now, there wasn't always a time Travis Ford would have been considered mentor material for the younger generation." Travis gave him a wry smile but didn't respond. "What changed?"

Travis flicked an intense look at the camera. "I met Georgie Castle."

A gasp went up in the living room, hands reaching out to steady her from all directions.

"I've met her twice in my life. This time, I was smart enough to fall in love with her." He took out his earpiece and swiped a hand through his hair. "She taught me more about myself than I ever learned with a bat in my hands. She's the reason I'm sitting here right now." With a deep breath, he looked into the camera. Right at her. "I didn't think anyone could love a broken-down has-been like me. That's why I didn't believe you actually loved me. I do now. You made me believe I'm worthy of it. And if I can be worthy of you, I'd consider that my life's greatest accomplishment." He paused. "I'm in love with you, baby girl. I want you for my wife. You think I'll stop at building you a mantel? I'll work every day to build my girl the life she deserves. If you give me the chance. Marry me, Georgie."

Georgie pitched forward, the wind leaving her. Dizzy, she caught herself on the television stand. Around her, the Just Us League was going absolutely mad, draining cocktails before they could be fully poured and repeating Travis's words in total swoon mode. Was this really happening? She pinched her forearm and yelped in pain, her hands flying to her mouth. *Oh my God.* Travis loved her. And not the Travis Ford who'd stared down at her from a glossy ceiling poster. The man behind the uniform. The most incredible man on the planet. Tears filled her vision and she turned in circles, about to burst from the pressure of love filling her rib cage. "What do I do now?"

"Do you love him back?"

"Of *course* I do!"

Bethany stepped forward. "It's only the third inning." With a knowing smirk, she tossed Georgie her purse. "Bye, bitch."

Georgie choked on a sob and spun for the door, only to be brought up short by Stephen. He stood at the edge of the crowd. Based on his relieved—and regretful—expression, he'd heard Travis's declaration of love on live television. "I've been wrong a lot lately," her brother said, jerking his chin in the direction of the door. "Come on. I'll drive you."

Travis sat at the front of the bus, bent at the waist, head in his hands. Behind him, the Port Jeff baseball team repeated Bombers chants, high off their VIP status at the game. They tried to make him join in, but he was frozen in time. For all the time he'd spent planning his proposal to Georgie, like an idiot he hadn't taken into account how long he'd be required to wait for an answer.

Had Bethany followed through on her end of the bargain and gotten Georgie to watch his debut in the booth? If so, why hadn't Georgie called him? Granted, it would be more poignant to accept his proposal in person. Then again, maybe she hadn't wanted to reject him on the air. Basically his fate hung in the balance as the bus he'd rented trundled down the Northern State Parkway. And when it slowed to a stop, blocked by bumper-to-bumper traffic, Travis couldn't take it anymore. He extricated his cell phone from his pocket, preparing to dial Georgie's number.

Her name and a picture of her in his Hurricanes jersey popped up on the screen.

Wait. She was calling him?

"Georgie?" Travis answered, standing up at his seat, the low tin roof keeping him stooped over. "Say something, baby girl. Please. I miss your voice."

"I miss yours, too," she whispered, sending relief cascading through his middle. "I thought I could make it to the stadium in time, but there's all this traffic—"

His laugh didn't hold a trace of humor. "I'm on my way to Port Jeff. Can you turn around?" He fell back into the seat, covering his eyes with a hand. "I need you to be there when I get off this bus. If I have to go another hour without seeing you, I'm going to die." He braced himself. "Did you watch the game? Did you hear what I said?"

"Yes. Travis, I—"

A horn honked on the parkway, drowning out what she said. But the beep came from two places. The road . . . and the other end of the line. "Georgie. Where are you?"

"On the Northern State Parkway. Near the Brush Hollow Road exit."

An incredulous sound fell from his mouth. He turned in the seat and scanned the westbound lanes on the other side of the divider. Neither side of the expressway was moving, not an unusual occurrence this close to Manhattan. It took Travis a few frantic seconds of searching, but he finally caught sight of a vehicle he never thought he'd be happy to see.

Stephen's fucking minivan.

"Don't move, baby girl. I'm coming to you." He hung up and pocketed the phone, despite Georgie's exclamation on the other end. Yeah, fine. It was pretty insane to get out of the bus in the middle of the expressway. And probably illegal. Ask Travis if he cared. When he said he'd die without seeing Georgie, his heart had backed him up. It ached like a son of a bitch as he hopped the divider and ran for the minivan, need and determination building with every step.

She didn't see Travis coming until he was a few steps away, her eyes flying wide on the other side of the passenger window. Her door flew open, her feet hit the pavement, and she threw herself into his arms, sending him stumbling back a step onto the shoulder.

"You're insane," she breathed into his neck. "You're insane and I love you."

The ground moved under his feet. "Present tense, right? Love not loved."

"Loved and love. Both." She looked him in the eye. "I've loved and love you in every single way."

Thanking the man upstairs with a whispered prayer, Travis eased back just enough to take her face in his hands. "I said those things to my father because he poisons everything he touches. He can poison anything he wants, except you. I couldn't stand your name in his mouth. I couldn't let him focus on you for a second, so I said something awful I didn't mean. I'm so fucking sorry."

"I know. I understand." She wrapped her arms around his neck, allowing him to lift her off the ground. "I'm sorry you had to face him alone."

"I'm strongest when you're around, but I'm going to get better at using that strength, even when you're not standing beside me." He laid the first of many kisses on her lips, almost drowning in the perfection of her taste. "If I ever start to lose strength again, I'll just think of how it felt to lose the girl who loved me, even when I couldn't love myself.

"And if you say yes to marrying me . . ." He had to stop for a breath. "If you say yes, Georgie, we're going to live the next five, six decades out together. We're going to fight and make up a thousand times. And we're going to have babies. I want to have babies with you, more than anything, because you make me believe I can. Be a father. Be a good husband to you." He dropped his face into the base of her neck and was reassured by the chaotic rhythm of her pulse. "Say yes," he whispered. "Please, baby girl. Be my wife."

Moisture filled her eyes. "Yes, Travis Ford. There isn't a single other person on this planet I could imagine those things with. I'll marry you," she breathed. "At least long enough for you to finish my fireplace—"

His laugh booming across the expressway, Travis wrapped her in a hug and swept her off the ground. "You said yes. Thank God." He staggered a little. "I thought I was fucked."

Around them, horns started to honk. One at a time, until it became a cacophony of noise. Clapping and whistling reached them through rolled-down windows. His relief and joy turned everything to a blur, though, and he promptly forgot about their surroundings, despite the loud ruckus taking place. He drew her hand up to his mouth, kissing her knuckles and palm, before sliding on the ring he'd been keeping in his shirt pocket, as even louder cheers and beeps erupted around them. Travis leaned in to breathe with an open mouth against her neck, his hands riding dangerously low on the small of her back. "You just wait until I get you home, baby girl." He drew her up onto her toes, grazing her neck with the barest hint of teeth. "I'm going to put you against a wall and—"

"All right. I think we get the idea," said a dry male voice.

Travis turned his head to find Stephen at the wheel of the minivan, the other man clearly battling a smile. "Fine, I'll be your best man. You don't have to beg."

Travis swallowed and brushed the hair back from Georgie's face. "Thanks, man." He looked at Stephen. "I'll make sure she knows every single day that she's the air I breathe. That's a promise."

Suspiciously teary-eyed, Georgie's brother gave a brisk nod and rolled up the window.

Leaving Travis and Georgie kissing on the shoulder, long after the traffic cleared.

Don't miss Rosie and Dominic's story!

Love Her or Lose Her

Coming soon!

Read on for a sneak peek . . .

CHAPTER ONE

Rosie Vega: a department-store shopper's worst nightmare.

Really, that's what her name tag should have said, instead of cosmetics consultant. In order to fulfill that title, someone would be required to consult her first, right? Problem was, no one ever asked to be spritzed with perfume. And really, that's all it was. Just a little spritz. Why wouldn't customers just let her make them smell good? Was it really so much to ask?

Rosie hobbled over to the Clinique counter in her high heels, scoping for her supervisor, Zelda, before performing a casual lean against the glass, groaning as the pressure on her toes and ankles lessened. One might surmise that Rosie was in the military instead of working as a glorified perfume girl at the mall. If Rosie was caught leaning, she wouldn't be docked pay or anything so serious. She would just get the shittier-smelling perfume to demonstrate tomorrow. Yes. The Zelda worked her evil in backhanded ways.

She leaned over the counter and checked the clock on the register. Nine twenty-nine. A little over half an hour to go and Rosie was exhausted from standing on her feet since three o'clock. The only customers left in Haskel's were buying last-minute birthday presents or shopping for impromptu job interview clothes. There were no pleasure cruisers at the mall this late, but she was required to stay until the very end. On the off chance someone wanted to smell like begonias and sandalwood right before bed.

A squeal rent the air and two children holding giant mall pretzels came tearing through her aisle, their mother sprinting after them with no fewer than three bags on each arm. Rosie managed to lunge out of their way, but one kid's legs got tangled in the other and they went sprawling, both pretzels turning end over end like tumbleweeds into a Dior display.

"Kill me now," the mother wailed at the ceiling, turning bloodshot eyes on Rosie. "Help us. Please."

Feedback screeched over the department store PA system. "Janitorial services to cosmetics." Both kids burst into noisy tears, neither one of them making a move to get off the floor. The PA system sent a ripple of static into the atmosphere forcing everyone to plug their ears, which Rosie could only accomplish with one finger since she was still holding the perfume bottle. "Bring a broom," the man on the speaker finished sleepily.

Rosie chewed her bottom lip for a moment, then set down her fragrance, thus committing a cardinal sin in the eyes of her supervisor. *Don't dawdle, always have a bottle.* Those words were on a plaque in the employee break room in size-seventy-two font. Desperate times called for desperate measures, however, and with her hands free, Rosie could stoop down to help the children to their feet, while their mother lamented the fact that she no longer smoked.

A teenager appeared on the scene dragging a broom behind him, music blaring in his earbuds, and Rosie ushered the kids over to their mother, waving off her gratitude, knowing she needed to find her bottle before—

"No perfume, I see," Zelda drawled, rising from behind the glass counter like a vampire at sundown. "How are we to entice the customer?" She pretended to search the immediate area. "Perhaps our commission will appear out of thin air."

Smile in place, Rosie picked her bottle back up and gave it a shake. "Armed and prepared, Zelda."

"Oh! There it is." Zelda sauntered off to go terrorize someone else. But not before calling to Rosie over her shoulder. "You're sampling the Le Squirt Bon Bon tomorrow."

Rosie ground her molars together and threw a thumbs-up at her supervisor. "Can't wait!" No one had ever sold a bottle of Le Squirt. It smelled like someone woke up with a hangover, stumbled into their kitchen without brushing their teeth and housed a cupcake, then breathed into a bottle and put it on shelves.

She was debating the wisdom of paying the janitor to hide every bottle of Le Squirt—an inside job!—when the sound of footfalls coming in Rosie's direction forced her spine straight, as if on command. She pushed off the glass and held her perfume bottle at the ready, a smile spreading her mouth and punishing her sore cheeks. A man turned the corner and her smile eased somewhat, her hands lowering. Even if he were to buy the scent as a gift for his wife, the dude definitely wouldn't want to go home reeking of women's perfume.

Rosie assumed the man would pass on by, but he stopped at the counter across the aisle, peering into the glass case for a moment. Then he straightened and sent her a warm grin.

"Hi." He shoved his hands into his pockets and Rosie performed her usual customer checklist. Nice watch. Tailored suit. Potential for an upsell if she could convince an obvious businessman that the three-scent gift box was a must have for his lady. "Shouldn't they have sent you home by now?"

Was he talking to her? Weird. On the cosmetics department floor, most people passed by Rosie like she was an inanimate object. A minor annoyance they had to successfully avoid for three point seven seconds, unless they needed directions or help wrangling their kids. She had the urge to glance over her shoulder to make sure the man wasn't addressing someone behind her. Maybe Zelda had doubled back to make sure she was spray-ready.

"Um." Rosie tried not to be obvious about shifting in her heels, transferring the ache between feet. "No rest for the weary, I guess. The mall closes at ten, so . . ."

Speaking to a man felt strange. Foreign. She hadn't even talked to her husband, Dominic, about anything of real importance for years. And God help her, someone giving enough of a damn to ask why she was terrorizing people with a perfume bottle at nine-thirty did feel important. Someone asking about her, noticing her, felt important.

For a split second in time, Rosie let herself notice the man back. In a purely objective way. He was cute. Had some dad bod going on, but she wasn't judging. With both hands in his pockets, she couldn't scope for a wedding ring. Some intuition told her he was divorced, though. Maybe even recently. There was something about how he'd approached as if intending to go straight for the exit that told Rosie he was only pretending to be interested in the jewelry case now. His tense shoulders and stilted small talk suggested he'd actually stopped to speak to her and wasn't overly comfortable doing it.

"Have you been working here long?"

This man was interested in her. In the space it took Rosie to have that realization, she realized her own wedding ring was hidden behind the perfume bottle. Without being obvious, she curled the bottle into her chest and let the gold band wink at him across the aisle. The light in his eyes dimmed almost immediately.

Rosie had been faithful to Dominic since middle school and that wouldn't be changing any time soon, but she allowed herself the feminine satisfaction of knowing a man had found her attractive. Had she even allowed that simple pleasure for anyone but Dominic? No. No, she didn't think so. And in the years since Dominic had returned from active duty, she hadn't gotten that light, bubbly lift from him, either.

Everything between them was dark, lustful, confusing and . . . so far off course, she wasn't sure their marriage would ever point in the right direction again.

Maybe it was silly, allowing this stranger's attempts at flirting to bring everything screaming into perspective, but that's exactly what happened. On a boring Tuesday night that should have been like any other. Suddenly, Rosie wasn't just standing in her usual spot beneath the fake crystal chandelier while boring piano music piped in over the speakers. She was standing in purgatory. Whose life was this?

Not hers.

Once upon a time, she'd been the straight-A student. A member of the Port Jefferson high school volleyball team—B Squad, but whatever. She'd been an aspiring chef.

Wait. Wrong. Rosie was an aspiring chef. She needed to stop thinking of that dream in the past tense. Something that faded with a long ago wish upon a star. Ever since she and her friends, Bethany and Georgie Castle, had formed the Just Us League, her dreams of opening a restaurant had been rekindled. Transformed from pipe dream to reality. They'd even signed her up for one of those crowdsourcing websites and people had donated. Invested in her dreams. Or at least given her a push to get started.

So why was she still standing there on her aching feet?

Rosie set the perfume bottle down on the Clinique counter and sent the man a wobbly smile. "How long have I been working here?" She laughed under her breath. "Too long."

The man laughed, seeming grateful that she'd broken the wedding ring tension. "Yeah, I can relate." He rubbed at the back of his neck. "Well, I guess I should get moving . . ."

He trailed off but made no move to leave. It took Rosie a tick to realize he was gauging her interest level, even though she was married. With a quick intake of breath, she nodded. "Have a nice night."

Rosie stood there long after the man left, still trapped in that out-of-body feeling. Whose life was this, indeed? In a few minutes, she would clock out from a job she hated and go home to a too-quiet house. A horribly, painfully quiet house where she would orbit around Dominic like they might catch fire if they make eye contact. Where had everything gone wrong?

She didn't know. But twenty-seven was too young to settle for unhappiness. Discontent. Hell, any age was too old for that. If she'd learned anything since helping form the Just Us League, it was that when a woman made a goal, she could reach it. Step one had been admitting she still wanted to open the restaurant. Step two had been validating that dream by letting the club sample her famous empanadas. Step three was . . . letting go. Running with her dream and facing the daunting possibility of failure.

Rosie swallowed hard. Okay, perhaps she wasn't quite ready for step three.

Perhaps she needed to correct another, more troubling aspect of her life first.

Dominic.

"I think I'm done," she whispered, the words swallowed up in elevator music, the sounds of cash drawers being pulled from registers and gates being pulled down at the entrances to Haskel's. Likewise, gates were coming down around a heart that was broken every time she passed through the living room and didn't receive so much as a hello, how are you.

I love you.

When was the last time she'd heard those words out of her husband's mouth?

She couldn't even remember.

She couldn't even remember.

Dominic knew about her dream. Knew it had been re-kindled. Yet he'd done nothing to encourage her. He let her walk out of the house in cheap pumps every day to go spray people with perfume, even though she gave every indication it made her miserable. If she had more courage, she would tell Zelda where to stick a bottle of Le Squirt Bon Bon. That bravery was missing, though. It had been for way too long.

Maybe Dominic was the reason she couldn't make the leap to step three of her aspirations. His lack of faith and encouragement—his utter lack of acknowledgment—was holding her back. She'd become content to waste away in this perfume purgatory.

What happened to us? We used to love so hard. We used to be a team.

With a chest full of crushed glass, Rosie leaned over the counter and checked the clock. Ten. She'd made it another day. Her marriage wouldn't.

ABOUT THE AUTHOR

TESSA BAILEY is originally from Carlsbad, California. The day after high school graduation, she packed her yearbook, ripped jeans, and laptop and drove cross-country to New York City in under four days. Her most valuable life experiences were learned thereafter while waitressing at K-Dees, a Manhattan pub owned by her uncle. Inside those four walls, she met her husband and her best friend and discovered the magic of classic rock, and she managed to put herself through Kingsborough Community College and the English program at Pace University at the same time. Several stunted attempts to enter the workforce as a journalist followed, but romance writing continued to demand her attention. She now lives in Long Island, New York, with her husband and daughter. Although she is severely sleep-deprived, she is incredibly happy to be living her dream of writing about people falling in love.

SEP 2022

BOOKS BY TESSA BAILEY

DISORDERLY CONDUCT

THE ACADEMY, VOL.1

One of Amazon's Best Romances of September & Best Romances of 2017

A 2017 RT Reviewers' Choice Award Nominee for Best Contemporary Love & Laughter

INDECENT EXPOSURE

THE ACADEMY, VOL. 2

One of Amazon's Best Romances of February

One of *Bookpage*'s Best Romances of 2018

"Sexy and emotional..." —*Washington Post*

DISTURBING HIS PEACE

THE ACADEMY, VOL. 3

"This terrific series continues to entertain, buoyed by great writing, a unique setting, and a tough-yet-vulnerable cast of characters that comes alive on the page. Bailey delivers another winning Academy romance smoldering with sexual tension and emotional angst."

—*Kirkus Reviews*

FIX HER UP

A NOVEL

"*Fix Her Up* was a complete, utter, unrelenting delight."

—Christina Lauren, *New York Times* bestselling author

HarperCollins*Publishers*

DISCOVER GREAT AUTHORS, EXCLUSIVE OFFERS, AND MORE AT HC.COM.

SEP 2022

BOOKS BY TESSA BAILEY

CHASE ME

A BROKE AND BEAUTIFUL NOVEL

"Bailey launches the Broke and Beautiful contemporary series with the gripping story of an independent woman and a generous man. [...] Honest emotions and real passion lead to [...] sex scenes that never feel gratuitous. Readers will appreciate these highly sympathetic leads and their powerful story of mutual self-discovery."

—*Publishers Weekly*

NEED ME

A BROKE AND BEAUTIFUL NOVEL

"Bailey puts a fun, super-sexy spin on the classic "hot for teacher" trope [...] The love scenes in *Need Me* are practically incendiary, and the author's sharp sense of humor provides a refreshing change from the usual heavy dose of dark angst that characterizes many other NA romances."

—*Booklist*

MAKE ME

A BROKE AND BEAUTIFUL NOVEL

"Hilarious, sexy, and absolutely addicting! I loved every character, and I'm dying to see what Tessa Bailey comes up with next!"

—Cora Carmack, *New York Times* bestselling author

HarperCollins*Publishers*

DISCOVER GREAT AUTHORS, EXCLUSIVE OFFERS, AND MORE AT HC.COM.